Time for a Highlander

by

Maxine Mansfield

Time for a Highlander

COPYRIGHT © 2016 by Maxine Mansfield

Contact Information: info@thewildrosepress.com

Cover Art by *Diana Carlile*

The Wild Rose Press, Inc.
PO Box 708
Adams Basin, NY 14410-0708

Visit us at www.thewilderroses.com

Publishing History
First Scarlet Rose Edition, 2016
Print ISBN 978-1-5092-0706-0
Digital ISBN 978-1-5092-0704-6

Published in the United States of America

Dedication

For all who dream of a second chance.

What would you do for one more smile?
One word, one moment, one more quick glance?
What would you do for one more hug?
One giggle, one snuggle, one more funny dance?
What would you do for one more summer?
One fall, one winter, one more fragrant spring?
What would you do for one more night?
One day, one evening, one more song to sing?
What would you do for one more story to tell?
One verse, one poem, one more silly rhyme?
What would you do for one more kiss goodnight?
One touch, one smell, and just a little more time?

Chapter One

The Callanish Stones, Isle of Lewis, Scotland
March, Spring Break, Present day

Bethany Ann Anderson couldn't remember the last time she'd been this happy. She'd scrimped and saved and dreamed of this vacation for years, and now she was finally standing on Scottish soil, listening to a real, live Scottish Highlander, in a Scottish kilt, speaking with a wonderfully Scottish brogue, and telling the tour group all about the standing stones before them, and the history behind them.

It was magical.

She took in a deep breath of brisk Scottish air, and at first, thought the dizziness she suddenly felt was due to her euphoria. But then the ground beneath her feet shifted and moved, and the tallest stone closest to her started to topple just as a child, who couldn't have been more than four or five, darted right in front of it.

She didn't think. She simply reacted.

Death wasn't anything like she'd imagined it would be. And that she was most assuredly dead was about the only thing Beth's panicked mind could comprehend.

After all, a stone slab more than four feet wide, eight feet tall, and weighing at least a ton, couldn't possibly have landed directly across her torso, where it lay pinning her to the ground, without killing her. Could it?

She glanced from side to side, and further evidence of her demise assaulted her senses. The entire tour group she'd been a part of only moments before had disappeared into thin air, and she was all alone in this silent place of ancient stones, on this sad little island off the coast of Scotland.

Alone except for the unfamiliar looking man who paced back and forth. He gazed directly at her, and for a moment, Beth's heart pounded with hope. Then, he simply shook his head and continued to pace, as if she weren't there.

Oh yes, she was definitely dead.

Of all the times Beth had contemplated the afterlife, not once had her vision included an angry-looking guy wearing a dress, with disheveled brown hair, and wire-rimmed glasses. Why on earth would she envision such a thing now?

She blinked furiously and fought to clear the fog her mind had become. When that didn't work, she scrunched her eyes closed and concentrated on the act of simply breathing in and out.

It didn't help. And her panic worsened as she realized breathing was exactly what she was no longer doing.

Her eyes flew open, and he was still there. He looked to be probably middle-aged, of average height and with average features. That is, other than the fact he was clad in what looked to be a dress of some kind.

On further inspection, however, she realized it wasn't a dress at all, but a long, white robe whose hem was frayed with age. He carried a worn-looking, gold-edged book of some sorts in his right hand, and unfortunately, he didn't have even a hint of wings or a halo.

She sighed. Well then, he probably wasn't a celestial creature here to welcome her into heaven. At least not one she recognized from any of the pictures in the old family Bible.

Beth wondered if perhaps he could still be a higher being of some sort. She hoped so. Because, considering some of her past mistakes, the alternative was too horrible to contemplate.

A strange sound emanated from his throat, not words exactly, but more a growl, mixed with an excited grumble.

Lord help her, if he wasn't an angel, then was he perhaps from the opposite end of that spectrum?

She didn't understand. Yes, she'd made that one unforgivable mistake, and she'd never tried to dispute it. But other than that, she'd always strived to lead a good and decent life. This entire situation wasn't in the least bit fair. Where were the bright lights and the streets of gold she'd read about in the good book? The harps playing while a heavenly choir sang? And—and—and real live angels with wings and halos instead of some guy with wire-rimmed glasses?

Her last memory had been of pushing the child

away from danger and toward his father as the earth had shook and the huge slab of stone that had been standing for centuries suddenly toppled over, crushing her beneath it. There hadn't been time for more than a moment of fear and then nothing.

"Umm, sir." She chuckled nervously. "Would you be so good as to call the equivalent of afterlife 911 or whatever it is here so I can get out from under this rock? It's quite uncomfortable. Where exactly am I anyway? God, I hope *this* isn't Heaven, or worse—" She gulped. "—Hell."

He covered his eyes with a hand and shook his head. His voice no more than a whisper. "This wasn't supposed to happen."

Mr. Wire-rimmed-glasses paced back and forth once more, weaving in and out between the standing stones as he mumbled. "How am I going to explain this one? There will be no hiding it like I did the last time. I'll very likely lose my job. But at the same time, I can't simply hold her here in Limbo indefinitely, can I?"

He shook his head. "Of course not. Someone would find her eventually, and then there would be memos and meetings and hearings. And I seriously doubt it would end before my entire reputation was completely ruined."

The confinement of the stone still lying upon her body became increasingly irritating. Not because it was painful, but simply because she found it impossible to move. "Mr. Whoever-you-are," she yelled. "If you aren't going to call someone, would you mind helping me get out from under this thing yourself?"

He briefly glanced her way, then continued pacing. "Help you? Is that all you're concerned with, madam? I can't believe you'd expect me to make matters worse by actually assisting you in your folly."

He wagged his finger at her. "You weren't supposed to be under there in the first place. That rock wasn't supposed to fall on you. It was meant to land on the child's father. He was supposed to be the one to save his son's life, not you." He stopped directly in front of Beth and glared. "Do you have any idea what a predicament you've put me in?"

Tears stung her eyes as Beth shook her head. It was the only part of her body she could move.

"Well, let me tell you then, madam, a true, I'll-probably-never-recover-from-it disaster, that's the kind of mess you've put me in. Lord save me from busy-body do-gooders. Don't you understand? It wasn't your time. You can't go taking someone else's turn. Makes a big mess of the time-space continuum, laws of nature, and all that"—he waved his hands about—"jazz."

She had to know. "The little boy, then? He's all right?"

The man balled up his fists, and his voice shook. "All right? Is he all right, you ask? Oh, yes, he's quite all right, and so is his father, who will be fine and peachy now for the next fifty-three years, seven months, two weeks, six days, eighteen hours, and forty-two minutes. That's the very next time his rotation will come around once more."

He glared right at her. "Do you now see what havoc you've caused, madam?" He wagged his finger again. "And before you threw yourself into a path that wasn't yours to take, did you even for a millisecond consider the ramifications of your actions? Do you have any idea all the children and grandchildren who might now be born because the person who should've died didn't? Not to mention how much extra work you've piled on top of me and my colleagues?"

Beth's heart soared, and she smiled. "I'm sorry about the extra work, really I am, but it's a good thing, then, my life for his. He obviously has a family to live for. I've been alone for, well, a while now. It's okay. Really it is. I don't mind. I just want out from under this rock."

For a moment, she feared the man was about to have a stroke as his entire face turned an ugly shade of deep purple.

"You don't mind? Who do you think you are? Who gave you permission to decide who lives and who dies? Even I don't get much of a say-so into such important matters, and I've been doing this job all my existence."

His face glowed an angry red, and for a moment, Beth worried he'd quit talking to her all together and leave her here all alone. He didn't, though. He continued to rant.

"I, madam, follow the rules. I pride myself in helping along the little unexpected things that catch people off guard and change the course of one's day-to-day life and death."

He stopped speaking, and for a moment, his eyes broke contact with hers and his lips grimaced. Then, he began again. "I admit, sometimes what I instigate can prove to be a tad, let's say, unpleasant, for the recipient, but not always."

Beth snorted. "You call being trapped beneath a huge rock a tad unpleasant? I'd sure hate to see your definition of really bad. You, sir, are the king of understatement."

He glared once more and then turned his back on her. "I'll have you know I am considered a perfectionist amongst my peers, madam. In close to four hundred years, three hundred and seventy-three to be precise, and on this very same day of March, I was indirectly involved in the only other small incident of my prestigious career. But I swear, other than what has transpired today, it was the only other irregularity to have taken place during my watch, ever. Just the one teensy, tiny, little mistake, but it was one I'll probably never live down.

"I was a rookie back then, though," he sighed. "And that debauchery wasn't any more truly my fault than what you've caused today. Quinton MacLeod, although a strapping example of manhood, was not, shall we say, graceful. And Lady Elspeth Frasier? Well, the fact of the matter is, she should've been paying more attention to her own business and concentrating less on her stepmother's."

He sighed again deeply.

On the one hand, Beth wanted to punch him in the nose for the fault comment, and on the other, she wanted to give him a hug and tell him everything would be okay.

Then she remembered she couldn't move, and she desperately wanted him to get through telling his story quickly and go get her some help.

He didn't seem to be the least bit in a hurry, however. He continued to reminisce.

"Poor Laird MacLeod, after what happen, he spent the remainder of his days blaming himself for the accident that took Lady Elspeth's life. He never did marry, you see. Died all alone, miserable, and more importantly, without the heir he should've been granted."

The man shook his head. "But when the boss gets wind of this latest mix-up, I'll be out of a job for sure. Or worse, he'll dock my pay and put me on plagues and pestilence duty again. I do so hate plagues and pestilence, they're such a nasty, smelly business."

He leaned in close to Beth and whispered, "He might be forgiving to others, but he can be a bit merciless with the hired help if you know what I mean. Demands perfection, that one does."

With a flip of his wrist the stone slab lifted away and fell off to the side, landing with a loud thud a few feet away.

Startled, Beth slowly rose and dusted herself off, amazed she didn't have a single bruise, ache, or twinge anywhere. She patted her head to make sure her tight, brown bun was still intact. And she pushed back in place the plain black-framed glasses she needed to read anything smaller than size fourteen font since turning forty-five last fall.

She held her hand out to the man. "I wish I could say I'm sorry about your possible, umm, job problems, but I'm not. Anyone who prides himself on causing mischief in other people's lives deserves to have their pay docked and put on plague and pestilence duty. The world could use a little more good will and charity and a lot less bad luck, if you ask me."

The man ignored her outstretched hand and folded his arms. "Nobody asked you."

She absently picked a piece of lint from her rust-colored cardigan and smoothed her skirt over hips no longer as slender as they'd once been. "So, what happens now? I expected to go toward the light or something like that. I thought I'd at least get to see, to explain, to be with…" She cleared her throat. "I've always tried to obey the commandments and be a good person."

The man chuckled. "Oh, I see how it is. You want to go dancing off into the light and have your happily-ever-after afterlife and leave me here holding the bag for *your* error in judgment."

He jabbed a finger in her direction. "You aren't going anywhere, madam. Not until you help me fix what you broke."

Beth sighed. "I don't know how to help you and preventing me from moving on would be…well, it would simply be wrong. Haven't you ever heard the old adage two wrongs don't make a right?"

Suddenly, the man's eyes lit, and a smile crossed his face. "That might be the answer."

He flipped through the pages of his book, then pulled what looked to be some type of high-tech smart-phone thingy from a pocket in his robe and began pushing buttons.

"If I add the co-efficient of the speed of light to the variable of time minus what happened yesterday and squared by the root of what's about to take place tomorrow…"

He fleetingly looked at Beth, then back to the instrument, then up again. He shook his head twice and glanced at his data.

"Two wrongs don't make a right, you say? If my calculations are correct, madam, I may be able to do precisely that. I'll make a right from two wrongs, thereby canceling them both out."

He poised a finger above the send button for a moment. "Shall we see if I'm correct?"

Then, he pushed it.

Time and the awareness of space itself became fuzzy and distorted. With a whoosh, Beth floated upward and away, toward an ever-growing pool of nothingness. Looking back toward the strange man fading in the distance, she shouted, "Who are you anyway?"

Only an echo found its way back before darkness completely enveloped her once more. "My name, madam, is Tobias Moiré. I am a third generation event manipulator, but you would probably know me better by my everyday title.

"I am Fate."

****

Beth's lashes slowly fluttered open, then her eyes widened. Above her head swung what looked for all the world to be a set of hairy testicles and a—a penis. She blinked and then blinked again while trying her best to avert her gaze. She couldn't really move very far away from the sight, however. Her head was bracketed by two big feet attached to two very long, sturdy-looking, bare legs, stretching out from beneath a red and black plaid …something.

Skirt perhaps?

Why was it, men who had the most to offer a woman in certain areas were almost always a little strange in others?

The cross-dressing, probably gay guy, whoever he was, stood with his booted feet planted right beside her ears. He suddenly bent over, and his hands reached down toward her. Big, strong-looking hands with long, thick, meaty fingers.

She sighed, and then another thought struck her.

If she wasn't mistaken, and Beth, when she managed to calm her racing heart, was pretty sure she wasn't, this man probably wasn't a gay cross-dresser at all. And the skirt probably wasn't even a skirt, either, but a kilt. And though the sight beneath it was quite impressive and had finally answered a question about what was truly worn, if anything, under a kilt, wherever she now was, probably wasn't the heaven she'd expected to see when she opened her eyes after the earthquake.

And if this wasn't heaven, then perhaps she wasn't as dead as she expected to be after pushing the little boy out of the way of the falling stone.

Conceivably, she could've been hit with just a glancing blow by the huge slab of rock falling over and simply been knocked unconscious. Seeing what she'd seen and having the strange conversation with an even stranger man in the interim could've been simply a hallucination of some sort or an undesired side effect of the sudden trauma.

Yes, that's exactly what must have happened.

People were talking excitedly, and Beth concentrated on the sound. The voices belonged to at least two men and one woman, and they were all speaking words she couldn't quite comprehend. The accent was vaguely familiar, though. It sounded Gaelic? Then she shook her head. Of course, it sounded Gaelic.

She was in Scotland, after all, in late March, on the last day of her spring break vacation, and on a guided tour of the islands. Had these three also been on the excursion with her? She didn't remember ever hearing their voices before, but then there'd been so many tourists, the company had needed to book two buses just to get them all to the ferry that took them on the day trip.

Suddenly, as if a switch flipped to the on position in her brain, she understood every word being said.

"Is she dead? Please, tell me she isna."

One of those big meaty fingers poked her in the chest, hard.

It was the woman's voice who answered. "I nae believe so. For a moment, I thought perhaps, but now it looks as if she's breathing."

The man with the set of impressive nether region parts backed up a little and leaned over even farther. Beth gazed up into the most amazing set of sea blue eyes she'd ever seen.

"Are ye all right then, lass? Tell me ye are."

Even though her head pounded like the devil, his voice flowed over her, filled her, and drowned out every other sound in the room. Beth managed a slight nod as she glanced back one last time hoping for another glimpse of his impressive intimate aspects.

It wasn't to be, however, as anything below his kilt was now well out of her line of sight. So she tamped down her disappointment and steeled herself to face him. Her cheeks burned with embarrassment, but she accepted his hand as he helped her into a sitting position and turned her until she faced him.

"Easy there, lass," he whispered.

Beth sighed again. He couldn't be more than twenty-five or -six, if he were a day. Thick, dark-brown hair curled playfully about the collar of his white tunic and teased at his neckline.

Her face burned even hotter when she grinned up at him, as if she were a teenager again. The idea that the hair on his testes looked as chocolaty rich as the hair on the top of his head had Beth clamping a hand over her mouth before she giggled like a school girl or said something completely inappropriate that would, no doubt, embarrass them both. What was going on with her today?

Then she looked into his eyes again and was mesmerized. They were the same shade of blue as a stormy sea and rimmed with long, dark lashes any woman would covet. Even a woman of her age couldn't be blamed for losing herself in their depths. Was there nothing about this specimen of prime manhood, who looked as if he'd stepped straight off the cover of a Highland historical romance novel, that wasn't perfect?

Her eyes wandered down his proud angular nose to his lips. They were luscious and full, so tasty-looking, with tiny laugh lines around the edges. His strong chin complemented his handsome face perfectly with its hint of a dimple. And his impossibly broad chest and tree-trunk sized arms were the stuff dreams were made of.

Wow!

A thought struck her as heat wicked up her insides from the pit of her belly all the way to the top of her head. If she were twenty years younger, forty—make that fifty—pounds lighter, and about three inches taller, she'd definitely be tempted to lie right to this man's face and tell him that, oh yes, she definitely needed his assistance in order to stand. What wouldn't she give for a chance to be lifted into those arms, held against that chest, if only for a single moment in time?

Heat filled her face again. Oh God. What would

her friends back home at the Tuesday night book club meeting think of her, a forty-five-year-old divorcee, having such naughty thoughts and desires? It would almost be worth the shocked looks and embarrassed laughter she'd be forced to endure if she were to tell them this story. They, of course, would snicker and label her the most terrible of fibbers.

But the chance to experience what it would be like to be held within the circle of those long arms, against a rock-hard, tight, beautifully muscled body like his just once in her lifetime, might well be worth their teasing.

"If you're through looking me over, lass, I'll be glad ta help ye up. If nae, then continue ta take in ye fill. I'm in nae hurry."

Even though her face burned like fire, she couldn't curtail the sigh that escaped her lips. All that gorgeous masculinity and a Sean Connery—in his prime—accent to boot. Perhaps this was heaven, after all.

He extended a hand, and even though she was completely embarrassed to be caught needing his help, she accepted it, with as much grace as she could muster, and stood. Waves of dizziness immediately enveloped her, and she had no choice but to cling to him or fall. Oh yes, the arms and the chest were even better than she'd imagined.

Tiny sparks of electrical energy scampered up and down her spine, and everywhere his body touched hers, she burned with the desire to wrap herself around him and never let go.

Thankfully, she hadn't totally lost her mind yet. She certainly didn't want to gross the young man out by forcing him to ward off the advances of a chubby, middle-aged, bat-shit crazy female who, just a little while ago, thought today to be her last. So instead of holding onto him as she would've liked, she took two deep breaths and forced herself to push away.

Beth glanced around the room to its other occupants. "I'm fine now, thank you. Really I am."

She wasn't fine, though. Something was very wrong.

For one thing, she was no longer out in the chilly open air surrounding the Callanish stones. Instead, she was now in a large room with a very high ceiling. Stone walls surrounded her, and a hot blaze roared and crackled in a huge blackened fireplace.

A scarred wooden table stood before her with scattered chunks of messy looking bread and—and eating utensils of some sort upon it. A runny-looking soup or stew of some kind, dripped from the table's edges. And an overturned bench lay at her feet, with what looked to be hay littering the floor all around it.

How had she gotten here?

Had someone picked her up and carried her to this place after the accident?

"Where am I?" she asked. "And who are you?"

Three voices rang out at the same time, but it was the gorgeous man who'd helped Beth stand whose voice she heard above the rest.

"Ye are home. Castle Frasier, in Stornoway on the Isle of Lewis. Where else would ye be, lass?" He grinned. "I'm Laird Quinton MacLeod. But, ta ye, I'm simply Quint or my laird. Do ye nae remember me, at all, lass? I'm so verra sorry. I didna mean ta cause ye harm. It was an accident, ye ken? Ye must believe me. I didna see the serving girl 'til it was ta late. I bumped the wee lass, and the hot stew went flying. I tried ta avoid it and, instead, landed right up against the board. The blasted table scooted forward, and ye toppled backwards and hit ye head. Ye are gonna have quite a nasty bump for a while, I'm afraid. Ye really did hit the floor hard, lass. Verra hard."

Beth shook her head. "What are you talking about? This isn't my home. That's not how…"

She didn't get another word out before the other man in the room grabbed her arm painfully and attempted to pull her away. "Come along, Lady Elspeth. I will personally escort you to your chamber. You've had more than enough excitement for one day, my dear."

But she pulled back and refused to budge. "Elspeth? Who's Elspeth?"

Why did the strange name sound so familiar?

"You've mistaken me for someone else, I'm afraid. I'm not Elspeth, I'm Beth."

He stopped any further words she'd meant to say with a cold, hard stare. Again, he squeezed her arm, and pain shot all the way up her shoulder. "Surely, you at least remember your own name, my dear? If not, then that most certainly must have been quite a blow to the head you took."

Even if his grasp hadn't been hurting her, there was something about this man that made her skin crawl. It wasn't really how he appeared so much as it was the way he looked at her. He had an expression of wide-eyed…almost fear, mixed with a cheek-twitching, sneer she'd only ever witnessed on one other face. It made her stomach suddenly want to empty itself upon the stone floor along with the spilled stew.

There wasn't really anything out of the ordinary

about him she could put her finger on. He was of average height and build, his hair a plain brown, his nose a tad long for his face, and his lips no more than a thin line. Still, there was something sinister about him. Something in those dark, wolf-like eyes that reminded Beth of her ex-husband of all people.

She shuddered.

The other female in the room suddenly intervened. "It won't be necessary for ye ta escort Lady Elspeth above stairs, my lord. I'll gladly see ta her well-being. It was a very generous offer of ye, though, but not in the least proper. And with ye being a titled viscount and a good friend of the king, I've no doubt you wish ta maintain proper decorum at all times."

The creepy guy stiffened beside her. "You misunderstand, Lady Lydia. Until after tomorrow morning's festivities, the girl is still my responsibility. And trust me"—he narrowed his eyes—"I take my responsibilities very seriously."

He suddenly smiled. "And after all, this is no time to quibble about protocol. Poor, dear Lady Elspeth has obviously suffered a grievous injury. The child doesn't even seem to know her own name at the moment. There's no telling what insanity she may spout next. I've seen this type of injury before, my dear, and have experience with it."

He waved his free hand. "You remain here in the hall where you belong and see to the clearing of this—" He gestured toward the table and the floor. "—mess. We shall continue with the remainder of our meal when I return. I'm willing to discount propriety just this once and personally see Lady Elspeth safely above stairs."

Beth shook her head again. *Child*? Had the creepy

guy really called her, forty-five-year-old Bethany Ann Anderson with more gray roots than brown these days, a child? Were any of these people for real? Not to mention, she had no intention of going anywhere, let alone up a set of stairs with the guy, and if he tugged on her arm one more time, she was going to make sure he knew it.

A moment later, though, Beth realized she needn't have worried. The Lady Lydia person took care of the entire situation and with only a handful of words.

"Nonsense, my lord, ye are a guest here at Frasier Castle. I cannae have it being bandied about that I encouraged improprieties or put my own responsibilities off on ta another, especially nae on such a prestigious member of King Charles's court. I'll personally see ta *all* of Lady Elspeth's needs, myself. I insist."

Beth racked her pounding head. Charles was king? When had that happened? And what of Queen Elizabeth? It was no secret the grand lady was getting up in years. Had she finally turned over her throne and her country to her eldest son, or had she, God forbid, died?

There was a good chance anything could've happened, and she wouldn't have been the wiser. Even though she was in the United Kingdom this very moment, she'd been so busy sight-seeing, she'd completely neglected current affairs everywhere.

She didn't even have a clue as to what was going on back at home, and she really didn't care. After all, she was on vacation. And that was why she hadn't bothered to turn on her cell phone when she'd first landed in Inverness or bothered to watch a moment of

TV or listen to a single radio station. Those things she could do anywhere. Scotland was for seeing where history had been made, up close and personal.

But she was curious as to what had happened to the queen, and it was right on the tip of her tongue to ask, when Lady Lydia spoke once more.

"Unfortunately the stew has been ruined, but there are still the main courses ta look forward ta. The servants will see ta the cleaning. And I will return in a few moments ta dine with ye both."

The MacLeod-Quint person simply smiled and nodded, but the creepy viscount sneered. "It truly is unfortunate the first course was ruined. I was so looking forward to watching you enjoy it."

He bowed slightly. "Until your return, Lady Lydia, and sleep well, Lady Elspeth."

Beth looked gratefully toward Lydia. She was young, probably even younger than the could-have-been-a-romance-novel-cover-model Quinton MacLeod. And she was pretty. Dazzling green eyes smiling, she had an air of confidence about her that immediately put Beth at ease.

But why was she and everyone else in the room calling her Elspeth? Perhaps it was the Scottish equivalent of Beth. That must be it. And what had Lady Lydia meant when she said Beth was her responsibility? Had this Lady Lydia person perhaps been one of the tour guides earlier in the day? For the life of her, she couldn't remember.

To her way of thinking, though, it didn't really matter. All that was important was finding a place to lie down, if only for a little while. Her head pounded so badly even the very root shafts of her hair hurt, but the touch of Lady Lydia's guiding hand was warm and comforting upon her own.

Beth took three steps forward, then stopped in her tracks.

Something was wrong. It was as if her body had suddenly forgotten how to function properly. Her legs wanted to move, but they were somehow foreign.

Where was the familiar brush of one thigh against the other? Why did they suddenly feel longer and stronger, but at the same time, her feet seemed smaller? And where was that everyday twinge of arthritis and the pain and popping in her knees she'd grown so accustomed to after the…

Beth cringed. She must have hit her head really hard when she'd fallen. She probably suffered some kind of concussion. Should she be concerned? Should she ask to see a doctor? Did she even care right now?

She shrugged and smiled to herself. She was simply too tired to worry about anything at the moment, even a brain injury. And if her head still hurt when she woke, then she'd be concerned, but not now.

Obediently, she followed.

It wasn't as if Beth didn't try to focus and concentrate on where she was and where she was going but nothing seemed right about any of this. Was it possible it was all simply a bad dream?

Perhaps she'd never even gone on a trip to Scotland in the first place. Perhaps right this very moment she was home, in Anchorage, Alaska, safe and sound, asleep in her very own bed.

Perhaps she'd made the mistake of eating turnips once again at dinner, even though they not only gave her horrible gas, but nightmares, too.

Perhaps, with a modicum of luck, any minute now she'd wake, refreshed.

Perhaps …

Lady Lydia escorted her up a set of narrow stone steps to a chamber, opened the door, and led her inside. A cozy fire warmed the room comfortably, and the large wooden-framed bed looked too inviting to resist. It was all Beth could do to keep her eyes open long enough to climb between the sheets.

She didn't remember what she'd been wearing, how she'd gotten undressed, or how she'd gotten into the bed itself, and she didn't care about any of those things, either.

All Beth wanted to do was slip into a deep slumber until this weird nightmare ended.

Even Lady Lydia's parting words of "Sleep well, my dear. Ye'll need ta be fully rested for ye wedding on the morrow" didn't faze her.

She giggled to herself as she dozed off.

Wedding? What freaking wedding, and to whom?

How silly.

Smiling into her pillow, Beth turned to her side and snuggled deeper under the warm furs, cocooning her. Now she knew beyond any reasonable doubt she was dreaming, or instead of this possibly being some weird version of heaven, it had to be her very own personal hell.

For there was no way on earth she'd agree to marry any man, anywhere, for any reason, ever again. One quick set of vows and nineteen long years chained to the hip of a madman had been more than enough marital unbliss to last Bethany Ann Anderson a lifetime, and then some.

Chapter Two

March, 1643

"Wake up."

Beth swatted away what she thought was a paw and rolled onto her side. "Five more minutes, Kato. Give me five more minutes, and I promise, I'll get up and let you out to pee. Good doggy, I'll even take you for a walk as soon as my head stops hurting."

"I'm afraid I'm not Kato, madam, and we don't have five minutes to simply dally. Time is of the essence. You need to wake now."

Beth's eyes flew open. Thin streaks of sunlight filtered through the cracks in the wooden closure of a stone-encased window and illuminated the room in a gentle glow. This definitely wasn't her apartment, and for sure, this wasn't her bed.

Where was she again?

She could just make out a man's outline standing beside her and hear the sound of his breathing.

Beth froze.

"You can't avoid this, madam. I know you're awake. I'm not leaving until I have my say, so you might as well look straight at me and face the day."

Slowly, she did, all the while terrified of who and what she was going to see.

After the earthquake and the strange conversation with the very strange man that followed it, she'd spent the remainder of the night convincing herself what she'd seen and heard had been some kind of weird reaction to something she'd eaten. And with the light of day, she wasn't prepared for it not to be.

But there he was, big as life and as strange as he'd been the day before. Mr. Tobias Moiré, the event manipulator, or Fate, or whatever else he might find to call himself.

"Where am I? What am I doing here? Did I really and truly die?"

He cleared his throat. "There isn't much time. Very soon now, that door is going to open, and I won't get another chance to explain, so please be quiet and listen until I'm finished. Then, if there is any time left, you may ask questions. Is that clear?"

She started to speak, but he held up a hand. "A nod will suffice."

Beth clamped her mouth closed and nodded.

"To begin with, yes, Bethany Ann Anderson's body is dead, mashed flat as a pancake. Trust me, not a pretty sight. You, madam, have been given a new body. Well, really, it's a very old body, as you are now in the past. Close to four hundred years in the past to be exact, in late March of Our Lord's year 1643. You are presently at Frasier Castle on an island off the coast of Scotland, and you are now in the body of one Lady Elspeth Frasier who, after suffering a rather nasty fall and fatal bump to the head during dinner last night, no longer has need of it."

Tears welled in Beth's eyes. "Mashed, flat as a pancake?" She shuddered. Though she'd never been what she'd call proud of her overabundant curves, they'd been hers, and the thought of complete strangers probably having to scrape what was left of her off the ground brought on a wave of nausea.

Fate sighed. "Your old body's condition should be the least of your concerns." He snapped his fingers. "We have much more pressing issues to discuss, so get past it, and let's move on. I need you to concentrate. This is important."

She swiped at her eyes. Concentrate? How the fuck was she supposed to concentrate? She'd just been told she was dead. Hysteria replaced the nausea.

"Today is to be your wedding day. In a matter of a very short period of time, you will be exchanging vows with Laird Quinton MacLeod."

Beth tossed back the furs and jumped to her feet. "No, oh no, no, no, and not just no, but oh hell no. I'm not marrying anyone ever again, especially not some guy I don't even know. And no one, not even you, can make me. If I'm really, truly dead, then I want to go to heaven, and I want to go right now."

She lifted her chin an inch in defiance, but she couldn't prevent her lip from trembling. "I've—I've earned it.

"And there are people there I need to see, to be with. I have things I need to explain, apologies to make." She flung her arms about wildly. "I didn't agree to any of this. I demand you get me out of here this minute."

Fate tapped his foot. "Are you quite finished with your little temper tantrum? There will be no getting you out of that body or this time period until the wrong, which you helped to create, I might add, has been undone. That is simply the way of things. Accept it and move on. And, madam, you certainly have met your prospective bridegroom. He is the man who helped you rise from the floor last evening after Lady Elspeth's untimely demise."

Beth gasped and shook her head. "I won't do it. You can't make me."

Fate simply smiled, and Beth had an almost irresistible urge to punch him.

"Oh, yes, I most certainly can, my dear. You will marry Laird MacLeod this very morning. For in the year 1643, young ladies wed whom they were told to wed."

She gulped at the memory of the man who would've made a gorgeous cover model and the feelings he'd elicited in her with no more than a smile.

"I won't. I'll show you. I'll tell the whole bunch of them all about you and who I really am."

Fate laughed. "It wouldn't be in your best interest to do so, madam. They burned females for making up less crazy stories than you have to tell. Remember, it is the year 1643." He leaned in close. "They thought them to be witches, you see. Very superstitious period in history. But considering you are, I mean were, a history teacher, I'm sure you're already aware of that."

The blood drained from Beth's face. After what happened to… Being burned alive was perhaps her greatest fear. She wouldn't give Fate the satisfaction of knowing that, however. Gathering her bravado, she faced him. "So be it. Let them burn me. Then I'll get to be with…"

"Your children?" He finished her sentence for her.

The lump in her throat impeded her speech as a sharp pang of longing squeezed the breath from her chest. She simply nodded.

"I know all about your two young sons, madam. One of the event manipulators for North America told me all about them. He's a cousin of mine. His name is Norbert."

Her mouth gaped. There was more than one?

"Oh please, surely you don't think I'm the only *Fate* there is, do you? There are many of us. Every major country has at least one, and some of the larger continents and providences have quite a few. It depends on population, you see? Itty bitty China for instance has five all to itself. It's like how your government goes about deciding how many senators each state gets. Though with Fates, we are all direct descendants of the original three Moirés.

"And before you even think to ask, no, Norbert was not the cause of the mishap that claimed your children's lives. There were other factors involved in that particular situation that I'm not at liberty to discuss."

He touched her arm. "No matter what you may have been led to believe, madam, their deaths were not your fault, and you could not have prevented them."

She buried her face in her hands as the taste of bile filled her mouth. His cousin Norbert may have told him the circumstances surrounding the deaths of her children, but one thing was for certain, Tobias Moiré had no idea what she'd said to her children only moments before the crash. And he didn't know why she so desperately needed to see them, be with them, beg their forgiveness.

Fate linked an arm about her shoulders. "Don't you see? The opportunity you have now been given truly is rare. Not only might you help fix my mistake, but this can be a fresh new beginning for you yourself. Not many people get the chance to do their lives over. Consider this a gift, not a punishment."

He slipped a hand into one of the pockets of his robe and pulled out a hand-mirror. "Look at how young and beautiful you are."

She took a deep breath, blew it out, and allowed Fate to place the circle of glass in her hand. What did it matter what she looked like? Inside, where it really counted, she was still a monster and she knew it. But look she did, and the reflection that stared back at her was that of a total stranger.

Lady Elspeth Frasier was pretty, of that there was no doubt. Golden curls hung down her back, well past her waist. Her eyes were large and sky-blue with thick, dark honey-colored lashes. A pert nose, peach cheeks, and a set of perfect, pouty, pink lips certainly didn't distract from her beauty either. Even her silly little ears were cute.

Beth ran a hand down the unfamiliar body. It was lithe and slender, perky in all the right places, and with enough curves to make any man with a pulse look more than twice and break out in a sweat. It was the face and body she'd always dreamed of. But a part of her missed the flabby, saggy, middle-aged, post-menopausal Beth she'd been yesterday. The knowledge she'd never again see the reflection of her own face once more brought tears to her eyes.

"Mashed flat as a pancake?" She sighed. "How old is she? I mean, how old am I?"

Fate smiled. "Twenty today. Happy birthday, madam."

Beth nodded. "I certainly don't feel twenty. I still very much feel forty-five."

Fate nodded. "Well, you did have a rather trying day yesterday. After the wedding, I'm sure you'll be able to find time to relax and get to know this new body of yours."

She cringed. "I can't do it. I can't possibly marry that, that young man. I'm old enough to be Quinton MacLeod's mother, for God's sake. It would be too weird, disgusting even, and probably illegal somewhere."

Fate chuckled. "Well, to be perfectly honest, madam, technically speaking, he's older than you by hundreds of years and older than Lady Elspeth by five. But then age isn't what matters anyhow. It's simply a number. And when it comes to relationships between men and women, the only thing that's truly important is what the heart feels. Trust your heart in this matter, madam, and you will be fine."

Beth sighed again. "So, what exactly do I have to do to make up for the mistake? I want this over with as quickly as possible."

Tobias Moiré smiled. "Your task is quite simple, really. Just give Quinton MacLeod the heir he was denied because of Lady Elspeth's untimely death."

She choked and sputtered. "Carry for nine long months and give birth to a baby again? His baby? And then what, just desert it, desert them? I can't. I won't. I'll do anything else, anything, please."

Fate shook his head. "The terms aren't up for debate, I'm afraid. That is the bargain, madam. An heir for Quinton MacLeod in exchange for being reunited with the children you lost.

"You now have approximately two minutes of privacy left in order to come to terms with your issues and lay them to rest. Do try and put a smile on your face before that door swings open."

He began to shimmer. "I must go for now, but I'll be close by if and when you truly need my assistance."

Beth panicked. "Wait, how do I get in touch with you? And I do have questions. I don't know this Lady Elspeth person at all. How am I supposed to be her? How did she act, how did she speak, what was her life like? Everyone is going to know I'm a fraud."

Fate was almost completely transparent, and Beth had to strain to hear what he said.

"When I'm needed, I'll know it. As far as acting like Lady Elspeth, simply tap into her memories, madam. Memories don't ever completely die, even when the body does. They fade over time and become particles of energy traveling through the universe. Until then, however, most remain hidden away in the subconscious.

"As a matter of fact, some memories, if powerful enough, have been known to remain behind for a millennium or more. Search for those memories, those deepest and closest to Lady Elspeth's heart. Start with her most recent ones. Those are the bits that can give you the clearest information.

"Good luck until we meet once again."

Then he was gone.

The door crashed open with a resounding bang and into the room walked the strangest assortment of people Beth had ever seen. In the lead was Lady Lydia, followed by another woman who looked surprisingly like a much older version of a Raggedy Ann doll, complete with a dull white smock but minus the striped stockings. Her hair was a mass of curly bright red, and she had rosy cheeks. Her freckles had freckles, even in her wrinkles, but her smile was open and friendly. Beth immediately liked her. She sought the recesses of Elspeth's mind and surprisingly came up with the name Bronwyn.

"It's your wedding day, my lady. Time ta break ye fast and have ye bath."

Beth searched her own memory for details from the numerous romance novels she'd read. Thinking that those stories, and the fact she'd been a middle-school history teacher for more than seventeen years, should be able to help in some small way. And suddenly, she knew. The Raggedy Ann look-alike must be her ladies' maid.

Beth raised her nose slightly, enjoying the moment of playacting the way she thought a noblewoman would, and said the first thing that popped into her head.

"Make sure the water is warm enough, Bronwyn. You know how I detest tepid."

The red-haired old woman laughed. "Didn't I tell ya she'd be right as rain this morn, Lady Lydia? It takes more than a little tumble and a crack on the noggin ta get the better of Mistress Elspeth Frasier, it does. Even though she'd been gone from us for nigh on eight years, I'd know that sassiness, anywhere."

Lady Lydia smiled and nodded as she directed the servants to set the wooden tub in the corner of the room, close to the fireplace. Bucket after bucket of steaming water was poured until the container was filled to her satisfaction.

Beth glanced at the platter of oatcakes and cheese that were set before her, along with a cup of tea, but all she longed for right this moment was a long soak in that steaming water to ease her aching head and muscles. Her stomach, however, chose that moment to remind her it hadn't eaten in a while, so she gave in to its demands and sat silently worrying as she nibbled on the fare.

How long would she be able to keep up this charade? How long before she made a mistake and was found out? Would they really think she was a witch? Would they really burn her alive if they did?

Beth shuddered.

Lady Lydia must have witnessed her unease and mistaken the reason behind it, for a moment later, she dismissed the servants, except for Bronwyn, and closed the door firmly behind them. With an almost sisterly expression on her face, the lady approached the bed.

She stood quietly for a moment, as if in deep thought, then began. "I was beginning ta think the day would nae come when I would have need of this conversation with ye. Though I'm certainly nae your mother, and with ye father sending ye ta the abbey so soon after I arrived here at Frasier castle, we never really got the chance ta become as close as I would've liked. But still, I do feel it my responsibility ta…"

Beth nibbled another bite to cover her grin, as the sight of Lady Lydia's cheeks pinkening told her exactly what discussion was forthcoming. What would the very proper young woman think if she had any inkling that Beth had taught more than her share of sex education classes over the years?

"I was fourteen years and ye were but twelve when I became ye father's wife and ye stepmother," Lady Lydia began again. "My own mother died when I was born and my ladies' maid had never married, so there wasn't anyone ta properly prepare me for what ta expect in the...marriage bed. I was terrified the first time, and I do nae wish that for ye."

The poor woman's face was now so red it glowed, and Beth wanted to stop her before she fainted dead away. She wanted to confide in her and let her know that even though this body was young and inexperienced, she was not.

But she didn't.

Memories flooded her mind, memories of her horrible marriage and of the maniacal brute she'd been attached to. The man who'd blamed her daily for the death of his children. The man who'd made sure she'd suffered for the crime he'd long ago found her guilty of. And he'd taken pride in punishing her for what he felt she did, over and over and over.

Beth shuddered, and Lady Lydia quickly continued.

"Please do nae mistake me, Elspeth, dear. Ye have nae ta fear. That is what I am here ta tell ye. Though there was no great passion between ye father and me, we did eventually become...friends, of a sort, long before his death."

Lady Lydia took a deep breath. "As ye know, ye are well past the age ta marry. 'Tis time for ye ta take ye rightful place in society as wife ta the laird and mither ta his children. If ye simply lie still and do whatever Quinton MacLeod tells ye ta do, the entire unpleasantness will be over with before ye know it. Granted, there may be a slight sting of pain, especially the first time or two, but nae so much as ta do...lasting harm. Ye will get used ta it soon enough. I did."

Bronwyn sputtered and laughed. "My lady, do nae be filling the lass's head full of nonsense. There's na finer in all the world than the feel of a braw mon betwixt ya legs. Take it from me, Lady Elspeth, ye'll be having yeself a grand ole time with that bonny mon of yours before ye know it."

The maid grinned and winked. "I caught a glimpse of the laird bathing in the loch this morn, and I'm here ta tell ye, he's got nae ta be ashamed of and plenty ta work his magic on ye with."

Lady Lydia blushed an even deeper shade of red, if that was possible. "Well then, I'm so glad we had the opportunity ta have this little chat." She nodded Beth's way, then hurried from the room.

Beth wanted to laugh with Bronwyn, but she wanted to cry for Lady Lydia more. Married at fourteen? And to an old man? Forced to endure sexual attention from someone she didn't even know or love? How horrid.

She'd studied her share of history from this part of the world and time period, and knew that what she was hearing and seeing really was the way it had been. Seeing it up close and personal, however, and hearing it straight from the lips of one who'd lived it was another story all together.

She couldn't bear living like that. She couldn't abide another bully like her ex-husband had been, and she wouldn't. It didn't matter how young or unbelievably handsome Laird Quinton MacLeod was. His new little wife wasn't going to lie there and do what she was told. Not again, anyway.

****

Quint paced the battlements like a man possessed.

In less than two turns of the hourglass he'd be married. And to whom? The she-devil, Lady Elspeth Frasier, herself. The same woman who for the last two days had, for the most part anyway, completely ignored his presence as if he were somehow beneath her notice.

It wasn't as if he didn't want a wife. Quint knew he needed to marry, needed to produce an heir. It was his duty to his clan and past time.

But Lady Elspeth Frasier?

The young harridan was known far and wide for her unreasonable temper and spoiled ways. Not only didn't he need that kind of woman for a wife, but his people didn't deserve someone who cared only for herself as their lady.

Could he tolerate the lass, even come to care for her someday? Quint shook his head. Probably not. He'd once freely given his heart to a much more deserving lass than Elspeth Frasier would probably ever become, and he'd had it handed back ta him in tatters. That, was one mistake he'd nae again make easily. But loyalty, kindness, and protection for the sake of his people, he could give her those.

But then, what of her loyalty? Where did it lie? She'd lived on English soil almost as long as she'd lived in Scotland. In the political and religious turmoil engulfing them, he could ill afford a wife he couldn't trust. And that he couldn't trust *her* was obvious.

For the last two years while Elspeth Frasier had been hiding away at court, one of her benefactors had been none other than the unscrupulous royalist, Lord Fredrick, Viscount Telford. The man was known to have not only the ear of King Charles, but his friendship as well.

What kind of influence did the viscount have over Elspeth? Did Quint need worry?

Though this island and his own were both very much a part of Scotland and so far, had been blessed to remain neutral in the struggle between the king's royalists and parliament, how much longer could he hold out?

And what of John Iain, the chieftain of Clan MacLeod? He was a staunch supporter of Charles and the royalists, while Quint's own beliefs tended to side with the forces of parliament. When would he be forced to bend a knee and swear allegiance to a king he no longer believed in or risk finding his head forfeit? And even if he was lucky enough to avoid John Iain's wrath…would there be a night in his near future when he'd lie down to sleep beside his young wife and not wake the next morning?

What choice did he have, though? He owed loyalty to Alec Mackenzie. The man and his army had stood beside him and clan MacLeod. And that was after his own chieftain, John Iain, hadn't. Even though the thieving MacDonalds had made good on their threats and tried their best to devastate his people and lands.

And when it was all said and done and the MacLeod lands were once more safe, Alec had come to him. He had asked Quint to take his sister, Lady Lydia's stepdaughter, Elspeth Frasier to wife. What else could he do but agree?

A small smile graced his lips. It seemed he'd need to perfect the skill of sleeping with one eye open apparently.

At least it wouldn't be too tedious a task to bed the wench. She was a beauty to gaze upon. More than simply beautiful, Elspeth Frasier had the face and body of an angel with a halo of golden curls. How would those luscious locks shine when spread upon his sheets while the rest of Elspeth Frasier's body was snug beneath him?

Quint's cock hardened and, unlike his brain, didn't have any objections at all to his choice of wife. But he did his best to ignore his erection's demands as it rubbed against the scratchy wool of his kilt. "Down, laddie," he hissed. "Behave. There'll be time enough for ye later."

Chapter Three

It was the most wonderful sensation she could remember in ever so long. Beth sighed as the back of her sore head rested lightly against the rim of the wooden tub. The heat of the water and the fragrance of wild flower petals strewn upon its surface seeped into her muscles and soothed her soul. Though cramped, and she had no choice but keep her knees partially bent, Beth knew she wouldn't trade this morning's bath for the fanciest spa treatment she'd ever seen advertised.

Running her hands along her skin, she closed her eyes and allowed her hands to explore. Oh, the wonders of youth. This body didn't have a single inch of fat or dimple of cellulite on it anywhere. She could clearly feel every single rib, and it even had…hip bones.

She smiled.

Beth couldn't remember another time in the last fifteen years when she'd actually been able to feel hip bones. And these breasts? She held them both in her hands and squeezed. They were magnificent, all round and perky, full and lusciously soft with pebbly hard, pretty little pink nipples.

God, here she was sitting in a tub of water, engrossed in the sight and feel of some other woman's body. Eww. What did that say about her as a person? Had she suddenly become some kind of pervert? After all, Elspeth's very female body was only twenty years old, and Beth's mind was an old forty-five.

She'd never been attracted in any way to female bodies before, at least not any more than the normal passing appreciation for a nice tight butt, flat tummy, long legs, or fine high boobs, cute haircut, pretty eyes, or full pouty lips. Why now did she suddenly wish to explore every single inch of this body she found herself in?

Along with her trip back through time, had her entire sexual orientation changed also?

She thought about it for a moment and shook her head. The memory of Quinton MacLeod's impressive...package as her very first glimpse into this time period had caused a warmth to flow through her insides that had nothing at all to do with the temperature of the water she sat in.

Bi then? She grimaced.

Not that she'd had anything against anyone's sexual preferences, ever, because she hadn't. It was just that she'd always had more than enough trouble figuring out relationship dynamics with men that she hadn't bothered with another after the disaster that was Bert. God help her, if she'd ever considered adding a women to the crazy mix that was her life.

So probably not.

She was pretty sure today's exploration was nothing more than simple curiosity. After all, hadn't her own saggy, flabby body parts and a few very useful toys with long lasting batteries afforded her hours of pleasure over the years? And if truth be told, they'd been her best and only real friends for longer than she'd like to admit.

Beth shuddered. Her poor flabby, saggy body parts

mashed flat as a pancake, how sad. How many strangers had it taken to scrape up the remnants of that mess? And what had they done with it when they were finished? Had they packaged her up in a really big, zip-lock freezer bag and shipped her remains back to Alaska? Had her sister and brothers bothered to make the long trip from Miami to witness the cremation?

What of her poor, old, almost blind Irish setter, Kato? Who was taking care of him now? And her three legged cat, George, whom she'd rescued from the pound as a kitten? And her mean-ass bird, Harley, who tried to bite her every time she filled his food dish? Her plants, and her classroom filled with eager young faces, and her little condo?

She shook her head. She couldn't afford to fret about all of that stuff. It would make her completely crazy if she didn't stop. What was she so worried about anyway? Her death hadn't even happened yet and wouldn't for almost four hundred years in the future.

Right now, there were more pressing issues to be concerned with, like her wedding to a complete stranger, a very young, very handsome, very sexy complete stranger.

Shivers ran down her spine.

The ceremony was due to start soon, and Beth had no clue how to prevent it from happening without getting herself burned at the stake. It made her brain hurt to think about it.

****

No wonder ladies in the sixteen hundreds needed personal maids to get themselves dressed. There was no way any one person could lace up, tie, tuck, and twist any of these garments into place all by herself.

Beth stood before the pounded to a shine piece of metal that served as a mirror and stared. Though a little blurry, Lady Elspeth Frasier was still an absolute beauty. The sky-blue day dress Bronwyn had helped her into fit like a glove and accented not just the curve of her high breasts but the slimness of her tiny waist. Her eyes glowed, her cheeks were a healthy pink, and her lips would put a ripe strawberry to shame. Her hair hung in golden ringlets about her shoulders and back, and a wreath of early spring flowers graced the top of her head.

But what was really weird was the fact that, though she was garbed in a multitude of layers, she wore no panties or bra beneath this gown. She pressed her thighs tightly together. It was the strangest sensation to be so very dressed from head to toe and still feel so utterly naked. From her study of history, she knew woman didn't begin wearing undies and such until a much later time period, but it still didn't seem right. As a matter of fact, it felt quite…naughty.

"'Nuff looking at yeself, my lady. Time ta get ye married, it is."

Beth took a deep breath, nodded, turned, and followed Bronwyn.

Through the soft leather soles of her slippers, the roughness of every stone step she descended imprinted on her mind, and it took much less time than she hoped to reach the bottom floor. To her right loomed the great hall from the previous night, complete with its long tables and huge fireplace. Those same tables had been wiped clean and were laden with what looked to be a great feast.

Her stomach rumbled.

Bronwyn chuckled. "Aye, I'm hungry meself, my lady. Looks like ye stepmother and her brother spared na expense for the occasion."

Beth didn't comment, she couldn't think, let alone speak. Every step led her closer to the kirk she'd been told lay outside in the courtyard and that much closer to her waiting groom. A morose thought flittered through her mind, and she suddenly giggled. Was this anywhere near to what men on death row felt when making *their* last walk to meet *their* maker?

Bronwyn stared at her as if she had lost her mind. She immediately sobered and concentrated on something she did have control over, the movement of her feet. Right foot, left foot, right foot. Clamping her mouth tightly closed, she breathed through her nose and simply walked.

The great doors of the castle opened, and she saw him. Laird Quinton MacLeod stood facing her, waiting silently at the entrance of a squat, stone building a few feet away, and he was…magnificent.

If she'd thought him handsome the night before, in the light of day he was beyond any romance book cover model she'd ever fantasized about.

The sun glinted off his dark hair as streaks of sunlight danced through each strand. His stormy blue eyes gleamed, and a velvety-brown stubble surrounded his oh so kissable mouth and chin, making him even more dangerously handsome. And his body, oh dear God, that body.

Quinton MacLeod's shoulders were so broad they blocked the sun, and his legs so long, he towered well above every other man present. What was it about a Highlander in a kilt, with a face and body like a god that made a woman hunger for something that had absolutely nothing at all to do with food?

Beth didn't remember the last few steps it took to close the distance between them, and even much later, if asked, she wouldn't have been able to repeat a single word she, Quint, or the priest had said.

But she'd always remember the kiss.

Quint's lips lightly brushed hers in a touch made of not much more than air, but they left a permanent imprint upon her soul as tiny sparks of excitement scurried along her spine. If a quick meeting of their lips could leave her so breathless and weak in the knees, what would it be like when he really did kiss her deeply, when he took her to his bed? When he…

Her mind was a muddle. As they walked hand in hand back to the castle a few minutes later, all Beth could think was, she'd gone and done the one and only thing she'd sworn she'd never, ever, ever do again.

She'd once more become some man's wife.

****

They sat at the far end of the great table and shared a trencher of food. At least, it had been meant to be shared. Beth's nerves had long ago killed any appetite she might have had today.

"Eat, my lady," Quint ordered, and Beth jumped at the sternness of his voice.

"I'm not hungry."

He scowled at her, and Beth gulped.

"When ye address me, lass, ye will call me, my laird, my lord, or my husband, or even simply Quint or Quinton, but ye will address me properly. As ye laird and ye husband, I am due that respect. Now eat."

She wanted to tell him where he could put his laird

and lord, but in the end she nodded. The last thing she wanted today was to start a fight with her new husband. Instead, she pretended to listen to what he said while scanning the room and Elspeth's memories for a glimpse of anything familiar.

He leaned in close, and she found it impossible to ignore him. "Lady Lydia and her brother the Mackenzie have gone ta a great deal of trouble ta prepare this celebration for us. It would be discourteous ta our hosts if ye don't eat, and I will nae have it be said a MacLeod was ever ill-mannered ta a friend."

Beth cringed. Here they'd been married less than an hour and her new husband was already issuing orders. Though quite handsome on the outside, it was obvious he was a brute where it really counted.

But then, weren't most men? And after all, this was Scotland, the spring of 1643, and Laird Quinton MacLeod was beyond any doubt a Highlander all the way to his toes. If he was anything like the Scots portrayed between the pages of the historical romance novels she so loved to read, she had no doubt she was in store for a whole lot more alpha male antics. The problem was, what could she do about it?

She wanted to ignore him. Not just ignore, but actually disobey him. For too many years she'd lived under the thumb of a tyrant, and the cost of her freedom had come at a very high price. She'd not live that way again. She couldn't and survive a second time. But this was no longer the twenty-first century. Women had no rights. They were chattel, property.

In some of the romance novels she'd read, even the nicest hero types had at times…censured their heroines. She couldn't abide being beaten again, and she knew it.

Also, it was well known that men of this time period felt it their due to have as many women as they wished. Could she tolerate blatant infidelity again? And if she dared speak her mind, would Quinton MacLeod have her punished for her insolence?

Beth took a deep breath and gingerly plucked a piece of mystery meat from the slab of dry bread being used as a plate. Taking a nibble of the cold, watery, spiceless lump, she almost gagged. She didn't though. Slowly, she forced herself to chew and swallow it.

She drew not just from Elspeth's memories, but also from the pages of her precious novels, for a proper response. Turning to her brand new husband, Beth forced smile. "Forgive me, my lord. I did not mean disrespect to you or our hosts. The day has simply been overwhelming to my delicate sensibilities. After all, it's not every day a girl marries."

Quint nodded.

They ate in silence, neither looking at the other until suddenly the sound of bagpipes filled the room. Her head popped up so quickly she was almost overcome by a wave of dizziness, but Quint's hand touching her shoulder steadied her. "Shall we dance, wife?"

She looked into Quint's smiling face and couldn't bring herself to deny him. But then, how could she accept? She barely remembered the steps to the stupid electric slide she'd learned as a young girl, let alone a country dance from seventeenth century Scotland.

Again she probed Elspeth's mind, hoping for a thread of help with the problem, and there it was, as if she'd danced Scottish folk-dance steps every day of her life.

Beth smiled back at Quint and nodded.

She wanted to laugh, and she wanted to sing. Dancing within Quinton MacLeod's arms was the most fun she'd had in ever so long. He spun her with ease, and his steady hands held her gently. Though the steps were intricate, and she had to concentrate on where she set her feet, she could've done this all day.

Then he spun her away from him, and the next thing Beth knew, she was in the arms of the creepy viscount from the evening before. She almost stumbled.

He leaned in closer than she was comfortable with and whispered, "What a beautiful bride you make, my dear. How are you faring today?"

His breath smelled of sour whisky, and his eyes glared at her with a gray, dark madness. Try as she might, however, this time Elspeth's memories let her down, and she couldn't remember a single thing about him except for his title. "I'm fine, my lord. Thank you for asking."

The expression on his face didn't change in the least as the fingers he had been resting lightly at her waist suddenly squeezed tight. Beth took a deep breath as pain shot throughout her side.

"Don't play games with me, Elspeth," he hissed. "If you think for a moment you can act the idiot and go back on your word, you'd better think again. Pay heed to our bargain, my dear, for if you fail to follow through with your promises, I'll make sure your husband hears all about your involvement. He'll run you through with his very own blade and position your head on a pike to decorate his castle gate before I'm through."

Beth's mind screamed. Oh my god, what had Elspeth Frasier gotten herself involved with, and who exactly was this man to her?

The viscount smiled. "I must leave in the morning. The king is in Yorkshire, and so I must be also, but I'll have eyes watching until my return. Don't think I won't. You have until such time to carry through with what we discussed, my dear. Pity our plans of last evening were thwarted. I would've enjoyed watching Lady Lydia slump over dead right in her trencher."

He laughed. "But at least you managed to fumble your way through the wedding, and if the look on your husband's face is any indication, getting him to do his part in our little plan shouldn't be a problem."

Then, with a twirl, Beth found herself right back in the arms of her husband. His eyes gleamed with questions, but she didn't have any answers and she certainly didn't want to dance anymore.

She wanted to run away, but since she couldn't do that, she wanted to lie down somewhere and sleep. She didn't want to wake again until this nightmare was over and she was back in her own time where the world might be bitterly cold and unbearably lonely, but at least, it made sense.

****

He wanted to heft his claymore and slice Lord Fredrick, Viscount Telford, into tiny pieces. What had the man said to Elspeth when he'd been holding her much too close than was proper? When the viscount had finally twirled her back to Quint, the lass had trembled beneath his touch throughout the remainder of their dance and even during the short walk back to their table. Or had it been the viscount at all? Did his new wife, by chance, still maintain a secret passion for the Englishman lost to her?

While she'd been at court for the past two years, the viscount had been known only as one of Elspeth's many benefactors. But what was it that Quint didn't know of their day-to-day relationship that he probably should? Had they become more than benefactor and benefactress? Lovers even?

Rage filled him. If the old red-haired maid hadn't already collected Lady Elspeth and taken her to his room to prepare for his arrival, he would've asked his brand new wife that very question and demand she answer him before the entire hall.

His heart pounded so hard in his chest, Quint worried it might burst forth. He gulped long draws of breath, his lungs burning. He'd not have another man's leavings, especially not the viscount's. If his young bride turned out not to be chaste, he'd send her right back to the abbey, and she could live out her days there alone. He'd never again set eyes on her.

Slowly, the rage cooled and simmered. He could breathe once again.

But what if she'd been seduced away from him already like Mairi had been? What if Elspeth truly loved the man, or even worse, was nothing but a pawn in Telford's political game? Would he hold the blame of a lost maidenhead against her then? Elspeth was so young, so small, so fragile, and the viscount…well, he was not.

And in the end, could Quint blame her for a single moment of weakness, if there had been one? Would he still send her away if that were the case?

His fingers itched to draw his dagger and sink its blade deep into the viscount's heart. It would serve the man right. Or he could always simply toss the despicable man off the castle's highest parapet as he'd been accused of doing to his good friend and cousin, Dougal.

Quint sighed. He'd found Dougal's dead body wedged between the boulders holding the sea back from the base of Brochel Castle. It was a sight he'd never forget. Even now, more than seven years later, the memory made him queasy.

There lay Dougal, the bastard son of the MacLeod chieftain, John Iain, in a grisly tangle of limbs, blood, and gore, and not even a full night after coming to Quinton and professing his love for Mairi. He'd even openly confessed to her seduction and informed Quint of the child to come from their union.

Knowing what it had been to be raised a bastard himself, Dougal had begged to be allowed to take Mairi as wife, to insure his own son wouldn't suffer the same shame.

Mairi. The woman his eighteen-year-old self had been desperately in love with and the only woman he'd probably ever give his heart to. Not of high birth, Mairi was a daughter of a lowly serving wench, but that didn't matter to him. From the first, when they'd been children growing up together, he'd had every intention of making Mairi and none other his wife one day.

Mairi, with her strawberry-blonde hair, her haunting gray eyes, her playful smattering of freckles across her pert little nose, and tinkling laugh from her kissable lips.

The very same Mairi, Quint had angrily sworn before every man, woman, and child present at Brochel that Dougal MacLeod would never call his own. Even though Quint had been well into his cups when he'd declared it and not of sound mind or thinking straight, those words had become his deepest regret.

He never gotten the chance to take them back. Before the sun rose the next morning, Dougal MacLeod was dead, and if Quinton hadn't been the cause, then it appeared to be by Dougal's own hand.

Quint would've relented eventually, and in the end, he would've stepped aside. He would've. Especially, if he'd known a few months later, his beautiful Mairi would be taken from him, too.

He shook his head. Even if he hadn't personally pushed Dougal off that parapet, both his cousin's and Mairi's deaths were still his fault and their blood was on his hands. He was well known for his quick temper and jealousy, always had been. It was no wonder they'd felt the need to hide their relationship for as long as they did. Dougal and Mairi had both known he couldn't be trusted with that particular truth.

With Elspeth, though, he wouldn't make the same mistakes again. He wouldn't let his unreasonable jealousy override his good judgment. After all, he had no cause whatsoever to doubt Elspeth's chastity or intentions. And for that matter, no real proof of any misdeeds by the viscount.

But soon now, very soon, he'd know for himself. He'd have firsthand knowledge as to the true relationship between Lady Elspeth Frasier MacLeod and Lord Fredrick, Viscount Telford. And then he'd decide whether the viscount needed to be dealt his death this night or would live to breathe for at least another day.

Right or wrong, Quinton MacLeod wouldn't lose or share what was rightfully his ever again.

Chapter Four

Beth closed her eyes as tightly shut as she could get them and tried her best to relax. It didn't happen, she couldn't. She was worried about what the creepy viscount had said.

Though she'd sought the very deepest recesses of Elspeth's mind for answers, none came. Try as she might, only fleeting glimpses of places she didn't recognize and snippets of conversations with people she didn't even know—and that made no sense whatsoever—were all her efforts were rewarded with.

Then there was Quinton MacLeod. What was she going to do about her brand new husband? Any moment now, the Highlander would stalk through the door, climb right into the very bed she lay in naked, completely, as the day she'd been born, and ravish her.

Her breathing quickened, and a heat she'd forgotten she was capable of flowed through her. The old maid hadn't wasted any time stripping away every last stitch of clothing Beth had worn and then left her all alone. And what had Bronwyn's parting words been? "Have a good night, my lady. May the MacLeod ride ye long and hard, and may his cock stay stiff 'til morn."

Beth shuddered. She wasn't afraid of what Quinton MacLeod meant to do. After all, she'd been married for nineteen of her forty-five years and had sex more times with her ex-husband than she could count. Granted, she hadn't personally had sex with anything that didn't require batteries for the last eight years since her divorce, and she hadn't ever actually had sex with any other living breathing man except for Burt Anderson, but it wasn't because she was afraid of men. Not precisely anyway.

Why hadn't she sought company from the male species after her divorce? Beth sighed, and could no more answer that question now than when she'd asked it of herself on so many other occasions. It was just the way it had been. Sex with vibrators and dildos and such had been safe, easy, and kind.

Toys weren't mean and never cruel. When having a relationship with plastic or rubber, she didn't have to be young, slim, pretty, witty, or even know how to talk dirty. And a sex toy never, ever forced her to do things she didn't wish to do. Things that shamed her, things that hurt.

Beth shivered and tugged the fur cover closer around herself.

One thing was for certain, Lard Quinton MacLeod didn't come with batteries, but he would come with expectations. With Elspeth's lithe, young body, she wondered if she'd be able to accommodate those expectations to his satisfaction. Heat surged up her neck, down her belly, and pooled between her thighs.

She was surprised to realize she was actually kind of looking forward to the handsome Highlander striding through the door and having his way with her even more than she feared it. Did that make any sense at all? Did it make her a bad person?

She groaned. At her age and with her history, she

should at least be ashamed that she was soon going to be in the arms of a very young, very handsome man.

But she really wasn't.

With that thought in mind, Beth drifted off to sleep.

****

She stood in a shadowed corner of the room and eavesdropped on the conversation between Elspeth Frasier and the creepy viscount. Though Beth realized she was dreaming and was now simply a witness to one of Elspeth's more protected memories, she still felt like the worst of voyeurs when she couldn't bring herself to look away from the scene unfolding right before her eyes.

"I hate her, and I'll be glad when she's dead." Lady Elspeth Frasier glared at the man sitting nonchalantly across the room with his legs sprawled and a look of complete boredom on his face. "Well, say something, Fredrick. Ye stand to lose as much as I do if I fail at killing Lydia and she succeeds in marrying me off to that, that MacLeod person on the morrow."

The viscount chuckled. "As if I would wish to impede your upcoming nuptials? Unless you do succeed in killing your dear sweet stepmother, this evening, I'll be counting on them. As a matter of fact, my dear, unless Lydia does indeed die, I will be dancing at your wedding to that filthy Scot come the morrow.

"After all, what Lady Lydia Frasier said is true. You have managed to thwart her attempts for years by staying first at the abbey longer than you should have and then by hiding away at court. But alas, my sweet, Beth, your time, our time has all but run out. And perhaps you should try calling him Quinton or laird, anything but that MacLeod person. I seriously doubt your dear husband would wish for his bride to be so cold and distant. Especially considering what you must do if you end up married to him."

She balled up her fists. "Do nae be calling me Beth. My name is Elspeth. Ye ken well I don't like it when ye call me by any other name but the one my father gave me. And I'll call the devil MacLeod whatever I like."

He laughed out loud. "Your Scots gets quite strong, my dear, when you're upset. You sound nothing at all like a proper, future countess should."

Elspeth stomped her foot. "Oh, now do you see what she's done to me? You, of all people, know how hard I've worked not to sound provincial."

She took a deep breath. "I refuse to allow Lydia the power to turn me back into that stupid, silly, little girl I was when I first left for the abbey."

The viscount smiled. "Perhaps you need only to calm yourself and consider embracing these nuptials as I've asked. That is, if by chance you fail in your task of this evening. Have you not been listening to anything I've been telling you for more than a sennight? Stop thinking with your woman's heart, Elspeth, and take a moment to use your head. Can you not see this marriage fits perfectly into our plans? Look at the benefits. When all is said and done, we'll end up with either Frasier or Brochel castle for King Charles, and that is all you need to know in order to stay on task. Now do us both a favor, my dear. Stop fighting this and either kill off your stepmother this evening or marry the Scot come morning."

Elspeth gasped. "You can't truly mean that even if

I fail with Lydia, I'm to still… I thought you weren't serious when you suggested… I mean, I thought you loved me, Fredrick. I thought you were going to announce your intentions to wed me yourself at tonight's dinner. Right before I…" She shook her head. "Are you telling me you could actually bear to have another man's hands and lips, and other parts touching my body? Don't you love me? Don't you covet the maidenhead I've saved for you?"

The viscount smirked. "Oh, my dear Elspeth, what a child in a woman's body you still are at times. You have but seen the passing of a handful of summers and know only the world the sisters at the abbey and your guardians at court allowed you to see. On the other hand, I'm a learned man of the world and have thirty-six years and two barren wives behind me. You hold that maidenhead of yours in such high regard, where as I see it only as a bargaining chip."

****

Beth's eyes flew open as warm hands gently shook her awake. "Elspeth, are ye or are ye nae still a maiden?"

She stared up into the stormy blue eyes of Lard Quinton MacLeod and shook her head no, then nodded yes.

"Which is it?"

She cleared her throat. "I swear to you, m—my lord, Elspeth Frasier MacLeod's body is still untouched by any man."

Quint smiled as he slowly brought his lips to hers. He chuckled. "Nae for long it isna."

The heat of his kiss as his lips captured hers burned Beth with a passion that seared her to the depths of her being. She was helpless, defenseless against the onslaught. She opened in surrender as his tongue slipped between her lips. It was heaven.

Her Highlander tasted of the tangy sweetness of ale mixed with honey and smelled of lust sprinkled with manly musk. With his beefy arms that now held her close, along with his large strong hands that caressed her and combined with his firm, forceful lips that devoured her, he was impossible to resist. But then she didn't really want to.

"Mine," he whispered against her still partially open mouth as his fingers slowly trailed down her body and possessively grasped her mound. "You'll find me to be a greedy man, my wife, my Elspeth, my Beth. I do nae share what's mine, nae ever."

The smoldering fire of his gaze bore deeply into her soul, seeking, searching for answers to questions she couldn't give him. She gulped.

His fingers delved through the curls, parted her folds, and captured her clit, stroking it, teasing it, tormenting her.

She thought she'd known what to expect, was anticipating it even, in a way. But the flash of pleasure that shot outward in every direction, from the pit of her stomach, to the tips of her toes and all the way back up to the very roots of her hair, caught her by surprise.

He rose above her and, with one leg, quickly parted both of hers. He settled himself snugly between them. His erection was hard and nudged her opening.

Beth took a deep breath and held it, trying to squash the panic threatening to overtake her. Oh my god, hadn't the pain of losing her virginity once in a lifetime been more than enough? She readied herself for the agony to come. Though she didn't want it to invade and tried her best to block it out, the memory of the first time she'd been in this very same situation came rushing back. She stiffened.

They'd both been seventeen. Their junior year of high school had just ended, and in a matter of a couple months, they'd be seniors. The summer, like the rest of their lives, lay long and lazy before them, theirs to enjoy, theirs to relish.

They'd been doing some pretty heavy petting in the backseat of his car at the local drive-in, and Burt had just slipped his letterman's ring, attached to a thin gold chain, around her neck. He'd been so sweet when he'd asked her to be his steady girlfriend.

So very handsome, Burt Anderson was all muscle and brawn, a hair over six feet tall, blond, with big brown eyes, and the star running back of their school's football team to boot. Even now, she had no idea why he'd picked her. He could've had any girl he wanted.

She hadn't wanted to have her first sexual experience that night, especially not in the backseat of a car. But he'd told her it was an expected part of agreeing to be his. And it would be the proof he needed that she really, truly was the one.

She'd wanted so desperately to be in love, to be loved. Coming from a completely dysfunctional home, any emotions, other than anger and apathy, had been in short supply for as long as she could remember. Being wanted and at least desired by the oh so popular Burt Anderson and unconditionally accepted into his large circle of friends had changed her life. No longer was she the weird bookworm nobody noticed, and no longer the sad little plain Jane either.

The cheap, vinyl upholstery of his backseat against her bare skin had been cold as death. She'd clenched her eyes as tightly closed as she could get them and grimaced as his hands roughly groped her body. The sharp pain came swiftly before she'd even been able to prepare herself for it. She'd cried.

Not only had the tearing of her virginal membranes been excruciating, but the pain hadn't stopped even when she'd begged him to. In retrospect, it really was over with rather quickly, but not quick enough for her taste.

It should've been a warning she'd heeded, but it hadn't. She'd married the jerk a year later and only because she'd been careless and gotten herself pregnant.

Beth's mind returned to the present and was embarrassed to find Quinton MacLeod rigidly still above her, staring at her, as if she'd suddenly grown horns and turned purple.

"Are ye all right then, lass? There's nothing to be afraid of. I'll take care of ye. Just breathe."

She swallowed the lump in her throat before nodding.

"Are ye sure ye are all right? Ye look skittish as a wild pony. Though I do nae deny there's a bit of discomfort a woman's first time round, I do promise, I'll make sure ye have pleasure to temper its bite. Trust me, my Beth. Ye are safe with me in this and all things, always. Do ye ken?"

She gazed into the sincere eyes of Lard Quinton MacLeod—his hair falling forward, his lips pursing in concentration, and the muscles of his shoulders bunching. She almost sighed. He certainly wasn't Burt, and that was a good thing.

Yes, her first sexual experience had been horrible, she couldn't deny that, but if she had no choice but be in the twenty-year-old body of Elspeth Frasier, then why not at least give it another shot?

Taking another deep breath, her body suddenly tingling with anticipation, she nodded once more.

He kissed her again, but this kiss was different, and Beth relaxed ever so slightly in his arms. Though his passion was certainly evident, for his erection rested against her thigh, his lips were gentle. They coaxed, prodded, and tempted, instead of taking.

She sighed and opened to him.

His tongue probed the recesses of her mouth, and she inhaled the breath he'd just breathed out. All memory of Burt and his backseat faded away, replaced by bittersweet euphoria.

The man feasting on her mouth was like a drug, and she couldn't get enough. He was a potent, narcotic aphrodisiac. A female version of the little blue pill on steroids. And she? Well, she was quickly on her way to becoming an addict.

Her nipples pebbled, and her skin tingled. Shivers of excitement raced along her spine, and he'd only kissed her for the fourth time ever.

She sucked in a deep breath as she realized something about herself. She and Elspeth really did have something in common. In this man's arms, she found herself as inexperienced as any twenty-year-old virgin. Where had the worldly forty-five-year-old woman gone?

Perhaps a little bit of the older woman was still there, too. Oh yes, she wanted to touch her new husband. Every single hot, slick inch of him. She wanted to run her hands across his corded muscles, she wanted to grasp his large cock, and she wanted to feel the power of the man coursing beneath her fingertips. Her hands itched with the desire, with the need to do just that, but she was too overcome with shyness to even try.

He must have sensed her nervousness and her need, because a moment later, Quint lifted himself off her and slid to her side. He took her small hand into his large one, ran it down the length of his body, wrapped her fingers around his cock, and held them there. "Every bit of me was made for ye pleasure, my Beth, as ye body was made for mine. There is nothing I will deny ye in our bed. Ye ken?"

She wanted to cry, and tears stung the back of her eyes. Burt had certainly never cared if she'd had pleasure. As a matter of fact, within moments of him getting his rocks off, he'd been snoring every single time.

Quinton MacLeod's shaft pulsed beneath her grasp, and Beth shook her head. She would not cry, and she would not let that monster of an ex-husband spoil this moment for her like he'd spoiled so many others before.

Beth banished the thought and memory of Burt Anderson from her mind and from her wedding night bed. With a smile Beth hoped her brand new husband would interpret as flirty and with a playful squeeze of what she held within her grasp, she gazed intently into his stormy-blue eyes. "I don't know what to ask for, my lord."

He chuckled, and the feel of his joy vibrating against her skin had tiny bursts of pleasure pulsing straight through her heart.

He rolled her onto her back once more and hovered over her. "First, I want ye ta call me, Quint, lass. It's what those closest ta me do. I long to hear the sound of my name upon ye lips while we make love. Oh—" He chuckled. "—and I've an idea or two of what ye may come ta like." He laughed once more. "It's just a guess, though, ye ken?"

His mouth devoured her—her lips, her ears, and then her neck. His tongue lavished her heated skin while his hands freely roamed the contours of her body. For a fleeting moment, Beth regretted the fact that the real Elspeth Frasier was missing out on this most exquisite experience.

Then the laird—no, she wouldn't think of him as the laird again, at least not for the remainder of this night—Quint captured a pert nipple between his teeth and nipped. She forgot about everything she'd ever known of passion except for the feel of his very talented mouth.

"Oh, Quint." She moaned.

His tongue traveled as his fingers led the way. Across her chest from breast to breast, down her ribcage, and stopping for but a moment to playfully lap at her bellybutton. Her insides throbbed and pulsed. Her blood heated to a fevered pitch as his kisses burned a path ever downward.

Beth gasped as she realized where his tongue was headed and what he meant to do with it. How many times over the long years of her marriage had she given blowjobs to her ex and never once gotten the female equivalent of that oral gratification in return?

Her face burned. How many times had she listened

to her girlfriends brag about their husbands and lovers? How many times had she contributed comments so they wouldn't realize she'd never personally had that particular experience?

Well, she meant to have it now.

Beth grinned in the darkness and spread her legs in anticipation. So what if it had taken a lifetime to finally find out what it would be like to have a man, an incredibly hot hunk of a man, kissing her, nipping her, licking her, and sucking her *there*.

As a matter of fact, in truth, it had taken more than her one lifetime, and she meant to savor every last second of it.

She held her breath, and then gasped as Quint's fingers gently parted her folds and his hot breath brushed across her tender membranes no longer than a heartbeat before his lips captured her nub and sucked.

Sparks of pure sensation streaked from her clit straight to her core. Exquisite, absolutely mind-blowingly, heart-stoppingly exquisite.

No vibrator ever manufactured could do Quint MacLeod's tongue justice. He was like a man on a mission, and Beth loved it. He lapped and sucked, nipped and teased. She convulsed with pleasure, one moment trying to pull away as the delight became too intense and the very next second grinding against his wonderful mouth, begging him for more.

Pressure built deep within as the throbbing pleasure intensified. Tremors of white-hot jolts skittered through her belly, and quivers shook her frame. She fisted her hands in his hair and rocked her hips, hard against the pressure of his tongue, seeking, searching for, demanding release.

When it came, her orgasm was like being struck by a bolt of lightning. Swift and shocking, catching her by surprise, curling her toes, and crossing her eyes.

Once the pulsing waves ebbed, Quint placed a kiss upon her damp curls and chuckled as he slid up the length of her body. "I think it's safe ta say ye liked that, my Beth."

She stretched beneath him, still marveling in her very first orgasm ever without batteries, and was taken totally by surprise when he entered her. He was big, oh my god was he big, and Beth froze, expecting pain. It didn't really hurt this time, though. There was a pinching sensation as the head of his cock broke through her maidenhead, and she couldn't help but wince as he buried himself deep within her. But the sensation she now had of being wonderfully filled had nothing at all to do with pain.

He held himself perfectly ridged above her once more. "Are ye all right then, lass?"

Beth forced herself to look Quint in the eye. She wanted to tell him not only yes she was all right, but *hell yeah*. She didn't though. She held her tongue, nodded, and slowly wrapped her legs around his waist, burying him even deeper. She rocked her hips up against his and let her body do her talking.

His breath let out in a whoosh as he began to move, sliding in and out, first slow and steady, then faster, harder, and deeper.

Beth forgot to breathe, and she forgot where they were and why they were even here. All she could remember was the rock-steady arms as her Highland husband held her, his muscular thighs between hers, and the most superb penis she'd ever seen or felt in any time period anywhere was now pumping furiously into her, over and over and over again.

If this wasn't heaven, it certainly should've been.

She clinched her legs and arms tightly about his torso as she sought to find her own rhythm. Stroke after delightful stroke filled her, and in response, pressure began building once more.

At first, she ignored it. Orgasms with toys had been hard enough to achieve, let alone a second one tonight during a real sexual encounter. It couldn't be happening. It simply couldn't. But still, with every downstroke Quint's thick cock made, the sensations grew until she found herself whimpering, "Don't stop, don't stop, for the love of God, please don't stop."

His chuckle sent a wave of shivers skittering along her spine. "Ye have nae ta worry about on that count, lass. Being inside ye feels like flying ta heaven and coming back home all at the same time. I could nae stop right now, even if our verra lives depended upon it."

With that, he redoubled his efforts and pounded into her furiously.

Her breath caught in her chest as a sense of wonder engulfed her. Spasms of pure pleasure flooded every fiber of her being a mere heartbeat before Quint stiffened above her and found his release.

She gloried in the feel of his hot semen coating her still trembling insides, and with a sigh of contentment, she drifted off to sleep, wrapped securely in Quinton MacLeod's arms.

****

Beth watched her husband sleeping, her eyes drowsily threatening to close. The warmth of his arms lulling her into an unfamiliar feeling of safety.

She smiled and almost laughed but covered her mouth to stifle the noise. She didn't wish to wake the sleeping Highlander beside her. For waking Quint might also awaken his seemingly insatiable hunger for her. What had it been, twice, no, three times he'd made love to her, with her, with such tenderness and passion his efforts had brought tears to her eyes.

Hmm. On second thought, perhaps she should wake him.

Beth did giggle then.

The thought of making love once more, then actually falling to sleep in his arms again, in the same bed as this man was so foreign to her, it struck her as funny. How long had it been since she'd made love, then peacefully slept the night through beside a man? She couldn't even remember. It was one of the reasons she hadn't dated since her divorce. She hadn't wanted to tell some guy that though they could join their bodies in the most personal of ways, he couldn't possibly spend the night.

Even after eight years of being single, being alone, there were still nights she'd wake in a cold sweat and fearful. Not knowing exactly where she was or what was about to happen.

It had been one of Burt's favorite games. He'd wait until she was sound asleep to attack. At first, it had been a quick hard shake or slap to the face. Then began the hours of yelling and the punishments.

"How dare you sleep when my sons are dead because of you," he'd scream. *"You killed them, and you don't even care. No one cares but me. You're happy they're gone, aren't you? Admit it, bitch."*

She probably would've survived with only

superficial wounds to her soul if shakes, slaps, and words had been where it stopped. It wasn't, though, it had only been the beginning. Next came the ripping off of whatever she'd worn at the time. Then the rapes. Though since they were legally married, she couldn't even call them that. Finally, the last year of their marriage, Burt had added the beatings to what he'd termed *what she had coming*.

Not long after that, he'd demanded she file for divorce. There truly was a God above, and he'd found Burt a new love on the Internet, six states away. Someone who'd promised to come to Florida and give him back what he felt Beth had taken from him. She couldn't have been happier to oblige. It had been the final straw that had freed her.

Actually getting away hadn't been as easy as it should've been. It hadn't taken Burt long to figure out Miss Internet Lover wasn't all she portrayed herself to be. He changed his mind about the divorce and demanded Beth put a stop to it. After all, without her income, who would support him?

But after the glimpse of freedom the idea of a divorce awarded her, there was no going back. That was the first time she'd out and out lied to him. The first of many more to come.

She even let him listen into the call she made to her lawyer's office telling him to stop the previously uncontested divorce proceedings Burt had already signed off on. But he didn't get a chance to hear the conversation between her lawyer and herself the next day when she'd assured her legal aid the call had been made under duress and to ignore it.

For the next three months, while the divorce

proceeded without Burt's further knowledge, Beth hid things she couldn't live without in her lunch bag. Instead of taking her normal apple and salad or soup and sandwich, she substituted treasures. She'd stashed her stolen booty safely in her locker at the middle school where she taught.

Every day, she'd taken something else, pictures of her children, their birth and death certificates, school report cards, popsicle stick Christmas ornaments, baked clay handprints, birthday and mother's day cards the boys had given her, articles of clothing she'd need, and anything else she couldn't bring herself to leave behind. She'd tucked all of it away and waited.

The day the divorce papers came she tucked those away, too, and started a job search on the Internet. Wanting to get as far away from Burt Anderson and Miami, Florida, as she could get, her job search took her to Anchorage, Alaska. It took less than a month to land a new teaching position beginning in the fall and even less time to horde away what she could from the household allowance and secretly purchase a plane ticket.

The last morning she'd seen Burt Anderson's face, she'd kissed him goodbye the same as she always had. She wished him a good day, told him she'd be late getting home because of a teachers' meeting, and walked out the door. By the time the last bell of the school day finished ringing, Beth had cleaned out their bank account, was thirty thousand feet in the air, and half way to Alaska.

Tears threatened at the memory, and she quickly swiped them away. She hated that even now, even almost four hundred years in the past, she still allowed her jerk of an ex-husband so much power to hurt her.

Quint stirred and wrapped an arm possessively about her middle. His voice was no more than a breath upon the air. "Why are ye crying, lass?"

"I'm not." She sniffled.

Quint chuckled. "I ken the sound of tears when I hear them, my Beth. Perhaps I can think of a way ta make ye forget whatever's causing ye sadness?" He nuzzled her neck and ear. "I'll nae have my wee wife weeping on her wedding night. Nae as long as there's breath left in my body ta prevent it."

And thankfully, that's precisely what he did as he parted her thighs and slipped his cock deep inside. Wonder replaced sadness as with stroke after stroke their bodies melded into one. Shivers of heat scampered along the curve of her spine, and a steady pulsating throb of delight tapped out a rhythm of ecstasy upon her clit until she was sure she'd die of pure pleasure if his attention went on for even one moment longer.

She didn't die though. On the contrary, she soared as the bliss of release once more shattered her soul into a million bright shiny pieces and then brought them all back together again, safely held within the confines of Quinton MacLeod's big, strong arms.

Beth contently closed her eyes and drifted off to sleep. For the first time in ever so long, she felt safe, truly safe.

Chapter Five

Quint studied his bride from the bow of the boat and shook his head. His wife sat huddled in her cloak, shivering against the brisk wind, as if she hadn't been born and raised, at least partially, in the Highlands. The crossing between the Isle of Lewis and the Isle of Raasay wouldn't take very long, but the small channel was well known for its invigorating breeze.

Who was this fey creature now his wife? It was as if she were somehow two different people, one by day and yet another by night. If he lived to be a thousand, he'd never truly understand the workings of a woman's mind.

As the light of morning dawned, Elspeth Frasier MacLeod had once more become the same spoiled, self-centered harridan he'd met a few days past.

After the wonderful night they'd spent in each other's arms, he had been so sure she'd be different, but she wasn't. She'd still ordered his people around, as if she were a princess and her needs the only ones important enough to be met. Even an entire boat had been required just to haul her trunks.

How could one wee female possess so much?

In all fairness, it hadn't actually been his Beth who'd shouted out demands. It was the red-headed hag of a maid, Bronwyn, who Lady Lydia herself had sent along to personally see to Elspeth's needs. No servant would dare do such a thing without her mistress demanding it, though, would she?

But Elspeth hadn't spoken more than a handful of words to anyone the entire morning. Not as they'd shared a trencher to break their fast, and not even as they'd said their goodbyes to Lady Lydia and her brother, the Mackenzie.

This...Elspeth was a direct contrast to the Beth he'd held in his arms all through the night. Though his Beth had been a shy innocent one moment and a demanding vixen the next, at no time had she ever been quiet.

He hardened once more at the memory of her soft sighs, moans, gasps, and squeals of delight. They'd made love four times before the first rays of sunlight streaked the eastern sky, and then once more for good measure before rising.

What had caused this change? The poor lass was no doubt a tad tender from his overzealous ministrations, but in all fairness, he had warned her. Could it instead have something to do with what the viscount had said to her as the two passed on the stairs?

As short as the conversation was, it couldn't have been much of an exchange. And Beth hadn't spoken so much as a single word in response to whatever the viscount had leaned in to say. The short conversation had been over almost before it began, and if he hadn't been watching for Beth, he would've probably missed it.

But whatever the viscount had said, Quint had every intention of finding out the moment they reached Brochel Castle.

The Beth he'd held last night couldn't possibly be

in league with Telford, and therefore a traitor to him and his people, could she? Not after what they'd shared. And which woman would he be presenting to his people this day as their lady when the boats landed, Elspeth Frasier of the English court or *his* Beth, his wife of the night past?

He hoped it was his latter.

****

God, she so needed to talk to Fate. Would he know where Quint was taking her? Would she be able to find a few moments of privacy to call for him?

Beth wrapped her cloak closer about her shoulders and shivered. Not knowing if the cold was from the wind or her fear. The words of the creepy viscount still rang in her ears. "I hope you got a good start on producing that heir, my dear. Remember, our plan counts on you delivering."

Our plan?

She had racked Elspeth's mind for any more memories that might give her answers and had come up empty. She wanted to sleep, maybe she'd remember then. Yes, she so needed a nap. Not that trying to remember Elspeth's memories had anything to do with the reason she hadn't gotten much sleep last night.

That thought brought a small secretive smile to her lips. Oh no, she certainly hadn't slept much last night, and though what sleep she had gotten between bouts of lovemaking had been short, she didn't regret that fact for a moment.

Quint had been amazing, and though she should probably feel guilty for doing what she'd done with such a young, hot, sexy man, she simply didn't. And not only didn't she feel guilty about it, but she couldn't wait for her next chance to do precisely the same thing.

Turning to glance at the man she'd been thinking, fantasizing, and daydreaming about, her breath caught in her chest. There, rising from the sea was the most beautiful castle she'd ever seen, and since she'd been on a tour of Scotland and its castles when she'd died, that was saying a lot.

It wasn't the biggest or the grandest, but with the sun glittering off the four tall towers, it looked magical. Why hadn't she noticed it two days prior when she'd been on her way to the Isle of Lewis and the standing stones?

Then a whisper so close to her ear it warmed her skin explained why. "That's Brochel Castle ahead, lass, our home."

Tears threatened. This was Brochel? The same Brochel that almost four hundred years from now would be no more than a single tower, a partial wall, and rubble? It hurt her heart to think time would waste away something so beautiful and formidable.

She looked at Quint and smiled, hoping the sadness didn't show in her expression. "It's lovely."

He touched her cheek tenderly. "Why so troubled, my Beth? Did I go too far last night? I should've kenned better than to have used ye so rough."

Beth wanted to kiss him. She wanted to rest her head on his shoulder and cry. She did neither, however. She smiled at her husband and whispered, "You did not use me too roughly, my lord. I enjoyed your attention." Heat warmed her chilled cheeks. "I am but tired and have need of a nap." Then she winked. "Perhaps you have need of a nap also, my lord?"

Quint smiled, nodded, and laughed.

****

She slipped from beneath his arm and out of his bed as stealthily as she could. Wrapping herself in his plaid and glancing back to make sure she hadn't awakened him, Beth sighed.

Laird Quinton MacLeod, even asleep, was really a more handsome sight than should be legally allowed. Dark brown, tousled locks of hair lay gently across his forehead, and his more than kissable lips moved ever so slightly as he quietly snored. A bare hairy leg stuck out from under the fur coverlet, and the outline of his fine ass lay less than the reach of a hand away. It was so tempting to give into her obsession for her new husband and snuggle with him, especially after what they'd once more shared.

Beth shook her head and looked away. Later perhaps, but right now, there really was something very important she needed to do first.

Slipping into the small chamber off the larger one where her highlander slept, she cupped her hands around her mouth and whispered, "Fate? Tobias? Mr. Moiré, I need you." She glanced around the corner to make sure Quint still slept, then whispered again, a little louder this time, "Fate, I'm not kidding. Get here now. I really need to talk to you."

The air around her began to shimmer, and suddenly, he was there. Mousey brown hair, wire-rimmed glasses, long white robe, and all. "This had better be important, madam. I was right in the middle of whipping up a storm, a very good storm if I do say so myself. You do realize I have a job to do, don't you? You aren't my only responsibility."

Beth took a deep breath. "Are you done with the

lecture? I need your help. I wouldn't have called for you if it weren't imperative." She paced back and forth across the small room. "The creepy Lord Fredrick, Viscount Telford, wants me to give Quint an heir as badly as you do, though I don't know why. He says it has to do with *our* plan. But I don't know what that plan is, and I wouldn't want any part of it or of him, even if I did."

Fate cleared his throat. "Do stop flittering back and forth, madam. You are making me dizzy. And how would I know what the viscount's plan is or was? In the history I know, Elspeth died remember? Whatever plan the viscount had must have died along with her. Did you search Elspeth's memories as I instructed you to?"

Beth scowled. "Of course, I did. That's why I called you. I've gotten no help from Elspeth's mind on this issue."

Once more, she peeked into the sleeping chamber to make sure Quint hadn't awakened.

Fate was the one to pace this time. "Time is a tricky thing. Since Lady Elspeth didn't die as she originally did, you are now rewriting history, so to speak, and I'm afraid you are quite on your own in this endeavor. Everything you do, everything you say has never been done or said before by Elspeth. Time really is like a ripple upon a pond. There's no telling how far reaching the changes may be."

Beth crossed her arms and glared. "Well, that's certainly no help. What if I make a mistake and someone gets hurt who shouldn't? What if the viscount now means to harm Quint in some way, and I'm part of that? And what about all the people who count on Quinton MacLeod as their laird? What will happen to them?"

Fate chuckled. "Why do you care what happens to people who lived almost four hundred years before you were even born? All you need do is give the laird his heir. That should be your only concern, madam. Then you get your wish and move on to be with your own children. End of story. We all live, or in your case, die happily ever after."

Tears stung her eyes. Fate was right. She shouldn't care. She did want to be with her children so very much. Not just wanted to be with them, but needed to be. Still, the thought of harm to Quint or the people who counted on him bothered her.

Beth shook her head. "I can't do it. I can't be part of your crazy scheme to make right a wrong you are responsible for. I won't do it, and you can't make me."

Tobias Moiré began to shimmer. "I don't need to make you, madam. You already carry the beginning of Quinton MacLeod's heir within Elspeth's body. I mean really, you did *it* at least five times before you ever left the Isle of Lewis, and then once here already. And I might remind you, without any form of birth control. What else did you expect would happen?"

He was almost transparent, and his last words drifted back to Beth on no more than a breath. "You won't see me again until it's time to give birth to Quinton MacLeod's son, so don't bother to call, madam, because I won't come. Until then, I do wish you luck."

Then, as if he'd never been there at all, he was gone.

After less than twenty-four hours of marriage, she was already pregnant? She now carried the MacLeod heir within her womb? She slumped to the floor, her hands protectively covering Elspeth's middle. What had she done, and what was she going to do about it?

The tears came fast and hot.

She couldn't do this. She couldn't be pregnant. She didn't want to be. As a matter of fact, being pregnant was the very last thing Beth had ever expected to be again. And especially not here and now. Even though she'd reluctantly agreed to give Quint an heir, part of her hadn't really believed it would happen.

This was 1643 for God's sake. There were no obstetricians, no hospitals, and no prenatal care. And—and no epidurals like in the time period in which she gave birth to her children. The mortality rate had to be through the roof.

Fear gripped her as she ran her hands down Elspeth's lithe body. Could someone so petite even safely deliver a child? And she'd bet her left big toe, that if they'd even been attempted yet, there weren't many successful C-sections in the year 1643 either.

Beth had read horror stories. Hour after endless hour of labor until both mother and child perished. She shivered, though not from the cold. If she really was rewriting history, and even Fate couldn't tell her how this story would end, what power did she have to change the outcome?

Fate was right. Why should she care about Quint, his people, or his son? This wasn't her time, and it wasn't her place. Hell, it wasn't even her body or her child. It was Elspeth's. Still, her hand lightly stroked her belly.

She would not love this child, and she certainly wouldn't love his father, no matter how handsome or charming he might be. If life had taught Beth anything, it was, if you love someone, they'll either be taken from you, leave you all alone, or drive you away. Beth wouldn't chance giving her heart again. It was no longer hers to give anyway. She'd left the biggest majority of it alongside a wet roadside in Miami, Florida, on a late July evening.

She wanted to be with her children in Heaven. She really did. Not only wanted to be there, but needed to be. There was unfinished business to attend to. That was what was important. Not Quint, not his castle, or his child, his people, or even whatever the creepy viscount had planned for them all.

Yes, with the decision made, she wiped the tears from her eyes. She needed to stop worrying about anything else and keep her mind focused on getting through this…pregnancy. It was her ticket out of here and into heaven, after all.

Nine months. That was it, and she'd be where she needed to be. A simple forty-week gestation period, easy-peasy. She could do it.

Beth shivered again. She only hoped, in the end, she wouldn't have to suffer a second death to get where she needed to be.

****

What exactly was the function of the lady of the keep?

That had been Quint's answer to her question this morning right before he'd kissed her soundly and walked through the wide wooden doors of the castle's great hall and out into the sunlight.

It had slipped out really, the question, that was. Beth hadn't even realized she'd asked it out loud. She'd simply been thinking. "What am I supposed to do with myself now?"

"Be the lady of the keep, of course. 'Tis who ye are," he'd said.

For not the first time in the past few days, she mentally kicked herself for not paying closer attention to the details in the historical romance novels she'd so enjoyed reading. Oh no, she'd been to wrapped up in the hero, the heroine, and their love story itself to care about what things were, how they functioned, or who did what.

She sighed. All the hours of research those poor romance writers must have done, and here she'd skimmed the majority of it in her quest to locate the next sizzling, hot love scene. She really was a dirty little old lady at heart.

Being a middle school history teacher wasn't much help either. She could rattle off the names of every American president in the order they'd served their country. She knew the dates they entered office, the years of their births and deaths, who they married, and even how many children they'd had.

Beth knew when the first ship landed on the eastern coast of the United States, when the first covered wagon crossed the prairie, and when the first spike was driven into the very first railroad to span the continent. She even knew when the first shot was fired in not only the Revolutionary, but also the Civil, the Spanish-American, First and Second World, Korean, Vietnamese, and Afghani-Iraqi wars. John F. Kennedy had been assassinated only a handful of years or so before her birth, and Martin Luther King and Robert Kennedy when she'd been but a babe.

As not much more than a toddler, she'd watched a man walk on the moon, and then a few years later, she'd stared in abject horror as a space shuttle blew apart right before the world's eyes. She'd been in shock when John Lennon had been senselessly murdered, and even more so when so many lives that shouldn't have been were lost in Oklahoma. Let alone the aftermath of the day the Twin Towers fell, and all of America lost its innocence forever.

She'd grown up, gotten married, given birth to, and watched her two best reasons to live die a horrible death. My God, she'd even died herself, once, so far. Yet, here in the year 1643, she didn't have a clue as what to call the table she now sat before or even how to begin to dress herself without help.

How sad was that?

She fisted her hands upon her hips and glanced around the great hall. The beautiful tapestry hanging on the wall above the fireplace and depicting fanciful mermaids rising from the sea was blackened in places with soot. The floor was littered with what looked to be dry hay, and *things* crunched beneath her feet. Even the table she sat at was so filthy it was impossible to tell what kind of wood it had originally been made from.

Perhaps she hadn't concentrated her studies on and didn't remember much about Scottish history and perhaps she'd even make a fool of herself for trying to make a difference here in what little time she had left to her, but one thing was for certain. All of her adult life she'd worked and she'd worked hard. She wasn't about to change now.

If she really was the lady of the keep, then, for the time being anyway, this was her home, her house, and she would clean it. There was no way Bethany-Elspeth Frasier-MacLeod was going to hide away in her room and do nothing for the next nine months.

She went looking for soap, hot water, a rag, a mop, and a broom.

Chapter Six

"My lady!" A stout, gray-haired woman standing before a brick oven in what must be the kitchen attempted a curtsy, and Beth couldn't help but smile.

Two other females, young girls really, who were kneading bread dough at a nearby table, literally froze in place, while a boy with a dirty face and an even dirtier plaid wrapped around his skinny little body stared up at her, as if seeing a truly frightening sight.

Beth cleared her throat. "Hello."

The stout woman found her voice. "The name's Annie, my lady, but most calls me Cook. Was the morning's fixin's nae ta ye liking?"

Her cheeks were rosy-red, probably from the heat of the ovens, and she wrung her hands nervously, as if she were standing before royalty.

Beth had an almost overwhelming urge to reach out and hug her. Instead, she held out a hand, and the other woman reluctantly took it. "It's nice to meet you, Annie. Please, call me Beth. The food was fine. I do, however, have a question for you. Where might I find cleaning supplies?"

Annie didn't release her hand, but she didn't answer the question either. She stared at Beth as if she had spoken a language the other woman couldn't comprehend.

She tried again. "You know, cleaning supplies, like

a broom, a mop, soap, water?"

The rosy-red of Annie's cheeks spread to the rest of her face. "What do ye want cleaned, my lady?" She pointed toward the two young girls still frozen in place. "Tell me, and I'll put me granddaughters, Lana and Elisa, right on it."

Beth shook her head. "No, no, you misunderstand. I just need to know where to find the supplies. I'm going to clean the great hall today myself."

The gray-haired cook let go of Beth's hand, as if it were too hot to hold onto, and bellowed at the top of her lungs. "Bronwyn!"

Within moments, the old, red-headed maid appeared. "What is it now, Annie? I'm busy. I have the laird's chamber along with her lady's things ta attend to. I don't have time ta be running up and down the stairs every time ye've got a question. I already told ye what her ladyship likes ta eat."

Beth almost laughed. Annie pointed toward her, and with her other hand, cupped her mouth as if that action would prevent Beth from hearing what the woman had to say, she said, "It's about our lady. I think she's taken ill. Says she wants a broom and such so she can clean."

Bronwyn sighed and took hold of Beth's arm, but it was Annie she addressed. "Aye, Lady Elspeth hasn't really been herself lately. Had a nasty fall a few days back, she did. Hit her head, and now she sometimes says the strangest things." She began backing out of the kitchen, pulling Beth along with her. "We'll nae be mentioning this ta the laird, now will we?"

Annie, the two young girls, and even the dirty little boy, all shook their heads.

****

"Who are ye and what have ye done with Lady Elspeth? Are ye a fairy then? A sprite perhaps? Or a witch?"

Sitting on the edge of the bed she'd shared with Quint MacLeod last night, Beth glanced at the maid. Bronwyn really did look frightened.

How was she supposed to answer the question? It wasn't as if she could tell Bronwyn that no, she wasn't any of those things. That in reality, she was a dead forty-five-year-old woman from almost four hundred years in the future, and she was simply using this body for the next nine months so she'd be allowed to join her dead children. How well would that go over? She caught herself before she could laugh at the ridiculousness of the situation.

"Well?" Bronwyn persisted.

Beth sighed once more and allowed memories from Elspeth's childhood to flow through her. Memories of being sent to live at the abbey when she'd been but twelve years old. Memories of lying awake in her bed at night, frightened, alone, missing her father, missing her home. Feeding her hatred for Lady Lydia, the one person she held responsible for being where she was.

Memories of never fitting in. Not with the nuns or even with the other girls in residence. Memories of always being considered the rich, spoiled little *lady* whose every want and need had been paid for in advance and had better be filled immediately or else. At least the wants and needs that didn't have anything to do with ever returning home again. Memories of never having any friends, of growing more and more bitter, more lonely, more angry as the years went by.

How sad.

"I am not a fairy, a sprite, or a witch, Bronwyn. I am Lady Elspeth MacLeod."

The old maid shook her head. "Ye do nae act like her, and ye haven't since ye fell and hit ye head. If'n ye truly are Lady Elspeth, then what was the last thing ye said ta me about ye soon-ta-be-husband before ye made ye way down the stairs ta supper that night? The same husband, I might add, that ye seem ta more than well enough like now."

Beth cringed, and once more drew upon Elspeth's memories, afraid of what she might or might not learn.

There it was, the scene, almost as if she were watching it unfold on a TV screen. Elspeth stood at the top of the stairs while Bronwyn made last minute adjustments to her hair and gown. The maid looked nervous.

"Now smile, my lady. After the fit he heard ye throw yesterday, it's important ta make a fine impression on the MacLeod laird this evening."

Elspeth had turned, a smirk on her face. *"Impress him? Oh, I'd like to impress him, all right. I'd like to impress my eating knife right into his black Scots heart."*

Beth shuddered as she recited the words of the memory to the maid.

****

It had been a day filled with vigorous training, and Quinton was more than ready for a hot meal followed by a long night spent within the arms of his pretty little wife. He threw open the doors of the great wall, and he and his men stepped inside.

He stopped dead in his tracks. The first thing he

noticed was the smell. He wrinkled his nose as the fragrance of…flowers assaulted his senses.

Flowers?

He gaped. Where was the tapestry depicting the frolicking mermaids? His mother had spent years stitching it. No longer did it hang in its place of honor above the fireplace. And where was the symbol of Clan MacLeod? The boar's head flanked by spears, proudly proclaiming the clan motto of *Hold Fast*? His father had fashioned it from bronze with his own hands and hung it himself above the laird's seat.

Why were there no rushes below his feet, and why did everything look so bloody bright? Even the birch logs his father had used to build the great board he ate his meals upon gleamed bright enough Quint could've seen his reflection in them if he'd a mind to do so.

His stomach churned, and his head pounded. There could be only one reason his castle had been turned into an English manor house, and he yelled her name. "Elspeth MacLeod!"

She came from the direction of the kitchen, but the woman who walked up to stand before him barely resembled the woman he'd brought here as his wife only yesterday.

This woman had her golden locks fashioned in a long braid down the middle of her back. The day dress she'd dawned this morning, though now covered for the most part by an apron, had spots and splotches upon it. She even had what looked to be a smudge of soot upon her cheek.

She wasn't alone either. The red-headed hag of a maid stood at her side, and almost every single castle servant was gathered behind her. Even Duncan, whose job it was to bring in the peat for the fires, was there. And, like his castle, they all appeared to have been freshly scrubbed. What had the lass done to bewitch his people?

"My keep smells of flowers, lass, and the rushes are gone and my mother's tapestry?" He hesitated a moment and took a deep breath. "Where is the MacLeod clan symbol? And the floors, the board, the benches, they're clean. Why?"

The wench had the nerve to actually smile, and Quint wanted to shake her. His servants were scowling, however, so he stopped yelling and gave Beth a chance to explain.

"Your keep needed a good cleaning, my lord. It smelled bad. Cleanliness is next to godliness, I always say." She gulped. "I mean, that's what the nuns at the abbey always said. And as for your mother's tapestry and your clan symbol, they are safe and drying. You should be so proud of your people, my lord. They were only too glad to help."

Heat crept up his neck as Quint heard snickering coming from his men. "This is a man's castle, Elspeth MacLeod. As a matter of fact, it's a Scottish man's castle, ye ken? We do not smell of flowers. We take pride in the fact we smell of an honest day's work and sweat. Ye will nae do this again, ye ken?"

Beth placed her hands upon her hips, and though Quint recognized the glint of stubbornness in her eyes, he was nowhere near prepared for what she did next. He was more than a little startled when she actually had the audacity to reach out and poke him in the chest.

"You said be the lady of the keep, did you not?"

He nodded.

"And as lady of the keep, does that not mean the running of this castle is *my* responsibility?"

Once again he nodded, but Quint also opened his mouth to retort.

Beth shook her head. "Oh no, you don't, MacLeod. You don't get to have it both ways. Either I run this castle as I see fit or I don't run it at all." She stomped her foot. "There's nothing wrong with being clean. It's important to me. And if you and your men wish to eat within the walls of this castle that I'm now lady of, then you'll take yourselves back outside those doors, down to the sea or to the loch, whichever you prefer, and wash your hard-earned sweat from your bodies. You, my lord, stink."

Quint crossed his arms. "No wee female tells Laird Quinton MacLeod when and where he will eat in his own castle or when he shall bathe, lass." The other men loudly added their own voices to his, and Quint looked toward Annie and ordered, "Serve ye laird his evening meal, cook, and be quick about it."

Annie glanced first toward Beth, and then back at Quint. "I'd be glad ta do that, my lord, and a fine supper it is we'll be having. Made a hearty fish stew, I did, and hot crusty bread the way ye like." She jerked her thumb toward her granddaughters. "Me and the lasses here will be serving ye supper up as soon as ye and the other laddies are finished washing up as our ladyship has so sweetly asked. Even though we ain't Catholics no more, we can't be snubbing our noses at the old church's teachings, now can we? Why, that'd be like going against God hisself."

****

She almost felt sorry for him.

86

From the corner of her eye, Beth watched her husband. Quint hadn't spoken a single word since he and his men had come back inside from bathing. He'd simply taken his rightful seat at the head of the table and waited as food was placed before him. He hadn't even looked her way, not once, not a smile, not a frown, not a touch, not even a grumble.

His men weren't doing much talking either. Everyone ate in silence, the great hall more a tomb than a place to socialize.

Well, she'd certainly made a mess of that, hadn't she? What had seemed like such a good idea a short while ago didn't sit so well now.

Beth blamed it on the romance writers. Not once had any of her favorite authors warned her about the realities of historical Scotland, especially the smell. The lust-filled love scenes certainly hadn't included the stench of unwashed bodies, and though Quinton MacLeod really was more handsome than should be allowed and sexier than any man she'd ever seen in any time period, the stench of day-old sweat was still the stench of day-old sweat.

Her heart pounded.

Quint was so very handsome it almost hurt her eyes to look upon him for too long. His chocolate brown hair was disheveled from the quick wash, and Beth longed to comb her fingers through it. But his eyes burned with anger, and the lines at the edges of his magical lips were tight and drawn.

What could she do to make him smile once more?

Beth thought about her day as she nibbled from the trencher she and Quint shared. After convincing Bronwyn she really was Elspeth and not some evil creature, winning over the majority of the rest of the staff, especially with tales she'd made up of the abbey and its rules, had been a piece of cake.

Servants had literally come out of the woodwork to do her bidding. They'd all been more than polite and eager to do whatever she'd asked of them. And once they saw their very own mistress wasn't afraid of a little hard work herself, they'd really put their backs into every task.

That is except for the young woman called Marta. With the very first mention of work, the beautiful, strawberry-blonde servant had scowled at her with a look of complete disdain and then simply disappeared.

She hadn't worried about it, though. And before Beth got the chance to even realize the day was almost over, not only had the great hall been cleaned, but the kitchen, a few of the upstairs chambers, and even the staff themselves now gleamed.

How long had it been since the castle was thoroughly cleaned before this day? She had wanted so very much to ask that question but was afraid she'd insult Quinton MacLeod's people, so she hadn't.

She giggled as the memory of young Duncan, the peat boy, and his particular bath invaded her mind. Talk about insult. The little ball of fury had fought as hard as any aged warrior.

Quint glanced her way, his eyes hard and questioning. Beth stifled her humor.

Yes, Duncan's bath wasn't something Beth was soon to forget. Just a few months past six years, according to Annie, and with what was obviously a severe club foot to boot and limbs so thin they could hardly be called more than twigs, he had certainly surprised her with his tenacity.

It had taken not only her, but Annie, her two granddaughters, and Bronwyn to wrestle the child out of his ragged plaid and into the big tub. Even with five people holding him down long enough to scrub away the filth, by the time they'd finished, not only was the water muddy, but they themselves were wetter than he was. Who would've guessed his soot black hair was really a sweet strawberry-blond or that he had an adorable smattering of freckles across his nose?

And the big tub itself...wow, what a pleasant surprise that had been. Almost as wonderful a surprise as the indoor well.

Annie had explained that, other than the MacLeod seat of Dunvegan, Brochel Castle was the only other to have such a wonderful luxury.

But the tub, oh my, the tub was magnificent. It was large and wooden and round. Big enough to easily hold two full grown adults without sloshing too much water over its side. The most amazing thing about the tub, though, was it could be easily drained.

Very close to the bottom edge of the round wooden tub, facing the outer wall, a pipe fashioned from a small hollowed out tree trunk had been inserted. It went from the inside of the tub, through a hole in the castle wall, and out onto a patch of ground somewhere behind the kitchen. A simple wooden plug made filling or draining it a breeze.

Annie had told her that Quint had built it himself when he'd been not much older than Duncan. It had taken him most of a year and been a gift for his mother.

The tub was used for many tasks. The washing of clothing, the dying of wool, the pressing of apples into cider, the making of ale, and yes, even the occasional bath.

Beth smiled to herself. An idea formed as to what might brighten Quinton MacLeod's mood.

****

"I'm tired, Elspeth, leave me be."

Beth glared at her husband who stood staring out the window of their chamber. "You only call me Elspeth when you're angry with me. Did you know that? I want to show you something in the kitchen. It'll only take a few minutes, my lord, I promise."

The stubborn man shook his head, crossed his arms, and firmly planted his feet in a stance not even a bulldozer could've moved.

"I've no concern for whatever ye wish ta show me, lass. I've had more than enough surprises this day. Anyway, the kitchen is for women, not warriors."

She wanted to stomp on his big arrogant foot. She wanted to grab his arm and drag him where she wanted him to go. She couldn't though. Even if she'd had the strength, she certainly didn't have the nerve.

What had she been thinking in the first place? Had she actually believed she could trick her husband into following her back downstairs and then seduce him with a hot bath?

She took a deep breath. Perhaps the old forty-five-year-old Beth with her flabby, saggy body couldn't, but she'd bet her life that young, pretty Elspeth MacLeod could.

She turned her back to her husband. "Fine then. Would you be so kind as to unlace me?"

The sound of his sigh and the heat of his fingertips through the fabric of her day dress bolstered her courage as nothing else could. Beth allowed him to undo and slip the garment from her shoulders and down over her hips. She even stepped out of layer after layer of shifts as he divested her of those also. She didn't turn to face him, however, not until she stood totally naked.

"Come to the kitchen with me, my lord."

Quint shook his head. "Ye are nae making sense, wife. 'Tis late, lass. Let's go ta bed." He held a hand out toward her.

She backed up three steps. "If you want me, my lord, I'll be in the kitchen."

The look on his face as she continued to back away almost stopped her. She had never seen such a look of total confusion cross anyone's face.

The moment the door opened and closed, she ran. Fear gripped her, and she glanced from side to side as she quickly descended the stairs. What had she been thinking? What if she'd been mistaken and there were still people up and about? They really would brand her a witch if she were caught running through Brochel Castle with her hair flying loose and not a stitch covering her body.

She heard a door above slam, and she ran faster.

****

He was going to kill her. Well, perhaps not actually kill her, but he'd make her think he was. And if another man saw her naked as she was now, he'd kill him, too.

Quint MacLeod took the steps of the stairs two at a time and was down them, through the great hall, and into the kitchen before he even realized where he'd been headed. He didn't see her at first. All he saw was the outline of the child, Mairi and Dougal's son, Duncan, fast asleep upon his pallet beside the fire and a makeshift curtain hanging before the tub he'd long ago made for his mother.

The fire suddenly flickered, casting shadows, and Quint's heart pounded. Beth was silhouetted behind the curtain. Standing, her hair draping about her slender shoulders, her breast high and proud, her waist slim, and her legs long. His throat went dry, and his cock hardened uncomfortably.

It took but two strides to reach her, and when he did, he threw back the curtain and gaped. She stood in the big tub, water steaming about her knees, and looking for all the world as if heaven had fallen to earth.

Quint glanced once more toward Duncan's sleeping form. "Have ye lost ye mind, lass?"

She didn't speak, just shook her head.

He stripped off his plaid and held it out. "Come now, enough of this nonsense. We'll go back above stairs."

Again, she shook her head no and beckoned him to join her.

"I've already had one bath today, remember?"

She smiled. "Not like this one you haven't, my lord."

There was something about the intensity of her gaze, the sly smile on her face, and the steam rising from the water that called to his soul. He tossed his plaid to the side and climbed in the tub.

Her hands were like silk as she prodded him to sit. The water rose to mid-chest level, heat seeped into his sore muscles, and he couldn't help but relax.

Beth straddled his legs and slowly lowered herself onto his lap, onto his throbbing, hard cock. "I'm sorry for not seeking your permission before cleaning your home today."

The minx had the audacity to wiggle her sweet ass. "Cleanliness is very important to me, my lord. I'm afraid the nuns had many years to firmly pound that concept into my head."

"The nuns struck ye?" He growled. "Though John Iain, the MacLeod chieftain, will nae be happy when he finds out. I and my clan here at Brochel Castle are Scottish Presbyterian now, not Catholic. I'd gladly have every single one of those zealots slain if they dared lay a hand on ye."

She shook her head. "The nuns touched me only with their words, my lord. I swear it."

Cupping her hands, she scooped water and slowly trickled it down his chest, following the path it took with her lips.

Quint sucked in a breath as her pert nipples raked his skin. Her teeth nibbled at his earlobe, and her warmth sheathed his cock. Slowly, she slid up and down its length.

"I promise to clean only what is really, truly important to me, Quint. Just a few places here and there. With as busy as you are training your men all day and seeing to the welfare of"—she waved her hand— "the entire clan. I doubt you'll even have time to notice."

Then she kissed him, and Quint forgot what they were talking about. It wasn't the kiss of a young woman who'd been a virgin only days before. It was the kiss of a trained courtesan, and he was her more than willing student.

Perhaps the keep was due for a thorough scrubbing.

After all, what could it hurt? When his mother had been alive, the entire castle had sparkled. Perhaps bathing on a more…regular basis, especially here in the confines of the tub he'd built, in steaming hot water, with his oh so tempting wife to see to his needs, wouldn't be such a grievous task either. That was, as long as the little vixen never again did what she'd done moments ago to assure he'd follow her here.

The sight of his Beth so bewitchingly beautiful and so completely bare was meant for his eyes, and his eyes only.

"Ye'll nae ever again run through the keep naked as the day ye were born, lass. Do ye ken?" he whispered against her ear before sucking its lobe between his teeth and nipping. Then he feathered her cheeks, her lips, her neck, and her shoulders with kisses as slowly she rode him.

The woman had the audacity to outright laugh, giggle really, and the action did the strangest thing to his deeply embedded cock. Her cunny contracted, cradled him, milked him, and caressed him as ripples of pleasure rolled up through him, threatening to cause his ballocks to explode. If he wasn't careful, not only would the bath water be more on the floor than in the tub, but this session of…*bathing* would be long over before it even had a decent chance to begin.

He took her face between his hands and forced her to look him in the eye. "I'll have ye word, wife. There'll be no more naked scampering through the keep. The next time ye ask me to accompany ye ta the kitchen, I'll know what ye have in mind and I'll come willingly, I give ye my word. But nae man looks upon what's mine and lives to tell about it. Do ye ken? So, if ye have a care for the men of the clan ye're lady of, keep that in mind."

Beth nodded and smiled as she once more slid up his shaft and back down again. "Yes, my lord, I understand."

Then, she began riding him in earnest, hard and fast, taking him deeper within her body with every stroke she executed. Quint grasped her hips and pumped as decadent spirals of pure delight ran the length of his cock. The water sloshed over the rim of the tub and onto the stone floor. But he didn't care. The floor would dry soon enough.

In the low light of the kitchen, with only the soft glow from a single candle to illuminate her face, his Beth looked just as he'd often imagined a wood sprite or fairy. Her head was thrown back, her eyes closed, and the muscles of her cunny clenched him tight as she rode, holding him close, caressing him, bending him to her will.

He could no more break this spell she'd cast upon him than refuse to draw his next breath, and he wouldn't if he could.

Any Scot worth his salt knew well the stories of the fae creatures and the magic they possessed, and if his little wife had even a drop of fae blood in her, then he truly was a lucky man. For the fae were well known for their powers of seduction, and seducing him beyond reason this night was exactly what his Beth had done.

His balls ached, not with pain, but with need, and the head of his cock throbbed in a rhythm that matched the pounding in his chest. He was close, so very close.

Quint slipped a hand between them, and found Beth's clit, all slick and hard. He kissed her, and she moaned and wiggled as he stroked. His cock responded to the sound by spasming once, and again, and then again. He pumped furiously as his body found its release.

"Yes, yes. Oh, my God, yes," she cried as her own tremors of pleasure overtook her.

He held her close and smothered her face and neck with kisses. "That was...that was amazing," he whispered. "Ye were right about baths, wife. We should do this more often."

She grinned against the skin of his naked chest.

And even after the water had long turned from warm to quite cool, neither one budged.

Chapter Seven

May 1643

Beth groaned.

God, what wouldn't she give right this very moment for a roll of toilet paper and a bottle of mouthwash? And while she was thinking about it, perhaps a good toothbrush, a stick of deodorant, zippers, real forks, a new romance novel by one of her favorite authors, and a lifetime supply of antacids.

Funny, in the three months she'd been in the year 1643, she hadn't really missed the cell phone that for so many years had been attached to her like an extra appendage, and she hadn't even truly missed cars, planes, bikes, TVs, fast food, computers, or even the Internet. But right now, she'd kill for the tummy-soothing and thirst-quenching effects of an ice cold glass of tea with a package of artificial sweetener thrown in for good measure and topped off with a wedge of fresh lemon.

"So much like ya dear departed mother, ya are, God rest her soul." Bronwyn sniffed, and smiled. "I'd wager she took the very first time ya Da had his way with her, too."

Beth raised her head from the chamber pot she'd been cradling every morning for the last two months. "Took?"

The maid chuckled. "Lady Elspeth Frasier

MacLeod, don't be trying ta tell me ya haven't guessed ye're with child? I know ye are smarter than that. And such a short time after wedding the laird, ta boot." The woman's smile suddenly faded. "The babe ye're carrying 'tis Quinton MacLeod's get, isn't he? Tell me the poor little soul wasn't sired by that horrid Viscount Telford?"

Beth retched again, even though there hadn't been anything left in her stomach to throw up for quite some time now. She scowled at Bronwyn. "If I am with child, and I'm not saying I am, and I'd better not hear about you spreading rumors because I haven't even said anything about the possibility to Quint yet. But if there is a *babe* on the way, it can only be Quinton MacLeod's child. I was chaste when I came to his bed."

The maid sighed with obvious relief. "Saints be praised. Ye can't blame a soul for wondering. Back at Frasier Castle before the wedding, ye and that viscount were thick as thieves and had ye heads together more often than nae. It was near scandalous, I tell ya."

"He creeps me out." Beth shuddered.

"Creeps, what mean ye creeps, my lady," Bronwyn asked.

Heat wicked up Beth's neck and overflowed her cheeks. Her choice of words was simply a slip of the tongue, and she'd have to be more careful. Or she really would find herself tied to a stake and burned alive as she feared.

She swallowed, hard, and then forced a laugh. "Creeps is a fairly new description I heard being bandied about court. It means, being in the vicinity of someone unpleasant can give one the feeling that something with many hairy legs is crawling upon one's skin, creeping, so to speak."

Bronwyn nodded. "Ah." And then she laughed. "Ye young people these days. There's no telling what ye'll say next. Creeps…I think I like it."

Suddenly, she grew serious again. "Well then, my lady, if the viscount makes ye feel as if spiders or some such were crawling all over ye, then why'd ye spend so much time in his company?"

Beth shrugged. "Familiarity, I suppose. After all, I hadn't been home since Father first sent me to live at the abbey. I knew the viscount better than anyone else present. It was simply easier to spend time in his presence, since we both had England and the court in common."

Bronwyn nodded. "I suppose that's true enough."

Beth cringed. When had it gotten so very easy to lie that untruths rolled right off her tongue without much forethought at all? And here she'd always prided herself on being such an honest person.

If there'd been one tried and true rule she'd learned from her mother, it had been, "Be truthful and honest above all things, and you'll always come out on top." Not that her mother's favorite saying had come in handy in every instance of her life, but it had in most.

Well, one thing was for certain. Honesty had certainly been the exception to the rule from the moment Beth had found herself in the year 1643 and not the norm. She wasn't very proud of that fact.

She made her way back to the bed. The very same bed she shared every night with Elspeth's husband. She had to think of Quint as belonging to Elspeth and not to her. The baby also. If not, then how could she stand to leave either one of them behind after the child she'd never hold, the child she'd never get to know or watch grow into a man was born?

And leave them she must. She'd made a deal with Fate, and she'd made a promise to apologize to her dead children for what she'd done, what she'd said. Apologies that were so very much overdue.

Was it wrong of her to wish it could somehow be different, though? Deep down inside, Beth wasn't sure. On one hand, she was already more than a little in love with Quinton MacLeod, and she knew it. Never had anyone loved her so tenderly or treated her with such goodwill.

And last night she'd felt the very first fluttering of his son moving within Elspeth's body. A stirring that not only reminded Beth that the child to come was truly real but had also brought back memories, both painful and at the same time glorious. Memories of two smiling little faces. Memories she wished she could forget, if for a moment. Because to remember every detail of the last glimpse she'd ever had of those faces was too painful to endure. But then, what kind of mother longed to forget the last sight she'd ever get of her children? Only a horrible one, of course.

Burt had been right all along.

Beth closed her eyes and for at least the millionth time, gave herself over to the nightmare that never ended.

****

"For the love of God, would you please stop kicking the back of my seat? I already have a headache." Bethany Ann Anderson glanced in the rear view mirror and scowled at her eight-year-old son, Brian.

"I'm hungry," he whined.

She sighed. "We're all hungry, but being obnoxious isn't going to get you fed any sooner." Beth turned up the wiper blades on her beat-up compact car yet another notch, in hopes she'd be able to see well enough to at least increase her speed from meandering turtle to donkey crawl.

Dinner was late, dinner was late, dinner was very late, and Burt was going to be so angry.

The late July drizzle and the on and off downpour in the Miami, Florida, area had been the reason both little league baseball games had taken so much longer than usual this evening. And it was the reason why, yet again, Burt was going to be pissed, really pissed. He didn't appreciate his supper being served after six. He'd always been that way. His mother had served dinner at six, not a moment before and not a moment after.

Beth glanced at her watch. It was six-fifteen.

"Can we have mac and cheese when we get home?" ten-year-old Ben asked.

Beth sighed. "Sure, why not."

It wasn't often she was allowed to give in to the whims of her children, but since Burt was already going to be upset, why not? But then again, Burt's preferences did have to come first, and she'd already taken a couple of steaks out to thaw before leaving the house. Her husband expected meat of some kind with every meal, and though she'd thought she'd just pop a few potatoes in the oven to go along with the steaks, she supposed mac and cheese would serve just as well, for the kids anyway.

"Why do you do that?" Brian argued. "You know we can't have mac and cheese. What'd Daddy say last time?"

Ben huffed from the back seat beside his brother. "I don't care what Dad says. He doesn't have to eat it if he doesn't want to."

Brian kicked the back of Beth's seat again. "Oh yeah, well, I bet you'll care when he throws it on the floor or at Mom again. Won't ya?"

She could hear the fear in her young son's voice, and it broke her heart. Shivers of dread skittered down her spine. He was right, and she knew it. "Don't worry about it, Brian. I'll make your father a nice big baked potato with sour cream and chives. Just the way he likes."

The kids were quiet for a few minutes, and Beth was thankful. If possible, the rain was coming down even harder and flooding the road enough that hydroplaning became an issue. She tapped her brakes, then sped up once again, pulled between getting home safely and getting home fast enough to prevent Burt from working himself into a total frenzy.

He hadn't wanted the boys to play little league. He'd said it was a waste of time and money. Both time and money that could be used for better means, like a new fishing rod for himself or yet another hunting rifle. Beth had argued her case, though, and after agreeing to teach summer school to make up for the extra expense, she'd won.

Ben and Brian were allowed to do so little that other children took for granted. She'd wanted to give them this one small thing. And they both thrived at it.

She glanced in the rearview mirror at her sons. God, how she loved them. Both blond and handsome like their father, with his same dark brown eyes and winning smile, they were the light of her life, her reason for everything.

Ben was the athlete, again so like his dad except when it came to attitude. That trait he'd gotten from her, along with the freckles across his nose and his ridiculously oversized ears. He was a straight A student with a sweet disposition that melted Beth's heart, and even at ten years old, already had the signs of a strong work ethic in the making.

And then there was Brian, the fourth of what Burt liked to call the four B's. Her little hellion. There wasn't a point he wouldn't argue or a cause he wouldn't champion. She had no doubt her eight-year-old son would someday grow up to be a lawyer, a politician, a preacher, or possibly even a, God forbid, prize fighter of some sort.

Boxer perhaps? But not a bully. Not like Burt. God, please not like Burt. But then Brian wasn't cruel, and he only ever fought to protect others.

How many times during this past school year alone had she been called to the principal's office because Brian had gotten himself into yet another altercation defending some smaller, weaker kid? And though it probably shouldn't and she'd certainly never tell him, she was proud he didn't back away from a fight. He wasn't a coward like she had always been.

"Give it back," Ben suddenly yelled.

Beth jerked out of the contemplation of her near perfect children and back into reality of the moment mode. Glancing once more into the rearview mirror again, the tension of the day, the weather, the lateness of the hour, and the knowledge that a fight, without a doubt, awaited her when she did finally get home, got the better of her. "Brian, give your brother back whatever you took."

Her eight-year-old sounded whiney again. "I just wanted to look at his stupid catcher's mitt."

"How many times do I have to tell you"—the sound of Ben's piercing screech went right through Beth's already aching head—"I don't want your greasy paws on my stuff. Give it back like Mom said."

Beth took a deep breath and slowly blew it out. Her normally even temper rising another degree. "Brian, give your brother back his mitt *now*. I'm not in the mood to listen to you two fight."

Instead of doing as she'd asked, though, Brian tossed the catcher's mitt into the front seat and out of his brother's reach. It landed on the passenger side floor board.

"Mom!" Ben wailed.

Beth seethed with anger as she unbuckled her seatbelt. Everything she did was for her children, and they couldn't care less they were making this trip home even more miserable than it needed to be. "Just a sec. Don't whine. I'll get it."

She turned her face slightly toward her children, enough so they could see she was serious. "Why must you two fight all the time? Isn't there enough of that at home? God, what I wouldn't give for five minutes of peace and quiet? I swear, there are days I wish I'd never had kids in the first place. Neither one of you appreciates anything that's done for you. Now, sit back and shut up before you cause us to get into a wreck. I don't want to hear another word out of either of you."

Suddenly, Ben's eyes became really big and round. Though he didn't say a word, he made his point with a single pudgy, little finger gesture toward the road.

Beth turned quickly, fear gripping her heart. There, right in the middle of her lane, coming straight for them, was a dark pickup truck with its headlights blinding her through the driving rain and its tires swerving dangerously forward.

She slammed on her brakes and tried to veer out of the way, but the guardrail to her right and the already occupied lane to her left, prevented her from making any adjustments that mattered. She threw her free arm over the backseat in hopes of somehow shielding her children from what was about to transpire

In the end, it didn't matter.

When the collision happened, the force of the unstoppable pickup truck coming in direct contact with her equally opposing compact car and combined with the fact that the glass of her car door window shattered on impact, Beth's unseatbelted body was flung free of the wreckage.

She didn't remember landing, but when she came to, she was lying on the side of the road. Beth wasn't sure how long she'd been unconscious. It could've been moments, or it could've been hours. All she knew was every bone and muscle in her body hurt horribly, and she could barely breathe or move.

She scanned the near total darkness for her car, and there it set, twisted about the guard rail with the front of the pickup truck embedded firmly within the compact's engine compartment.

There was no movement, only deathly silence.

Beth panicked. She blinked back the rain and blood fogging her sight and started crawling toward her car, toward her children. Pain ripped through her lower extremities, but she ignored the odd angle her legs lay in and the fact that she could no longer feel sensation of any kind below her knees. Inch by excruciating inch, she made her way closer to the wreckage, closer to her children.

Then she saw it. A small round fist pounding upon the glass of the backseat window. Brian, thank God, he was still alive. Faster she crawled, every movement threatening to take her consciousness from her once again. She saw Ben's frightened eyes, his face pressed up against the window beside his little brother's fist, and she heard both of their screams.

That was the last sight she ever had of her children before the car suddenly exploded into a ball of fire. Though their excruciating screams pierced the night as they burned to death right before her eyes.

It was the last thing she remembered before totally losing consciousness, and the first thing that came to her mind five days later when she finally woke in a hospital bed.

Two days later, Burt came to see her. It was the first and last visit she'd get from him the entire six weeks of her hospitalization or the subsequent three-month stint in the rehabilitation center in order to learn how to walk again. He'd stayed less than a minute and had only two words to say. "They're buried." He turned, walked away, and didn't even bother to come when the rehab center phoned for him to pick her up. Instead, after waiting another twenty-four hours, she'd simply called herself a cab and made her own way home.

He didn't look at her when she'd hobbled through the front door on legs that, though once more functional, would never again be quite the same. Instead, he popped the top on another beer. "I'm hungry. Get supper cooked. And this filthy house needs cleaning."

"Don't you even want to know what happened?" she asked.

Burt shook his head. "I know everything I need to know. My kids are dead, and you aren't." He shook his head again. "A real mother wouldn't have let that happen. If she couldn't have gotten them out of the car, she would've had the decency to die with them."

Beth didn't have anything else to say.

For days, she'd wondered around the silent rooms of her home, within her own mind, begging her children to forgive her as she picked up and washed the glasses they'd drunk milk from while munching cookies before the game that day. She silently pleaded with them to understand she'd gladly take their place if only she could as she collected two small sets of jeans and T-shirts they'd discarded at the foot of their bunk beds before donning their black, white, and green Miami Gator uniforms.

She'd even prayed for death as she picked up and put into boxes little toy trucks and cars, story books, baseball cards, and well-loved stuffed animals.

But Beth didn't say another word out loud, and neither did Burt, at least not until a few months later. For the longest time, they both wandered through the days like a pair of strangers being forced to share the same space. It hurt that Burt acted like she didn't exist, but at the same time, Beth hadn't realized how preferable that sentiment was to what lay ahead.

Chapter Eight

June 1643

God in heaven, she was beautiful to behold.

Quint watched his Beth walk across the bailey and felt guilty. Instead of not being able to draw his gaze from his wife whenever she was anywhere near, he should be paying closer attention to his men's training, pushing them harder, making sure they were prepared for what he feared was coming.

A single Macdonald had been spotted yesterday trespassing MacLeod land. But where there was one Macdonald you *did* see, there were a hundred right behind him that ye didna. They were like so many other forms of vermin that plagued the Highlands, plentiful and hard to kill.

He sighed, wishing he could lay aside, if only for a short while longer, the tedious responsibility of having to take the lives of others in order to keep his own safe and the equally ominous summons he'd received this morning from the MacLeod chieftain, John Iain, himself.

"Ye will attend me presently," was all the scrap of parchment had read.

He glanced again Beth's way right before she and the small boy following close upon her heels disappeared through the keep's doorway and out of sight. Should he take her with him? Did he dare?

A trip from the Isle of Raasay to Dunvegan Castle upon the Isle of Skye really wasn't that long or arduous a journey, but it could be uncomfortable for a woman in Beth's delicate condition if the winds weren't favorable. Though his Beth had yet to inform him of his pending fatherhood, he'd lived in a keep filled with females all his life and had seen the same symptoms she was exhibiting enough times to recognize when a woman was increasing.

A part of him overflowed with joy while an even bigger part trembled in fear. He didn't want to lose her. He couldn't. He wouldn't survive it. Not this time. Already the little vixen had begun to wrap herself securely about his heart. A feat since the time of Mairi that Quint believed an impossible task for any woman to accomplish ever again.

Was the opportunity to become a father, to produce an heir, really worth the risk to Beth's life? And what good could come from worrying about the situation after the fact anyway? It's not as if he had the power to change the future or the past. It certainly wasn't within his power to prevent even the woman he'd come to care for, the woman he hoped to spend the rest of his days with, from being taken from him, if it was the Lord's will.

In truth, men were a powerless lot when it came to the women in their lives, and he well knew it. After all, his father hadn't been able to save his very own wife or the small second son who'd never taken a breath. And try as he might, Quint hadn't been able to save Mairi.

Thinking of the only woman ever to break his heart made Quint remember the little boy who'd been dogging Beth's footsteps a few moments ago. He sighed again. Duncan. What should he do?

It had been so much easier to forget the child existed when he'd simply been the soot-covered peat boy who slept on a pallet before the warm kitchen fire each night. But now that Beth had cleaned the child up and Duncan had become her almost constant companion, he was increasingly hard to ignore. Dougal's same serious solemn, brown eyes stared back at Quint every time Duncan glanced his direction. And Mairi's playful little smile graced Duncan's face at times when he wasn't even aware he was being watched.

Especially, when the child looked at Beth.

Plain and simple, the six-year-old lad obviously loved Beth, and Quint couldn't blame him. Annie the cook, and her two granddaughters had done all they could for the child, but it was clear Duncan was starved for a mother's love that should've rightly been his to claim. Like the love of a father, of a family. Though not on purpose, a love Quint had stolen and withheld from him.

He might not have physically pushed Dougal MacLeod over the parapet and to his death with his own two hands, but he might as well have when he'd declared Dougal would never, ever have Mairi as wife. Quint knew it wasn't technically his fault that Mairi died giving Duncan life. He also understood that even before the night her son was born, Mairi had succumbed to a broken heart. Probably the very same moment the father of her child died.

Quint felt powerless. What could he do about any of it now?

He couldn't bring Dougal and Mairi back from the

grave and give Duncan the parents he deserved. Even if he could somehow accomplish that miracle, he certainly wouldn't turn back the hands of time and not lie with his wife so she'd not be carrying his child and endangering her life. And try as he might, he could keep the next invasion of Macdonalds at bay for only so long, and though he dreaded it with every fiber of his being, when the sun rose in the morning, like it or not, he'd have no choice but answer the summons from his chieftain.

Perhaps there was one small thing he could do. Perhaps he'd take Duncan to the Isle of Skye with him instead of Beth. After all, the boy had never stepped a foot off MacLeod land let alone onto a ship or across a sea. It would be an adventure. Something Quint could offer since he couldn't give back to the child what he'd taken.

Yes, he'd take Duncan to Dunvegan. That was, if he could manage to pry the child from Beth's skirt tail long enough to make the journey. After all, wasn't it well past time John Iain, the sixteenth chieftain of clan Macleod, met his grandson face to face?

****

"Lady Elspeth?" Duncan whispered.

From the comfort of the day bed in her private solar, Beth forced her breathing to stay slow and steady, and her eyes to remain closed. She wouldn't acknowledge him, and he'd go away, eventually. He always did.

"Lady Elspeth?" He tugged ever so slightly on her sleeve.

But Beth didn't even twitch. God, what had she done to deserve such unwanted devotion? She couldn't help it. She gulped.

It hadn't taken much to garner little Duncan MacLeod's affections. All she'd done was toss a discarded scrap of fur onto his small, flat pallet, but only because she hadn't wanted to see the piece go to waste. Though the tattered bit had been more holey than not, Beth hoped it would allot the child a little more comfort, a little more warmth.

And yes, it was true. She'd been known to slip the boy an extra portion or two at meals. An apple tart here, a chunk of warm crusty bread there. But it wasn't her fault he was so very small, so skinny, so all alone.

With those two kindnesses, she'd created a problem.

Why couldn't the child simply go away and leave her be?

"I picked these for ye, my lady." His voice trembled. "I thought they were pretty. They're the same color as ye eyes."

Beth held her breath and prayed. *Go away, go away, go away.*

She would not open Elspeth Frasier MacLeod's blue-blue eyes even if it killed her not to. She would not look at Duncan's gift, and she would not thank the always too solemn, too serious, too sad little boy. She couldn't. It wouldn't be fair to start something she had no intention of sticking around long enough to see finished. She would not love this child, and she'd not allow him to love her either. It would be too hard, hurt too much to care and then simply abandon him like she'd—

She wouldn't do it, even if it broke both their hearts.

She heard his sigh, and then the awkward shuffling sound as he turned and hobbled back toward the door. Years from now, Duncan's condition would be an easily fixable inconvenience at the most, but in the year 1643, a club foot made one a cripple and an outcast.

She squeezed her eyes tighter. He wasn't a stray puppy. He was a human being. She would not love him. She wouldn't. She couldn't. It wouldn't be fair to love him and then leave.

Beth wasn't going to be in this time period or Duncan's life long enough to make a difference. He was going to have to grow into manhood all on his own because as soon as Elspeth's body was delivered of Quinton Macleod's son, Bethany Ann Anderson would be long gone.

The door quietly clicked closed, and she took six deep breaths and silently counted to one hundred before peeking. Tears filled her eyes to overflowing, and her heart pounded hard in her chest. There, upon her lap, set a bunch of wild blue pansies. Their stems mostly broken, and their delicate petals mostly crushed from small hands gripping them too tightly. They were without a doubt, the prettiest flowers she'd ever received.

A thought began to form, an idea really. Not much more than a seed.

Perhaps she no longer had the capacity or the time left to love little Duncan MacLeod as he deserved. That depth of emotion and choice had been stripped from her along with her children. But was there something else she could give the child without destroying either one of them in the process? Something she still knew how to give? Something she was even considered good at?

Something she'd done for so many others?

Could she possibly teach Duncan MacLeod to stand proudly upon his own two feet, no matter what obstacles lay in his path? Could she show the child who had no one to guide him, how full his world could become through the simple basics of reading, writing, and arithmetic?

Perhaps?

For the first time since waking and finding herself in the year 1643, Beth's heart filled with true hope.

****

"What do you mean you're taking him with you to Dunvegan tomorrow?" Beth cried. "You can't do it. You simply can't."

Quint stared at his wife, not understanding her outburst. "Of course I can, I'm laird."

Beth paced their bed chamber like a caged animal before once more turning on him. "No, I won't allow it. He's too little to be on a great big ship out in the middle of the sea all by himself. And…and Dunvegan is much too far from home for him to be traveling. He could get hurt. He could fall overboard. For God's sake, Quint, he could drown."

Quinton MacLeod shook his head. "Ye'll nae allow it? As if the choice is yours ta make?"

She folded her arms across her chest and tapped her foot. "He's not going."

Well, what did one make of that?

Though Quint had little choice but show his wife that his word was law and would be obeyed, the fact that his lady would fight like the most ferocious mother wolf for one of the lowliest cubs in the clan filled his heart with warmth. Elspeth Frasier MacLeod was truly becoming the lady of Brochel Castle, and she was doing it right before his eyes.

He gentled his voice. "My Beth, ye don't understand. Though a cripple, young Duncan is a Highlander, a Scotsman of the north. The sea's in his blood, in his soul, part of his legacy. I'll nae keep him from it any more than I'll try and hold back the winds. It's past time the boy had his first real voyage. And it's past time he bent a knee ta his grandfather."

"But—but—but he can't go," she cried.

Quint wrapped his arms about her. "Do ye nae trust me, wife? When I was his age, I spent almost as much time upon water as I did upon land. My father demanded it, expected it. I'd nae send the lad away without a care and allow harm to come to young Duncan. If ye believe nothing else of me, ye must believe that."

She nuzzled into his embrace and sighed. "I do believe you. It's just that, well, I've been making plans."

"Plans?"

Beth nodded and glanced up into his eyes, a tinge of heat warming her cheeks. "Brochel is immaculately tidy now, my lord, and leaves little to keep me busy. While at the abbey, the nuns were forever telling us that idle hands are the devil's playthings, and I took their council to heart. I've been thinking of trying something with Duncan first, and if it works out, perhaps even with some of the village children." She lifted her chin and looked him straight in the eye. "I'd like to teach him how to read, write, and figure numbers. In my spare, time of course."

Quint laughed. "Duncan MacLeod read? The child

can barely walk without falling over his own two feet let alone read. And what need do village children have for such folly? It would only make them dream of heights beyond their reach. Better they stay content with what they have and ignorant of what they cannae obtain."

Beth shook her head and pushed herself from Quint's arms. "You're wrong, especially about Duncan. He's a very intelligent child. And someday, someone is going to have to replace the castle's steward, why not Duncan?" She took a deep breath. "James, though very efficient at his tasks, is an old man. Who better than Duncan to fill the role he'll vacate when the time comes?" She placed her hands on her hips. "Since his crippled foot limits him, it's not likely he'll ever become much of a warrior or fight by your side. Allow him this one small dignity, husband. Give Duncan the chance to serve you and his people in a capacity greater than that of a…a peat boy, please."

Quint ran his hand through his hair and shrugged. "And the other children? Why waste ye time on them?"

She stood silent for a moment, then gazed up with tears brimming her eyes. "Perhaps for no other reason than to see the joy on their faces when they first read the words of a story they've never heard told before. Perhaps so that when they are grown and take the fruits of their labors to market, they'll not be cheated. And perhaps for no other reason than teaching children what they do not even know they hunger for will bring me joy. Isn't that enough?"

She was right, and what could it hurt? After all, the more his people knew, the better. And his Beth really hadn't asked for much. Being laird, there was so many times he had no choice but to say no to so many people, and so many times he had to put the good of the clan before his own happiness or hers. But this one small thing he could give her, and would if possible.

Quint nodded. "Aye, tis. But make no mistake, my lady. I'll still be taking young Duncan ta Dunvegan with me on the morrow. If the lad returns, then ye can teach him and any of the other weans whatever ye wish."

"*If?*" she croaked.

Quint stroked the soft, warm skin of Beth's cheek. "John Iain Macleod is the boy's grandfather, lass, ye ken? It's only right he has a say so in what's to become of the lad." He leaned down and planted a quick kiss on her abdomen, then winked up at her. "Just as it will be my right and responsibility when my son is born."

"You know?" Beth gasped.

He straightened and kissed her forehead. "Aye, lass, I've suspected for a while now, and we'll be discussing why ye didn't see fit to inform me yeself before I had ta figure it out on my own."

Beth nodded. "I wanted to tell you. Really, I did. There never seemed to be the right time."

Gently, he cupped her chin and forced her to look him in the eye. "Did ye think I would nae be pleased, my Beth?"

She shook her head. "It's not that. It's just that you've had so very much on your mind lately, and this marriage is still so new. You don't really know me yet, and I don't really know you."

She tried to glance away, but he held her chin steady. "What are ye afraid of, lass?"

Her throat bobbed as she swallowed. "What if I'm

117

a failure as a mother? Some women aren't meant to be, you know? And some children are better off without them."

Quint gathered her into his arms and held her tight against his heart. What had happened at that English abbey to make his sweet, kind wife think she wouldn't be a good mither? He was of a mind to shake himself a few nuns until he found out the truth of the matter. Beth was right about one thing. There really was much they still didn't know about each other. One thing he did know, though, his wife was good, and she was kind. What better qualities could any man ask for in the woman who would raise his children?

"Do nae fash so, my Beth. Ye are the only woman I want to be the mither of my children, and I believe in ye. Ye'll do a fine job. Ye'll see."

Chapter Nine

Quint stood in the middle of Dunvegan's great hall and waited while his uncle and chieftain, John Iain MacLeod, stuffed yet another chunk of mutton into his mouth and downed it with a single gulp of ale while pretending his nephew and grandson weren't even in the room.

Typical. Though he'd always respected his father's brother, not only as the leader of their clan but also as blood kin, there were times, like now, when he wished he could shake him and tell him to stop being an ass. It was one thing to ignore a full grown man, even if that full grown man was a laird in his own right and one's blood, but it was entirely another to knowingly hurt a little boy who'd already been hurt so much in his short life.

Without looking up, the old man suddenly motioned toward Duncan. "When I summoned ye ta come before me, Quinton MacLeod, I dinna tell ye ta bring Dougal's bastard with ye."

Carefully controlling his expression and making sure his visage remained completely passive, Quint bent a knee before his father's oldest brother and the leader of clan Macleod. He kept his backbone straight. It wouldn't bode well to display any form of weakness while in the presence of John Iain. The man considered sentiment an unforgivable flaw.

Quint nodded. "Nae, ye dinna. But it's past time the child knew from whence he came and where he belongs."

The MacLeod chieftain motioned to Duncan again and grimaced as the little boy hobbled close to Quint's side and clumsily attempted to bend a knee, too.

"Stand straight, child," John Iain commanded. "There'll be time later ta show ye respect. Come closer so I can get a good look at ye."

Duncan shuffled until he stood with his face peering over the table top, across from where his grandfather sat.

The old man suddenly smiled at the little boy and relief flooded Quint. "Ye have the look about ye of your father and even some of ye grandmother, too, God rest their souls. Do ye know who I am, lad? Do ye ken you're my bastard grandson?"

"I—I—I know ye are my grandfather, sir," Duncan stuttered. "Be—be—because Laird Quinton told me so, and I—I k—k—ken I'm the crippled bastard son of ye bastard son Dougal MacLeod, sir."

John Iain nodded. "So, ye be not just a bastard, but a crippled bastard, ye say?"

The little boy gulped. "I have a crooked foot that does nae work as it should. Aunt Marta says it's my rightful due for killing me mither."

Quint grimaced. Though he'd thought in time Marta would've gotten over her unreasonable attitude concerning Duncan, it seemed she hadn't. And like it or not, when he got home, he'd have no choice but to deal with the situation.

The chieftain nodded. "I see, and did ye indeed kill ye mither, Duncan MacLeod?"

Again, the boy gulped, and it was all Quint could do to not rush to the child's defense. He didn't, though. He stood waiting for Duncan's response like everyone else present.

"Aye, my lord, 'tis sorry ta say, but I did." He sighed and hung his head.

John Iain chuckled. "Well, lad, women die birthing babes all the time for many reasons. I'm pretty sure it's nae something ye could've prevented. Do nae take what ye Aunt Marta says ta heart."

Then, shaking a finger toward Duncan, the MacLeod chieftain bellowed, "But as far as being a cripple, now there's something ye do have power over, lad. A man is only as frail and helpless as he allows his differences ta make him. Ye very well may have been born on the wrong side of the sheet, but ye are a MacLeod still, and MacLeod's are nae cripples."

Duncan stood a little straighter and nodded.

"No son of John Iain MacLeod has ever been or has ever sired a cripple. I won't hear of it. And ye, lad, are as much MacLeod as any other man ever born ta the name. Ye will grow tall and ye will learn ta heft a sword high in defense of those 'tis ye duty ta protect, and ye will follow this clan's motto until the day ye die and hold fast. And ye'll do it just as every other MacLeod man before ye has done since time began or fear my wrath." He waved his hand through the air. "Being a cripple is a state of mind, lad, nae a condition of the body. Ye are the grandson of a clan chieftain and nae a cripple. Do ye hear?"

Duncan nodded once more. "Aye, yes, sir."

John Iain MacLeod motioned toward the back of the castle. "Now, get ye ta the kitchen. If ye are ta grow tall enough and strong enough ta ever watch ye laird's back, then ye need much bigger muscles on those scrawny arms and legs. Go find cook while I talk with ye cousin. She'll see ye fed right proper."

Duncan bowed before his grandfather, quickly glanced back toward Quint, and then hobbled off.

The moment the child was out of sight, John Iain glared at Quint. "How dare ye bring that lad into my lady wife's home, right under my lady wife's nose. What were ye thinking, nephew? Do ye have so little care for your aunt's feelings? Do ye nae realize the only reason I sent his father away in the first place was to protect my Sibylla. That, though I was verra fond of his mither and felt sorry for the boy when she passed, I'd nae embarrass the woman who has born me two fine legitimate sons and four beautiful daughters by forcing her ta gaze upon Dougal MacLeod's countenance every day of her life? Let alone ask her ta foster his bastard son, Duncan."

Quint ignored the question for a moment and instead, asked one of his own. "Why did ye summon me, then, if nae ta meet ye grandson?"

John Iain slammed down his eating knife. "Ye know good and well why I summoned ye. It's high time ye swore allegiance ta ye laird and ta ye king. War's coming, boy, and I ha need of knowing what side of the battle I'll be seeing ye on. I do nae wish ta fight me own nephew, but we both know exactly where ye father stood when it came ta the royalists and parliamentarians. Are ye of a like mind?"

Taking a deep breathe, Quint let it out slowly. So, it had finally come to this. Time was up, and he had only two, possibly three, choices before him. Swear fealty to his uncle and his sword to King Charles or back his religion and the new parliament, though that choice would undoubtedly put his people at risk of retaliation. Or if God were willing, he'd think of some way to, if only for a while yet, keep his people out of the fray.

He cleared his throat. "I am my father's son, Uncle, and can be nae other. If forced ta fight, then I'd prefer the side of parliament. But at the same time, ye are my chieftain, and nae matter what is decided this day, ye'll always have my loyalty and my sword. Know this, nae matter the outcome of what's ta come, nae matter what either one of us believes, I'll nae ever raise my sword ta ye or yours, and nae will any of my men. Wars can be verra long and drawn out, sides change over and over again. Why nae simply keep Brochel and what she has ta offer in reserve for the time being?"

John Iain shook his head. "I'll nae be changing sides. I was born a king's man, and I'll die one."

Quint nodded. "I understand, Uncle, but in good conscience, I cannae back the king. We both know Scotland would be better off without Charles's strangle hold upon her."

The MacLeod chieftain pounded his fist on the table. "Have a care, nephew. Ye are speaking treason. I'll nae see the head of my favorite brother's only son upon a pike if I can prevent it. I am but one man among many, though. There's only so much I can do."

Again, Quint nodded. "Aye, my laird, I understand."

John Iain stood, paced, and glared. "I'll tell ye what I *can* do. Ye take young Duncan back ta Brochel with ye. Train the lad ta fight. Ensure me he'll at least be able ta defend himself if and when the time comes. And keep him safe and away from this conflict. For the time being anyway, I'll simply forget ta mention ta the king that I have further resources at my disposal."

He stopped pacing a moment and looked Quint straight in the eye. "But if the need arises, do nae think for a moment I'll nae be sending ye aunt and girl cousins ta Brochel, and I'll be expecting ye ta protect them. Do I have ye word, Quinton MacLeod? Will ye keep my family safe if and when the time comes when I canna?"

Quint bent a knee once more before his uncle. "On my life, I swear I will."

****

Beth ran a finger along the dusty window ledge of the room she'd been working on all morning and sighed. It'd been seven long days and six even longer nights since Quint and Duncan sailed away and out of sight. How long could one wee trip between two little islands take? And when Quinton MacLeod finally returned home, would Duncan still be at his side, or would Quint leave the little boy behind? She still wasn't sure which she hoped for more.

"Ye asked for soap and water ta be brought ta ye?"

Beth turned toward the sound of the one voice she'd least expected to hear, especially in this room. "Marta?"

The young woman stood straight and tall with a bucket of steaming water in one hand and strips of cloth in the other. Marta's long strawberry blonde hair, the exact same shade as Duncan's, was tied back from her face with a strip of wool, and her gray as Scottish heather eyes glared daggers right through Beth. Her mouth, though normally lush when relaxed, was flattened in a pinched straight line, and her unusually dainty, freckle-kissed nose rose in the air until it tilted ever so slightly higher than proper for a servant.

It was obvious to anyone with two eyes and capable of looking that Marta didn't like Elspeth Frasier MacLeod one little bit. But the question was, why? Beth couldn't think of a single thing she'd ever said or done to warrant the other woman's disdain.

She probed Elspeth's memories once again, but came up with nothing.

"Well, where do ye want it?" Marta hissed.

Beth motioned to a small table set up against the wall. "There's fine."

The other woman plopped the bucket down, sloshing water upon the table top, and turned to leave.

"Just a moment, Marta."

The servant squared her shoulders, turned, and folded her arms across her chest. "Was there something else ye be needing…my lady? I've other duties ta be seeing ta, ye ken?"

Beth cleared her throat. "Why do you dislike me so?"

Marta laughed. "Why do ye care?"

Beth shrugged. "I'd like to understand, I suppose."

Marta laughed again, though there was nothing humorous about the sound. It was almost a cackle, wild and on the outer fringes of sanity. "Ye have everything that should've already been mine but isna, yet." She made a production of turning in a circle and encompassing the room. "But considering we stand in the middle of the nursery, I take it ye are well on ye way ta fulfilling ye promise ta the viscount at least?"

Beth couldn't have been more surprised if Marta had reached out and slapped her. "My promise to the viscount?"

The other woman winked. "Don't ye be worrying overmuch. I won't give away ye little secret. I'm counting on ye ta give Quinton MacLeod his heir almost as much as Viscount Telford is. After all, once the little brat is born, Quinton will be disposed of and ye will be wed ta the viscount and well on ye way back ta England where ye belong. I'll finally be Lady of Brochel, as I should've been long ago. Just as the viscount promised me I would be if I kept my eyes open for information he might find useful."

Beth pointed. "You? You're the viscount's spy?"

Marta grinned. "Spy is such a treasonous term, do ye nae think? I prefer ta consider myself as being verra observant for a price."

"Bu—but why?" Beth sputtered. "What could Quinton MacLeod have possibly ever done to earn such disloyalty? He's a good man, Marta. A good laird."

The other woman shook her head, and for a second, Beth saw a sheen of tears cloud Marta's eyes. "Good man? Good laird? Quinton MacLeod is just as responsible for the death of my sister as that ugly, little, crippled spawn of hers. I hate him. I hate them both, and I want them dead. If he'd only allowed Mairi and Dougal ta wed when they'd first asked, everything would've been fine. I know it woulda. She wouldn't have died birthing that thing. She would've had Dougal as a reason ta go on living. Quinton MacLeod would nae allow it, though. He wanted her for himself, and it did nae matter the cost."

Beth gulped. "Duncan's mother was your sister?

You're his aunt?"

Marta nodded. "We shared the same womb, the same face, the same voice, and even loved the same man. She was my twin sister and the only family I had left. Quinton, Dougal, and Duncan MacLeod took her away from me, and though Dougal is dead and buried, the other two still draw breath even though they have nae right."

The young woman closed her eyes, and Beth wasn't sure that Marta was even talking to her anymore but simply releasing some of her pain. "I found Quinton upon the parapet that night," she whispered. "He and Dougal were well inta their cups. I even offered ta take Mairi's place and become his wife, so Mairi could be free ta wed Dougal. He laughed at me. Told me I'd make a piss poor substitute for Mairi, and Dougal agreed with him." Marta took a deep breath. "I had nae choice, ye ken? Honor demanded I make them pay. And though I tried my best ta…" She shook her head. "It does nae matter what I tried. What does matter is, Quinton MacLeod did nae care enough ta even remember I was there come the next morning. It would've served him right if I had killed him.

"And one of these nights, when Duncan is sound asleep before the kitchen fire, I'll find a way ta make Mairi's bastard son pay for his role in my sister's death, too. And then, perhaps, Laird Quinton MacLeod will finally speak up and take responsibility as he should."

"You'd do that?" A shiver ran up Beth's spine. "You'd stoop so low as to…to murder an innocent little boy who has never done or said an unkind thing to anyone?"

Marta opened her eyes, and this time the gleam of

insanity was a shining beacon of just plain scary. "Oh, aye, I've killed before when left with nae other choice and will again if need be. Especially if someone dares ta get in the way of what's rightfully mine." She grabbed Beth's arm and twisted. "Ye won't be telling anybody, though, now will ye? After all, we both have secrets we share, remember? Secrets we would nae want known."

With that, Marta spun on her heel and walked away.

****

A trickle of sweat ran down her neck, itching as it went, but Beth was powerless to stop it or even reach up and wipe it away. Not only could she not control the functions of the body she now found herself in, but she couldn't control its thoughts either.

"*Eat, you stupid spredith,*" Elspeth's mind screamed. "*Eat every single bite and die.*"

Beth had fallen asleep, safe and sound, in her bed in Brochel castle and was undoubtedly dreaming, but she felt completely trapped within this old memory of the real Elspeth Frasier and had no idea how to get out. She didn't want to be here. She didn't want to watch what she was afraid was coming. Yet she also couldn't seem to look away.

Why had she tried so hard to conjure up more of Elspeth's memories on this night when she was so very alone, so very lonely, and so very confused? But then she already knew the answer to that question. It had been the strange conversation she had with Marta earlier in the day. What was the true connection between Elspeth and Lord Fredrick? And how exactly did Marta figure into the mix? She needed to know.

Beth gazed out through Elspeth's eyes. Over the last few months, she'd come to consider this body as hers, if only on loan, but she'd never before had the distinct impression she was sharing it with the ghost of its real owner, at least for this one night anyway.

For one thing, she was back in Frasier castle, in the very same room she'd first awakened, and dinner was being served. A meal she definitely had no recollection of being present for. And unlike the previous times she sought out Elspeth's memories, she was no longer on the outside looking in. Oh no, this time she was being granted the very distinct unpleasure of Lady Elspeth Frasier's up close and personal brand of downright crazy.

And she didn't like it one bit.

Lady Lydia sat to her left at the head of the table, and Marta, of all people, was ladling some kind of stew like substance onto Lydia's trencher while two other servants placed food before Elspeth and the viscount.

Shivers of excitement skittered along Elspeth's spine as the smell of roasted meat mixed with gravy and vegetables had the woman's mouth watering. She hesitated tasting the fare set before her, however, and looked directly at the viscount, waiting for his slight nod before dipping the tip of a single finger into the sauce and bringing it to her mouth.

"Umm." Elspeth grinned. "Lady Lydia, your cook has certainly outdone herself this evening."

The viscount made a production of spearing a large chunk of meat with his knife and quickly devouring it. "Yes, very tasty."

They both turned and simply stared at Lady Lydia.

Beth wanted to scream. She knew without a doubt,

the dish Marta had placed before Lady Lydia was poisoned. She could even remember the exact conversation when Elspeth and the viscount planned the murder.

The union between Lady Lydia and Elspeth's father had never produced an heir. And if by chance her stepmother died before the vows with the Scot were spoken on the marrow, then Elspeth would be free to marry the viscount instead. And together they could grant her deceased father's crumbling castle on the Isle of Lewis to the king, and she and the viscount could return to England where people were civilized.

But it all hinged on Lady Lydia eating her stew.

After all, it would be so much simpler to kill off her stepmother than it would be to wed Quinton Macleod, pretend to like him long enough to give him an heir, and then kill him off in order to procure his lands and castle for the crown.

Beth wanted to alert Lydia. Her mind screamed for her to do just that. But she couldn't utter a single word, let alone shout a warning. Elspeth's mind was too strong, and her tongue wasn't the least bit inclined to obey anyone else's commands.

Beth was nothing more than a helpless onlooker in a nightmare she couldn't escape or control, and she hated it.

"More ale, girl," Lord Fredrick bellowed.

Marta made quick work of doing his bidding, and the look that passed between the two would've sent shivers along Beth's spine if it hadn't been Elspeth's body she was in.

The viscount lifted his goblet and smiled at his ward. "To your nuptials on the morrow, my dear."

Though Beth tried to prevent it from happening, Elspeth's hand reached out and grasped her goblet, holding it high. "Indeed, my lord, to my nuptials."

Lady Lydia cleared her throat. "We really should wait for the groom ta arrive at the board before we begin our meal, don't ye agree?"

Beth had never felt a glare from the inside out before, but she did now. Elspeth's eyes literally burned with animosity toward her stepmother. "And why should we wait? If the MacLeod laird wished to be included in this pre-wedding supper, then he should've already been present."

She popped a morsel of meat into her mouth and chewed, then she smiled and gestured toward Lady Lydia. "Quinton MacLeod will arrive when Quinton Macleod arrives. You know the man only does as he wishes and in his own time. But as for you, dear, dear stepmother, please eat. You know I worry so for your health. With Father forever gone from us, you're the only real family I have left."

The man they'd been speaking of walked into the room and pulled out the bench across from Elspeth. She didn't spare him a glance. She was too busy watching Lady Lydia lift a bite of stew toward her mouth.

Euphoria filled Elspeth's mind to overflowing while Beth's brain screamed a silent, "*No!*"

Suddenly, the heavy table shifted, and Elspeth's body toppled backwards. An excruciating pain slashed through her brain, and then there was quiet. She was all alone once more in Elspeth's body, her dead, cold, empty shell of a body. Alone and trapped in the midst of a never ending nightmare.

Beth screamed.

"Shh, easy there, I've got ye, lass."

Her eyes flew open, and at first, Beth thought she must still be dreaming. Then the sight of Quinton's handsome face came into focus, and the warmth of his arms enveloped her.

"You're home." She sighed. "I'm so glad you're home."

He kissed her, and the world once more righted itself.

Chapter Ten

Beth trembled in his arms, and Quint stroked her back. "Bad dream, my lady? Don't fret, I'm here. Ye are safe."

She shook her head.

He chuckled. "Ye can't fool me, my Beth. What was ye night terror about, being forced ta endure idle hands with no work ta be found for them or a smudge of dirt on something somewhere ye could nae remove?"

She shook her head again. "Really—" Her voice broke. "—there were no night terrors. I'm simply chilled."

Quint kissed her neck. "I know the difference, Beth. Now, be a good little wife, and tell ye husband what or who has caused ye distress?"

She didn't answer him. Instead, she asked a question of her own. "Did you bring Duncan back with you?"

He sighed against the soft skin of her neck. He wanted his wife to feel comfortable enough to confide in him, but at the same time, he hadn't seen her, touched her, been with her for nearly a sennight and attempting to pry information Beth obviously didn't wish to impart right this moment was the last thing on his mind.

"Aye," he whispered. "I did."

Quint nuzzled his way back up her neck to her ear

and across her cheek before finally capturing her lips. Her tongue flicked out and intertwined with his, drawing him into a kiss that shook his control with its intensity, its need. The heady taste of summer-ripened berries mixed perfectly with her sleepy warmth and quenched a thirst his soul hadn't realized it hungered for while her soft, tempting flesh beneath his fingertips enticed and excited his already overheated ardor.

God, he'd missed her.

She stilled in his arms, and her voice suddenly sounded strained. "Perhaps you should've left Duncan with his grandfather. Is it too late to take him back?"

He sighed, tamped down his fervor, and forced his cock to behave long enough to get to the bottom of whatever was troubling his wife. He rose, lit a candle, then sat back down on the side of the bed.

"Out with it, my Beth. What has transpired in the short time I've been away ta make ye so fearful?"

She gulped. "Nothing really. It's simply that I've come to realize Marta doesn't like him very much, and I'd hate to see Duncan hurt. That's all."

Quint paced. "Everybody knows Marta does nae like the child. She ignores the lad every chance she gets and ridicules him when given the opportunity. She's made nae secret of the fact she blames him for her sister Mairi's death. But she'd never actually harm him, Beth. Trust me in this. Marta and I have been friends since we were children growing up together. At the end of the day, Duncan's still her blood relation, the only one she has left. And she's still a MacLeod. MacLeod blood does nae harm MacLeod blood. It goes against everything we believe in. Nae without dire consequences anyway."

Beth shook her head. "What if I told you I'm sure she does mean to do Duncan harm? That I heard her say those very words? Would you believe me then?"

Quint smiled. "Perhaps ye have, and perhaps she did, but it nae matters. In the end, she will nae. Anyway, I promised his grandfather I'd teach the lad how ta defend himself. It will nae be long before Duncan MacLeod can watch his own back. Until then, it'll be good that ye are willing ta engage him in studies when he isn't in the lists with me. Between the two of us, Marta will be hard-pressed ta find young Duncan alone long enough ta cause any mischief, let alone harm."

He winked to distract her. Marta was his problem, not his pregnant young wife's worry. "Now, can we put away the rest of ye worries 'til morning? I'd very much like ta make love ta my wife. I've missed ye something fierce, and my poor cock has been threatening revolt if it does nae get relief soon."

She smiled, and he blew out the candle.

The reverberation of Beth's gasp and then giggle as Quint quickly pinned her to the bed and proceeded to lavish her face, her breasts, and her belly with kisses was the most welcome sound he'd heard in ever so long.

Tingles of anticipation skittered along Beth's spine as an urgent throbbing began deep in her core. She nudged against him, rubbing, rocking, seeking to get closer than nothing but skin between them would allow.

His voice broke as he shuddered above her. "Forgive me, my Beth. I can wait nae longer ta have ye. I'll do better next time. I give ye my word." He parted her thighs and plunged forward with one long, strong, steady stroke.

Beth sighed happily as she wrapped her legs around her husband's fine ass and met each of his thrusts with an answering force of her own.

He laved her nipples, first the right and then the left before taking turns sucking them deep into his mouth. They hardened beneath his attention, and spirals of delight scurried from the top of her head to the bottoms of her feet.

His pace increased, and so did hers. Over and over, he joined with her, giving then taking away, filling her with his thick girth as she clenched tightly around it in an attempt to make the pleasure of every single stroke last as long as possible. It was wonderful. Quint was wonderful. The entire world was wonderful.

Beth giggled again as joy and pleasure filled her to overflowing.

"Ah, ye think my lovemaking ta be a laughable matter, do ye?" He chuckled. "I suppose I'd best put more effort into it and show ye what ye husband is capable of." He smiled against her skin. "I want ye breathless beneath me, my Beth. I want ta hear ye scream with ye happiness, ye satisfaction, ye bliss. And I want ta hear the sound of ye voice shouting my name when ye find it."

Beth sighed, tightened her legs more securely about him, and arched, drawing him in deeper, daring him to do precisely as he threatened.

Quint growled, nuzzled her neck, nipped her bottom lip, and doubled the pace and intensity of his thrusts.

She gasped as spasms of pure pleasure exploded seemingly everywhere at the same time. Her eyes crossed, her nipples tingled, her thighs quivered, her clit contracted, and deep within, her soul discovered the true meaning of unbridled passion. "Oh, my God. Oh, my God. Oh, my God," she yelled.

Two strokes later, Quinton stiffened above her as the warmness of his cum filled her. Beth smiled as she held him tightly, enjoying the aftermath of what they'd shared.

A moment later, Quint's shoulders began to shake, and at first, she didn't understand what was wrong.

"Though I do appreciate the comparison, my Beth." He laughed. "I am nae a god, but simply a man."

She swatted him on the shoulder. He laughed again, harder this time as he turned until he was flat on his back with her nestled against his side and close to his heart.

He yawned loudly and chuckled again. "Ye never fail ta surprise me, and ye even scare me a little with ye insatiable hunger for me attention, lass."

Beth swatted him again as heat wicked up her neck and filled her cheeks.

This time, instead of laughing, he cupped her chin and forced her to look him in the eye. "Never feel embarrassed of what we have between us, my Beth. 'Tis a rare gift. Know this, though. I've come ta care for ye more than a prudent man probably should a wife, and I trust ye with my very heart as I hope ye will someday trust me with yours."

He kissed her, a soft peck, and within moments, he was snoring.

Beth didn't sleep though. She watched Quint slumber, and a lump formed in her throat. She forcibly swallowed it down. Now was not the time for emotion.

Now was the time for planning. He cared for her as she cared for him, and she'd—well, really, not she herself but Elspeth—had betrayed him. What was she going to do to remedy that fact?

Earlier, she'd failed to make him understand how much danger Duncan was in, and she'd botched it so badly because of her fear of losing the very first real love between a woman and a man she'd ever known. If she were any kind of good and decent person at all, she would've forced Quint to stop doing the wonderful things he'd been doing and she would've made him listen to the retelling of the entire conversation she'd had with Marta.

And if truth be told, she shouldn't even think of stopping with that one little tête-à-tête either. She should expose every single detail she'd uncovered about the viscount and Elspeth's involvement from Elspeth's memories.

After all, what right did Bethany Ann Anderson have to withhold information that could potentially save both Quinton and Duncan MacLeod from what had been set in motion when Elspeth Frasier hadn't died as she once had? Especially since Beth herself had no intention of remaining in this time period after Quint's heir was born.

She couldn't stay here, even if a part of her wanted to. It wasn't possible. She simply had a job to do, and then she'd be with her children again, and she'd not think of it in any other way.

Beth bit her lip and stroked her slightly rounded tummy where Quinton's son safely grew. Yes, she'd tell him. He wasn't just any man. Quint was Laird of Brochel castle and her husband, for the time being anyway. He had every right to know what dangers lay ahead. It was her responsibility as his wife to inform him of anything that might affect him, his people, or his child.

Beth swallowed a sob as Quint's eyes fluttered open, and he smiled lecherously at her. Leaning over, he captured one of her nipples between his teeth and nipped. Startling spasms of pleasure ricocheted throughout her body landing right between her thighs. She couldn't help herself. She rocked against his growing hardness, seeking to get closer. Her body begging for one more time. Possibly the very last time.

Oh, yes. She'd tell him everything…well, almost everything anyway. And she'd do it first thing in the morning. Really she would. Her conscience demanded it of her. But for the remainder of this one last night while they were still safe within their chamber and she was still wrapped within his arms, she'd be greedy and gift herself these last few hours of pure bliss.

The last moments she'd ever know before she stood before him and watched his beautiful eyes cloud with surprise and fill with disgust as he came to realize his wife, Elspeth Frasier MacLeod had been as set on his downfall and destruction as Marta and Lord Fredrick ever were.

For, Quinton MacLeod, Laird of Brochel castle, protector of small children, and thoughtful, wonderful, oh so sexy lover who had just told her he'd come to care for her, hated disloyalty above all else, and she knew it. She also knew there was no way to tell him the truth about the viscount or the woman he'd thought to be a lifelong friend without revealing the involvement of the before-Beth's-time, Elspeth Frasier.

****

Beth was fairly certain she hadn't dozed for more than a few moments at a time the entire night, and yet it still surprised her that the sun had risen and she'd better rise herself and prepare to face the day.

She watched her husband dress and contemplated where to begin with what needed to be said, for begin she must. She couldn't allow another day to go by without making sure Quint understood that he, Duncan, his people, and even his castle were in imminent danger.

But where to start?

She chewed her bottom lip. There was no way to tell him that his sweet, young, pretty little wife was in reality a forty-five-year-old flabby, saggy, dead woman from four hundred years in the future. But then again, she couldn't very well tell the man that, though she was indeed Elspeth Frasier MacLeod, she wasn't the same Elspeth Frasier MacLeod who'd willingly plotted against him with Lord Fredrick. The very same Elspeth who'd betrayed him before she'd spoken a single vow. If she tried to tell him anything close to the truth, he'd probably have her locked away somewhere and throw away the key. Or have her burned as the witch he'd undoubtedly believe her to be.

Beth placed a hand protectively across her belly, and the sensation of fluttering butterflies danced beneath her fingertips. There had to be another way to explain what she knew, without revealing who she truly was and putting their—Quinton's child in jeopardy.

The man she'd just been thinking about headed toward the door, and she knew she'd run out of time. "Quint, there's something I need to speak with you about before you leave, please."

Her voice sounded squeaky and nervous even to her own ears. She gulped.

He turned and faced her. "What is it, my Beth? I'm in a hurry ta get out onto the lists, but if it's important, I'll gladly make time for ye first. Today is ta be young Duncan's first lesson with a sword." He chuckled. "Ye can have a go at him after supper, though, I promise. However, the lad may be too worn out ta pay much attention ta ye reading lessons by then."

She wrung her hands and took a deep breath. "What I have to say won't take long. I simply need to tell you—"

A loud knock sounded on their chamber door, and Beth yelped.

Quint didn't flinch. He simply bellowed, "Enter."

The door swung open, and a man Beth recognized as one of Quint's many warriors walked in. His face was red, his clothing stained with soot, and his eyes filled with anger. "My laird, a MacDonald has been captured and brought ta the great hall. He's there now, awaiting ye justice. But he was nae caught before setting fire ta two coffers and causing the deaths of five of our kinsmen."

Quint shifted into full Highland chieftain mode right before Beth's eyes, as in not much more than a whisper, he hissed, "How did a thieving MacDonald manage ta slip past the guards I ordered on lookout?"

The warrior lowered his head, and his voice shook. "He did his mischief in the middle of the night, laird. Tavis MacLeod, his wife, and their three weans did nae have a chance ta escape. Luckily, old Angus was nae at home. He's still visiting the people of the husband to his oldest daughter."

Quint glanced at Beth for a moment, and the pain in his eyes broke her heart. "Stay here until I return for ye, my Beth. The great hall is nae a place for a lady right now. Ye understand? I do nae wish for ye ta witness what's ta come. Clan justice can be unpleasant at times. Ye'll get ye chance ta tell me what's on ye mind when I'm done. I swear ye will."

Beth nodded, and without another word, Quinton walked out and closed the door.

She counted to one hundred and then followed. She was disobeying Quint's dictates, but her curiosity was stronger than her fear. Silently, she crept down the stairs, far enough to still be hidden in the shadows, but close enough to observe the goings on.

There stood her handsome Highlander of a husband with a bloodied mess of a man lying at his feet.

"Stand him up," Quint ordered.

Two MacLeod men hurried to do their laird's bidding.

"Who are ye, and who sent ye ta do such evil?" Quint's voice dripped with malice.

The bloodied man lifted his head and stood up straight. "Does nae matter who I am, and nobody *sent* me anywhere. Whatever I may have done or will do in the future, I do all on my own. I answer ta no man."

Quint pointed to the green and black plaid kilt. "Ye wear the colors of the MacDonalds. Do ye claim not ta be one of their numbers, then?"

The man spit at Quinton's feet. "I wish I was a MacDonald. Me mum belonged ta their clan before she married me da. They at least have honor. The MacDonalds do nae steal a man's land out from under him because he likes ta take a drink now and again, and they sure as hell do nae give his land over ta another less deserving."

Quint moved in a little close to the man and tipped his face up. "I think I do know ye. Aren't ye old Shamus MacLeod's son? The same Shamus MacLeod who I threw off my land because he was drunk all the time and refused ta work it?"

The man nodded once. "Aye, I am Clach, and after ye tossed me da, me mum, and meself off *ye* land without a care, ye gave it over to that greedy Tavis MacLeod. We had nae place ta call home. Nae people ta depend upon, and nae help from anyone. Me da and mum both died last winter because of what ye, Tavis MacLeod, and that liar, Angus, did. It was him and Tavis who went ta ye with the tale of me da's drinking."

Chills ran down Beth's spine as a smile suddenly split Clach's face. "Though I could nae make Angus pay for his part in the deed, at least, Tavis MacLeod will nae be harvesting the fertile fields on me da's land any longer. I made sure of that."

Tears stung Beth's eyes. Tavis and his entire family had been burned alive, his innocent wife and three small children killed, and for what? For nothing more than a stupid chunk of ground? Anger filled her to overflowing. She'd never wished for someone else's pain, but she fervently hoped Quint would severely punish Clach MacLeod and cause him a great deal of suffering.

Quint nodded. "Ye are right in that. Tavis MacLeod and his family have nae more need for the land or anything else except for burying, and I have nae more use for ye." He hefted his claymore, and with a single swing, sliced opened the belly of the man standing before him.

Screams rent the air as a stream of bloody intestines tumbled toward the floor like wet, red, dangling ropes.

Beth gagged.

"Disgraced or nae, kicked off land or nae, ye and ye da and mum were still MacLeods with MacLeod rights and privileges. Ye could've asked at any door and not been turned away." Quint shook his head. "Instead, ye chose to betray ye own people, kill ye own kinsman? Disloyalty and betrayal I cannae abide. Ye, Clach, son of Shamus MacLeod, are hereby sentenced ta be staked outside the gates of this castle, so ye may gaze upon the fertile MacLeod fields that will never be yours while ye die a coward's death. What's left of ye after the buzzards finish we'll burn without a prayer said or a care taken, like ye did Tavis and his family."

He gestured to two of his men. "Take him away, and do as I've commanded. May God have mercy on his soul, for I have nae ta spare him."

As the two guards dragged the still screaming man away, leaving a trail of blood and gore in their wake, Beth ran for the safety of her room.

She gulped in deep breaths of air and backed as far away from the door as she could possibly get. She'd known ancient Scotland was a violent, uncivilized place, and Highlanders in particular. After all, they were a barbaric race of people, especially during the early ages when the small country was rife with all manner of war and strife. But nothing could've prepared her for the brutality she'd just witnessed delivered from her husband's own hand.

Bile filled her throat, and Beth made a mad dash for the chamber pot.

As she knelt there, emptying her belly of what little was in it, one thing became adamantly clear. She couldn't tell Quint about the viscount's, Elspeth's, and Marta's plans now. At least not yet. She couldn't take the chance he'd do the same to her. She couldn't take the chance he'd harm the child she carried.

Not that she would mind going to Heaven and being with her children right this very second, for she'd welcome the chance. But not in such a horribly brutal fashion. Not with buzzards pecking at Elspeth Frasier MacLeod's innards.

Over the years, Beth had experienced more than her share of pain. The beatings from Burt she'd thought would never end. The black eyes she'd covered with makeup. The sore ribs, the bruises, the scratchy throat from the chokings. The raspy voice she'd made excuses for, more times than she cared to remember.

Instinctively, she rubbed her throat. The choking had been the very worst part of her ordeal with Burt. Especially when the spots formed in front of her eyes and the blackness descended. Every single instance she prayed would be different. That she'd never awaken. That the nightmare her life had become would finally end.

But she did awaken, time after time after time. And when she could no longer keep her eyes closed but was forced to once more look into the hate-filled gaze of her husband, Burt would smile and begin the process all over again.

The chamber door flew open, and Beth jumped as

it banged against the stone wall.

"Ye disobeyed me, Elspeth Frasier MacLeod, and do nae try and deny it. I saw ye with my own eyes hiding on the stairs." Quint's roar reverberated off the walls. "I'll know why ye'd do such a thing, and I'll know the way of it this very moment, wife?"

Beth gulped. "I—I c—c—couldn't help m—m—myself. I needed to see what kind of man would be so evil as to set f—f—fire to a coffer and b—burn an entire family to death."

He strode forward until he stopped inches from her. The memory of her very large Highlander husband slicing open Clach's middle and the man's intestines falling to the floor played over in Beth's mind, and she flinched as she wrapped her arms protectively about her own middle and the child nestled within. "I'm sorry."

Quint sighed, but instead of doing any of the things she feared, he gathered her into his arms, nuzzled her neck, and whispered, "That's why I did nae wish for ye to see what was about to happen, my Beth. Being laird sometimes means meting out justice. Cruel, hard, swift justice. Even when warranted, it's nae for the eyes of a lady, especially my lady wife who carries my child."

She snuggled into his embrace and breathed in the warmth and safety mixed with the scent of wood smoke and leather that was Quinton Macleod. He kissed the top of her head, and Beth lifted her face toward him. "I know you only did what you had to do, and—and though it's not a sight I'd want to see ever again—" She shuddered. "—I'm glad I witnessed what I did today. You are a fair and honorable laird Quinton MacLeod, and Clach was not a good man. He deserved his punishment."

He nodded. "Aye, he did, lass, but enough about Clach. What was it ye wished ta speak about?"

Beth's entire body stiffened. There was no way she could tell him about Elspeth's memories, the viscount, or Marta's plans, especially after watching how her husband dealt with those who betrayed his trust. So, what then, what could she say to him that wasn't a lie?

He nuzzled her once more. "Come now, my Beth. There is nothing ye cannae discuss with me."

Gazing up into the kind eyes of the man she was losing her heart to a little more every day, she decided to tell him of the one other worry that had been plaguing her all week long.

"The nursery." She chewed her bottom lip. "I've been working on the nursery, and I have a favor to ask of you."

Quinton MacLeod chuckled. "What is it, my Beth? Ask, and if it's within my power, I'll grant it to ye."

Beth's heart filled to bursting with a mixture of love, respect, and guilt. This wasn't right. She shouldn't hesitate to warn him of the dangers coming. And she should do it right this very minute instead of waiting until it was possibly too late to avoid them. But Quint was looking at her with such care, such tenderness, and perhaps, even with a hint of love. She simply couldn't risk it. Not yet anyway.

She cleared her throat. No, she wouldn't tell Quint the real reasons behind what she wanted to do, but maybe, just maybe, if she pulled this off, at least the one person who was in imminent danger might be safer. For a little while anyway. "I know you have your own plans for Duncan, husband, and I agree he needs to be trained to handle a sword and fight like a man. But I'd like your permission to move his sleeping quarters from the kitchen to the nursery." She held up her hand when it looked as if Quint might argue. "I know what you're thinking. That no good can come from coddling the child, but please, hear me out."

Beth took a deep breath. "Duncan's place in this castle and this clan is about to change. No longer will he be the peat boy, but a valuable steward in training. And with you teaching him how to wield a sword, and me placing him in the nursery and getting him used to it, by the time our child is born, he'll have a ready-made guard with him at all times. I've already spoken to Bronwyn, and she's agreed to be nurse to them both."

Quint rubbed his chin. "If Bronwyn is ta be nurse, then who is ta be ye maid? Ye need a maid, lass. I've seen ye try and dress yeself."

Beth shrugged. "I thought of asking one of Cook's granddaughters."

"Nae." Quint shook his head. "Cook needs their help in the kitchen. But then if nae one of Cook's granddaughters, it'd probably have ta be Marta, and I don't trust her anymore. Especially around ye or Duncan. So one of Cook's granddaughters it'll have ta be. Since ye are lady of the keep, inform Marta she's ta now help in the kitchen."

Beth gulped, remembering how Marta had been part of trying to poison Lady Lydia. "I'm not sure the kitchen would be such a good place for her either, Quint."

He shook his head again. "Ye are probably right, my Beth. But if not the kitchen, then what are we ta do with her? I'm the laird, but tis ye who runs this keep."

"I don't know what to do with her." Beth shrugged again. "I just try to stay as far away from her as I can."

Quint nodded. "That's probably for the best. At least for the time being."

Chapter Eleven

July 1643

The lad was hopeless, and that was all there was to it.

Quint sighed as he raised his sword. "Stand fast, Duncan, and prepare ta defend yeself."

It took the child three attempts to heft his newly acquired blade as far as his shoulder. When he finally did manage to lift it above his head, he lost his balance and ended up on his backside in the dirt yet again.

Quint let his own sword drop to his waist. "Even for a wean, ye are bad, really bad, lad. Ye do ken this, don't ye?"

Duncan nodded. "Aye, me laird."

"Ye've been carrying peat for the fires for more than a year." Quint shook his head. "At least a few muscles should've developed on ye scrawny arms by now. What am I ta do with ye?"

Again, Duncan nodded, but this time his chin quivered. "Aye, my muscles should've grown, and I do nae know what ye are ta do with me, my lord. I am not much use."

Quint knelt to the child's level. "Do nae fash. I'll put one of the smaller lads ta gathering peat from now on. If ye are ta build a real man's muscles, then it's time ye moved up ta hefting stones."

Duncan's eyes shone with surprise. "Really, like

the older lads?"

"Aye." Quint chuckled. "It takes a lot of strength ta wield a sword, young cousin. And nothing hones a man's body faster than hefting chunks of rock ta build new fences. First thing in the morning, after ye break ye fast, report ta old Alaric the stonecutter and tell him I sent ye. A few sennights or so of lifting and carrying stone under his watchful eye, and we'll give ye sword arm another try."

Duncan nodded and slowly held out the shiny new blade Quinton had gifted him with only a short time before. "I suppose I will nae be needing this for a while, then."

Quint shook his head. "A man nae willingly hands over his sword ta another man, not even his laird, as long as he has breath left in his body ta heft it and fight, lad. Ye remember what ye grandda said, don't ye?"

"Aye." Duncan once more nodded.

"Ye were born ta be a MacLeod guardsman, and a MacLeod guardsman ye shall be. Keep ye sword at ye side at all times. Ye never know when ye'll be called upon ta use it."

"Aye, my lord." The boy smiled.

Quint patted him upon the head. "Now, off with ye, and find Cook. See what old Annie has ta fill up ye belly. Then report ta ye lady. My Beth has another surprise in store for ye."

As fast as his crippled foot allowed, Duncan hurried toward the keep, and Quint watched him go with a lightness in his heart he hadn't felt since before the child's parents died.

****

God, she was tired.

As a matter of fact, Beth couldn't remember another time she'd been so tired. Though she'd taught middle school for years and was used to the antics of pre-teen juveniles, medieval six-year-olds were apparently another whole story. Now, she remembered why she'd adamantly refused to teach the elementary grades to begin with. Young children had the attention spans of toadstools.

Their first reading lesson, which had consisted mainly of recognizing letters and simple words, had been met with rolling eyes, fidgeting, and yawns while the math problems were barely endured at all. Duncan couldn't seem to grasp the idea that the apples she'd collected were for counting and not eating. All the child seemed to want to do was play with his blasted sword.

Then had come supper and bath.

Supper hadn't been too bad. Though it was Duncan's first time eating at the long trestle table in the great hall with the adults instead of in the kitchen with Annie and her granddaughters. Only three times did Beth have to remind him to sit up straight and quit squirming. But if Beth thought the first bath she'd helped give Duncan was a trial, then this one had to be described as a full out war.

The child wrestled out of her and Annie's grasp numerous times and had even managed to hobble into the great hall once, stark-assed naked except for his confounded sword. Beth had no doubt she was wetter than he was by the time she managed to grab him up and finish the job.

Quint hadn't been any help either. The dratted man had hefted his tankard of ale in a salute to Duncan's tenacity, and every man in the hall cheered along with him.

Her head hurt, her belly was queasy, she was tired, and all she wanted to do was go to bed. And she would, as soon as she could get young Duncan into his.

He jerked from Beth's grasp and tried his best to dart through the still open doorway. But his club foot prevented him from getting very far, very fast, and again she scooped him up and deposited him back into the middle of the small trundle bed for the fourth time in as many minutes.

"Nae, I won't do it. Ye cannae make me," Duncan shouted. "I want ta go back ta me pallet in the kitchen. I cannae sleep here. Only bairns sleep in a nursery. I'm nae a bairn. I'm a man, a MacLeod guardsman. Ask the laird. He'll tell ye."

Beth sighed again as she sat beside the boy and looked him straight in the eyes. "I know well you are no bairn. Why else do you think you were chosen for this honor in the first place? The laird assured me himself he will trust no other guardsman but you to watch over his son. After all, you're the laird's blood, his cousin, and will be blood relation to the babe also, once he's born."

She playfully tweaked his nose.

He swatted her hand away and tried once more to escape. "If'n it's truly what the laird wishes, then I'll do it. I'll sleep at the bairn's side once he's born, but nae until."

Beth shook her head. "No, Duncan. Starting tonight, this is the room and the bed you will sleep in."

The little boy crossed his arms across his chest and adamantly shook his head. "I will nae."

Beth sighed. "Quinton trusts only your loyalty and

only your bravery to see this task done. He told me so. It's a duty you must prepare for like learning how to use your sword to fight or becoming proficient in reading and ciphering so you can someday become steward of all Brochel. It's an honor your laird is bestowing upon you, Duncan, not a punishment. Becoming familiar with every inch of this room, learning to sleep in here every night, where Laird Quinton MacLeod's son will be sleeping, is just the beginning of carrying out that task."

Duncan pointed toward Bronwyn, his eyes frantic. "But I cannae be caught sleeping in the same room as a lass, even a verra old one. 'Tis nae manly."

Beth hugged him close and whispered, "The laird sleeps in the same room with me every night, and he's very manly."

The little boy sputtered. "B—b—but I'm sure it's nae because he wants ta. Aunt Marta said the laird has nae choice but allow ye ta share his bed. 'Tis his duty."

Beth grimaced. "Well, Quinton has done his duty, and still, he lets me share his bed so that I may sleep in peace and am not afraid." She pointed to her maid. "Perhaps you being here will keep poor old Bronwyn from being scared of the dark. She's got to get used to sleeping in this chamber every night as you do. She's to be the babe's nurse when he's born." She hugged him close. "Can you do this one small favor for me, Duncan? For your laird, for the babe, for Bronwyn?"

Though she could see he didn't really want to, the child slowly nodded once and sighed. He slipped under the cover without another word and laid his head upon the pillow.

Beth leaned over and kissed his forehead while

tugging at the sword the child still had gripped tightly in his hand.

"Nae." Duncan tugged back. "A man nae willingly hands over his sword ta another as long as he has breath in his body ta fight. Laird says so."

She let go of the weapon, tucked the covers up and around the child's shoulders, and stood. She'd fought enough battles for one day.

After all, considering the way Marta felt about her one and only nephew, Duncan's sleeping with a huge, razor-sharp knife that would have any twenty-first century child yanked from his home by children's protective services, probably wasn't such a bad idea after all.

****

Quint watched his wife sleeping peacefully at his side and smiled. Beth was as beautiful in slumber as she was wide awake, even more so, probably. At least in sleep, the worry lines that creased the length of her forehead these last few sennights were relaxed and gone. And though he had no doubt it was a case of pure exhaustion and not simply his presence in the bed that allowed her to rest so deeply, he was still thankful.

He caressed her soft cheek, kissed the top of her head, and breathed in the scent of fresh soap and warm woman. God, how he loved her.

The thought startled Quint, and he sat straight up. He loved her? Not just cared for Beth, but actually loved her? Was in love with his wife? Unthinkable.

He shook his head. He couldn't be. Could he? After Mairi, he'd promised himself he'd never be so stupid as to fall prey to the wiles of another woman. Especially a woman like Lady Elspeth Frasier was known to be.

He laid back and watched the candle light flicker across her face. The Beth who lay beside him was in no way like the mean, spiteful Elspeth Frasier who'd met him with snarls and harsh words when he first arrived at her home. She wasn't anything like the little scared rabbit of a lass who he wedded and bedded two days later.

As a matter of fact, the woman he'd come to know as wife wasn't anything like either one of those women. His Beth was the complete opposite. She was loving, confident, strong willed, giving, protective of Duncan, patient with his people, and more than a little responsive to his lust. She was everything he'd ever hoped for in a wife, and she was carrying his child ta boot.

Yes, he loved her. He loved everything about her. He loved her tendency to snuggle up under his elbow and rest her head upon his chest right where his heart beat. He loved the way she smiled, the way she smelled, the way she tasted, and the sound of her laughter. He loved the way she chewed her bottom lip when trying to determine how to best get her way, and he loved how she looked up at him with adoration in her eyes, as if he were her champion even when he'd told her no.

Quint chuckled. Telling his Beth no did nae do a bit of good. The lass did about whatever she pleased while doing her best ta convince him, after the fact, that it was his idea in the first place. Like Duncan sleeping in the nursery.

Quint knew damn good and well he'd nae told Beth to change the lad's resting place from a pallet in front of the warm kitchen fire to a cold bed in the empty nursery down the hall this soon. He'd thought she meant to move the boy when her time to deliver grew near. But by the time she'd finished talking and by the time her eyes had misted with tears, she'd about persuaded him that it'd been his idea all along.

Their argument of earlier in the evening ran through his mind.

"I'm only trying to do what I thought you'd want." She poked him right in the chest. "You said you'd make a MacLeod guardsman out of him or die trying, didn't you? You said you promised his grandfather you'd train him." Then, she'd sniffed, and a single tear had escaped and slid down her cheek. "How better for Duncan to learn how to become a guardsman than to make him the personal sentinel of your son, our son? And how can he be our son's sentry if he continues to sleep in the kitchen?"

Quint realized that in truth, their exchange hadn't really been an argument at all. An argument meant a disagreement between two persons, and the only one doing any talking about anything had been his little wife.

She'd placed her hands on her hips and glared up at him. "And since Duncan's to become steward of Brochel one day, he needs to learn how to sleep in a proper bed as befits his station."

Quint laughed out loud. Nae, their conversation hadn't been much of an argument at all, and his Beth was sly as a fox. As a matter of fact, the only comment he'd made during the entire exchange was the very first question of the evening. He'd simply inquired if she'd found a suitable position for Marta. A question, Quint now realized, Beth had avoided all together.

He sighed, snuffed out the candle, snuggled his wife in closer, and stared into the darkness. His Beth was tricky, all right, but she wasn't the only one who knew how to go about getting their way. That is, as long as he could keep from revealing the nature of his true feelings for her.

Love could weaken even the strongest of men, and in the hands of the wrong woman, become a powerful weapon. Hadn't Mairi taught him that lesson in spades? A lesson he wouldn't soon forget.

Aye, he might be in love with his young wife, but it'd be a cold day in hell before he admitted it to her or anyone else. Lairds didn't show such weakness.

She wiggled her soft arse right against his already expanding cock, and Quint knew he was lost. "Lass, ye must desist. Ye need ye rest. Think of the bairn."

She had the audacity to giggle. "And miss out on a midnight tryst with my husband? I think not, my lord. The babe is restless anyway. Perhaps he needs his father to rock his mother to sleep."

Carefully, so as not to disturb the growing child too much, Quint deftly positioned Beth even more onto her side and slid deeply into her welcoming warmth. He sighed with satisfaction as her heat, her moisture, the very essence of the woman he loved surrounded him, drew him in, cradled him as closely as her womb cradled their son, and held him tight.

She sighed her pleasure into the darkness as her body moved in rhythm with his, meeting his thrusts halfway. Giving as good as she got. "Have I told you lately how much I love you, Quinton MacLeod? How much I love making love with you, like this, all alone, in our room, in the middle of the night? How much you make me feel so very loved, so special, so complete?"

He breathed in the scent of her hair and skin and grinned. She smelled of fall even though it was still the middle of summer. Something fruity, spicy, warm baked apples and cloves perhaps. Something Beth. He wanted to nibble upon her, taste her, feast upon every delectable inch of woman set before him.

Instead he did exactly what he'd told himself he would nae do. "I love ye, too, lass, with all that I am and ever hope ta be. You and our bairn. Never doubt that for even the passing of a single moment."

No more words were said, but then, no more words were needed as Quint quickened their pace. Deeply, he filled her as her sheath surrounded him and strove to hold him close. Daring him to leave her warmth. Begging him to take them both over the top, to take them to ecstasy.

At last, sighs of pleasure filled every corner of the room.

Sleepy kisses were exchanged, caresses traded, and love wonderfully made.

Chapter Twelve

October 1643

A single tear slid down Beth's cheek and for at least the sixth time in as many hours, she swiped it away. What the hell was wrong with her today? She wasn't unhappy. As a matter of fact, it was finally her favorite time of year—fall—and the season was progressing wonderfully. Things couldn't be better.

Quint was an amazing, loving, caring husband. The baby was growing very nicely inside her. Duncan was progressing even better than she'd expected in all of his studies. And even Marta had stopped spouting the majority of her craziness, at least within the range of anyone else's hearing.

Beth wasn't in pain. She wasn't sad. She wasn't angry, and she wasn't even uncomfortable today for being as extremely fat and clumsy as she was.

So what then was her problem?

She sighed as a chilly wind sliced through her thin shawl. She pulled it close around her shoulders and hurried toward the granary. She needed to check the progress of the season's last barrels of stout Macleod ale and *uisge beatha* being brewed, and even the scent of snow upon the air wasn't going to prevent her from doing her task.

Shaking her head, she hurried through the door. Where had the time gone? Summer had sped past in the blink of an eye, and autumn was quickly becoming winter. The larders were practically full to brimming with an abundance of fish, meat, fruits, and vegetables. The fields had all been harvested, fresh rushes collected for the floors, and peat gathered to keep all of Brochel toasty warm until spring.

So why then, why was her heart so full of despair and dread?

A nudge from the inside out brought a smile to her face, and Beth rubbed her swollen belly. "Shh, little man. Everything's all right. Don't be so impatient. You'll be out here with the rest of us before you even know it." A sob suddenly caught in her throat. "Oh yes, you'll be here very soon, and then I'll be gone."

Another tear escaped and rolled unchecked down her cheek. If she allowed herself to think about it, she knew exactly why she was so melancholy lately. Time was running out, and she couldn't stop it.

In a little over two months, Quinton MacLeod's heir would be born and Beth's part of the bargain she'd made with Fate would be complete. He'd come for her. And even though she wanted desperately to be in Heaven with Ben and Brian, she wasn't yet ready to let go and leave behind the only home she'd ever truly felt safe in and the only sense of family she'd known in longer than she wanted to think about.

A swift hard kick from the inside reminded her yet again of what leaving behind everything here entailed. What would Quint name his son? Would the child have dark brown wavy hair like his father, or would he be a sunshine blonde like Elspeth? Would his eyes be stormy blue like Quint's or a paler blue like her own? Would they twinkle with mischief? Would a row of freckles grace his small nose and cheeks like tiny angel kisses, and would his pink little bowtie mouth whisper secrets to the castle cats some day? Would the sound of his laughter fill the halls to overflowing? And when the day was said and done, who would be there to kiss his hurts all better, tuck him into bed, dry his tears, and calm his fears?

One thing was for certain, it wouldn't be her.

The tears did come then, fast and hard. What kind of woman chose death over a life with a wonderful man like Quinton Macleod and their child? A coward, that's who. But then she'd always been a coward, hadn't she? Even in her previous life. The fact she was more mouse than lioness was the one certainty Burt had made sure she'd never forget.

Beth shook her head. She couldn't afford to think of her decision to leave with Fate as taking the coward's way out. Her real children, her Ben and Brian were waiting for her in Heaven. She had to get to them. She had to explain. She needed to apologize. She'd waited for so very long. *They'd* waited.

She shook her head again. This feeling sorry for herself was a total waste of time and energy. In reality, probably nothing more than a hormonal surge. Not that it mattered. For even if she wished with all her heart and soul the baby she was carrying was really and truly her own, he wasn't and would never be.

This child belonged to Laird Quinton and Lady Elspeth MacLeod. The very pretty, twenty-year-old Elspeth who'd died before her time. Not the smashed-flat-as-a-pancake, forty-five-year-old Bethany Ann Anderson, the surrogate from the twenty-first century.

And what of Quint?

In truth, he wasn't really even her husband. Though late at night, when he held her so tenderly in his arms, whispered endearments meant for her ears only, and made love to her with such gentleness her heart nearly exploded with love, she could almost believe he was. But she wasn't and couldn't be the woman he'd thought he'd spoken vows with and given his name to. No, Beth was nothing but a fraud, and she knew it. She'd been right in the decision she made when last she talked with Fate.

Quint and the babe would both be better off without her. As a matter of fact, all of Brochel and its inhabitants would be.

Why, before long, every trace of Beth's existence would be washed clean from the castle and the lands. And in no time at all, it would be as if she'd never been here in the first place.

She cried harder.

****

Quinton Macleod was a happy man.

He smiled into the darkness as he wrapped his arms about his sleeping wife and snuggled her warm, soft backside against his groin. The babe protested the sudden weight and with a swift kick, reminded Quint of his presence.

He chuckled.

Aye, life was very good within the walls of Brochel castle right now. Beth was happy, healthy, and if the pink of her cheeks and the smile on her face each morning were any indications, she was more than content to be his wife and lady of the keep. She thrived upon it.

But the child in her belly was growing bigger every

day, taxing not just Beth's small frame, but her energy, too. He was strong, active, and showing off his impatience to be born. He was being so energetic, in fact, that Quint had instructed Bronwyn this past morning not to allow her mistress to overexert herself unduly.

Had his Beth listened to him or her maid, however? Nae, she hadn't.

This past afternoon, he'd found her in the granary, crying over a spilt barrel. Though she'd sworn the loss of good ale was the only reason behind her tears and not because fatigue or carrying the babe caused discomfort. Something about the fact she couldn't quite meet his gaze when she spoke, made her statement ring false. The dratted female seemed determined to take on every task around the keep herself, no matter how big or small.

But soon, at Hogmanay, the child was due. Things would be different after his birth. Beth would gain back her strength, and he'd be able to worry less.

A smile lit his face. A new year would begin, and at last, they'd be a family. A real, honest to goodness family.

He rubbed her belly, and she moaned. Tomorrow, he'd not simply suggest she begin to take things easy, he'd insist upon it.

When had the welfare of Lady Elspeth Frasier MacLeod become so very important? He knew when. It had been the moment he'd claimed her as his own. The very first moment she had willingly come into his arms and wiggled her way into his heart.

Quint shook his head and chuckled once more. He still hadn't told her again that he loved her, not in words anyway. Since that first time, it had seemed unnecessary. But then, words shouldn't need to be spoken if action was taken. And after all, it wasn't manly to go on and on about one's feelings.

Beth should already know by the way he held her, by the way he made love to her, and by the way he kept her and his people safe and fed. By the way he provided a sturdy roof over their heads, and by the way he smiled at her, touched her, kissed her.

Still, a part of him longed to give her the words again. He leaned in close and whispered against her cheek. "I love ye, lass, and will forever."

Another part of him longed for her to wake and repeat those same words to him. Instead, she simply sighed.

Quint squeezed her tighter within his embrace, and though Beth twitched twice, she did not awaken.

****

Burt held her down so tightly, she couldn't breathe. "Come on, fight back, bitch. You know I like it when you get feisty. It gets my juices flowing."

Beth shook her head as he ground his alcohol soured mouth against hers once more. Bile rose in her throat, and she gagged. "I won't fight you, Burt. Do whatever you want. Just be quick about it."

He slapped her hard, and even though somewhere deep in the back of her mind she knew she was dreaming, it still hurt.

"You fucking cunt. You killed my kids, and now you aren't even willing to try and turn me on? You know goddamn good and well I can't stomach touching you when you act like a scared little mouse. You owe me."

Again, she shook her head. "Beat me all you want. I'm not going to fight you."

He shoved her away and rose from the bed. His face red with anger, and his speech slurred from his week-long drinking binge. "What the fuck good are you, anyway? You can't screw worth a shit. You can't get pregnant anymore and give me back what you took away. And you're so fat you can barely fit through the door, so ugly I should do the world a favor and put a damn bag over your head."

Even in her sleep, tears still threatened.

She wasn't going to give into the recollections, not this time. She wasn't going to allow Burt to pull her down into his darkness.

"No," she whispered.

He laughed. "I can't believe you failed at the one thing even women in third-world countries are capable of. You couldn't keep your own children alive. Did you laugh while they burned, Beth? Were you glad they were gone and out of your hair?"

She shook her head once more.

Again, he slapped her, but this time she hardly felt it. She had already begun her descent into the cold dark place she'd existed in for ever so long after the deaths of her children.

He punched her once, right in the mouth, but she no longer felt anything. As the cloak of darkness covered her head she heard Burt's snide voice. "You can't even cook a decent meal, and this house is a filthy pigsty. I bet you haven't even told Quinton MacLeod he's in danger yet, let alone poor little Duncan, or God forbid, Quint's child. Now have you? Yeah, that's you, all right. Hide your head in the sand, scared little Beth, and maybe the bad guys won't see you. All you've ever cared about is protecting yourself."

If she wasn't sure it was a dream before, she was now. Beth tried to respond, but no sound came out when she opened her mouth.

Instead, Burt's voice kept taunting. "Scared little mousy. All you've ever done is stay in the shadows, playing it safe. How many people have to suffer and die before Bethany Ann Anderson finally stands up for something? How many more? Weren't Ben and Brian enough for you?"

Beth jerked awake, her breathing coming in quick little bursts. Sweat cooled her brow, and her heart pounded. Dream Burt was right. She was a mouse, always had been. Even growing up she'd never once taken chances or made waves. She'd always been the good daughter. The one who followed the rules. The one who never talked back. The one who always colored between the lines.

Her biggest act of rebellion had been allowing Burt Anderson to have his way with her, and even that had been because she'd been too afraid he'd stop loving her, wanting her, if she'd said no.

She hadn't even bothered to argue when her parents found out she was pregnant and told her she must marry Burt. She hadn't disagreed when Burt insisted she be the sole bread winner and he the stay-at-home parent after she finished night school and completed her teaching degree. And she hadn't even disputed the fact that the wet roads could've been a contributing factor in the accident that took her children's lives. Even though there was proof positive the driver of the other vehicle's blood showed more than twice over the legal limit, and he had swerved directly into her lane.

She hadn't wanted his family to have to pay for his bad judgment. After all, they'd all lost so very much already.

Beth glanced at Quint still sleeping with his arm securely about her waist. Burt had never been right about much, but he was right about her in one regard. She had been a mouse all of her life. But that was going to stop now.

She nudged Quinton.

He half opened his sleep-filled eyes. "My Beth?"

"We need to talk," she whispered.

****

Beth paced back and forth before the fireplace. How exactly did one go about explaining the unexplainable?

With her next pass, Quint pulled her onto his lap and nuzzled her ear. "It's the middle of the night, my Beth. Ye said we need ta talk. If neither of us says anything, its nae talking, ye ken?"

She blew out a breath and looked her husband straight in the eye. "I'm not who you think I am."

Quint chuckled. "Who are ye then? Ye look like my wife. Did the *sidhe* steal in through the window in the middle of the night and carry off my Beth? Are ye simply a pretty little *boobrie* they left in her place?"

Beth shook her head. "*Sidhe*? *Boobrie*?"

"Do nae be telling me ye mum or the old nuns at the abbey never told ye the stories of the fey people?"

She shook her head again and cleared her throat. "I'm serious, Quint. I'm not who you think I am. I'm not really Elspeth. I mean, I may look like her, and I may sound like her, but inside where it really counts, I'm not her."

His smile faded. "If ye are not my wife, Elspeth Frasier MacLeod, then who be ye?"

Beth crunched her eyes tightly closed and took a deep breath. "I'm Bethany Ann Anderson, a dead forty-five-year-old woman from almost four hundred years in the future." She opened her eyes again and held her breath, waiting for Quint's reaction.

A moment later, he fondled her breast playfully and nipped at her earlobe. "Ye are a fine looking lass, my Beth, for being so verra old, let alone, dead."

She slapped his hand away. "I'm trying to be serious here, Quint."

He picked her up, carried her across the room, and deposited her back onto the bed, then he began to pace. "Why are ye saying such things? How can ye be an old woman from four hundred years in the future? Are ye trying ta get yeself burned as a witch? Who else have ye told this nonsense?"

She held up a hand. "I'm not trying to get myself burned, and I've told no one but you. I traveled through time, Quint. Or at least Fate sent me back trough time."

He stopped right in front of her. "People do nae go traveling through time. It's nae possible. And even if they could, they do nae go around possessing other people's bodies. I'll admit ye have surprised me since we wed, and ye do seem much different than the Lady Elspeth Frasier I first met when I arrived on the Isle of Lewis, but I'm nae prepared ta believe ye are somehow from four hundred years in the…the future."

She wrapped her arms around herself. "I've been a coward all of my life, afraid of my own shadow, but I refuse to be afraid anymore. You and this child I carry are more important than any fear I may have. Come back to bed, Quint, please, and I'll try to explain everything."

For more than an hour she talked, babbled really. She told him in as simple terms as she could about America, and she told him about being a teacher. She told him of her vacation to Scotland and how she'd originally died saving the little boy. Beth even told him about Fate, and how Elspeth's fall had given her the opportunity to right a wrong, the error of his never having produced an heir.

When his eyes began to cross, she tried to tell him bits and pieces about cars and trains, airplanes and rocket ships that had landed on the moon, even microwave ovens, computers, cell phones, and iPods. But from the look on his face, she was pretty positive he didn't have a ghost of an idea what she was talking about.

She didn't tell him anything about her marriage to Burt, however, and she certainly didn't say a word about Ben and Brian. Those pains were too great to share even with Quint, too personal.

When Beth finally ran out of energy and things to say, she glanced at the man who'd lain silently by her side the entire time with his arm thrown casually across her waist. She couldn't read his expression. He didn't appear any different this moment, than he had when she spoke to him of routine castle matters.

But he looked tired when he looked at her. "If this story be true, then why did ye wait until now ta be telling me?"

Beth swallowed her fear. "Because now you're in

danger, Duncan's in danger, this babe I carry is in danger, and all who live within the walls of Brochel are in danger. I love you too much not to warn you. Your safety, their safety, is more important than whatever you may think or decide to do to me."

Quint grinned and squeezed her. "Ye love me then, do ye?"

"Of course, I love you, you silly man. How could I not?" Beth sighed.

He squeezed her again, closer. "We'll discuss this matter of ye great love for me later, but for now, where do ye perceive this danger ye speak of is coming from? Some great future army from across the ocean? One of ye so called machines with wheels that don't require horses ta pull them along? Or perhaps a—what was it— oh yes, rocket ship ta the moon?"

She rolled her eyes. "This is not a jest, Quint. Lord Fredrick means to kill you, and Marta means to do great bodily harm to Duncan if not kill him outright. They've been plotting for a very long time. After this babe is born, they mean to take Brochel and possess it for King Charles. The king desires land of his own in Scotland, other than Sterling castle, that is, which belongs to the people, not to the king. The viscount means to provide him with it."

She could feel the heat creeping up her neck and overflowing her cheeks, but still she forged ahead. "And—and I—I mean Lady Elspeth Frasier was a very integral part of their plans before she died."

Quint looked skeptical. "If indeed, the real Lady Elspeth Frasier died before we were ever wed, then how is it *ye* know of the viscount and Marta's plans?"

Beth swallowed hard. "Fate told me memories

never truly die, even after a person does. I've been having dreams, nightmares really. I've seen her memories. And Marta told me right to my face of their plans, and of her hatred for you and Duncan. She blames you both for her sister's death. She doesn't realize I'm not the same Elspeth she knew."

"Ye swear ye haven't spoken of this to anyone else?" Quint asked.

Beth shook her head. "No, of course not." But she could still see the wheels turning in his head through the shadows of his eyes. Did he believe what she'd told him? Should she be worried about what he would do with the information? And now that he knew she wasn't the Elspeth Frasier he thought he'd married, would he send her away? He hadn't really said much. He just continued to stare at her as if she'd grown a second head. But then her story was a lot to process.

"Good," he finally said. "See that ye don't." He tucked her in close to his side and kissed the top of her head. "Sleep, wife, whoever ye be. We'll speak more of this on the morrow."

Chapter Thirteen

In the first rays of the morning sun, Quint studied Beth. But then, that's what he'd been doing for hours. Lying in his bed, wide awake, staring at a woman, who'd earlier last evening sworn to him she was from another time and place. But for the moment, in this time and in this place, she was sleeping peacefully by his side, as if this were just another morning, while he certainly hadn't slept much at all.

He shuddered, yet still couldn't bring himself to feel even a grain of fear toward his wife. And she *was* his wife, even if what she said were true. Especially if what she said was true.

After all, if the real Elspeth died the night before their wedding, then it had most assuredly been his Beth and not Elspeth Frasier who'd spoken back to him the vows of their marriage. And if that was the case, then it had been his Beth and not the high-and-mighty Lady Elspeth he'd taken into his arms that very first night and claimed as wife.

Even now, though he still wasn't sure if the woman he knew as his wife was telling him the truth or if somehow the fairies had addled her brain, his cock roared to life and stiffened with the memory of her tight warmth enveloping him, holding him close, welcoming him home.

Beth from the far away future or Lady Elspeth

Frasier, it made nae difference. He desired his wife, this wife, and it didn't matter to him how he'd acquired her. What mattered was he aimed to keep her, forever. Even if the lass had gone completely doo-lilly on him. Even if keeping her meant keeping her secret from every other living, breathing soul in Brochel...forever.

He'd do it if he must.

He'd nae lose her now.

He couldn't. He loved her too much.

Quint took a deep breath and blew it out. But then, what if she were telling the truth? Should he really be concerned about Telford's coming and trying to wrest his castle and lands from his grasp?

He chuckled. Quinton Macleod was a Scot through and through, and nae Scot worth his salt would ever allow an Englishman ta take what was rightfully his and live ta tell about it. Nae, the viscount wasn't really that much of a concern yet. Nae even if he brought an entire army with him. On a good day, a handful of MacLeods could outfight a full regiment of Englishmen without ever breaking a sweat.

He knew that for a fact.

He'd trained them himself.

But then, if the viscount wasn't really a threat, was Marta?

He'd promised Mairi on her deathbed he'd take care of Marta and see to Duncan's well-being. The child's future was set. Every day he became stronger, faster, more proficient with his sword, and every night, Duncan surprised him and Beth both with how quickly he learned. Mairi and Dougal would be proud of their son if they could see him today.

Marta was another story, though. The woman was

surly at the best of times. She'd even taken Beth's offer to work in the kitchen and thrown it right back in her face. She'd insisted that being the aunt of the laird's cousin put her in much ta high a position ta be a mere scullery servant, and for the moment, Beth was allowing it.

Quinton hadn't argued the point. He wanted to give Beth the chance to be the lady of the keep as she saw fit, without the heavy hand of the laird interfering. If she needed his assistance in dealing with the help, she'd ask for it.

And he'd nae even blamed Marta for being the way she was, or even for hating him as she did. God knew there were days he hated himself. It really was his fault her sister Mairi had died. It didn't matter whether he was directly responsible for Dougal's death or if the man had thrown himself off the battlements. It was still he who'd denied his cousin's request in the first place. And it was still he who'd watched the life fade from Mairi's eyes a little more every day she'd carried the shame of Dougal's bastard.

But what could he do about any of it now? He couldn't bring Dougal or Mairi back, and he couldn't undo his decision to nae allow them to marry. He'd been an arrogant, selfish, immature, doo-lilly himself back then. The experience had changed him, though. It had forced him to grow up and learn to put his people's needs before his own.

So, what was to be done about Marta then? He had no idea. The best plan he could come up with was to wait, watch, and pray that, in the end, Beth was wrong about Marta's change of loyalty and that he'd nae be forced to go back upon the promise he'd made to her sister.

****

Beth snuggled farther under the covers of their bed. It'd been only a few hours since she'd told her husband she was from a different time, and already he was waking her up and wheedling all the information he could from her. It wasn't that she didn't wish to tell him, at least not precisely. It was more that she was worried whatever she might say would or could somehow change the future, and perhaps not for the better. She had to be careful.

But at the same time, would it truly be wrong to tell him some tidbit that might someday give him a small advantage over others? Just a little something? Or even a few little somethings? Especially if she meant to leave him here all alone in 1643 with a castle to run and a newborn to take care of?

"No, I didn't say cars were carts without horses. I said cars were kind of like carts but without the need for horses to pull them along. They're made of metal and leather. They have engines and use gasoline to make them go."

"Now I know ye are trying to confuse me, lass." Quint grinned. "Metal? Engines? Gasoline?" He smacked her soundly upon the rump, then rubbed it all better for good measure.

Beth chuckled. "I'm not trying to confuse you, really, I'm not. I don't know how to describe the stuff from my time in words you'll understand."

"The metal." He sighed. "Start with the metal they use. Is it forged iron like we use ta fashion our weapons?"

Beth hesitated a moment, and then shook her head.

"It is, but it isn't. In the future, metals will be…mixed. Don't ask me the exact process because I don't know all the particulars. But I do know that if you melt iron ore and chromium together, you get what's called stainless steel. It's much more durable and flexible than plain forged iron. And you can put in some nickel or carbon if you have any lying around and make your metal stronger and more pliable."

She didn't dare go into the process of making any other types of metals from her time period. She couldn't imagine trying to describe some of the more complicated metal alloys, aluminum foil, or God forbid, fluorocarbons like the Teflon series to a man from the seventeenth century.

Quint got a faraway look in his eyes. "Hmm, I think I'll have a word with the blacksmith later today. But let's forget about metals and engines and this so-called gasoline for the moment. What can ye tell me about Scotland in your future world? Is she free from English tyranny? Does Brochel still stand? Is the MacLeod name still uttered with respect? Do my future clansmen still keep close to their hearts our motto of Hold Fast?"

Beth hesitated. Being an American history teacher, she really should know more English history than she did. But knowing from the beginning exactly what she wished to teach, she'd never really paid that much attention. If truth be told, she'd leaned more English, and especially Scottish history, from the romance novels she read, than she ever learned in the classroom. But there were a few things she did know details about. The only problem being, they were things she wasn't sure Quinton would want to hear.

She looked him straight in the eye. Though perhaps she wouldn't tell him the whole truth and nothing but the truth yet, there would be no more lies between them. "Scotland, in my time is a proud prosperous country. It's part of what's called Great Britain. Scotland, England, and Wales eventually form an alliance that works very well for all three of them. There's no more war. And together, with Northern Ireland, they become what's called the United Kingdom. You'd be proud of your people's descendants, Quint. They've learned to live together in peace."

He smiled as he playfully drew a single finger across her lips to her ear and back again, following the pathway he'd made with his mouth. "And Brochel? Does she still stand?"

Beth hesitated again. What to tell him of Brochel?

The memory of the last day of her previous life and the sight of the more-rubble-than-structure tower, standing all alone and barren upon the edge of the small Isle of Raasay came clearly to mind.

She cleared her throat. "Brochel still stands, at least a good part of it, anyway. It's a very old castle in my time, remember?" She leaned into his caress. "And you'd be pleased to know that Dunvegan is still held by the MacLeod clan. And yes, like all the MacLeods before them, they still Hold Fast."

He nuzzled her neck, and his grin against her skin brought an answering one to Beth's lips.

"That makes me happy," Quint whispered. "I'm glad that even hundreds of years in the future, a MacLeod still sits upon the seat of power at Dunvegan." He nuzzled her neck once more. "But enough about things that have nae happened yet, I've plans of my own for this night."

His hand slipped down Beth's body, and then back up again, coming to rest finally on her breast. He squeezed gently before taking her nipple between his teeth and nipping, sucking, and thoroughly licking it.

Beth gasped as spirals of pleasure skittered along her spine and landed in her clit. She leaned in closer. Oh yes, they'd have plenty of time for talking, later.

Quint suddenly lifted his head. "Ye truly were forty-five years old in your time?"

She nodded.

In the flickering light of the candle, his face took on a very serious expression. "I ken for a fact, Lady Elspeth Frasier MacLeod's body was chaste when I first bedded her. But what of the woman ye used ta be, my Beth? Forty-five years alone is a verra long time. Is coupling different in the future? Did ye have a husband ye loved? A fine home, laughing children? Am I and Brochel a disappointment compared ta what ye once had?"

Beth shook her head. She still wouldn't tell him about Burt or the boys, at least not yet. But perhaps she could be honest about her feelings for him. "I love you, Quinton MacLeod, and I love our home. I can honestly say I never knew what it was to be truly loved by any man before you showed me the pleasure to be found in your arms. And believe me, no man, in any other time period ever, could begin to come close to you, in bed or out."

He kissed first her lips, then her neck, her shoulder, her breasts, and her tummy as he gently lifted her until she was straddling him. Tingles of intense desire shot straight through her gut and landed right where she wanted his cock.

A moment later, he complied with her wishes as with one hand upon her expanding midsection and the other on his full erection, carefully he rose to meet her waiting cunny. "Well, then—" He chuckled as he entered her and began rocking back and forth. "—I suppose I'd better do my duty and make sure ye do nae forget what pleasure this *young* man can bring ta such an old lady."

Beth gave him a sultry look as she leaned forward and rubbed her pert nipples against his chest. "I'd like that, my very young lord. I do believe I'd like that very much. But we shall see who pleasures whom first."

She winked and slowly rose up the full length of his cock, then plunged back down.

He moaned low and long, and Beth did it again, and then again, and then again.

Quint grabbed her hips, "Ye wee vixen," he laughed. "I'll nae lay here and let ye slowly torture me ta death, even if ye are now big with child and we have a need ta be careful."

In a single motion, he flipped her onto her back, lifted her legs until they rested upon his shoulders, and slid his cock so deep into her cunny its head kissed her cervix.

Beth whimpered as tiny shockwaves of pure pleasure radiated outward with every stroke he executed. God, how she loved this man.

"I'm nae hurting ye, am I, wife?"

The concern on his face brought a sheen of tears of joy to her eyes, and Beth smiled up at her husband. "You'll only be hurting me if you stop too soon," she laughed. "Big and pregnant or not, I need this, I need you, and I need you right where you are."

With that, Quint doubled the speed of his strokes, and within moments, they were both shouting their releases to the dawning sunrise and quivering as shudders of bliss filled them both.

****

From their chamber window, Beth stared down into the bailey, watching Quint work with his men. She shook her head and smiled. The man was driving her completely bat-shit crazy and had been for the last three days. Since she'd first told him she was from the future, at least once every few hours, he'd come to her with a question. And that didn't even count the queries he'd kept her awake half the night with.

Questions like, if she truly were from the future, then what kind of weapons did man use to fight battles and what kind of horses did they ride? How did they manage hunting enough food for an entire army, let alone the wood it would take to cook it? Were red-tail deer still plentiful? Fish? Fowl? Was wool still used for clothing, leather for boots? What did she mean by skyscrapers, and how did one possibly build structures that could even come close to scraping the sky? And what happened to the sky once it was scraped?

It never ended, and it was at times, as if he were trying to trip her up and force her to make a mistake he'd recognize as an untruth.

She'd tried to answer his questions as thoroughly as she could, but more than once, disbelief filled his eyes, and she couldn't blame him. After all, who in their right mind, in the year 1643, would ever believe man would one day cook his food without first needing to build a fire, let alone scrape the sky or walk on the moon?

Suddenly, he glanced toward their chamber window, and Beth shook her head as he turned over the training of his men to another and headed for the keep. She recognized that look of determination on his face. Quinton MacLeod had more inquiries to make.

She had barely counted to ten before the door to their chamber burst open. "What happens with King Charles?"

Beth motioned for Quint to take a seat before the fire. "Why do you keep asking all these questions? You don't really believe anything I've already told you. One minute, you swear I truly must be from the future, and with the very next breath, you're just as positive I'm not. You are making both of us crazy, Quint."

He nodded. "Aye, I suppose I am, at that, my Beth. But I still need ta know what happens with King Charles in the end. Does he wrest Brochel away from me? Do the royalists finally get overthrown by the parliamentarians? Do ye nae see, this knowledge is important for the safety of our people? My loyalties, our loyalties, must be in the right place at the right time. Our duty is first to those who reside behind the walls of Brochel, not to our personal beliefs."

Beth paced the room, trying to decide how best to answer. She knew exactly what had happened in her lifetime, but that was a period of history before Quinton MacLeod had an heir on the way, changing the stakes, and that was a time before Elspeth Frasier Macleod had failed to die as she once had. Had history changed? And if so, what to tell Quint?

She stopped right before him, knelt, and took his

hand. "I understand your concern for our people. Really, I do. But I can't be one hundred percent positive what will happen to King Charles now. In my time, he was beheaded in either 1649 or 1650 by Oliver Cromwell and his followers. I can't remember which year for certain. And yes, parliament overthrows the royalists. But that was before *we* changed history, Quint." She rubbed her belly with her free hand. "That was before this child was created."

Quint rose abruptly to stand and pace. "Forty-nine or fifty is only a few years away. Our child will still be a young lad. His existence shouldn't have any effect on the king's fate."

Beth shook her head. "No, not on the king's fate, but perhaps on the future of Brochel. The viscount will be determined to procure this castle and lands for Charles once this child is born. It is his mission."

Quint got that same stubborn look on his face she'd seen so many times before. The eyes-narrowed, lips-pursed expression that Beth had come to realize meant hell would freeze over before he'd allow anything or anyone to threaten what was his. "He'll nae take Brochel. Nae as long as I draw breath."

Beth nodded. "That's what scares me the most about all of this, Quint. I know you'd die for Brochel, and I know you'd willingly exchange your life for the lowliest of your people. But then, what's to become of your son? Who will see to his welfare if you aren't here?"

Quint stopped pacing, stood right in front of her, and took both her hands into his. "I do nae plan on dying and leaving ye, my Beth. But if it should happen, ye'll be here ta safeguard our lad, ta tell him of the father who loved him, ta watch him grow into a man."

For a moment, her breath left her body. Just the thought of a world without Quinton MacLeod in it was too horrible to contemplate. "No, you must live." She sobbed. "You must raise your son. Promise me you will."

She turned away from Quint and crossed to the other side of the room. How could she explain to the man she'd come to desperately love that she herself meant to betray him even more than Elspeth Frasier had ever hoped to? How could she tell him she meant to leave him the moment his son was born? And not simply walk away into her happily-ever-after afterlife, but leave him all alone here on this cold, cruel earth in the year 1643 and in the middle of the fight of his life?

His arms were warm and comforting as he wrapped them around her. "I will nae promise ye something I do nae know for sure. Ye are the one who claims to know the future, lass, not I. What I will promise ye, though, is ta try my verra best ta remain at ye side until God calls me ta him. And I expect the same from ye. Do nae ever leave me, my Beth. My life would nae be worth living without ye in it."

Beth gulped as her heart ripped in two.

Part of her wanted desperately to stay in this past with Quinton and the child he and Elspeth had made, but an even greater part of her heart screamed no, she couldn't, she didn't dare. Ben and Brian were waiting for her. They had been for ever so long. They deserved to hear the words she'd failed to say to them the day they died. They deserved to have their mother back. They deserved an explanation, and she meant to give them one. She intended to finally give them all peace.

Even if delivering that explanation in person meant losing Quint, his son, Brochel, and all the people she'd come to care for.

Instead of making the promise Quint longed to hear, Beth cupped his chin, drew up on her tiptoes, and gently kissed his lips. "What will be, will be," she whispered. It was the best she had to offer.

Quint didn't seem to recognize her discomfort, however. He simply nodded. "Aye, ye have the right of it, lass. What will be, will be."

He turned to leave and then back toward her once more. "I'll be going whaling on the morrow." He held up a hand. "Aye, I ken ye opinion on the matter. We've discussed it ta death. But with the threat Telford may verra well be upon our shores shortly, we must gather provisions. People need ta eat, my Beth. They need light and warmth. I cannae take the chance of not being prepared for a siege. Ye do ken that, aye? The sea provides for us. It always has, and it always will."

He did know well her opinion of the practice of whaling. And he was right. They had discussed its benefits, its disadvantages, and its dangers ad nauseam. Living in Alaska in the twenty-first century and being a history teacher to boot had brought her much closer to the subject of whaling than she'd ever hoped to be.

In Alaska, whaling was a way of life and had been for centuries. Entire communities counted on the bounty. If not for the whaling and salmon industries, people would go without food, without clothing, and without shelter. But at the same time, she couldn't wrap her mind around the devastation to the species the practice would one day cause.

She'd been born and raised a PETA generation

baby, and there were some things, even being transported back in time by four hundred years couldn't change.

At least in Alaska, in Bethany Ann Anderson's time, laws had been passed to protect the whales, and a number of yearly catches had been established in order not to hunt the various species into extinction. But in 1643 Scotland, there were no safeguards in place yet, and though Quint and his people certainly didn't seem reckless or greedy, they'd already gotten one whale this year.

Beth opened her mouth to protest, but he again raised a hand for silence, and there was something in his eyes, something that prevented her from saying any of the things on the tip of her tongue. Was it sorrow perhaps, guilt, defeat?

She wasn't sure. So she clamped her mouth shut, willing to at least hear him out before her own conscience made him feel bad for seeing to the welfare of his people. For looking out for the residents of Brochel even to the detriment of himself had always been first and foremost in Quinton's heart. It was one of the reasons she loved him so much.

"I'll not just be whaling. I mean ta bring home cod, seal, and otter, too." He smiled, as if hunting the other creatures of the sea would somehow make up for the whaling part.

But he looked so sincere. And even in Alaska, in the twenty-first century, two whales a year were allowed. And it wasn't as if the whales he would be hunting tomorrow were the really big, endangered kind. They weren't bowheads, humpbacks, grays, and orcas, after all.

The waters around Raasay sported what would someday be known as the minke whale. They were probably the most abundant species of whale even in her day. Though only twenty to thirty feet in length and weighing approximately five tons, they were still a very abundant source of meat, oil, hide, and baleen. Most of the things the people of Brochel relied upon daily to survive.

So instead of complaining or once more giving her opinion as she really wanted to, Beth simply smiled back. "I only meant to wish you safe travels, husband, and fair winds and calm seas." She patted her tummy. "And hurry back to us. We'll be here, waiting for your return."

Chapter Fourteen

November 1643

Quint had always loved the sea. Even as lads, he and Dougal couldn't wait for whaling season to begin and with it the opportunity to board his father's ship and be counted among the men.

And though Dougal could no longer be here ta feel the cold, salty mist wetting his face, fight ta keep his balance during the riding of a turbulent sea, or race him ta the top mast like they used ta do, his son Duncan could. It was the only legacy left from his father that Quint could give him. The right of every MacLeod man ta take care of his own from the bounty the sea had to offer.

He watched the lad work the ropes as every other MacLeod before him had done, and he thought of Beth. How did one explain the sea was nae a thing ta be feared, but more a proud calling, a destiny so ta speak, in the verra blood of his people? More than simply a source of food, bounty, or adventure, the waters surrounding the Isle of Raasay were more a religion than anything else. They gave and they took away, like the good Lord Himself did. They sheltered, they fed, and in the end, if necessary, they even buried their own.

It hadn't been enough that his pregnant little wife refused to understand the importance of the sea and his need ta take Duncan with him, but she'd even tried her best ta make him feel guilty about catching ta many fish. As if that were possible.

The lass simply didn't understand. Ye didn't take anything from the sea. The sea gave what it wished ta give ye and nae else.

And right now, the sea was being a verra greedy mistress. Though over the last four days, she'd blessed them with an abundance of cod, salmon, otters, and seal, not one single whale had been sighted let alone pursued. It was as if the sea itself were taking Beth's side over his and punishing him for defying his little wife and taking Duncan against her wishes.

After all, the only thing she'd asked, well demanded, really, was he leave Duncan behind with her. He'd tried for hours to explain why he should take the lad, but on that point she'd adamantly refused ta budge or see reason. They'd parted still angry with each other, a fact that ate at Quint's soul.

Not that his Beth had cared one whit about him taking any of the other MacLeod males along with him. On the contrary, she seemed more than happy ta be rid of the lot of them and the mess they brought inta *her* castle. Oh no, she hadn't cared enough about any of them ta keep him awake all night ranting and raving. It had been only his taking of Duncan she'd objected to vehemently.

Quint sighed. Why hadn't he simply given in to her this once? After all, she was getting quite large with his child and as emotional as most women carrying tended ta be. What would it have hurt?

He chuckled as he remembered exactly why the stubborn little chit hadn't gotten her way.

His wife, his Beth, had actually stomped her

delicate little foot, as if the limestone beneath it wouldn't dare ta not shake with her wrath. She'd fisted both her hands upon her hips and glared at him when he first tried ta inform her Duncan would nae be present for their daily lessons for a while. She'd had the audacity ta tell him no, as if she were laird instead of him. She'd looked so adorable in her rage, kissable, and if he hadn't been afraid she'd bite him if he'd tried, he would've.

It wasn't as if any of her dictates had made a bit of a difference in the end anyway, because they hadn't. He'd still taken the lad with him as he planned. After all, it was important Duncan learned what it meant ta provide for the needs of the people of Brochel. Especially if he was someday expected ta become steward as Beth wished.

Didn't the lass realize there was more ta running a keep than what could be learned within the pages of a book? And were lads so coddled in the time she'd come from that she couldn't see her fears, her verra kindness, kept Duncan more a cripple than his foot ever could?

Though he'd not be the one telling her that.

What had really happened in the four hundred years between his time and hers? Not that he truly believed every single word she said about that either, because he didn't.

Men could nae possibly ride around on moving carts without horses, and there was no way anyone would ever be able ta cook food without first starting a fire. Let alone talk right ta each other while nae even being in the same keep. Or fly ta the moon or fly anywhere as far as that mattered. Had future man somehow sprouted wings? He thought not.

Still, he'd listened to every word, wanting only ta hear more. If his Beth was telling half-truths at most and making up the rest, her stories still made her the best *seanchaidh* in all Scotland ta have ever spun a tale.

But then maybe he enjoyed her stories so much because he really wanted all of it to be true. Maybe he wanted ta believe that someday Scotland and England really could come to live in peace, and that the MacLeod name, even four hundred years from now, did still *Hold Fast* and stand for something.

Either way, the lass had certainly burrowed deep under his skin and straight into his heart. She was his first thought in the morning and his last thought at night. And if she were really that concerned about Duncan's welfare, he'd keep an extra vigilant eye on the lad. He'd even make sure they only took as many damn fish as they needed ta survive a siege and not a single one more.

He shook his head and smiled. It must really be love he felt for his little Beth, because what else could occupy a man's mind so completely, and at the same time, drive him stark raving mad?

"There she blows," a deck hand shouted.

Quinton grabbed his harpoon and headed across the deck. So the sea obviously wasn't as angry with him as he'd feared. And it was time ta show her the respect she deserved for the bounty she was about ta provide.

He grinned again. There'd be blubber a-boiling in the vat come the morrow.

****

It was everywhere, the oil, that is.

It was in her nose, her ears, her hair, her eyes, and had even seeped deep into every pore of her skin. Not to mention, the smelly substance coated every single surface of every single table, chair, and the floor itself of the room she stood in.

Beth cringed as she wiped her oily hands upon her oily apron.

No matter how much oil covered everything, the large copper cauldron in the middle of the big processing shed still boiled on and on and on as the raw blubber was rendered into yet more of the odious whale oil.

It didn't matter in the least to her that the oil would provide hours of much needed light come winter or that the MacLeod men, and especially, Quint had spent five full days and nights watching and waiting, capturing and working their fingers to the bone to bring back what the sea had gifted to their people. Oh, no. The only thing that mattered to Beth, that occupied her mind, was the need for a long hot bath she wasn't going to get and didn't have the time to take even if it was offered.

She sighed and felt guilty. She should be grateful they'd returned with such an abundance, but she simply couldn't be. Whale processing was disgusting, all of it. For at least the tenth time in the past hour, she wished desperately for a twenty-first century grocery store where she could hop into her car and go pick up a few packages of light bulbs and a couple dozen candles instead of dealing with one more drop of disgusting whale oil.

God, how it stank, and if she didn't get out of this room soon, she was going to lose what little food she'd managed to keep down since starting the harvesting process first thing this morning.

Beth shuddered.

Not that she didn't like seafood, because she always had. But her problem today was that, in her present condition, the sight and the smell of so much raw fish in so many different forms and in such a confining place was more than a little overwhelming.

On one table alone sat huge slabs of whale meat right next to filets of cod, chunks of otter, and large deep-sea salmon with their heads still intact. Their cold, dead eyes stared up at her accusingly, as if she'd been the one to pull them up from their deep-sea home and to toss them willy-nilly upon the deck to flop around until eventually suffocating.

The memory of twenty-first century grocery stores once more flittered through her mind with their neat, clean aisles and shelves stocked with whatever food stuff one could dream of wanting. A place where all forms of seafood were packaged neatly under tight layers of see-though plastic wrap or easy open cans and pouches. One had no need whatsoever to even contemplate where it had all come from and what it had taken to process it. It was simply there to be placed into one's shopping cart, paid for with plastic, and taken home to be consumed.

Though rife with many other problems like disease, hunger, war, and plain old-fashioned cruelty, the twenty-first century had certainly become very civilized as far as food packaging went. Not once in her many years of walking up and down grocery store aisles had there been a single sight of bloody entrails on display when she arrived at the meat and seafood section, let alone bits of gore upon the floors, barrels of fermenting guts sitting around and spilling onto the floor, or anything else unpleasant to the eye and nose. And the local deli sure as hell hadn't been covered with stinky whale oil.

She made the mistake of glancing back at the gut barrels and gagged once more as a big yellow-striped cat sat licking his bloody paw. Though she truly didn't want to, she found herself both grossed out and mesmerized by the sight.

And though she completely agreed there should be as little waste as possible, the thought of what the inside of those particular containers would smell like come spring when their contents would be mixed into the compost used to fertilize the vegetable gardens and fields had bile rising. She ran for the door.

She wanted to help with the processing. Really, she did. After all, as lady of the keep, it was her responsibility to make an accounting of all food stores. But today, she simply couldn't stand one more minute in this place.

Beth hadn't taken more than three steps outside the door of the shed before she was reminded of her duty.

"What good is a *lady of the keep* who cannae complete the most basic of tasks." Marta's lip curled with malice. "Perhaps our laird should be looking for a more sturdy wife. One who isna so delicate he fears he'll break her while plunging deep inta her cunny with his fine cock."

Beth glared at Marta, then smiled. She wasn't in the mood to let the other woman see weakness on her part today. "I haven't heard any complaints from Quint concerning my sturdiness as the lady of this keep or in his bed either. As a matter of fact, from the smile on his face this very morning, I'd say he's quite content. But if by chance, in the future, he does voice any such fears, I'll be sure to pass yours along also."

She stiffened her spine, raised her chin a notch, and walked off, leaving the strawberry-blonde harridan with her mouth hanging open.

Beth needed these few minutes of fresh air, and come hell or high water, the likes of Marta wasn't going to prevent her from enjoying them. After all, she'd had more than enough foul odors and oily individuals to contend with for one day. She'd have her five minutes of peace, and then she'd get back to work.

****

Quint yawned, wrapped his arm a little more snugly around his sleeping wife, and grinned into the darkness as he sniffed her hair. His Beth wasn't going ta be the least bit happy come morning when she realized she still smelled of whale oil. And that was even after soaking in a tub of hot water for more than a full turning of the hourglass after he'd done her the favor of pissing on her.

He laughed out loud at the memory of the look upon her face when he'd done just that.

How, in her time, did they go about ridding themselves of the stink of whale if not with a concoction of human urine mixed with blubber ash? He'd have ta ask her in the morning. *If* she were talking to him again by then.

He laughed once more. He couldn't help himself. Just the look on her face when he'd dropped his kilt and sprayed her naked body with his urine. Then he'd rubbed her down with the nasty ash while she stood bare-arsed, waiting for her bath ta arrive. It had probably been the most fun he'd had for ever so long.

She didn't seem to share his opinion of a good time.

She'd screamed, squealed, squeaked, and even tried her best ta claw his eyes out a time or two.

But then she hadn't really put up *that* much of a fuss when he asked her to reciprocate in kind. As a matter of fact, the little wench had quickly straddled the chamber pot. Before he'd even had the time to realized what was about to happen, she'd dumped a good size handful of blubber ash in with her piss, and then smeared every inch of his chest, his belly, and his groin in the warm, wet, ashy mixture. When she was done, she'd doubled over in a fit of giggles until tears streamed down her cheeks.

Quint hugged her even closer and smiled.

His Beth, his life, his verra own wife was a wonder ta behold. She'd worked side by side all the day long with every other able-bodied inhabitant of Brochel, and she'd done it without complaint. Not only had she worked as hard as everyone else, but she'd also made sure his people had been rewarded with a tasty oyster stew ta fill their bellies at the end of the day.

And it wasn't until the verra last worker had left the processing shed for the night that she'd taken to her bath and finally ta their bed.

He worried for her, though. She was growing bigger each day with his child and looking more tired. Was it safe for her ta work so verra hard? He couldn't lose her. He wouldn't. Tomorrow he'd make her rest. After all, he was laird. And what would she have ta say about his dictates on morrow?

Quint chuckled. Riding out a storm at sea was simpler than preventing his Beth from doing whatever she set her mind ta. What would he do if he couldn't curtail her enthusiasm to be so helpful? He wouldn't have her overtaxed. It wasn't ta be born. But then, if yesterday had been busy, it was nothing like what the morning would bring, and they really would need all the help they could get.

Yesterday, they'd barely begun the processing of the one small whale. Tomorrow, the real work would start. It would be dawn ta dusk, nonstop cutting, chopping, salting, smoking, and drying of not just whale, but of the cod, salmon, otter, and seal, too. Not to mention the continued boiling down and rendering the blubber into the much needed whale oil.

Beth had seemed so verra surprised by the whole harvesting process. But then she hadn't yet been comfortable enough to join in and help with the first whale they'd captured earlier in the year. She'd only stood on the outer periphery, watching, with a look of abject horror on her face.

That memory brought a new question to Quint's mind. One he'd ask her the next time they were alone and she was speaking ta him again. What did the people of her time use for light if not whale oil? And how did they preserve their food through the long winters? Were there even still such a thing as a long winter? Or had future man conquered weather as they apparently had so many other things?

He wasn't sure he truly wanted to know.

Though he certainly enjoyed his Beth's stories, he couldn't imagine a world where only select men were allowed ta hunt and fish in order to provide for the many. And only if they'd first been awarded a mysterious parchment called a license. If not seeing ta the needs of one's family, what was left for a man ta occupy his day with?

And without a doubt, he wasn't sure he'd even want ta live in a time where he wouldn't be allowed ta openly carry his claymore ta protect those weaker than himself.

And what kind of horrible world did away with talking face ta face with ye fellow man? How did one man look another in the eye and determine his truth, his worth, if it wasn't a requirement ta even be in the same room let alone the same keep or country? iPhones and Internet, as she'd called them, had ta be instruments of the devil. There was no other explanation for it.

He shuddered.

To Quinton, his Beth's future seemed impersonal, barbaric, and he was infinitely glad she was here with him, in this time, where the world was sane and civilized and he still had his strength, his claymore, and his castle walls ta keep her safe.

But could he really keep her safe in his time if Telford arrived upon their shores with an army in tow as his Beth was certain he soon would?

Though without a doubt Quint would die to protect her, their child, and his people if it came to it, he hoped she was wrong. Just like his liege lord, John Iain, the viscount was one of the king's men. Quint would rather not be the one to start the war coming. But he would if given no other choice. And he'd not just start the fight, but he'd do it by running his claymore straight through Telford's black heart if the man dared threaten what was his.

He squeezed Beth closer, and the bairn within protested his overzealousness with a swift kick. That made him chuckle.

What a strong bairn his lad or lass already was.

He should hope for the son his Beth was so sure she was carrying. After all, he was laird and had need of an heir. But at the same time, he could so clearly picture a sweet, little lass with her mother's golden curls and beautiful smile.

That didn't mean he would mind a braw lad. Someone to teach how ta ride and hunt, ta fish and sail, ta fight and protect what was theirs. Someone ta take his place when the time came. Someone ta look after his mither and care for Brochel.

Beth's eyes suddenly fluttered open. "I'm sturdy enough, aren't I."

He stared at her. Was his little wife truly awake or simply talking in her sleep as she often did?

Not wanting to take the chance of incurring her wrath again, especially after the pissing incident, he decided it really didn't matter. She'd asked him a question, and he'd answer her anyway. "Aye, lass. Ye are verra sturdy indeed."

Beth smiled. "Good. I thought so." She patted the hand resting upon her belly. "You were right, you know. About taking Duncan along with you. The child literally glows with health. His cheeks are pink, and he hasn't stopped smiling since you got home. And I swear he's grown a foot, at least, while you were gone."

Quint patted her tummy. "I'm glad ye are nae longer angry with me, my Beth. On the morrow, though, I want ye ta take it easy, do ye ken?"

She chuckled. "I will if you will." She closed her eyes and slept once more.

Quint shook his head. What a fey, stubborn

creature his wife was, and she thought she'd gotten the last word ta boot.

But he knew better.

He'd show her tomorrow.

Chapter Fifteen

December 1643

Beth stood upon the castle's parapet, facing the sea wall with her cloak clutched about her shoulders, and breathed in the chill morning air hoping for some small semblance of peace.

The preparations for winter were behind them. Stores of dried, salted, or smoked whale and fish, red deer, and mutton lined the larder, as well as baskets of kale, peas, broad beans, chard, potatoes, onions, and leeks. Not to mention, wild raspberries, apples, pears, plums, and cherries. And of course bundles of wild thyme, blocks of salt, rounds of cheese, and bins of flour for the day's bread.

But she didn't care about any of those things. All Beth cared about today was the fact it was truly winter and she was running out of precious time. With every rise and setting of the sun, faster and faster the days sped by. She counted them, each and every one, knowing full well that, soon, her last moments with Quinton would slip away like the grains of sand trickling through the hourglass.

She no longer wanted to leave, but neither could she stay.

Winter really was upon them, and though there was no snow to speak of upon the heather-clad moorlands, forests, or sea cliffs, she still felt the cold finality of what was about to come to pass.

How could she simply go away with so much unsettled?

Quint was still in danger from the threat of the viscount. His son was still in danger of being used as a pawn. And poor, little Duncan was still in danger from the likes of his crazy aunt.

No, she didn't want to leave before the situation with Lord Fredrick was seen to its fruition and Brochel and all who resided within its walls were safe. Yet how could she not? And what was the freaking viscount waiting on anyway?

She'd thought he would've shown up on their shores by now, but he hadn't. And it was all but too late. He wouldn't dare attempt to traverse the tempestuous winter seas this late in the year. Surely, he'd be forced to wait for the spring.

By then she'd be gone, and who'd be here to watch Quint's back?

She'd lost her chance to be helpful. The cowardly viscount would bide his time and wait for the optimum opportunity. From Elspeth's memories of the man, memories quickly fading into oblivion, she knew that, though Lord Fredrick was greedy, selfish, devious, and conniving, he certainly wasn't stupid.

Which meant, when the viscount did finally arrive, there'd be no one other than old Bronwyn, the cook Annie, and Duncan close enough to keep Quinton safe. His men wouldn't give the English viscount a single second look. They thought their laird to be invincible. She'd seen the truth of that written all over their faces every time they looked his way, every time they sparred with him in the bailey.

What of Marta? Who'd be watching her? Would she and the viscount work together to kill Quint and Duncan both?

And the baby. Who'd take care of Quint's son if neither of them were here to raise him? Would Marta take her place as his mother, and the viscount take Quint's as his father? That couldn't be allowed to happen. It simply couldn't.

Beth shuddered.

God, what a coward she must be to even be contemplating leaving those she cared for while they were still in danger. How could she walk away from the man she loved with all her heart, let alone a helpless newborn, and a crippled boy while she went traipsing off into her happily-ever-after afterlife with Ben and Brian?

She couldn't. Yet, she must.

She was so confused.

Hogmanay was only a couple of weeks away, and with the beginning of the new year would come the birth of Quinton's son. And just as Fate had promised, she'd be with her children.

Then why wasn't she happier about the situation? She was getting exactly what she'd asked for, wasn't she? So what was her problem?

In her heart, Beth knew exactly why she was troubled. Brochel hadn't originally been meant for *her*. The people residing within its walls were technically not *hers*. Quint wasn't truly *her* husband, and the child she carried wasn't really *hers* to claim and could never be. Still, she longed for what rightfully belonged to another woman.

Beth longed for a full lifetime of years with Quint,

and she longed to watch his son grow into a good man like his father. Though, in truth, it was probably for the best she didn't. There was no telling what mistakes she'd make this time around, and she wouldn't see another child harmed, or worse, because of her incompetence.

Burt's words came rushing back to haunt her. *Stupid fucking cunt. You let them die and did nothing to stop it. You laid your fat, lazy ass on that road waiting for someone else to come along and rescue you while you watched my children burn to death. A real mother would've found a way to save them. Or at least a real mother would've died trying. They're better off dead, you know, than they ever were with you.*

Tears ran unchecked down her cheeks.

She'd always believed the old adage, *It's better to have loved and lost, than to have never loved at all*, but she didn't anymore. Life had taught Beth her share of hard lessons. The hardest of all being that some wounds never do completely heal. They simply fester, scab over, and kill their victims slowly. Just a little bit more every day, they're forced to endure the pain.

Being separated from her children was pure, unending agony. Ripping herself from Quinton's loving embrace was going to shred the very last vestiges of her already tattered-beyond-recognition heart.

She should've remained aloof.

She shouldn't have fallen in love with him, and she really shouldn't have begun to wonder what his son's tiny body would feel like snuggled in her arms, feeding at her breast, and cooing for her ears alone while, at the same time, wrapping his little fingers securely around her heart.

To him, she needn't be a fraud. He'd never known the real Elspeth Frasier MacLeod. She could actually be his mother in truth if she dared, and he'd never know the difference.

But then again, she couldn't. She really couldn't. Ben and Brian were waiting for her, and it was to them she owed her loyalty.

What was she going to do? She couldn't stay. Yet, she couldn't imagine leaving, either.

Beth wrapped her cloak closer about her body and shivered. Why on earth was she standing out in the cold when she could be in the warmth of her solar, in the sleeping chamber she shared with Quint, or in the great hall, overseeing the running of Brochel?

She'd simply been so very restless this morning— big, fat, very pregnant, and…and emotional.

Just a couple more weeks by her calculations. Two more weeks, and the Yule log would be burning brightly as a brand new MacLeod made his entrance into the world.

Tears threatened once more. Yes, two more weeks of waking content in Quint's arms each morning, of making slow, tender love with him each night, of talking for long hours, of laughter, of joy, of feeling loved, of being loved.

God, how she was going to miss him. And not just him, but the baby she carried, Duncan, Bronwyn, Annie, Brochel, and the whole frigging seventeenth century, stinky whale oil and all.

As if thinking about Quint conjured him to her side, she heard his voice. "What are ye doing out here in the cold, my Beth?"

She turned to face him, swiping tears from her

eyes. It wouldn't do to let him see she'd been crying. He'd only ask questions she wasn't prepared to answer.

She took one deep cleansing breath, and then another. "I suppose I was feeling—oh, I don't know—in need of more air than the inside of the castle holds today." Patting her huge belly, she smiled. "Your bairn is getting quite big, my laird, and there are times it's hard to breathe around him."

Quint placed his big, warm hands over hers. "I cannae wait ta see him and hold him." He suddenly blushed. "Or her. I'd nae mind a lass, either, ye ken? Whatever ye give me, my Beth, as long as I have ye by my side, will be fine."

"It's a boy," she whispered. "You'll have your son, your heir, Quinton MacLeod."

"How do ye ken?" he asked.

Beth smiled and shrugged. "It's not like it's the first time I've told you he's a boy. I just know, and perhaps this time, you'll believe me."

****

Quint held his wife close in the night and groped for something, anything to say. Since their short conversation on the parapet the previous sennight, his Beth had become even more withdrawn, to the point of being deathly silent.

She hadn't once joined in the festivities of the hanging of the holly, the baking of the mince pies, or the decorating of the hall with rosemary and ivy. She most assuredly hadn't participated in any of the dancing, singing, or the games, and she certainly hadn't been anywhere in sight for the consuming of great amounts of *uisge beatha* that literally screamed tomorrow was the eve of Christ's Mass.

Was his little wife a puritan at heart? Did she despise the frivolity of the holidays as the English Protestants did? He hoped not.

Though he and all of his people were Presbyterians, they did still enjoy the twelve days of banqueting, feasting, and drinking, not to mention the exchanging of gifts and distributing of boxes to the servants, tradesmen, and the poor. It was a fine way to end the old year and begin the new.

Christ's Mass was a tradition he very much liked, and one he wished to share with his wife. But the closer it got to the new year and the lighting of the Yule log, the further away from him Beth seemed to slip.

Perhaps it was the weight of carrying the bairn taking its toll, and she'd be her old self once more after the birth of their child. But then again, perhaps not.

Were the holidays so much different in her time? Mayhap that was the problem. Perhaps the lass had no idea how to celebrate Christmas, because there was no Christ's Mass to celebrate where she'd come from.

Or perhaps something had happened in her old life to make her not like this time of the year? There were many times he wondered what his Beth's life had been like. Though she willingly talked about machines, wars, buildings, and other such marvels, she confided little if nothing about her own day ta day life.

He shouldn't ask. Her life before him wasn't his business. Still, he had ta know.

He nuzzled her warm neck. "I've a question, wife."

Though she remained silent, her muscles stiffened, ever so slightly, beneath his touch.

"Do nae pretend sleep, my Beth. I ken better."

She sighed. "I'm not pretending anything. I'm

simply tired." She yawned. "Go on, then. Ask whatever it is you feel you simply must know in the middle of the night and get it over with."

He chuckled. "I was wondering about Christmas. Is it still celebrated in your time much as it is now? I ken well I shouldn't take such pleasure in one day above another since I and my people are Protestant and the church has ruled the Yule time as a pagan practice to be shunned for the most part. I cannae seem ta help myself. I do enjoy the frivolity."

She turned in his embrace, and the flickering candlelight illuminated her glare. "Quinton MacLeod, I am huge with child and barely sleep as it is, and you woke me to ask about Christmas?"

Quint chuckled once more. "We both ken ye were nae asleep." He swatted her playfully on the rump. "So quit dallying, my Beth, and answer the question."

She huffed. "Yes, there is still Christmas in the time I came from."

He waited, and waited some more, until it became painfully clear she wasn't going to offer anything else. "Well, lass, what is the Christ's Mass like in ye time, because ye certainly don't seem happy with ours?"

Her eyes misted over a heartbeat before she answered. "Christmas in this time, here with you, is fine with me, Quint. I'm just tired, very tired, because I can't seem to get comfortable anymore."

He placed a hand on her taut belly, leaned down to kiss it, and was rewarded with a swift kick to the jaw. That made Beth giggle, and it was the prettiest sound he'd heard from her in days.

Then she sighed. "You really wouldn't like Christmas much in my time. People actually go into debt to outgift each other. In the time I came from, the real reason for the holiday has all but been forgotten, and in its place is a make-believe fat old man in a red suit who flies through the sky in a sled driven by magical reindeer. He brings toys to little children while eating their cookies and drinking their milk.

Quint shuddered. "Really?"

She sighed once more. "Yes. But like in this time, as far as most adults go anyway, Christmas is a good reason to throw a party and get rip roaring drunk."

He ran a finger along her cheek. "And what of family, my Beth? How did ye family celebrate Christ's Mass? Did ye husband light the Yule log, and did ye children sing songs and dance happily around the fire? I would nae be jealous if ye'd had a family ta love before me. After all, in ye time, ye had already lived a much longer life than ye have with me. Is there someone in the far future waiting and hoping and wishing for ye ta come back ta him? Someone ye miss? Is that why ye seem so sad?"

She closed her eyes, but not before a single tear escaped and ran unheeded down her cheek. Her bottom lip quivered. "There is not one single, living, breathing soul waiting for me in any time period anywhere, my laird. Of that, I can promise you."

"But ye did have a family once, didn't ye?" he asked. "Or at least, I hope ye did. No one should be alone, my Beth, especially not at Christmas."

Her throat bobbed as she swallowed and shook her head. "No. I no longer had a family when I traveled back in time. At least, not one I want to talk about."

Quint nodded and hugged her closer. So be it. He was a patient man. He could wait. After all, they had a lifetime together stretching out before them. His Beth would eventually tell him whatever it was hurting her, but like everything else about her, she'd do it in her own time.

****

Christmas?

Quint wanted to know about her past Christmases of all things? How could she tell a man who obviously loved Christmas that she felt nothing but dread for the holiday?

Not that she'd always disliked Christmas or any other holiday, for that matter. It had just been since the death of her children. Before that horrible day on a wet Miami highway, she'd been the queen of Christmas, and Ben and Brian her little elves.

She could still hear Brian's little voice singing "The Twelve Days of Christmas." It was his favorite holiday song and one that, after his death, she could no longer stand to listen to.

And the tree... Oh, my God, how he loved to decorate the tree. He'd sing and dance the entire time he hung lights and bulbs, his cheeks glowing a healthy little boy pink while the words of that song lisped through a gap where he'd recently lost a tooth. And he'd sing it over and over and over.

Ben couldn't care less about the tree or the songs but couldn't wait for his mother to open whatever treasure he'd found for her that year. He didn't seem to care about what he himself received, but the look on his face when she or Burt opened their gifts and smiled and hugged him was beyond price.

One year, when he'd been about five or six, Ben had found a small framed, canvas picture of a pair of ducks flying past a bare branch in the neighbors trash bin. The edges were scuffed in a couple of places and mold discolored one side. The thing was hideous, but he'd thought it beautiful. So he'd wrapped it up for her and squealed with glee and pride as she opened it.

That precious beyond words picture still graced the wall of her small condo bedroom. Where she could glance at it each morning when she first opened her eyes. Or at least it had graced her bedroom wall until her death. There was no way her sister or brothers would've known what that old, beat-up picture meant to her. They'd probably thrown it right back into the trash, and hopefully some other little boy had rescued it for his mom.

Even Burt hadn't been so horrible during the holidays. He'd always taken pleasure in putting the boys' toys together, in the wrapping and the stuffing of the stockings. The only real problem he'd had was with her cooking. No matter how hard she tried, the turkey was never quite as good as his mother's, the potatoes as creamy, the stuffing as moist, the pies as sweet, or the cranberries as fresh.

It didn't matter, however. The boys seemed to like her cooking fine, especially the cookies they helped bake for Santa.

But then the wet Miami road and the drunk driver did happen, and Ben and Brian were no longer there. Christmas, along with every other holiday, became a nightmare.

She dreaded the weeks of school not being in session from right before Christmas until after New Year's, for that meant more time spent at home with Burt. Time he'd spend drinking most days and yelling at her most nights...or worse.

After she'd moved to Alaska and far away from Burt, she'd never again decorated her home for the holidays. Though she still owned a box of ornaments, like the Popsicle stick squares with the boy's pictures on them, she didn't open the container. It sat in the storage area of her condo, sealed, in the dark, safe and sound, but never again used.

She couldn't help herself. Though she treasured every piece, she couldn't put any of it out for display. The sight hurt too much. But she couldn't stand to part with a single piece either. Just like the cards she'd received over the years with Happy Birthday Mom or Happy Mother's Day scribbled in smudged crayon or the hand print turkeys for Thanksgiving or the cotton ball Easter rabbits. She'd kept them all.

And soon, very soon, she'd be with Ben and Brian once more. It simply meant leaving Quint and his son behind, in danger, and all alone in the seventeenth century.

God, how she hated Christmas.

Chapter Sixteen

Beth smiled up at Burt as he handed her a cup of eggnog. It wasn't often, even in a dream such as this, that he was remotely nice to her. And though it seemed odd, she extended her hand to accept the gift anyway.

Just as she'd almost grasped it, he snatched the cup away. "Lying, cheating, murdering bitches don't deserve anything for Christmas." He laughed. "Not even a lousy cup of nog."

For good measure, he slapped her across the face.

"Hey," Quint yelled. "Ye'll nae be hitting my wife. Who do ye think ye are, anyhow?

Burt laughed again, but this time, it sounded more like a snarl. "She was my wife long before she was ever yours, so I'm entitled to the first discipline of the day. But you're welcome to slap the cunt around a few times if you want. She's a useless piece of shit. Bet she didn't tell ya she couldn't manage to keep my kids alive long enough to grow them into men." He pointed to her huge stomach. "I hope she does a better job with *your* son than she did with mine. But then again, it's not as if she could do any worse, now, is it?"

"Ye really were her husband?" Quint asked. "And ye had bairns with her? She never said a word about ye ta me in all the time I've known her."

Beth tried to speak, to explain, but no words came out of her mouth.

"Oh, I was her husband, all right." Burt chuckled. "But considering you're four hundred years older than I am, and she went back into the past in order to marry the likes of you, that probably makes her your wife first."

Quint shook his head. "I suppose ye are right. And though I hate ta admit it, ye are probably right about her being a useless piece of shit, too. At least, our Beth had the decency ta stick with ye for a while after she killed ye bairns. She's leaving me the moment my son is born. And she doesn't care that the viscount means ta kill me as soon as she's gone. It's pretty obvious, all Bethany Ann Anderson ever cared about in any time period was herself."

Tears stung her eyes, but she didn't bother to swipe them away. What was the use?

Quint shook his head once more. "And here I thought she wasn't anything like the real Lady Elspeth Frasier when, all along, they were exactly the same."

Burt cackled. "Like I said, stupid cunt. Stupid, stupid cunt, that's what our Beth is. Always was. Always will be."

Quint nodded. "Aye, I'm afraid ye might be right about that."

Beth sat straight up in the bed, sweat beading her brow and her breaths coming in short little pants. Oh, my God. Now, both her husbands were talking to each other in her nightmares? And agreeing as to what a horrible person she was? Hadn't the one-sided night terrors with Burt been bad enough?

Quint wrapped his big strong arms around her and pulled her down into his embrace. "What's got ye so upset tonight, lass?"

What was she going to say? It wasn't as if she could tell him about Burt and the boys. Not now, not after so much time had passed. Could she?

"Just a bad dream," she whispered.

"Ye can't keep shutting me out, my Beth. I have a right ta know what's troubling ye."

She closed her eyes and snuggled deeper into his embrace. Perhaps she could tell him part without revealing the whole. "You asked me if in my time I had a—a husband, and...and yes, I did."

She shivered, and Quint held her tighter.

"He...he wasn't a nice man, and there are times, like tonight, that I have nightmares about him. But then I wake up with you right beside me, and I feel safe once more."

Quint rocked her gently. "And bairns, my Beth? Did ye have a family with this man who wasn't nice ta ye?"

A sob caught in her throat, and all she could do was nod.

"I'll not press ye ta say anymore, lass," Quint whispered into her hair. "I ken ye are hurting, and ye'll tell me in ye own time what ye wish me ta know."

She nodded once again. "Quint, would you make love to me, please?"

He patted her bottom. "Ye are so far gone with child, I fear I'll do ye harm."

She shook her head. "You won't. I know you won't, and I need—I so need you inside me tonight.

Quint sighed against her skin. "Aye, lass," he whispered once more. "I'll make love with ye, slow and careful, mind ye, and while I'm at it, I'll do my verra best ta replace some of those unpleasant recollections with brand new good memories of us."

His hands were gentle as they caressed her back, her sides, her breasts, and her ass. When he lifted her hair out of the way and nuzzled her neck and nipped her earlobe, she sucked in a breath and gloried in the shivers of excitement racing down her spine.

She loved this man, honestly loved him with every fiber of her being, and the thought that she soon must leave him was tearing her apart. But then he kissed her, and the warmth of his lips and the force of his tongue invading her mouth drove away almost all coherent thought.

But a single leftover tear escaped.

Perhaps she did have to leave him soon and perhaps there really wasn't anything she could do to stop time, to postpone her fate. But for tonight, for this one glorious night, she could still know what it meant to be loved by this man and to make sure he knew he was loved by her.

He deepened the kiss, and the reason for the single tear was forgotten. All that was left in the wake of her grief, her guilt, was absolute, wonderful sensation.

Feather-like wispy tingles of pleasure flowed over her, landing deep in the pit of her belly as Quint positioned her onto her side and slowly entered her. He was big, but she was wet and ready, and a moan of pleasure escaped her partially opened lips.

"Are ye all right then, lass?" he rasped.

She ran her fingers up the side of his thigh and laughed. "Aye, my laird, I am verra well."

He wrapped an arm about her big belly and the baby kicked as he quickened the pace, thrusting in and out, over and splendidly over. Within moments, she adjusted to his tempo and met his driving force with a momentum of her own.

Her toes curled, the roof of her mouth tingled, icy heat streaked, down her thighs, and the muscles of her pussy contracted about his girth as stars formed before her eyes.

Still, he didn't slow.

"I love ye, my Beth," he shouted. "With my body, my soul, and all I am and will ever be."

"I love you, too, Quinton MacLeod, so much it hurts. And no amount of time, distance, or even fate can ever change that."

With another shout, this one of pleasure, he found his release, too.

Beth closed her eyes with a smile on her face and slept. This time, no bad memories and no nightmares invaded her dreams.

****

Quint opened his eyes in the early dawn to the sound of soft rapping upon his door. The very first rays of the eve of the Christ's Mass morning sun graced the wooden opening of the slit in his outer wall as he called, "Enter." At the same moment, he made sure his sleeping, naked wife was well covered.

"My laird," his man at arms said in a hushed tone. "I did nae wish ta wake our lady, but ships ha' been sighted a ways off shore, and they be a flying an English flag. What would ye have us do?"

"How many?" Quint asked.

"Three, my laird."

Quint glanced at his wife and sighed. He would not wake her with this news. She looked so tired these days, so fragile. She needed her rest. Without the need of

217

seeing it in her eyes, he knew well her fears of what was to come, for three ships flying English flags could mean only one thing. Telford was about to land upon the shores of Raasay and with a force at his back. And he was doing it now, in the middle of winter, when least expected.

Quint might respect the man a little for having the ballocks to at least try and wrestle a Scottish castle from a Scot, but that didn't mean Lord Fredrick had any chance of succeeding. Though Quint might admire his adversary for his show of courage, he wouldn't let it cloud his judgment. He'd protect what was his, and he'd not give over his legacy, his son's birthright, and his people's home without a fight to the death. But then Brochel wouldn't be that easy ta take herself, either. Her high sea walls were all but impenetrable when need be.

That was, if the ships came to start a war at all. There was always the possibility, though slim, they were about other business. Quint wouldn't be the one to fire the first shot. He wouldn't give the viscount that kind of leverage to use against him and his people later. But he'd sure as hell fire the second if need be, and almost hoped it was an obvious fight coming his way and not a cloaked intrigue as his Beth feared.

"Alert the men," he ordered as he rose and quickly put on his kilt and boots. "Let us go greet our English *guests*, and see if they be calling themselves friend or foe this day."

As quickly as he could, he made his way down to the sea. Though the gray winter morning was crisp and mist laden, he easily made out the ships on the horizon, growing ever closer with every ebb and flow of the tide.

"Didn't I tell ye, laird?" The man at arms gestured toward the looming sight. "Three English ships of war heading straight for us."

Quint squinted his eyes. His man at arms was right about the first two ships, anyway. They both flew the king's colors, a red, white, and blue Union flag with Saint George's cross plainly placed over the Scottish cross of Saint Andrew. In other words, two ships of the Royal English Navy.

The third and last ship, however, was harder to make out from this distance, and when it finally came clearly into view, the sight of the Scottish white cross upon a field of blue, and a second flag below with a black bull's head dead in the middle with staves at each side upon a blood-red background was like a punch straight to his gut.

So his liege lord and chieftain, John Iain MacLeod, was personally accompanying the viscount to Brochel? Why? John Iain hadn't even bothered to visit Brochel and pay his respects when his bastard son, Dougal, died. What then could be so important as to bring him to the shores of Raasay on this day? Quint hoped he was wrong about his own guess as to the answer to that question.

But only one thing kept pounding through his mind, over and over.

The MacLeod was a king's man through and through, always had been. And whenever the need arose, it was the king's business John Iain saw to. So the only pertinent question left to ponder was, in the end, which loyalty would win out, that to his king or that to his blood? For whether out right or by deception, a fight was coming, and God knew no man could serve two masters. Only time would tell how this day's beginnings would eventually end.

He glanced toward his man at arms. "Ye stay behind with me and greet our guests, but I want the rest of the men behind the gates of Brochel, at the ready."

A grumble began, and Quint turned with his fists upon his hips and a scowl upon his face. "Aye, I know well there be English bearing down upon the shores of Raasay, but I'm not a stupid man and neither are any of ye. I won't give them a reason ta attack us outright, if'n I can prevent it. We have lasses and wee bairns and weans within the walls of that castle and in the village ta protect. We must think and act carefully. We can nae afford ta be rash. But I swear ta ye this day, if there be killing that needs ta be done this fine Scottish morning, then I'll be the first ta be doing it."

His small army of Highlanders raised their shields and claymores in support, nodded, and slipped into the shadows as they headed back toward their posts.

****

Beth was in a tizzy, but then she had been since the moment Bronwyn awakened her with the news of the English ships approaching. It had to be Lord Fredrick, for it could be no other.

She wasn't sure which to do first, have old Annie put on another pot of pottage or grab up a sword and go help defend her husband. Either was fine with her and both needed doing, but one thing was for certain, she'd lose her mind and the respect of her people if she didn't stop cowering in the corner like a scared little mouse and do something.

"I am not a coward. I am not a coward. I am not a coward," she whispered over and over to herself. "I can do this. I'm not afraid of the viscount. I won't be afraid. I won't."

But the years spent at the mercy of Burt had taught her well what lengths some men would go to when defied, and Lord Fredrick was, without a doubt, one of those men. Elspeth's memories had confirmed that fact. Not that he'd been physically cruel to Elspeth, because he, for the most part, hadn't…yet. But then she'd given him no reason to be, either. As a matter of fact, Lady Elspeth Frasier had followed him around like a puppy most of the time. Doing whatever the viscount asked of her without question.

That wasn't the case now, however. Beth couldn't be the Elspeth the viscount remembered, and even if she could somehow pull it off, she didn't want to be. Lord Fredrick wanted Quint dead. And he wanted to take possession of her—no, not hers—Quint's son, Quint's castle, and Quint's lands, and for no other reason but to impress some stupid king.

Though the viscount hadn't been physically abusive to Elspeth, the young woman who'd once occupied this body had certainly witnessed his mistreatment of others plenty of times. She'd seen more than her share of bruises and scars he left behind on those who dared defy him. If there was one thing Beth meant to do, it was defy the viscount at every turn.

She gazed at the handful of warriors standing around waiting to break their fast in the great hall. "Your laird has gone to greet ships approaching our shores. Perhaps you should all join him."

One of the big burly Highlanders she knew only as Ralf answered for the group. "Nay, my lady. The laird has ordered us ta remain here in the keep, and ta guard ye and the other lassies with our verra lives."

"We don't need protecting. Your laird does." She stomped her foot. "He's the one who's in danger, not us. I order you to go to him this moment."

Ralf chuckled, and the other warriors smiled at her, as if she were a silly little child throwing a temper tantrum.

"We cannae do as ye ask, my lady. Though ye be fierce, 'tis our laird's wrath we fear more."

She shook her head. The big Highlander was right. No one with more than two brain cells to synapse together would dare defy an order straight from Quinton MacLeod. So instead of arguing a lost cause further and trusting her husband's judgment, Beth forced herself to head toward the kitchens before she did something silly like take up a sword and head after Quint herself.

"Annie," she yelled. "Put on another pot of pottage. It appears we may have guests. And have your wee granddaughters prepare the sleeping chambers in the tower opposite the rooms the MacLeod uses. It wouldn't do to put strangers too close to the laird before we ascertain the true reason for their visit."

Then she was off to the larder to check on the availability of meat and vegetables. She had no idea how many men a ship could hold or how many they'd be expected to feed, but she didn't want to be caught unawares either. From there, she headed to the granary where the MacLeod ale and *uisge beatha* was kept fermenting and instructed a couple of the men to bring in a few casks of each. After all, this was Christmas Eve, and if by chance the ships' arrivals warranted friends and not enemies as she hoped, ale and whiskey would both be expected.

And then it was up the stairs to the rooms the viscount would be granted. Though she'd spent little time in this tower, she had to insure herself there were no short cuts between the two. When Quinton MacLeod next laid his head down to sleep, it wouldn't be with the fear of a sneak attack from the other side of his very own castle.

Next, she stopped by their own rooms to make sure, just in case it wasn't the viscount, that she didn't embarrass her husband by showing up in a wrinkled skirt or a smudged tunic. And while she was at it, she ran a comb though her sleep-tousled curls, and added a ribbon for good measure. After all, it could be Lady Lydia and her brother, the Mackenzie, come to spend the Christmas with them just as easily as it could be the viscount. Though no Mackenzie worth his mettle would ever be caught flying an English flag, and she knew it.

With a swish of her skirts, Beth was off and onto her next task, and by the time she heard the castle doors swing open and saw her husband, the viscount, and another Highlander she'd never seen before saunter through them, she was ready to face whatever Lord Fredrick or anyone else thought to throw her way. At least, she hoped she was ready.

But when she met his eyes, she knew she was not.

The viscount was exactly as she remembered him from their brief encounters and from her nightmares. The same cruel beady gaze, the same twitchy little moustache, the same arrogant, malicious smile upon his face.

Quint's voice reverberated off the stone walls of the great room. "Look who has come ta break their fast

and ta celebrate Christ's Mass and the Yule with us."
He gestured toward Beth. "Ye remember his Lordship
the Viscount Telford, don't ye, wife?"

Beth nodded.

Quint gestured toward the other man. "And this,
my Beth, is our liege, John Iain, chieftain of the
MacLeod clan. We've certainly been blessed this year,
haven't we?"

Beth forced herself to smile at John Iain. Quint had
told her he was a king's man and not to expect any help
from that direction. But no matter how hard she tried,
she could not force herself to smile at Lord Fredrick.

Not only could she not smile at him, but it was
almost impossible not to pull her hand back in disgust
as he kissed the very tips of her fingers and winked at
her while almost crowing.

"My, my, just look at how you've blossomed, Lady
Elspeth. When we left the king's side, we had no idea
we were in for such a wonderfully anticipated event as
what's apparently about to take place here at Brochel."
He turned toward Quint. "Good show, laird. Oh yes, a
jolly good show indeed."

He smiled so widely at her that Beth had no trouble
counting the yellowed stains upon his teeth, and her ire
boiled over. The creepy viscount was in for a very big
surprise when he came to realize the Elspeth Frasier he
left behind really wasn't the same Elspeth MacLeod
he'd now be required to deal with. And though she did
find herself tamping down a few skittish nerves, and
though she'd really had no choice but to compel a
breath or two to calm herself, and even though she'd
finally given in to the temptation to swipe her sweaty
palms upon the brocade of her shirts, she'd at least won

the first of what could be many battles to come.

She hadn't cowered.

After all, she was a MacLeod.

She hadn't so much as blinked an eye when the viscount turned his wicked gaze upon her. She wouldn't give him the satisfaction. For Bethany Ann Anderson-Lady Elspeth Frasier had become a MacLeod through and through, and in the words of Quinton MacLeod, Laird of Brochel and the man she'd love through whatever time she found herself in, *A MacLeod does nae cower. A MacLeod does nae show fear. A MacLeod always and forever, Holds Fast.*

And hold fast she would—today, tomorrow, and as long as it took to see Quint and his son safe.

Maxine Mansfield

Chapter Seventeen

Beth wanted to punch him right in the mouth. Not just once, but at least twice. Maybe then he'd shut up for at least a freaking minute. The viscount was giving her a headache on top of the rampant case of nerves she'd neither been prepared for nor desired to endure this day. She was very pregnant, she was very hormonal, and she was already on edge.

Wasn't that enough to deal with?

It had been going on all day long, too—his veiled threats, his cruel little whispered innuendos, like, "Oh my, Lady Elspeth, but don't you simply look ravishing, and in such a late stage of pregnancy. I'm so glad to see you've been quick to do my bidding. And to think impending motherhood tends to wash so many out, but not you, my dear."

He'd said that as he leaned in close and kissed her cheek when he returned to the great hall after being shown his rooms. When they'd made their way to the board in order to partake of the eve of the Christ's Mass meal, he had the audacity to actually pinch her ass...hard. She'd almost tripped over the hem of her skirt. If it hadn't been for the steadying hand of Quint, she probably would have.

The moment they'd been seated, he leaned across the table and whispered again, but this time just a little louder. "You, my dear, literally glow with good health.

Not at all like the Lady Elspeth Frasier I knew *so* well back in England. That girl, if I remember correctly, was quite sickly at times."

Then he'd sneered. "Perhaps it's the Scottish air that's been so good for your constitution? Or is it by chance that big Scottish laird who has you glowing? Pray tell, my dear. Do be kind enough to impart upon us mere mortals the secret of your sudden good health. You haven't gone and done something stupid like fall in love with the wretch, though, have you? That would be unfortunate. After all, we have an understanding. And if by chance you have, you better get over it quick, Beth. I mean, my Lady Elspeth."

Then he winked, and Beth shivered as he continued. "On second thought, keep your tender feelings for the oaf for the time being. It can only further our cause if Quinton MacLeod doesn't see what's coming. It'll be our little secret, Beth. And it's been my experience that deceitful women like we both know you to be, whoever you really are, wherever and whenever you truly came from, do so love to keep their surreptitious little morsels of information close to their devious little hearts."

He chuckled from his place across from her at the evening meal as he lifted his tankard in a salute, and downed MacLeod ale.

Had he really guessed she wasn't the Lady Elspeth Frasier he thought he left behind to do his bidding? Or was he simply fishing for information? He'd certainly had plenty of time to ponder the differences he undoubtedly noticed while on the Isle of Lewis for Elspeth and Quint's wedding.

But was he really smart enough to have put the

clues together and correctly guessed she, in fact, wasn't Elspeth Frasier? Or that she could possibly be from another time, another place? Had he convinced himself that Beth and Lady Elspeth Frasier were two completely different people? Only witchcraft could explain that. Was he, in his own scheming way, threatening to expose her as a witch if she failed to further cooperate with him?

The thought of burning at the stake had shudders skittering along her spine, and whatever food she'd managed to swallow, formed a rock-hard ball in the pit of her stomach. She had no way of knowing without coming right out and asking Lord Fredrick what he meant, and that she certainly wasn't prepared to do. She couldn't, especially not in front of the MacLeod, John Iain, who was looking at her as if he had a few questions of his own to ask.

But then again, she really and truly was a MacLeod now, and the reality of the beady-eyed Lord Fredrick didn't scare her half as much as Elspeth's memories of him had. The man sitting across from her was obviously desperate. He needed her cooperation in order to complete his mission, and he was going out on a limb by attempting to use the same scare tactics he'd used on Elspeth in the past.

Well, he was right. She wasn't Elspeth, and this time the viscount's tactics wouldn't work. She was Bethany Ann MacLeod, wife of Laird Quinton MacLeod of Brochel, and if her ex-husband had taught her anything, it was, if she kept her cool, if she didn't show fear, if she played the game well, she could not only outlast the viscount, but she could win. Lord Fredrick might very well think himself a master at manipulation, but compared to Burt Anderson, he was simply a novice.

She'd beaten Burt at his own game, and with Quinton MacLeod at her side, she'd best Viscount Telford, too.

Beth forced herself to smile as she lifted her tankard of ale to her lips. "Whatever do you mean, my lord?" She chuckled. "What understanding do you speak of? I'm afraid I barely remember you or anything we may have spoken of before my fall on the eve of my wedding." She sighed deeply. "You do remember my nasty fall, don't you? As for my husband, of course I love him. Isn't that a wife's duty? And there's no need for petty little secrets of any kind when one has the *truth* on one's side."

The gauntlet had been dropped, and she saluted him back. "Don't you agree?"

For a moment, confusion clouded the viscount's eyes. She'd caught him off guard. That obviously wasn't the response he'd been expecting. He thought she'd show fear. He thought she'd grovel. He thought she'd crumble and cry like the old Elspeth would've done. Or at the least, he thought she'd ensure him she was still in his corner. But she hadn't. Instead, she'd confused him, challenged him, dared him to disbelieve or attempt to expose her even.

She had the viscount right where she wanted him, perplexed and unsure of himself.

Marta ruined the moment as she sauntered into the room with her strawberry-blonde hair hanging loose and curling about her hips and her lips smiling wide, especially in the direction of the viscount. She walked up to the high-board and boldly took a seat right beside him, as if it were her right by birth.

"Forgive my lateness, my lords and my lady," she practically sang. "I've been ever so busy seeing ta the comforts of our guests. I do so hope I've nae missed anything of real interest?"

Lord Fredrick literally beamed at her. "Not at all, my dear lady. As a matter of fact, now that you've arrived, in truth, the feast and the festivities can begin."

****

Quint stared out into the darkness of his bedchamber and pondered the day. Though his Beth slept, even if it was fretfully, no sleep, in any form, would come his way.

What were his guests really up to, and what should he do first to ensure the safety of his wife, his child, and his people? He would've liked to talk it over with Beth. She always seemed to have a way of putting things in the proper perspective. But he hadn't had the heart to wake her. She'd looked so tired when she excused herself a couple of hours ago and retired to their bed.

From the moment John Iain and Lord Fredrick had stepped out of the small boat and onto the shores of Raasay, Quint had known he was being lied to. He'd so wanted to believe his uncle's reason for visiting was the holidays and the wish to see how his grandson, Duncan, fared. Yet, he couldn't. And the same could be said for Telford's excuse of wanting to look in on his ex-ward Elspeth.

Both men insisted the English warships were simply escorting John Iain back to the Isle of Skye after being in Hampshire at the request of the king. And since they were already so close, they'd decide to simply *stop* by.

John Iain, Quint's liege lord, his chieftain, and the man he'd respected all his life, almost as much as his own father, hadn't even blinked when explaining why he was at the foot of Brochel castle, in the dead of winter, with two English ships of war and a viscount in tow.

Quint had no choice but to welcome the MacLeod and the viscount into his home, but he sure as hell didn't have to trust either one of them. All through the evening meal, well into the night, and even after both men were well into their cups, they still continued to insist their visit was a matter of simply being in the right place at the right time.

A coincidence so to speak.

Quint didn't believe in coincidences any more than he believed the men of Beth's stories had really walked upon the surface of the moon. John Iain had told him many times he was a king's man and always would be. So, if they weren't here to openly try to take Brochel away from him, then what other king's business might they be about?

He was so deep in thought, he almost missed the soft rap, but still he managed to make his away across the room with his claymore fisted before the door's hinges had a chance to creak.

From the candle light illuminating the hallway, he could just make out the sober face of his uncle, and for a moment, he wondered if he should do them all a favor and just kill the lying bastard right now, before being forced to endure any more of his lies.

With a sigh, he lowered his claymore. Good or bad, king's man or nae, John Iain MacLeod was still his liege lord and had the right to be heard.

"Follow me, nephew." John Iain beckoned.

Quint shook his head. "Nae, 'tis late. Whatever ye have ta say, ye can say ta me on the morrow."

The Macleod bristled. "Do nae be obstinate with me, lad. What I have ta say must be said tonight and will take a while in the doing."

John Iain gestured toward Beth. "But nae here. I'll nae be responsible for waking ye little wife. I have one of me own, ye kin? I know what it is ta arouse the ire of a female, especially one that far along inta her carrying."

Quint looked back a Beth and sighed. "Ye are right about that. She needs all the rest she can get."

"So where can we go where we can be sure unwelcome ears won't be listening?" the Macleod asked.

Grabbing a fur, Quint headed out the door. "If'n it's privacy we be needing, then let's go onto the parapet. Only an idiot or a man who really does nae want anyone else ta hear what he has ta say would venture out into the cold wind found upon the top of a Scottish castle in the dead of winter."

His uncle chuckled and wrapped his own fur closer around himself. "That, my nephew, sounds like a fine idea."

The moment they exited the door to the parapet and the northern wind hit him square in the face, Quint rubbed his hands together for warmth and pulled his fur closer about his shoulders. "Well, Uncle?" He leaned in close to be heard above the howling of the wind. "What's so important it couldn't wait for the morning?"

"Telford means ye harm, lad," John Iain said. "And I'm afraid ta say, so does the king. I overheard them discussing ye imminent demise in Hampshire. If'n it's a son ye little wife bears ye, they mean ta kill ye outright and take ye castle and lands for the crown."

Quint chuckled. "Aye, I know. I've known for some time now, Uncle."

If the shock on John Iain's face hadn't been so sincere, Quint might have laughed. Instead, he did his best to explain. "My Beth warned me long ago."

The MacLeod's mouth gaped open. "She told ya? So she's nae in league with the viscount like he thinks she is?"

Quint shook his head. "Nae, she isn't. My wife is loyal ta me."

John Iain scratched his head. "I'm glad ta be hearing that. I ken ye care for the lass. But what are we going ta do about Lord Fredrick. We cannae let him kill ye. Not even for the king. I may be a royalist at heart, Nephew, but even I don't care ta have the king for a neighbor. I sure don't want him setting up a household right between the Isles of Skye and Lewis. And do nae forget I am still the MacLeod and ye uncle. My loyalty is ta ye first, nephew, before king or country."

A weight Quint hadn't even been aware of lifted off his chest, and for the first time all day, he took a real deep breath. "Well then, I suppose we'll simply have to find a way to prevent him from succeeding."

The MacLeod nodded. "The bairn could be a lass, ye ken. If it is, that'd solve all our problems. At least, until the next time ye got ye wife with child."

Quint shook his head. "It's a lad. Beth swears it is, and I believe her."

"Damn," John Iain said. "And they usually know. My wife did, anyway, every single time, without fail."

Suddenly, a smile broke across his face. "Maybe we can outwait him. I heard the king tell Lord Fredrick his ships have ta be back in London by the middle of next month. If ye can just keep her from delivering until then, it'll at least buy us a little more time ta come up with a solution ta this problem."

Quint shook his head again. "Beth's due anytime now, Uncle. Within the next sennight, during the time of Hogmanay at the verra latest. And it's not as if I or anyone else can stop that process once it's started. Bairns come when bairns come. Ye know that better than most."

"Aye," the MacLeod answered. "I suppose I do. So then, if you've known about the threat for a while, ye must have a plan?"

Quint nodded. "I mean ta kill the viscount before he can kill me."

John Iain shook his head. "Ye cannae just go about killing a viscount, especially one so close ta the king. Trust me, Charles would nae take it well. And those two English warships out in ye channel…they've orders ta flatten Brochel ta nothing but a pile of rubble if anything happens ta Lord Fredrick."

The MacLeod took a deep breath of his own. "What ye need, Nephew, is friends at ye back and a reason for those English ships not ta fire upon ye. I have one ship sitting out there and ready ta fight, but we need at least one more ta help balance the odds. Would the Mackenzie come ta ye aid if'n we could find a way ta get word ta him in time?"

Quint thought for a moment. The last thing he wanted to do was involve his friend in his troubles let alone possibly put him right in the middle of a war. But the Mackenzie was more than just a friend. He'd always been like a brother, and in his heart, Quint knew he'd do the same if asked. "How do ye suggest we get word ta the Mackenzie? He's at his castle on the Isle of Lewis for the holidays, and it's not likely those warships out there will simply let one of my boats slip past them with a message."

John Iain MacLeod chuckled. "Nae, they'd never allow such a thing, but I bet they wouldn't look twice at a skinny, little lad just out fishing?"

Quint shook his head once, then shook it again. "Ye can't mean Duncan? I have nae doubt he can do it. I taught the lad ta sail myself. But I cannae allow it. Lord Fredrick won't have need ta kill me. My Beth will do it for him if anything should happen ta that child."

This time John Iain laughed out loud. "Aye, Duncan's exactly who I mean. He's perfect. Who'd even pay a passing glance to a poor crippled lad in a tiny, little fishing boat? My grandson may not be able ta do some things as well as others can, but he's a MacLeod just the same. The sea's in his blood. And I'm betting the lad can sail a fishing boat across the channel ta the Isle of Lewis and get a message ta the Mackenzie without batting an eye or drawing suspicion."

Quint hung his head. Not Duncan, anyone but Duncan.

God help him. He'd rather face the wrath of Lord Fredrick, Viscount of Telford, the King of England, and the two ships of war out in his channel a hundred times a day than be anywhere in the vicinity of his Beth when she got wind of this latest plan.

****

Beth couldn't believe it. She simply couldn't.

There had to be a mistake. What she'd been told when awakened by Bronwyn a few moments ago couldn't possibly be true. And the dire reality of the situation certainly wasn't anything like she'd envisioned her Christmas morning to be.

Quinton MacLeod, the man she thought she knew, the man she respected above all others, the father of the babe she carried, the husband of her heart was a monster. For only a real, true monster would encourage a little crippled six-year-old boy to go out upon a treacherous, winter sea, in a tiny boat, all by himself. For that was exactly where Bronwyn had told her Duncan was when she'd asked after the child.

Quint knew how she felt about Duncan. And she'd always thought he felt the same. Yes, she understood MacLeods were *men* of the sea and that the sea was in their blood, blaa, blah, blah, blah, blah.

But not at six years old and not all by himself. It couldn't be true. It simply couldn't be.

The moment he entered their chamber with his liege lord, John Iain, in tow, she knew it was. Quint couldn't even look her in the eye and neither could the MacLeod.

"What have you done?" she cried.

Quint finally looked at her and raised a hand for silence. "Do nae question my decisions, wife. I am laird and have my reasons."

"Reasons?" Beth scoffed. "What insane reason would have you for endangering the life of a little six-year-old boy?"

"Seven," Quint said.

Beth shook her head. "What?"

Quinton crossed his arms. "He's seven today. He

was a Christ's Mass bairn. The boat and the fishing trip, all on his own, mind ye, was a present I've been waiting ta give him. Duncan's a MacLeod." He gestured toward the man standing beside him. "And John Iain's grandson ta boot. Do ye really think I'd put the MacLeod's own flesh and blood in danger if I thought he really would be? The lad can sail as well as any MacLeod and swim like a fish now. I worked with him all summer. Ye cannae keep him a bairn forever, my Beth. Ye must let him grow inta the man he'll someday be."

She stomped her foot. "I am not simply being overprotective, and you know it. And birthday or not, he's still too young." Tears filled her eyes, and though she strove to prevent them from falling, they did, wetting her cheeks.

Quint wrapped his big, strong arms around her, and Beth couldn't help but snuggle into his embrace. She knew in her heart he wouldn't purposefully put Duncan in danger. It was simply the stupid alpha male in him that made him think all MacLeods were invincible, even the little ones.

But then Quint had never lost a child.

She had, and she wouldn't stand by and watch it happen again.

"Go after him, please," she cried. "Bring him back, Quint, bring him back now."

Quint sighed and ran his hand through his hair. "I cannae, my Beth. And I cannae be untruthful with ye any longer either. Ye are my heart, and ye will have the truth of the matter from me always. Duncan is nae on a fishing trip. I sent him on a mission."

At first, his words didn't sink in or make sense.

Sending a little boy out in a boat to go fishing in the middle of winter had been bad enough, but a mission? What kind of mission did one send a child on?

She pushed herself out of Quint's embrace, and though the hurt on his face broke her heart, still she had to know. "Tell me about this mission."

"It was my idea, lass," John Iain spoke up. "Ye know all ta well the viscount means Quint harm as soon as that bairn ye carry is born, and so do those two warships waiting out in the channel. We sent Duncan ta take a message ta the Mackenzie. Not one single sailor aboard either one of those ships will pay any mind ta a scrawny lad in a fishing boat. It was the only way. And if ye could just do us the favor of keeping that bairn where he is for a few more days, a sennight or two at the most, all will be well. You'll see."

The weight of all of their welfares upon the shoulders of a crippled little boy? It wasn't fair. Yet, Beth could see the wisdom of Quint's and John Iain's plan. She might not like it and she certainly wasn't ready to be happy about it, but she could understand it.

That didn't mean she was ready to forgive Quint for lying to her in the first place and for sending Duncan anywhere for any reason in the second. She turned her back on him and crossed her arms. "I'll do my best to do my part and keep this bairn inside. But God help you Quinton MacLeod, and you, too, John Iain, if anything happens to that little boy."

Beth didn't need to turn around to realize the two men had left the room without another word. She heard the door open, and she heard it close. Then she heard nothing but the silence of her tears.

God, how she hated Christmas.

Chapter Eighteen

The first contraction hit as the evening sun was setting, and with a gasp, Beth woke from a fitful nap and sat straight up in bed. Pain clutched at her back and radiated low in her belly. Though this particular contraction didn't really last very long, she had a good idea things were about to get much worse.

She took a deep breath and tried not to panic. Perhaps it was simply one of those false contractions, the Braxton-Hicks variety. The kind that stretched things out and made the body ready for real labor but in themselves usually didn't last very long or hurt that badly.

Another one started in the middle of her back and worked its way around to the front. Still, she told herself, it might not be true labor. After all, with both Ben and Brian hadn't she had Braxton-Hicks contractions for weeks before either one of them had been born?

Then she remembered. Oh yeah, this wasn't the same sturdy, boxy body that had born her children. This was Elspeth's body. So there was no way of telling if this particular, smaller, daintier, slimmer body was truly in labor or not.

Only time would tell that tale.

As soon as the pain completely subsided, Beth lay back, took a deep breath, and tried her best to relax. It wouldn't do to put herself into real labor by worrying.

A few minutes later, another hit, this one just a little bit harder, and lasting a heartbeat longer.

She wished Quint were here. But she hadn't seen even a glimpse of him since their…conversation earlier.

Not that he hadn't tried to see her, for he had, twice. Once for the Christmas morning breaking of the fast, and then again for the official afternoon Christ's Mass. But she'd told Bronwyn to bar the door and not admit him to their room unless he had Duncan with him.

She was being unreasonable about the entire situation, but she couldn't seem to help herself. So instead of being at her side, where a husband and expectant father should be at a time like this, Quinton was no doubt in the great hall with his uncle and Viscount Telford, getting rip-roaring drunk.

And it was all her fault.

To make matters worse, she'd already dismissed Bronwyn for the evening. Just because she was in no mood to celebrate Christmas, didn't mean the old maid should miss out.

But that also meant no one would be coming to check on her anytime soon. Probably not before morning. She could die giving birth right here in this bed, and no one would be the wiser.

Tears stung her eyes, and she swiped them away, refusing to give in to the panic. She was being silly. If she really was in labor or had need of assistance, all she need do was yell out. Someone would hear her. Someone would come. Surely, they would.

The next pain hit. This one all but took her breath away with its intensity.

Beth sighed as her frustration grew. Well, hell. Since they were already coming one after the other and gathering in intensity, the pains probably weren't Braxton-Hicks, after all. And it looked like she was about to break her word to her husband and to the MacLeod. Because like it or not, it seemed Quint's son, just like Duncan, had determined Christmas was a right fine time to be born.

Glancing around at the room's four cold stone walls, the remnants of a smoky peat fire, and the rush covered floor that hid God only knew what creepy-crawly creatures, Beth shuddered. What had she been thinking? She couldn't do this, she couldn't have a baby today, especially not here and certainly not in the frigging seventeenth century.

She didn't even have a stupid watch to count down the contractions. How was she to know if they were getting closer together or farther apart? And what had been the stupid rule anyway? Head to the hospital when the contractions got to be five minutes apart? Right? It had been so long ago since she'd given birth to Ben and Brian, she'd forgotten.

Beth laughed, but even she recognized the edge of hysteria in her voice. There would be no trip to the hospital with her carefully packed little bag this time. God, what wouldn't she give right this minute for a sterile delivery room, a competent obstetrician, and an epidural?

Another pain hit. For a moment, this one took her breath away. Then she remembered her old Lamaze classes and forced herself to close her eyes, relax, and slowly breathe through the pain.

When the contraction finally subsided, she

chuckled. Oh, my God. After Brian's traumatic birth, she'd never thought she'd ever have need of Lamaze again. She'd had an emergency C-section and a hysterectomy because a big part of the placenta had detached from her uterus and the doctors couldn't control the bleeding. Though she hadn't felt a thing other than pressure, it had been the strangest sensation to hear the cry of a new life beginning while her own slowly seeped from her body.

Tears that had nothing to do with labor pains stung her eyes as she remembered Burt's reaction to the fact she'd never again bear him a child.

"Can't you do anything right?" he'd asked when she woke. "Cook a decent meal and give me four kids like my mom gave my dad. That's all I've ever asked of you. Don't get me wrong, I'm grateful to have another big, healthy boy, but I wouldn't have cared if the other three kids had been girls. At least I would've had my four. Just like my brother and both my sisters. You know how important grandchildren are to my mother."

He'd ran his fingers through his hair. "But no, you couldn't do it, could you? One little complication, and you let those quacks rip out your whole fucking uterus. And you did it without having the decency of making sure they'd asked me first."

"I didn't have a choice, Burt, and neither did they," she'd said. "They couldn't stop the bleeding, and they were afraid they'd lose me."

He'd turned and walked away. "I wish they had."

He'd mumbled the words under his breath, but she'd heard every one of them just as if they'd been shouted.

Beth took a deep breath as yet another contraction

hit. Well, there was one thing for certain, this time, whether she was bleeding to death or not, this was 1643 and there would be no C-section performed this day.

****

Quint sat in the shadows of the great hall wishing he were anywhere but where he was. And especially wishing he could climb the stairs and celebrate the Christ's Mass with his wife instead of sitting here watching a bunch of sloppy-ass *blootered* men get themselves even more *blootered.*

Not that he was stupid enough ta think for a minute he'd be welcomed with open arms inta his own chamber, even though it was well past midnight. Beth had made it more than plain the last time he'd tried that she didnae wish ta endure his presence today. And it wasn't likely she'd be in the state of mind ta forgive him before Hogmanay, either.

But here in the great hall, Telford had been sneering at him all evening. As if Quint were purposefully keeping Beth from him and as if he knew for a fact it was the Laird of Brochel's fault his wife had not descended the stairs even once during this day and graced the stupid count with her presence. But then again, Quint didn't care if Lord Fredrick was right or not. It was his fault, and he'd pay the price.

Then he chuckled.

Considering Beth's mood of the moment, the viscount should probably count his lucky stars she had remained above stairs. Because in her present foul temper, she just might give in ta the temptation of doing in Lord Fredrick herself...when she was done doing bodily damage ta her husband, that was.

Duncan. Quint sighed. Why couldn't he make her

see she was being completely unreasonable when it came ta the lad?

In the time where she'd come from, were young, strapping males coddled like bairns until they were full grown?

He shuddered, thankful his father hadn't been one ta pamper anyone, especially his son, and hadn't allowed his wife ta do any cosseting either.

By the time he was Duncan's age, it had been one of his duties ta hang from the high mast and be a look out for whales, he and Dougal both. The only time they'd been allowed ta come down was to help slice up the great fish, once one had been spotted and captured.

They hadn't even come down for meals, ta take a piss, or even ta sleep. Food, mainly bread and fish, and bottles of weakened ale were sent up by way of a little basket and a pulley system. And as far as pissing, they simply yelled look out below and hoped they didn't hit anyone who'd later hit them back. He and Dougal both had become experts, the hard way, when it came ta sleeping. Just like every watcher before them, they'd learned to link their scrawny arms and legs through the rigging of the mast and hold on as they napped in their makeshift beds or rode out a storm.

If Duncan's legs had been studier, he would've had the lad do watcher duty right along with all the other boys his age on their last outing. He hadn't though. He hadn't been sure the lad could hold on, and the thought of Dougal's son falling to his death on his watch was more than Quint could stomach.

Perhaps he was becoming as soft as his little wife, after all.

Beth simply didn't understand what it meant ta

grow up MacLeod. It was an honor, not a punishment, ta be tasked with something so important as delivering a missive. He himself had certainly not been any older than Duncan was when his father had first sent him back and forth across the channel, bearing communications for one laird or another.

Yes, he understood, and he wasn't an idiot. The practice could be dangerous. Over the years, a handful of lads had been lost at sea, and though they'd been grieved for sorely, stories of their bravery had been told around the fire and there was never a shortage of volunteers for the next assignment.

But if one didn't send a lad, how would one get messages sent across the channel in the first place? No laird worth his salt would ask a full grown man ta walk away from his duties or even the older lads ta leave their training just ta deliver or gather news. After all, it was one of the simplest of tasks. Even a MacLeod lass could do it, probably.

Why then did he feel so guilty?

His tender-hearted, little wife was going ta be the death of him yet.

Quint chuckled, and with a sigh, stood, stretched, and headed up the stairs. Perhaps his Beth didnae wish ta see him, but he had a powerful need ta see her. She was simply going ta have ta bear his odious presence like it or nae.

If he could make it past the old maid Bronwyn and the barred door this time.

****

Beth wasn't exactly sure how long ago her water broke. All she knew was, she was extremely wet, cold, and uncomfortable.

Between contractions that were coming closer and closer together, she slowly made her way off the bed and over to her trunk. She desperately needed to get out of her soggy shift and replace it with a dry one so the shivering would stop, she could once more think clearly, and with any luck, the incessant chattering of her teeth would cease.

How she longed for the warmth of Quint's arms right about now. Just a few minutes of bliss, just long enough to drive the ice from her bones and replace it with his glorious heat. For there was certainly no other source of warmth in this room. Even though a fire had been stoked earlier, over the course of the last few hours, it had been reduced to nothing but embers.

Her maid was no longer by her side, either. She'd sent Bronwyn off before the contractions ever started. She hadn't wanted the old woman to miss out on the Christmas festivities because she was being a stubborn blockhead. And since her maid hadn't peeked her head through the door once since then, she must have taken her lady up on her suggestion to go and have some fun.

Fear she'd been striving to keep at bay seeped in right alongside the cold. No one was coming to check on her, and there was no way she could make it out of this room and down the stairs in order to seek help. Even if she could, she couldn't take the chance it would be the viscount she'd encounter instead.

Gently, she placed her hand upon her belly. God help her and Quint's son both, because she was going to have to deliver this child all on her own. As an American history teacher she knew many things. Birthing babies, sure as hell, wasn't one of her specialties.

"Tobias," she cried in desperation. "Come help me please. I can't do this." But the only response she received was the increased pounding of her heart.

Another pain hit. This one so hard it had her knees buckling and a cry escaping her throat.

Beth hadn't been aware anyone had entered the room until her husband's warm, strong arms wrapped around her and pulled her in close.

"My Beth," he whispered. "What is it, lass? Why are ye shivering so? And why did ye cry out? Is it the bairn?"

She managed a nod as he picked her up and carried her toward the bed.

"Where is ye maid?" he scolded. "Why did ye not have her come for me? Surely, ye cannae be so angry ye'd keep me from the knowledge of this?"

She shook her head. "I told her to go and enjoy Christmas hours ago, before any of this started. And then by the time I realized I truly was in labor, I couldn't make it far enough to yell for help." Leaning into his embrace, Beth cried. "I'm sorry for being so unreasonably angry with you earlier, Quint. I know you'd never ask anything of Duncan you thought would bring him harm. It's just that he's so little."

She buried her head against his chest, the heat of him seeping into her bones, warming her. Another contraction sliced through her, this one burning low in her back, radiating to her front, and lasting so long she thought it would never end.

"Let's get ye back ta bed, lass." Quint's normally rock steady voice shook.

"It's wet," she whimpered. "My—my water broke some time ago."

He gulped. "Oh."

If the situation hadn't seemed so dire, she would've laughed. She wasn't sure it was because she actually found their particular dilemma funny or because she was just so grateful he was here now and she didn't have to face the birth of his son all alone.

He turned with her in his arms, one way and then another, as if trying to decide where to set her down in order to go for help. But in the end, he simply walked to the door, opened it, and bellowed at the top of his lungs, "Bronwyn."

A moment later, the sleepy-eyed maid peeked from behind the nursery doorway. When she saw Beth being clutched in Quint's arms, she rushed toward them as quickly as her old bones would allow.

"The bairn's coming," Quint roared.

Bronwyn walked right past him and into the room, as if he hadn't even spoken. "Aye, I kenned that," she cackled. "Though I do think she'll have an easier time of it if ye put her in the bed, laird."

Beth almost smiled, but then another contraction hit, this one a whopper, and all she could do was moan and hold onto her husband.

"I ken she'd be more comfortable in the bed, ye old harridan, but 'tis wet."

"Ah," Bronwyn said. "Then give me a moment ta see things put ta right."

Quint paced back and worth with her in his arms, and though he was making Beth quite dizzy, she didn't complain. She was too grateful for his presence. When Bronwyn signaled, he placed her gently between the clean sheets and covered her with the warm fur.

The moment he stood back up, she knew exactly

what he was thinking and what he was intending to do, and panic had her calling out, "Stay, Quint. Please don't leave me."

He looked as if he were going to be sick. With both Ben and Brian, she hadn't wanted Burt in the labor room, and he'd been more than happy to wait for word from the comfort the neighborhood bar. But with Quint, it was different. Beth didn't want to be alone this time, and more than anything, she wanted desperately to share this miracle with him.

Though they were not fated to be together as Quint raised his son into manhood, they could both be witness to the first breath the child took.

"Stay," she pleaded once again as the next pain hit, and he took a seat on the edge of the bed and grasped her hand.

"Are ye sure, my Beth?" he asked. "I do nae know what ta do ta help. I fear I'll be in the way."

She smiled as the pain let up a little. "Stay with me. We were together when this child was made, and we should be together when he comes into this world."

Quint smiled back at her, and then glanced toward his wife's maid. "Ye heard what she said. I'm ta be ye servant this time. Just speak plain and slow, Bronwyn, when ye tell me what ye need me ta do. This being my first time midwifing and all.

From almost the moment Quint had gotten her back to bed, the contractions came one after the other and each one stronger and longer than the last. It got to the point where Beth could no longer tell where one began and another ended.

Something was wrong. Nothing could possibly hurt this badly and be normal. With Ben and Brian, there had been a lovely epidural in place by the time labor progressed to this point, so she really had no idea what normal was anymore. All she knew was, she hurt horribly and all Quint and Bronwyn could do about it was sit and watch. Though the old maid did cool her brow with a damp cloth, and her husband held her hand and whispered sweet encouragement to her, no matter how tightly she squeezed his.

"Ohh," she moaned long and loud, and they both jumped. he grabbed both her hands and began frantically patting while Bronwyn flipped back the furs, lifted her shift, parted her thighs, and stared.

"Looks like 'tis still going ta be a while yet," was all she said.

Beth shuddered. How had women done this without the advent of modern medicine? God what she wouldn't give for a hefty dose of morphine right about now? Then she chuckled, morphine be damned. Who was she kidding? She wanted another dose of the anesthetic they'd used to completely knock her ass out for Brian's C-section.

A sobering thought struck her. Many women hadn't successfully done this at all, especially as far back as the seventeenth century. More than a few had died trying to do exactly what she was attempting this very moment.

She tightened her grasp on Quint's hand. "If I don't make it through this, promise me you'll care for and love this child with all your heart and never hold against him the fact his mother died giving him birth. It's not his fault, and I'd gladly give my life for his."

Then another thought struck. Perhaps this had been Fate's plan all along. Perhaps she'd been destined to die in childbirth and that was how she'd be reunited with Ben and Brian, the children she'd lost, the children she hadn't appreciated enough until after it was too late, the children she'd said horrible, unforgivable things to only moments before their deaths.

Her children. Her real, true children.

Quint shook his head, fear evident upon his face. "Ye'll nae leave me, my Beth. I won't allow it. Do ye hear me? I'd nae survive without ye, and neither would our bairn. We need ye. Take my strength, take my very breath, and the last beat of my heart if ye have need of them ta get ye through this. But please, I beg ye, do nae go."

Chapter Nineteen

He was one of the most beautiful babies she'd ever laid eyes on.

Beth couldn't bring herself to look away from the child she held close to her heart and had been holding since the moment he made his presence into the world, red-faced and screaming bloody murder as the sun began peeking its head above the mountains.

She glanced toward Quint and smiled at her peacefully sleeping husband. Though now exhausted, he'd shown no signs of it throughout the long night. He'd stayed right by her side and held her hand, without letting go even once during the entire process. He'd whispered words of encouragement when she'd needed them most. He'd even held his squirming wet son as Bronwyn cut the cord, and he'd been the one to gently place the infant into her outstretched, waiting arms.

God, how she loved him.

She glanced back down at his son. The baby had his father's dark brown hair, but his was still the fuzzy, soft down of a newborn. And he had his dad's cute nose, strong jaw, and full lips, though Beth was pretty sure it was Elspeth's ears the little boy had inherited. No matter which parent contributed what, there was no doubt about it; he was absolutely, undeniably beautiful.

And he was already tugging hard on her

heartstrings. He felt so very right in her arms. And after he'd fed at her breast, he'd grabbed onto her pinky and held on for dear life, just as if he knew she'd be gone soon, that she planned on leaving him.

With that thought, the air around her suddenly began to shimmer, and Beth felt an added presence in the room. She didn't look up. She didn't want to see Tobias Moiré, third generation event manipulator, better known as Fate.

At least, she didn't want to see him today.

She wasn't ready.

He cleared his throat, and Beth swatted at the air. "Go away, Bronwyn. You'd think after the long night you had, you'd still be sleeping."

"We both know I am not Bronwyn, madam. Do stop pretending and have the decency to at least look me in the eye."

Beth glanced his way. Well, actually, she glared. And though she'd pleaded with Fate to come to her rescue last evening, it still distressed her to actually see him standing right beside her bed today. "Tobias?"

The event manipulator rolled his eyes. "I assure you, it is I, madam. And this isn't a social call. You summoned me, remember?"

He pulled his cell phone looking thingy from his pocket. "I see you've made good on your part of the bargain and have given Quinton MacLeod his heir. So I take it you're ready to be reunited with your children as per our agreement?" He pushed a couple of buttons. "A simple case of birthing bed fever should do the trick nicely."

"No." Beth scurried from the bed with the baby still in her arms and led Tobias into the same little alcove they'd spoken in the last time he'd been here. It wouldn't do for Quint to wake in the middle of this conversation and see a strange man with wire-rimmed glasses, wearing a long white robe, standing in the middle of their bed chamber.

She clasped the infant to her chest. "I can't go yet," Beth whispered. "Lord Fredrick is somewhere in this very castle as we speak, and the moment he finds out Quint's son has been born, he means to kill him. I can't just leave Quint and this helpless little newborn baby all alone in the seventeenth century without first knowing they'll be safe."

Fate scoffed. "Surely, you jest, madam. With or without the influence of the viscount, there certainly was no such thing as a guarantee of safety in the seventeenth century, for anyone, of any age."

He shook his head. "I mean, really, you were a history teacher in your old life. You know as well as I only approximately twelve percent of all infants born in this time period lived to see their first birthdays, let alone grow into adulthood. Even if they happened to make it past infancy, there was still mumps and measles, chicken and small pox, dysentery, cholera, consumption, whooping cough, typhus, yellow and scarlet fever, influenza, and let's dare not forget about the black plague to deal with. And that's not even taking into consideration all the accidental and intentional ways people found to meet their demise."

Tears misted Beth's eyes as she rocked the sleeping child back and forth.

"Trust me, madam." Tobias Moiré sighed. "You're better off leaving right this moment before you get too attached. You've already suffered the loss of two children. Why take the chance of putting yourself through the possibility of a third?"

He took off his wire-rimmed glasses and cleaned them on the sleeve of his robe. "You have successfully fulfilled your part of the bargain, and now it's my turn. It matters not how long or whether Quinton MacLeod and his son live or die. As far as I know, the heir simply had to be born in order to fix my, umm, mistake."

The event manipulator once more started pushing buttons on his contraption. "Let's see, if you aren't keen on birthing bed fever, perhaps a nice quick, painless hemorrhage will be more to your liking?"

"Stop," she yelled and held the baby so tight he began to squirm. "I can't, not yet anyway. Just a little more time, please?"

Fate frowned. "If you weren't ready for me to fulfill my part of the bargain, then why did you call?"

Heat crept up Beth's cheeks. "I'm so sorry. At the time, I was all alone and didn't know what else to do."

Tobias Moiré glared at her. "Do I look like a ladies' maid to you, madam? I know for a fact I've told you before I'm a very busy man. Floods, tornados, earthquakes, car accidents, but not yours, of course. Wet slippery floors, falling rocks, and the such. I don't have time for nonsense. So don't call me again until you're truly ready to complete our transaction."

Beth gulped down the lump in her throat that had formed at the mention of the car accident that took the lives of her children.

"It's no skin off my nose, you know?" he continued. "And I couldn't care less if you decided to spend the rest of your, I mean, Lady Elspeth Frasier MacLeod's natural life right here in the seventeenth century. I'll still return and reunite you with your children even if you die in your bed in your sleep in the middle of the night when you're eighty. But I do so detest having my time wasted, madam. Time is important, and as you well know, almost impossible to get back once it's gone."

She nodded. She did understand, probably better than most. Time was a precious gift. What happened in the blink of an eye or a careless moment could never be taken back or changed. So it was infinitely important how time was used.

And she also understood what Fate was offering her, and for a moment, her heart soared. If she wanted to, she could stay right here in 1643 with Quinton MacLeod and his son, and still be reunited in Heaven with her children when Elspeth's life had run its natural course. But wouldn't that be selfish? Hadn't her children already waited long enough?

It was on the tip of her tongue to ask when Fate shimmered, and in the space of a heartbeat, completely disappeared.

****

From the open doorway, Quint took in the image of his wife feeding his son. What a magical sight it was to behold. One, after what had transpired with Mairi, he'd all but given up hope of ever seeing for himself. The bairn lost his grip on the tit for a moment and started loudly smacking his lips while frantically flailing his chubby little fist.

Beth smiled down at him and quickly gave him back what he'd been searching for.

Quint chuckled. "Since we cannae come ta an agreement on a name, perhaps we should simply call him Verra Hungry MacLeod and be done with it."

There had been an ongoing discussion as to what to name their brand new prodigy for most of the day, and this latest suggestion was met with the same scowl the previous ones. The only difference being, at least Beth laughed with him this time when she was through with her scowling.

However, she hadn't laughed at his first suggestion of the name Bertram, after his great grandfather. As a matter of fact, she'd almost looked as if she were going to be sick. And she hadn't liked Torquil, after the founder of the clan Macleod, any better. Nor Archibald, Ewan, Fergusson, Hamish, or any of the other strong male names he'd come up with.

So he truly had no idea what to call his son.

He'd had months to ponder the question and knew it was his responsibility. He simply hadn't given it much thought. Though he certainly didn't consider himself a superstitious man, he also hadn't been willing to tempt fate, the fey, or whatever else might be out there lying in wait to snatch away his happiness by settling a name upon a child before the lad had even taken his first breath.

Not that he'd been good at naming anything ever, for he hadn't.

Once, his father had brought home a puppy from the mainland, and he'd told Quint he could be the one to decide what it would be called. But he'd taken so long trying to come up with the perfect name, the poor creature had ended up being just plain Dog his entire life.

He'd do better this time. After all, his son couldn't go through life being called Son. It wasn't dignified, and it wasn't proper.

Quint chuckled as he imagined the lad standing upon his grave and cussing as an old man after years of being laird, when people half his age, and well beneath his status, or God forbid, his own children, still addressed him as Son.

Nae, he needed, deserved, a name he could be proud of, a name worthy of the next Laird of Brochel.

"Though he does seem to have a very healthy appetite," Beth giggled. "I'm afraid you're simply going to have to come up with something better than Verra Hungry MacLeod."

Quint nodded. "I thought about naming him after my da. But his name was Charles, just like our dreadful English king, and I'll nae have my son called the same as the man who wants ta steal his birthright and murder his father."

She shook her head. "No, perhaps Charles wouldn't be such a wise choice." Then she smiled. "But then he's only a few hours old, my love. Take a day or so to think about it, and I'm sure the perfect name will present itself." She giggled once more and snuggled the now sleeping infant close to her heart. "Until then, I think I'll just be content to call him ours." Suddenly, her head popped up. "So how did the announcement of his birth go downstairs?"

Quint stared at his wife, dreading this moment. His Beth knew him so well. It would be difficult to outright lie to her and tell her all were overjoyed. But then again, perhaps he could give her the gist without revealing the whole.

He forced himself to smile. "Old Annie said ta tell ye she'd be making ye a special supper ta celebrate.

And our liege lord, John Iain, said ta tell ye how proud he is of ye for delivering me a son even if it was before our agreed upon date. And ye should see the wee village. There are banners hanging everywhere declaring this ta be a true day of celebration."

He didn't tell her Marta's reaction or the viscount's. There was no reason to give Beth more than she already had to worry over. But he couldn't help but be a little more than simply concerned, especially about the state of Marta's sanity.

The woman had risen from her seat next to Telford and sauntered to Quint's side. When she'd reached him, she'd stood on tiptoes, wrapped an arm about his neck, and whispered close to his ear as if they'd been lovers. He almost stepped back, but in the end, his curiosity as to what she'd have to say got the better of him, and he leaned in closer.

"So ye witch has given ye a son has she? Do nae be surprised I know her ta be a witch. I have eyes and ears. But that'll be our little secret, won't it? As long as ye keep mine, I'll keep yours. I'd hate ta see the poor wee lad have ta grow up without his mother like our Duncan is. And ye better be watching ye back, Quinton MacLeod, or the viscount is going ta be taking what's yours, if he hasn't already. I've seen the way he looks at ye little witch of a wife, and how she looks at him."

He'd pushed her away. "I ken well I made mistakes when it came ta Mairi and Dougal. Mistakes I regret every day of my life. I should've allowed them ta marry when they first asked, and I ken it well now. So do nae think for a moment I've forgotten any of my shortcomings or limitations. At the same time, tread verra carefully, Marta. For ye own sake, do nae make me believe ye ta be a true threat ta my wife or my child, because ye won't like the consequences of that decision. Just because I made a promise ta look after ye ta ye sister on her death bed, does nae mean ye can do or say whatever ye please ta me either. As long as I do draw breath, I am laird."

He cleared his throat. "And as far as the viscount planning ta take my wife, my castle, my lands, and my son, aye, I ken he means ta try. But trying and doing are two verra different things, ye ken?"

Marta laughed, and the same full, red lips he'd so loved on the face of her sister, Mairi, snarled back at him. "Only time will tell, laird. Will it nae?"

Quint groaned. Nae, he would not tell Beth anything Marta said.

And Lord Fredrick, Viscount Telford? What of his reaction to the news of the birth of a MacLeod heir? In truth, his had been even more disturbing than Marta's. The man had simply smiled, lifted his tankard in salute, tipped it toward his mouth, and downed its contents. Then he'd slammed the receptacle back down on the table, stood, and walked out of the keep.

Oh yes, the fight of his life was about to begin, and though he well understood that fact, he also knew he wouldn't be imparting that little piece of information to his wife, either.

****

Beth sighed as she slowly rocked the sleeping infant in her arms.

Didn't the dratted man realize he needed to be more truthful, more forthcoming, with her? How else was she to know how to help him when the time came? And the time was coming, of that there was no doubt.

Time for the viscount to make his move.

Time to thwart Marta's plans.

Time for her to leave.

She rocked faster.

But Quint wasn't being truthful with her. He was lying, and she knew it. Well, not precisely lying. His story had been more one of omission than lie, for he simply hadn't told her what the viscount or Marta had to say about the birth. She hadn't specifically asked, but she was relatively sure both of them had plenty to say on the subject.

And Beth needed to know exactly what had been said before she dared contemplate leaving.

Time was running out.

Their relationship had always been one of saying mainly what the other wanted to hear. What they were both comfortable with. Don't ask, don't tell, if it wasn't pleasant. It made everything so much easier and more congenial. He hadn't insisted upon details about the family she'd had in her previous life, and she hadn't prodded him for information when it came to his relationship with Mairi, his cousin Dougal's death, or even his lesser enjoyable duties as laird.

In truth, all they'd ever really fought about was Duncan, and even in that, he hadn't been unreasonable, usually.

But she would be leaving soon. Had no choice but to leave, even if Fate had said she could stay. Her children were waiting for her, so she needed to know how to proceed.

God, she was so tired of the façade of their relationship. She didn't appreciate feeling like an outsider in her own marriage. And yes, perhaps it had been Elspeth's body who had married Quint in the first place, but it had been her words that spoke the vows and her mind that first felt a connection with him and her emotions. Oh my God, the emotional bond they'd formed over the last few months, and how she loved him with every fiber of her being.

Right this moment, postpartum as she was, she had emotions in excess, raging even. To make matters worse, those rampant emotions were playing havoc on what little was left of her sanity.

She couldn't go, yet she couldn't stay, and she couldn't even discuss it with him. He wouldn't understand. He'd be angry. He'd be hurt. Wouldn't he?

Guilt filled her. Hadn't she had enough of being shut out of important decisions and discussions while married to Burt? Why would she allow or do the same thing to Quint? Everything had to be Burt's way without question. Quint wasn't like that. Though protective, he was willing to at least listen. That was, if she could manage to come up with the courage to discuss what needed to be discussed.

For yes, she did need to tell Quint she planned on leaving and why. It was only fair. But there were also questions she deserved the answers to. Quint should have truthfully told her what had been said by the viscount and by Marta. And he hadn't.

But then how did she come clean herself and start a conversation that began with "By the way, I plan to leave you, Verra Hungry, and Duncan all alone here in the seventeenth century as soon as the viscount has been dealt with. Because what I've neglected to tell you is, Fate himself is going to come get me and take me to be with my children, my very dead children, who are patiently awaiting my arrival in Heaven."

Even without voicing the words out loud, they sounded insane to her ears. So how was she supposed to say them to Quint and expect him to understand?

Chapter Twenty

For the last turn of the hourglass, Quint had stood upon the parapet of his castle with John Iain by his side and watched as his friend, Alec Mackenzie, made his way toward the shore. It had been three days since the birth if his still unnamed son. Three verra long days of constantly watching his back and waiting for the viscount to slip a knife between his ribs while at the same time, trying ta make sure his wife did nae have cause ta worry and fret as she had a tendency ta do.

But the laird of the Isle of Lewis had arrived and his ship flanked one of the English warships while the MacLeod's flanked the other.

Quint sighed with relief.

Not that Alec himself could prevent whatever was to come to pass, but at least he would be another set of eyes, just like John Iain. Even better, he'd have Duncan with him in that little boat he rowed toward shore. Thank God for that. Now perhaps his Beth would cease her worrying about the lad.

The waves brought the skiff the last couple of feet onto the shore, and Quint smiled as his old friend quickly disembarked with Duncan on his heels. They made their way toward the castle, but after just a few moments, the lad could no longer keep up with the Mackenzie's long strides and began to lag behind.

Alec stopped in his tracks and waited patiently for

the child. When he caught up, the Mackenzie hefted him up upon his shoulders. Duncan's laughter could be heard echoing upon the wind, and his wide smile could be seen even all the way up to the top of the parapet.

Quint smiled, turned, and headed toward the stairs.

"I already like ye friend," John Iain said. "A man who is Highlander enough ta lead a clan the size the Mackenzies are rumored ta be, yet knows when and how ta be gentle and see ta the needs of a little crippled lad, is a good man indeed. His father was a friend of mine, and he would've been proud of how his son turned out. But I myself have nae laid eyes on the lad since he was no bigger than Duncan himself."

"Aye," Quint nodded. "Alec Mackenzie is a good man and a good friend. But do nae be thinking ye grandson that weak or crippled, my laird. Duncan's been working every day with his sword, just like ye tasked him ta do. And he can match any lad his age when it comes ta rock piling and peat cutting." He smiled at his liege lord. "Duncan MacLeod does a fine job at whatever he sets his mind ta. And it seems we can add messaging ta that growing list. Though my Beth isn't apt ta like it one bit."

John Iain chuckled. "Aye, I can see Duncan is well received here at Brochel, even if he does have a foot that does nae work quite right. I ken he's especially well liked by ye wee wife."

Quint chuckled again. "I thought the lass was going ta flay the skin right off my arse when she found out we'd sent Duncan off ta give a missive ta the Mackenzie. She mothers him, and that's a good thing. He needs one."

The MacLeod suddenly got a faraway look in his

eye. "I'd hoped me own wife would've done the same for Dougal once she got ta know him, but it had been ta much ta ask of her."

Quint couldn't stop himself; his eyes automatically darted toward the spot on the parapet where Dougal's broken body had been found on the rocky ground below. "Why did ye nae come when he died, Uncle?"

John Iain seemed to age right before his eyes. His uncle had always been so strong, so vibrant, so verra sure of himself, but now, he just looked tired.

His voice was no more than a whisper when he finally spoke. "I wanted ta. But I was never the father ta Dougal I should've been. Ye da did a much better job of raising him than I. So since I had nae been there often while he was alive, I did nae feel I had the right once he was nae longer. And I did nae think Dougal would've wanted me at his wake anyway. When I last saw him, we did nae part on good terms."

The MacLeod shook his head. "But I did nae think him ta be so weak as ta take his own life and over a lass, ta boot. That did surprise me. I kenned well ye both wanted Mairi, and I kenned she was carrying Dougal's child and ye would nae allow them ta marry when he asked. But ye and he would've hashed it out eventually. Ye loved each other like brithers."

Quint gulped down the lump forming in his throat.

"But ta take ye own life is a mortal sin, Nephew." The chief of clan MacLeod sighed. "And I do nae like ta think of my son burning in hell for all of eternity."

Quint cleared his throat. "I wish I could remember what really happened, uncle, so I could set your mind at ease. I do nae think Dougal threw himself off this parapet, any more than I would throw myself off. But we were both so deep inta our cups that night, anything may have happened. Neither one of us was thinking straight. All I can figure is he got ta close ta the edge and lost his balance, because the alternative is ta horrible ta contemplate. We were the only two up here. And though I do nae hope he took his own life, either, I pray it wasn't me who did."

John Iain scoffed. "Do nae fash yeself. Whatever happened, ye did nae kill ye cousin, and especially not over a lass. Of this I know. Perhaps someday we'll both find the truth, and be able ta put Dougal's soul ta rest, even if it is in Hell." He gulped, and once more headed toward the stairs.

Quint took two deep breaths and then two more before following his uncle. "I suppose we had better make it ta the great hall before the Mackenzie does. I would nae want ta keep Alec waiting, and I cannae wait myself ta see the look on Telford's face when he gets a glimpse of our latest guest."

****

Where was Duncan? What was taking him so long to come see her?

Beth glanced toward her chamber door, then out her window for at least the tenth time in as many minutes. She'd seen the child follow the Mackenzie right through the castle gates, but she hadn't caught another glimpse of him since, or heard any small footsteps approaching her door.

She'd thought he would've come straight away. She thought he'd be eager to meet his brand new cousin and see her once again, too, as much as she wanted to see him.

What was she thinking, and what had she allowed

267

to happen?

Beth sighed.

How could she have permitted one small boy to weasel his way so deeply into her heart that she longed to see him? Especially since she planned on leaving him, on leaving all of them, and very soon. But she obviously had, and there was nothing she could do to undo it. Weaseled into her heart or not, she still desperately needed to simply look him over, ruffle his hair, listen to every detail of his adventure, and ensure herself he was whole and well and truly back home where he belonged.

But he hadn't come to her yet, and she couldn't go to him. She wasn't allowed to step even one stupid toe outside her chamber doors for at least two more very long days.

Curses on the seventeenth century and their superstitious customs.

Quinton MacLeod's son had been born three full days ago, and she had yet to see the outside of this room. She was going just a little bit stir crazy. Something about the scent of freshly birthed woman's blood flow or some such rot inviting bad luck and the fey to enter and harm the newborn child or even steal him away.

According to both Bronwyn and old Annie, she didn't dare venture out before sundown on the fifth day after his birth, when supposedly, the smell of the blood or the bleeding itself would be all but gone, and the child would once more be safe.

Whatever.

But then she smiled. What would she have given to have been so pampered after delivering Ben, or especially Brian since his birth had been a C-section? But Burt Anderson had never been one to coddle or indulge, and with her first born, she'd only stayed the one day in the hospital before being discharged home and back to her duties.

Even now, she shuddered at the memory of that first night home.

One of Burt's old high school buddies had dropped by with a couple of six-packs of beer to offer his congratulations, and after he'd left, her ex-husband had lost his mind. He accused her of being attracted to his friend. He'd thrown her across their bed and raped her.

His words still echoed through her mind. "*Lay still, and take it, bitch. I couldn't be certain that first time in the back seat of my car, but I'm going to make damn sure I'm the first to get there now, before you go and get yourself knocked up again. I won't be raising some other man's brats.*"

The two small stitches the obstetrician had placed during her episiotomy broke that night, and though walking and especially peeing had been horribly painful for quite a while, she hadn't told anyone what happened. She'd been too ashamed.

A soft knock upon her door drew Beth out of the disturbing memories of her past, and she darted toward the bed. It wouldn't do for Bronwyn to catch her up and about before that fifth day. She settled and smoothed the firs about her. "Enter."

She'd been expecting Bronwyn for a while, for the old maid had been trying her best to wrest the baby out of Beth's arms and take him to the nursery with her almost from the moment of his birth. But as of yet, Beth had avoided giving in. She'd be gone soon, and her time with Quint's son would forever be gone. She meant to cherish each moment.

But as the door opened, Beth couldn't help but smile. It wasn't Bronwyn at all, but a little tow-headed strawberry-blond who stuck only his foot and nose completely through her door and waited.

"Duncan," she sighed. "I'm so glad ye are home safe and sound. Come in."

The boy smiled shyly as he made his way into the room with his ever present sword clutched tightly in his little hand. "I'm nae bothering ye, am I, my lady? I was told the bairn had been born, and I wanted ta see my new cousin for meself. I went ta the nursery first, but old Bronwyn told me he was in here with ye."

Beth gestured toward the small cradle nestled beside the bed. "Come see for yourself."

Slowly, Duncan tiptoed in Duncan fashion until he stood directly before the cradle staring down in wonder. "My, but he's a wee one, isn't he, my lady? What's he called?"

She chuckled. "Aye, Duncan, I suppose he does look very little to you now, but he'll grow fast. And I don't know yet what his name will be. Quint hasn't made up his mind. For the moment, we simply call him Verra Hungry MacLeod because he has quite the appetite." She sighed with contentment. "But you just wait and see. In no time at all, he'll be big enough to follow you all over the great hall."

Her voice caught, and her heart suddenly ached. If she chose not to take Fate up on his offer, she wouldn't be here to see them play together. Or to watch either one of them grow into men. Or even to give them words of comfort when their hearts or heads or arms were broken. Let alone rejoice with them when they both found true love and married. And she certainly wouldn't be around to bounce their bairns upon her knee or grow old with the man she loved.

But she'd made a promise so she'd be leaving soon. Time was running out.

Duncan's lip suddenly trembled. "I'm glad he's so little. At least, he did nae kill his mither like I did."

Beth shook her head. "You did not kill your mother, Duncan MacLeod. Sometimes things beyond our control simply happen."

The child shook his head back at her. "Nae, I ken I killed me mither. Aunt Marta told me so. She said it was cause I was ta big and my crooked foot got caught up ta long and Mairi bled ta death."

His voice caught on a sob. "I did nae mean ta kill her, though, ye ken. I think I would've liked ta have had a mither, especially if she'd been nice like ye are to me. But nae if she'd been mean like Aunt Marta. She hates me, ye ken? She told me so. But I do nae blame her. She says I am the spawn of the devil and should never have been made in the first place. And I deserve ta drag my foot along behind me like a wounded animal. It's my just punishment for what I did."

Beth bristled as she grabbed up the little boy into a tight hug and placed him on the bed beside her. "I don't care what Marta says or thinks. You are not the spawn of the devil, and your foot is not a—a punishment. You haven't done anything to be punished for, do you hear me?"

Duncan looked solemnly into her eyes and slowly nodded.

"You are kind," she continued. "You are brave and

strong, and Quint and I both love you very much. Never forget that."

She gasped as she realized what she'd just said aloud. Yes, she did love the child, but then, who wouldn't love a little boy who worked so diligently at every task put before him? One who did his best to swing his too big sword in an attempt to protect others, and at the tender age of seven. He practiced every day to become a MacLeod guardsman, and then did his lessons every single evening without complaint in hopes of someday becoming the steward of Brochel.

His lip trembled once again. "Ye and the laird love me?"

Beth nodded.

"No one has ever said that ta me before." He smiled. "Old Annie and her granddaughters tell me they like me sometimes, especially that little red-haired one, but ye are the first ta say ye love me. It's nay mushy or girly at all. Nae like the other lads say it 'tis. And even if it 'tis, I still think I like it."

He jumped off the bed and grabbed up a discarded fur from a nearby chair and proceeded to make himself a pallet directly between the cradle and the door.

"What are you doing, Duncan?" Beth asked.

The usually solemn boy giggled, and it was like music to her ears. "Guarding my cousin, Verra Hungry, just as ye and the laird tasked me ta do. I gave ye my word, my lady, and a MacLeod always keeps his word and holds fast, ye ken?"

Within moments, Duncan MacLeod was fast asleep upon his pallet with his sword clutched tightly to his chest, and Beth realized that somewhere along the way, little boys sleeping with very sharp objects had become a perfectly normal occurrence.

****

Quint rubbed at his temples in an attempt to lessen the throbbing in his head, let alone the grumbling in his stomach. He wasn't exactly sure what was causing this particular headache. Or the one he'd had all day yesterday, for that matter, or the one the day before that, or the day before that. But there were certainly enough reasons, of late, to be experiencing both headaches and stomach troubles, so he didn't give the whys of the matter much thought.

But it was hard to put his discomfort very far from his mind when one of the biggest reasons, Lord Fredrick, Viscount Telford, sat at the high board in the great hall, immediately to his left, where his good friend Alec Mackenzie should've been sitting. The English viscount was doing so, as if it were his God-given right. Just as if he were a most loved and valued guest here at Brochel, instead of being the sneaky, murdering, little weasel he truly was. The man even had the audacity ta wear that self-same smug, condescending smile he'd been wearing for days on end. The same hateful smirk Quint longed to wipe right off of his face with his fists.

But he couldn't. He was Laird of Brochel, not a simple serf. He wasn't free to do as he wished. At least, he couldn't do what he wished *yet*. Lairds were held to a higher standard than others, as they should be. Without solid proof of treachery on the part of Lord Fredrick, Quint's hands, and especially his fists, were tied.

John Iain was right when he'd said the viscount was a favorite of the king and beyond reproach. Beyond reproach or nae, Quint still wanted to kill him now and be done with it. He was tired of waiting for the man to strike, tired of watching his back, and tired of expecting a knife to slide between his ribs at any moment.

He took another gulp of the too sweet, off-tasting *uisge beatha* and grimaced. It wasn't bad enough he'd had to put up with unwelcome guests and treachery in his hall, but now he was being served an almost undrinkable tankard of whiskey ta boot? MacLeod *uisge beatha* was known far and wide for being smooth as velvet and as strong as steel, but never sweet. And what he'd been served all week long, he wouldn't place in front of his worst enemy, even if Lord Fredrick hadn't been inclined toward the isle's stout ale instead.

It was his own fault this particular batch hadn't been up to the normal quality, however. He'd been so busy this past year with a brand new wife and more young Highlanders to train than ever before. But with the coming of the next year, he'd make sure to personally oversee the preparations of Brochel's fine Scots whiskey. The recipe had been handed down for generations, through his father's fathers, and this batch definitely left much to be desired.

No Scot worth his kilt would willingly settle for the likes of this pigswill. And he was ashamed to be serving it to his guests.

It was on the tip of his tongue to demand a new barrel be brought forth when Alec's words reached his ears. Though the man was seated half way down the huge table, his voice resonated throughout the great hall and Quint couldn't help but chuckle.

The Mackenzie had yet to be at Brochel a quarter of an hour, and the man was already poking at the wasp's nest with a sharp, pointy stick. "I did nae say I was here ta outright attack ye two little ships, Telford. What I said was, according ta the Solemn League and Covenant promises recently set forth, I *should* attack ye ships since the Scots army is duty bound ta aid ye English parliament, against ye English king. Ye ken there's a difference, aye?" He smiled broadly. "But seeing as ye are a guest of my good friend, Quinton MacLeod, I'm willing ta overlook the fact there be English warships in our channel, for the time being, and ta let ye and ye men live another day or so."

The viscount sputtered. "You're willing to *let* us live? I'd put my money on the Royal Navy against your bunch of uncivilized barbarians any day of the week."

Alec Mackenzie held up a hand and smiled again. "Aye, I'll *let* ye live, as long as ye can learn ta be civil. It goes against our sacred Scottish rule of hospitality ta be the one ta take any other course first. And I for one, would nae ever do something so underhanded as ta take the life of a man who's done nae harm ta me or my friends. After all, I'm all Scot. There's nae a drop of coward's English blood ta be found flowing through my veins."

Quint chuckled out loud this time and belched loudly. He couldn't help himself.

Telford didn't seem to see the humor in the Mackenzie's statements in the least. He puffed out his chest, and his face turned a bright, angry red. "Friend of Quinton MacLeod's or not, how dare you sit there and smugly insult not just any peer of the realm, but a close confidant and friend of your king. And yes, like it or not, Covenant or not, he is still your king, and your words, sir, are treason. For do not think, for a moment,

Charles does not still sit securely upon the throne of both England and Scotland, as God himself divined it to be, for he does and will until the day he dies."

John Iain raised his tankard. "Long live the king." He winked at Quint.

Quint couldn't help but raise his tankard in salute and chuckle once more. After all, it was an appropriate use for such poor *uisge beatha*.

The viscount glared right at Quint when he paused, as if searching for the exact right words. "And as far as your sacred rule of hospitality is concerned, look first to your good friend Quinton MacLeod here, for the man has already shattered that myth. I traveled a great distance to simply ensure myself of the well-being of my young ward, Elspeth Frasier, and to see with my own eyes she is being treated well. And yet have I been allowed close enough to even lay eyes upon the lady in question for the past three days?"

He took a deep breath. "No, I haven't. She could've died giving birth for all I know. Even her child could be dead and buried, and I wouldn't be the wiser, because your *friend* here, refuses to allow anyone who isn't her old hag of a maid to see either of them. And he has caused further damage to English-Scottish relations and insult by allowing you, a common thief and an unlawful reaver no less, to speak to me, a viscount, as you have. And by threatening the king's ships with the hostile presence of your own."

The Mackenzie only laughed. "I'll have ye know reaving is still a time-honored tradition amongst us Highlanders, especially when it comes ta the MacDonalds. Unlike ye thieving English, we do nae steal anything we aren't willing ta have stolen back from us. It's all in good, clean fun."

God, how his head pounded and his stomach rolled, but Quint managed to lift his voice loud enough to be heard over Alec and the viscount's bickering. "Gentlemen, enough." He raised his tankard once again. "Now is nae the time or place for talk of deceit, threats, politics, insults, reiving, or even why my bonny, little wife and bairn remain above stairs and are nae at my side. All those things can be addressed later.

"Right now, let us drink this, umm, fine Scot's whiskey and be merry. My good friend Alec Mackenzie has traveled here ta simply congratulate me upon the birth of the first of what I hope ta be many fine sons. And, of course, ta spend the Hogmanay amongst friends and help welcome the coming year." He made direct eye contact with the viscount. "This be a time of cheer and goodwill, and nae else will be tolerated."

The chief of the MacLeods, John Iain, and the laird of the Mackenzie's, Alec, raised their tankards and downed their drinks in agreement, but Quint couldn't manage more than another tiny sip of his own to flow down his throat, even though he was thirsty beyond reason and had been for quite some time. He gagged.

Telford, however, did nae toast at all. He stood and stomped from the hall with his handful of men following in his wake.

Quint gestured toward his guardsman, Ralf. "Follow him and report back ta me."

The man nodded, and the laird of Brochel watched as his warrior headed out the front doors of the castle. That was the last thing Quint saw clearly before blackness descended.

Chapter Twenty-One

As Beth was putting the just fed, now sleeping infant back in his cradle, the door of the chamber she shared with her husband burst wide open. In staggered John Iain and Alec Mackenzie, dragging her seemingly unconscious husband between them.

"Oh, my God," Beth cried. "Has Quint been injured? Is the viscount responsible for this?"

"We do nae yet know for sure what has happened, if anything, my lady," John Iain said. "One moment, he was giving a toast, and the next, he was face down in his trencher. Perhaps he has simply overimbibed and needs ta sleep it off."

She ushered the two men toward the bed and helped them gently lay Quint upon it.

"My husband rarely, if ever, overimbibes," she huffed. "He knows I do not tolerate a drunkard very well." She shook her head. "Did either of you at least check to make sure he isn't bleeding or otherwise wounded?"

They both looked sheepish as they shook their heads.

Quickly, she gave his body the once-over, and then laid one hand upon his forehead to assure herself that, yes, he was still warm to the touch. She placed the other upon his chest to make sure he still breathed. It was only after she felt the slow, steady up and down movements that she was able to draw her own next breath.

In the commotion, Duncan stirred and the baby woke with a loud squall. She ignored them both, and after a moment, Verra Hungry once more settled, but the little boy did not.

"What's happened ta the laird, my lady?" he asked.

Beth placed her hands upon her hips "I'm not yet sure, Duncan, but I'm about to find out."

She took a deep calming breath and faced Quint's good friend and his uncle as she impatiently tapped her foot. "Well, out with it, both of you. What really happened here? Are you two by chance responsible for the condition of my husband? Or know who is?"

John Iain and Alec looked back and worth at each other and shrugged.

"I do nae think he's simply blootered," the Mackenzie finally said. "I've had many occasions ta enjoy a pint or two with Quinton, and it's almost always I who finds himself carted off ta bed, not our friend here. He has a gut of stone and can outdrink almost any man standing. I do admit, though, we did all have a wee dram or two or three during the evening meal, but nae enough ta even make wee Duncan fall flat on his face, let alone Quinton MacLeod. I be thinking there's something else causing him ta nae wake."

He opened his mouth to say more, but out of the corner of her eye, Beth caught the shake of John Iain's head, and Alec immediately clamped his mouth and simply shrugged.

She glared directly at her husband's liege lord and chieftain. "Out with it, and this time tell me the truth. I am no child to be coddled and protected. What do you really think happened, and why is Quint in this state?"

John Iain hung his head. "We do nae ken for sure, lass, but we fear he may have been poisoned."

She almost tripped over Duncan as she hurried toward the door, but the little boy was quick enough to get out of her way. Throwing the door wide open, she yelled down the hallway toward the nursery. "Bronwyn."

She turned back to Duncan. "Hurry to the kitchen and bring Annie back to me. Don't say a single word to anyone about the laird's condition or about anything you've heard within these walls. Understand?"

The child glanced back at the unconscious Quint, and then up at his grandfather before once more facing Beth and nodding. "Aye, my lady, I understand."

As Duncan shuffled out the door, Bronwyn came through it yelling, "Ye should nae be out of bed, my lady, and ye well ken it. How many times must I tell ye 'tis bad luck before—" She stopped speaking the moment she saw Beth and the bairn weren't the only ones in the room.

"It's Quint," Beth cried. "He won't wake, and the MacLeod and the Mackenzie fear he's been poisoned. What can we do to help him?"

The old maid went immediately to the bed. She placed her ear against Quint's chest, and then after a few moments, she sniffed his breath. "Aye, his heart is pounding verra fast, as if he's run all the way across the Isle of Raasay without stopping ta catch his breath, and he smells of tomatoes, but ones that be ta sweet and unpleasant, as if they rotted on the vine before they ever had the chance ta ripen."

She glanced at Beth and shook her head. "I fear

they may be right, my lady. Our laird has been poisoned, I do believe, and with deadly nightshade, ta boot. And if that be the case, there's little we can do but wait, watch, pray, and hope for the best."

Beth wasn't good at waiting around anymore or at hoping for the best, as far as that was concerned. If two lifetimes had taught her anything, it was that waiting around for someone else to fix a problem and hoping divine intervention would somehow save them at the last possible moment from bad things happening was a false and cruel hope at best.

And anyway, she was no longer Bethany Ann Anderson who stuck her head in the sand so she didn't have to see, and covered her ears so she didn't have to hear every time something unpleasant occurred. She was a MacLeod, now, and MacLeods didn't wait, watch, and hope for the best. They held fast to those they loved and didn't easily let go of what or who was important to them without a fight. They did whatever was necessary to succeed in their task, no matter the cost.

Quint had taught her that, and now he was the one who needed her to put her newfound convictions into action.

Deadly nightshade? What did she have stored away in her memory about deadly nightshade other than the fact it was also called belladonna?

Being an American history teacher for as long as she had been, she must've run across some reference somewhere to the effects and treatment of deadly nightshade at some point. Mustn't she have? After all, there were many different poisons that played significant roles throughout history.

And even if she couldn't remember specifics from her studies, there were still the yearly basic and advanced CPR classes she'd taken in order to address any and all student emergencies that might arise. Surely, poisons and their antidotes had been covered during at least one of those long and boring case study lectures?

Hadn't there?

She forced herself to calm and let the teaching professional she'd once been take over. And that professional part of her brain told her to take things one rational step at a time. She could almost hear the voice of the lecturer speaking, as if he were in the room with her.

"First, when dealing with the ingestion of an unknown and potentially poisonous substance, it is imperative to have the subject expel as much of said substance as possible."

She hurried back toward Quint and moved the baby's cradle well away from the bed.

"Help me get him onto his side," she said in a voice that at least sounded calm to her own mind, even if it still held hints of hysteria to anyone else's ears in the room.

Both the MacLeod and the Mackenzie rushed forward to do her bidding, and the moment they had him positioned the way she wanted, she pried open his jaw and shoved a finger down his throat.

Immediately, Quinton MacLeod puked all over the floor, all over Beth, and all over everyone and everything within puking distance. She continued to make him gag over and over until not a trace more of liquid came forth.

Old Annie walked into the room while Quint was still puking, and the moment he was finished, she said, "I'll just be going and gathering the cleaning supplies then, my lady."

Beth held up a hand. "Yes, please do. But first, there is something very important I need to know."

The cook nodded. "Aye, my lady, anything."

"Who's been helping in the kitchen of late?" Beth asked. "I mean other than your little granddaughters? For it appears your laird has been poisoned."

Annie's eyes grew big as a look of horror crossed her face, and then she shook her head. "Nae anyone else, my lady, I swear. Just as ye asked, no other hands have touched the food I've prepared but my own. Though I do have ta admit, Marta has been especially kind since our guests have arrived. Though she's nae helped with the cooking, mind ye, she's been more than willing ta serve the ale or whatever else the men have had want ta drink."

Beth sighed. Marta. Of course it had been Marta, for who else would it have been? It wasn't as if Quint was the first person the odious woman had ever tried to poison, either. But as God was her witness, he'd be the last.

She couldn't think about Marta now, though. She needed to concentrate on Quint.

Step two, step two, step two. What was it she was supposed to do after ridding the body of whatever leftover poisonous substances there might have been? She'd made him puke in glorious puking fashion, but what was next?

For a moment, Beth closed her eyes and allowed the memory of the case study on ingested poisons from her advanced CPR class to run freely through her mind.

One, induce vomiting. Check.

"Step two, transport to a medical facility so an antidote can be given. And in the case of no known antidote, treat each symptom as it arises."

Well, this was the seventeenth frigging century, and there were no handy-dandy medical facilities to transport him to, let alone labeled vials of deadly nightshade antidote lying about anywhere. So that suggestion wasn't of any use.

Beth could feel herself starting to lose it, and she staunchly pulled herself back from the brink. *Think, think, think.* So what if she didn't have an antidote? She still had symptoms she could treat. Things she could do to help increase the odds of Quint living, not only through this night, but through the entire ordeal, hopefully.

For one thing, Bronwyn had said his heart was racing. What could she do, if anything, to slow it down?

This time, it was American history that came to her aid. There had to be a bottle of laudanum somewhere in this castle, because before there were many other medicines available to treat anything, the opium derivative had been plentiful and easy to obtain, basically worldwide. If Quint's heart was beating too fast, then a sedative would probably slow it down. That was, if she could somehow get him to swallow it.

She turned to Bronwyn. "Is there laudanum available? Please tell me there is."

The maid nodded. "Aye, I have some. I always carry a bottle with me in case of need. Almost gave ye a dose the other day when ye were trying ta deliver the bairn and making so much noise doing it. But it was just childbirth, and it would've been wasteful. Better ta save it for someone who's really suffering."

If Quint hadn't been desperately ill and if Beth hadn't needed Bronwyn's cooperation so badly, she would've probably shown the maid the definition of really suffering, right upside her head with whatever was close at hand. But she did need Bronwyn, and she needed her conscious.

So, instead of becoming violent, she spoke in a completely calm and controlled voice. "Go and get it, please. I have no idea if Quint is in pain or not, but we need to decrease his heart rate. I know for a fact laudanum will do just that. I'll try and trickle it down his throat and hope he swallows."

She turned to Annie. "When you bring back supplies to clean up this mess, please bring a bucket of cool, clean water, and cloths. Your laird is burning hot to the touch, and if I bring his temperature down, that might help slow his heart some, too."

Both women nodded, and without another word, left to do her bidding.

As soon as the door closed, the Mackenzie spoke. "What can I do ta be of help, Lady MacLeod?"

Beth shrugged. "I don't know. You could undress him I suppose. It'll be easier to cool him if he's naked."

Alec got right to his task

"And I, my lady? How shall I be of assistance?" the MacLeod chieftain asked.

She was so tired and already felt as if the weight of the world had been placed upon her shoulders in the last few minutes. She didn't have the first clue as to how to answer John Iain, because she couldn't see past the too still form of her dying husband to anything else that might be needed. But what she did know was the MacLeod was a liege lord and a laird in his own right. As a matter of fact, he was Quint's laird.

Beth took a deep breath and looked John Iain in the eye. "Quint can't lead his people right now, so Brochel will need someone else with a steady hand, wisdom, and the MacLeod name to do what he can't until he once more can. Confusion and hysteria is the last thing any of us needs right now. Especially not with Lord Fredrick in residence and Marta walking around free poisoning people. We must show a united and strong front if we hope to maintain any semblance of order."

Her voice cracked, and she took another deep breath as tears threatened. She fought them back. This wasn't the time for weakness or fear. She'd cry later if there became a true reason for it, but not now. Quint needed her to be tough and stalwart, and she'd not let him down.

"Oh," she added, "and while you're at it, find Marta and see she's put under lock and key. For whether Quinton MacLeod lives or dies, that woman's going to answer for what she's done."

****

Beth rested her head against her folded arms and fought to keep her eyes open and her mind sharp. If by some miracle, Quint did wake, she needed to be alert enough to see it for herself.

It'd been two full days since the poisoning, and the biggest majority of two full nights. During all of those hours, she'd been sitting beside his bed, keeping watch over her husband and talking. She'd finally told him all about Ben and Brian, the color of their eyes, the sound of their voices, their likes and dislikes, and ultimately what had happened to them, and why she had no choice but to leave when he was better and the viscount and Marta had been dealt with.

She told him about Burt and what her marriage to the monster had really been like. And over and over she told him how much she loved him, and how it was going to rip her heart right out of her chest when the time came to leave. She even shared with him every name choice she could think of for poor little Verra Hungry. And she begged him to open his eyes and come back to her.

Yes, she sat there for two very long, worry-filled days and nights imparting her words of love along with small doses of laudanum when needed to keep his heart rate slow and steady. And when she wasn't talking to him or spooning medicine down his throat, she was giving him the occasional cool bath in order to keep his fever down. And not once, in all those hours had he opened his eyes and assured her he was still among the living, still here with her in body and soul, even if his mind was drifting elsewhere.

Not that she was complaining about the work, because she wasn't. And not that she'd even had to do everything herself, for she hadn't. Bronwyn and Annie had been godsends, especially with the baby, Duncan, and the various daily duties of the lady of the keep.

Poor little Verra Hungry. The only time she'd seen her son since Quint had taken ill was when he needed to be fed.

The MacLeod and the Mackenzie had pitched in, too. They'd taken over Quint's duties, and Brochel was running almost as smoothly as if Quint himself were giving the orders. He would've been proud.

Though the two men had both failed miserably at the one other task she'd set before them. Marta was still out there somewhere, free to poison her next unsuspecting victim, and Lord Fredrick was rumored to be on one of the two English warships sitting in the channel. Out of their reach.

God, she wished Quint would open his eyes and talk to her. She so missed the sound of his voice.

Suddenly, he gasped and his chest rattled.

"No," she cried. "Don't you dare leave me. Don't go, please don't go, Quint." She lowered her voice to a whisper. "I need you. Your son needs you. Duncan needs you, and Brochel needs you. Fight to stay here with us. Fight with every bit of that great strength I know you possess. No matter how hard it may be for you to do so. I'm begging you, my love. Don't leave me here all alone. Please don't go."

No more than a whisper of air reached her ear, and at first she thought the sound she'd heard was her imagination. Then she heard it again, stronger this time.

"I'll stay if ye will."

She sat up so quickly she almost tumbled from her chair. With her heart pounding hard within her chest, she stared into the most beautiful set of stormy blues eyes she'd ever seen.

"You're awake," she cried. "Oh, thank God, you're awake."

Quint chuckled. "Aye, it appears I am. Though I'm sore thirsty."

She held a tankard of water to his lips as she pressed kisses to his forehead, and then to both of his cheeks, his chin, and his ears. After he'd drunk his fill, she kissed his lips, too, long and thoroughly. "I was so afraid I'd lost you."

He sobered. "I'm more afraid of losing ye than I am of ye losing me."

She shook her head. "I'm right here."

Quint nodded. "Aye, for the moment ye are. But for how long, my Beth?"

She could feel heat creeping up her neck. "What do you mean?"

"I heard what ye said, lass, every single word, though at times I was afeared I was dreaming." He sighed as she shook her head. "Aye, I did. I did hear ye. For more than a sennight, I've wondered what ye were fighting with yeself about, and now I ken."

She opened her mouth, but he raised a hand. "I ken about the bairns ye lost, my Beth, and I ken about the bargain ye made with Fate. I even ken why ye feel ye need ta be with them, really I do. I've made my share of mistakes, and I've said things I've come ta regret later. Things I cannae take back. But if what ye say is true, Ben and Brian have nae even been born yet and will nae for almost four hundred years ta come. Ye'll still have plenty of time ta go be with them long after I'm gone. I'm nae asking for forever, my heart, I'm only asking for the here and now."

Tears blurred her vision, and a lump formed in her throat. He loved her and wanted her to stay even after he'd heard all the horrible things she'd done in her other life, the mistakes she'd made, and what she'd endured. But could she? Would it be selfish? Would it be wrong?

He leaned up and kissed her. "Life is a precious gift ta nae be thrown away, and ye've been given the rarest of all gifts—two lives. Ordinary people like me only get the one, and that one will be more than enough if I can spend it with ye. Just give me forty, fifty, or sixty more years. That's all I ask, and ye children will be there ta welcome ye into heaven when ye get there. If Ben and Brian are anything like their mother, they'd want ta see ye happy. And I'll use every day, every morning, and every night ta make it worth ye while, I promise. And those times, when ye pain gets ta be ta hard ta bear, then ye can lean on me, my Beth, and I'll share it with ye. Just promise me ye'll stay."

He pulled her down until she was snuggled in his arms and close to his heart, and she went willingly. "Do nae go, my Beth. Do nae leave me here all alone. I need ye. Ye son needs ye. Duncan needs ye, and Brochel needs ye. Fight to stay here with us," he pleaded. "Fight with every bit of that great strength I know ye ta possess. No matter how hard it may be for ye ta do so. I'm begging ye, my love, do nae go."

Beth smiled against his shoulder. He really had heard her, the real her. He'd heard every single word she'd said to him, and he'd come back to her just as she'd asked him to do. And yes, he was right. Ben and Brian hadn't been born yet, technically. They would want her to be happy, and they would still be there waiting for her, if she did agree to remain in the seventeenth century and spend what was left of Elspeth's life with Quint and their offspring. But the knowing didn't make the decision any easier. So she closed her eyes, said a quick prayer her children would understand and made a difficult choice.

She lifted her head and looked into the face of the man she would love forever, even long after time itself no longer existed. "I'll stay as long as you do."

Chapter Twenty-Two

The sun was beginning to rise as Quint held his wife in his arms and kissed the top of her head. He was happy to be alive. "I really slept for two full days without waking once, even ta piss?"

She nodded.

"That means today is Hogmanay, and we missed first-footing," he sighed. "I truly am sorry about that, my Beth. Ye would've liked that tradition."

He could feel her smile against the bare skin of his chest. "I don't mind," she said. "There's always next year, and right now I'd rather be snuggling with you."

Quint chuckled. "Aye, ye are a bonny lass ta be passing the morning with, that's for sure. But trust me, first-footing is a tradition nae ta be missed if ye can help it. After the Yule log is lit and the midnight hour has come and gone, the visiting and gifting begins. And since I'm a dark haired man—" He laughed. "—'tis especially lucky for whoever's threshold I step across first. So even if I weren't laird, I'd still be in great demand. And there's the singing and dancing, and eating and giving of gifts, especially salt for good luck. 'Tis a grand time for sure, and the only proper way ta welcome in the New Year."

He stroked her cheek. "What of when ye came from, my Beth? How did ye start the New Year?"

She shook her head. "You'd be disappointed in

New Year's traditions in America, in my time, I'm afraid. For the most part, people get drunk, watch a big ball drop in Times Square, and then kiss whoever they're dancing with."

"What's a Time Square?" he asked. "And watching a big ball fall? That sounds boring. I swear, the more I hear about ye time, the more I appreciate me own, and the more I'm grateful ye've decided ta share it with me."

He heard her gulp, and for a moment feared she'd changed her mind. But then she laughed. "Times Square is a huge park in one of the biggest cities in America, and actually it's kind of fun to watch that stupid ball drop. But I don't blame you one bit for appreciating your time period more than mine. I'm beginning to like yours a lot, too." She poked him in the chest. "Except for the food, that is. Holiday food in my time is amazing. There's turkey and dressing, prime rib roasts, leg of lamb, mashed potatoes, and cranberry sauce." She licked her lips. "And pies and cakes. Oh yeah, food in my time is much better."

His stomach suddenly rumbled, reminding him they'd probably missed yet another meal whiling the hours away talking. "Ye have nae had Annie's holiday feast then. Every dish all but melts in ye mouth. But food of any kind sounds good right about now. I'm near ta starving this morning."

Beth quickly sat up. "I bet you are. What a horrible wife you are saddled with, husband. You haven't eaten a bite of anything for more than two days, and here I lie, snuggling instead of seeing to your needs."

He kissed her and winked. "Ye are all the feast I be needing, my Beth." He cupped a naked breast and lowered his head as he slowly took a nipple in his mouth and sucked.

She swatted him away. "That particular food source is for your son. I'll go get bread and cheese for you."

"But nae *uisge beatha.*" He grimaced. "I doubt I'll ever be able ta drink Scot's whiskey again and nae puke."

"Ah, then I see the poisoning wasn't a total waste," she teased. "Ale it is."

The moment Beth exited their room, John Iain and Alec entered in her wake.

"'Tis good ta see ye even more alert than ye were just a few hours ago, Nephew," the MacLeod said.

"Aye, he's a right bonny sight, for sure." Alec Mackenzie grimaced. "Ye almost died on us, my friend. Do nae be doing that again any time soon, ye ken? Ye little wife almost worked us in ta our graves because of it. She's a fierce one, she is."

Quint nodded as pride filled him. "That she is." And before his wee tyrant returned, there was business ta be dealt with. "Did ye do as I asked?"

"Aye, we did," John Iain answered. "We sent word ta both the English ships that ye had perished from the poison, and we'd be holding a wake for ye later today. The MacLeod banners have all been taken down and sheets of black hang in their place. Even the great hall has been prepared for mourning. Every mirror has been draped. If that does nae bring that little weasel scurrying back here, nothing will."

"And what of Marta?" Guilt filled Quint. It was his fault and his alone that Mairi's sister was out there somewhere, and God only knew where or what she'd do next. He'd let a promise to a dying girl cloud his judgement—lesson learned, and not something that would happen again anytime soon. "Has she been found?"

Alec Mackenzie shook his head. "At last word, she hadna. But Ralf did say he had a lead as ta where she might be hiding, and he went ta look. If she's anywhere in the vicinity, ye guardsman will find her. I swear that man's half bloodhound the way he sniffs out a trail. I'd hate ta be Marta if and when he does find her. He didnae take word of his laird being poisoned on *his* watch verra well, ye ken. None of ye men did."

Quint nodded. "Aye, Ralf is a good mon. But right now, I need a hand before my wife returns. I do nae want her ta see I'm still as weak as a bairn. So if I could get some help getting dressed and down those stairs, I'd verra much appreciate it."

John Iain's face lost all color. "Should ye even be outta bed so soon? I do nae object ta helping ye all I can, ye ken that, but I gotta admit, ye wee wife scares me just a little. While ye were sleeping, she was like a crazed wolf watching over her cub, and she told the both of us if we even dared touch ye, she'd tie us down and slice off our bits, and with a dull blade ta boot."

"She's nae bigger than a healthy shit." Quint laughed. "I'm pretty sure ye bits are safe. With or without ye help, I'm still going down those stairs and in ta my hall. And that's exactly where I'll be sitting when Telford arrives. I may nae yet be quite up ta snuff, and I'm nae sure I can even heft my broadsword above my head, but the viscount will nae be the wiser. When he walks through those doors, all he will see is a Scottish laird sitting in his rightful place of power."

He ran fingers through his hair, tugging out tangles as he went. "So, are ye gonna help me or nae?"

****

Beth stood in the kitchen with Annie, watching the cook prepare the Hogmanay meal while waiting for a chance to bother the woman for a quick plate of food for Quint. He was still very weak, and if he hoped to get his strength back anytime soon, he needed to eat.

But as Annie rolled out and cut the dough she was so diligently working on, Beth's curiosity got the better of her. "What are those for?"

Annie looked up from her work table and grinned. "For my famous Scotch pie of course. There cannae be a proper Hogmanay without them. I stuff the crusts plum full of beef and onions, and then bake them up in the oven right alongside the black bun."

"Black bun?" Beth shrugged.

The cook stopped for a moment and placed her flour-covered hands upon her hips. "Aye, my lady, the black bun. What kinda Scot are ye if ye do nae even remember our cake filled with raisins, almonds, ginger, cinnamon, and just a wee touch of brandy? 'Tis tradition, lass." She shook her head. "What kinda nuns raised ye at that abbey? English ones?"

Beth shrugged once more. "I honestly don't know."

The old cook chuckled. "Well then, ye are surely in for a treat today, 'cause we be having ourselves a full-on Scottish New Year's meal ta celebrate the fact our laird still lives. Haggis, clootie dumplings with custard, and a right nice cullen skink chock full of smoked haddock is gonna be served, right along with the bridie and the black bun. Oh, and of course, my shortbread. Hogmanay would nae be a holiday without me shortbread, ye ken?"

Beth smiled. "It all sounds wonderful, Annie, but I don't suppose you have anything already prepared I could take up to Quint, do you? I'd rather he stay abed and rest as long as possible."

"In these kitchens, there always be food for the laird." Annie pointed toward a big pot hanging over the open fire. "Take him up a bowl of the cullen skink there a simmering. And a big piece of this morning's fine crusty bread slathered with freshly churned butter. That'll put some strength back in his step."

Thanking the cook, Beth gathered up the meal and headed back toward the stairs. She hadn't made it a half dozen steps into the great hall before she realized her efforts to keep her husband in bed were in vain, because there he sat, big as life and twice as handsome. She wasn't sure which she wanted to do first, kiss the man for being so stubborn and refusing to die or hit him over the head with something and drag him back to their chamber.

In the end, she walked over, slammed the bowl of fish stew upon the table, and tossed the bread beside it. "Just what do you think you're doing?" she hissed close to his ear so the Mackenzie and John Iain, who were both sitting close by, wouldn't hear.

Quint calmly picked up the crust of bread, dipped it into the stew, and bit off the end. "What's it look like I'm doing, wife? I'm eating."

She wanted to hit him. But then she'd been wanting to hit something or someone for days now. "You shouldn't be out of bed yet, and you know it."

Her husband smiled, and Beth's heart skipped a deep. "I tried ta stay there longer. Because I ken ye wish it. But I simply could nae, and I hope ye understand, my Beth."

Though she wanted to be angry, she couldn't keep up the effort. She'd missed that smile too much, and she'd missed that Quinton MacLeod stubbornness, too. All she could manage to do was smile right back at him and nod.

The doors of the great hall opened, and Beth's smile died on her face as in walked Ralf, half prodding and half dragging Marta along behind him.

Sadness filled Beth as she realized the smirking woman standing before them was much too pretty for her own good. Even with brambles in her strawberry blonde hair and the dirt and mud smudging her tight-fitting frock, Marta could still bend any man in the room to her will if she so desired. And she'd been Mairi's twin. No wonder Quint had loved her sister so. What man wouldn't?

Beth was on the verge of confronting Marta herself when the woman's eyes suddenly widened with fear as they locked on Quinton MacLeod sitting in his usual place at the board. There was no way she could've missed his anger reflecting back toward her.

For a moment, Beth almost felt sorry for the woman about to face judgment at the hands of the man she'd tried her best to kill. But then Marta opened her mouth, and any sympathy Beth might have felt fled in the face of her words.

"I see I should've made ye drink a wee bit stronger, laird." She winked. "Perhaps next time, aye?"

"How much did the viscount pay ye, lass, ta poison ye laird?" Quint asked.

Beth was proud of her husband. He didn't lose his

temper, and he didn't yell. His voice was controlled and perfectly even, as if they were all simply chatting about the weather instead of his attempted murder.

"I do nae understand," he continued. "I cared for ye after Mairi died. I gave ye a home, a roof over ye head, clothes on ye back, food in ye belly. Why would ye do such a thing?"

Marta glared, and her eyes burned with hatred. "My sister did nae simply die. It was ye who killed her. Ye and Dougal, and that crippled bastard of hers. But it was mainly ye when ye would nae allow her ta marry Dougal MacLeod. Ye struck her just as dead that verra day, as if ye'd stuck ye dagger right in her heart." She suddenly laughed. "And then, ye stupid *blootered* arse could nae be bothered ta even fall off the parapet as ye should've when I did my best ta push ye. Oh no, it was nae ye who fell over that wall and broke upon the rocks below. It was Dougal.

"Even though ye'd denied him the woman he loved and the child that was rightly his, he was still so loyal, so trusting, like a pathetic lap dog. He wedged himself between the two of us that night when he kenned my intentions. And ye should've seen the surprise on his face as he fell ta his death. Though I hated him, too, for getting Mairi with child in the first place, I hate ye more, much, much more."

Beth's blood ran cold. There was certainly no remorse to be found in Marta MacLeod's eyes, only craziness. The woman continued to dig herself into a deeper hole as she smiled brightly and just kept on babbling.

"And now it looks as if I've failed again. For here ye sit, Quinton MacLeod, big as life. If ye but give me one more chance, I'll be sure ta get the dosage right this next time. And we both ken there'll be a next time, do we nae? For ye made a promise ta, Mairi, ta watch over me and keep me safe, and the Laird of Brochel would nae ever break a promise made ta the woman he so loved. Nae even if it meant his own death."

Beth wasn't sure which she wanted to do first, hug her husband and wipe away the look of hurt and betrayal from his eyes or scratch Marta's out. In the end, she did neither. Quint would not welcome comfort or interference right now, especially not in front of his men.

And as for Marta?

Beth let out the breath she hadn't even been aware she'd been holding. Marta's ultimate fate was in Quint's hands, not hers. After all, it had been him the woman had tried her best to harm. Unlike Marta, though, Beth had no doubt whatsoever her husband would mete out whatever justice he felt was deserved. For it was Laird Quinton Macleod Marta faced, not the young man who'd loved her sister.

She counted the seconds as they ticked by, waiting to see how Quint would deal with Marta. She'd just gotten to forty-two when he spoke once more. "I'll ask ye again. What did the viscount offer ye ta betray ye laird?"

Marta shrugged. "What does it matter? I did what I did, and I freely admit it."

Quint shook his head. "I'd still like ta ken?"

Marta chuckled. "Lord Fredrick, Viscount Telford promised me I'd be lady of the keep if I'd help him. So I did. After all, Mairi would've been if she hadn't died, and I look just like her. Ye should've taken me as wife when she and Dougal betrayed ye. It should've been me ta have given ye an heir." She sighed. "And then it would've been me the viscount would've wanted ta marry after ye were dead. I deserve ta be a countess more than Elspeth does. And the stupid little chit does nae even want it. But want or not it does nae matter, for a countess she will be. For ye will nae best Lord Fredrick, and he means ta see ye dead, marry ye wife, and give over ye lands and ye son ta the king."

The woman gasped and grabbed at her waist as a growing pool of dark red oozed through her frock and down the front. At first, Beth wasn't sure exactly what had happened until Marta dropped to her knees.

"Ye said ye would nae kill me," she said in a voice barely above a whisper.

Quint gestured toward the man standing at her back. "I kept my promise, Marta. I did nae take ye life, lass. Ye did that ta yeself the day ye pushed John Iain's son ta his death. It was the MacLeod himself who has passed judgment on ye and carried out ye sentence. A life for a life, ye ken? 'Tis the Highland way."

And with that, Marta slumped over, dead.

A wave of dizziness overcame Beth, and she was forced to sit before she fell. She'd seen death up close and personal, first her children's and then her own. Yet, the suddenness, the finality of Marta's ending, shook her to the core, and she feared what was yet to come. What would happen when Lord Fredrick decided to make his entrance? For there was no doubt he was coming. After all, he thought Quint to be dead, and he'd be wanting to collect his prize—her, her newborn child, and all of Brochel.

****

Glancing down at Marta's unmoving form, Quint thought he really should be feeling more than he was. After all, she'd been identical to Mairi, in features if nothing else. But try as he might, he couldn't muster much more than simple irritation that her blood was now staining his floor, and he wondered if it was truly that he did nae care or that he really was even yet beyond exhaustion and should be abed.

He glanced toward his wife. There was no way he'd ever admit ta her that he was nae yet up ta snuff. His wee wife would have him back up the stairs and between his covers before he kenned what was happening, and that he could nae afford. At least nae yet. For there was still the viscount ta deal with.

He turned to his wife who sat beside him so quiet, so motionless, her eyes big and frightful, and brimming with tears.

"My Beth," he whispered so as nae ta frighten her, "how is it with ye, lass? Ye look as if ye are about ta be ill."

Beth took a deep shuddering breath. "I know Marta tried to poison you. I'm even glad she's gone and can never harm you again. But it all happened so very fast, and I know her sister was your first love, and I'm just so very sorry things had to end this way."

Quint nodded. "Do nae waste ye pity on Marta, lass. Ta tell ye the truth, I ken she almost welcomed the ceasing of her misery, for she never stopped grieving for her sister, and in the end, it cost her her mind. And as far as Mairi...aye, I did love her once. But 'twas the love a lad has for a pretty lassie, and nae more. I ken that now. 'Twas nae meant ta last a lifetime, only a little while. Marta had the right of it. Mairi did nae love me. She loved Dougal. Nae allowing them ta marry was the biggest mistake and deepest regret of my life."

He took a deep breath and released it slowly. "But my feelings for her were nae ever anything like the love I have for ye. The love a full grown man has for the woman he hopes and prays he gets ta spend the rest of his life with and die beside, safe in her arms, in their bed, when they are both verra old."

He took her hand into his and gloried in the love shining in her eyes. "It's time we both let Mairi and Marta rest in peace, ye ken? For nae other woman means anything ta me or ever will. Ye are my life, my Beth, and my reason for living. Ye are my next breath and every beat this man's heart takes. I love ye beyond reason, beyond all time." He lifted their joined hands to his lips. "Of that, nae ever doubt."

He was on the verge of emphasizing his words with a slow, thorough kiss upon her lips when Bronwyn bellowed from the stairs. "My lady, Verra Hungry MacLeod has decided he's verra hungry once more."

Beth chuckled, and the sound was like music to his ears, but then she punched him right in the shoulder, hard, as she rose from her seat. "Your son is almost a week old and as yet does not have a proper name."

She held up a hand as he opened his mouth to speak, so he quickly shut it. He'd been married long enough to understand the futility involved in interrupting a woman in the middle of her lecturing.

"I realize you woke only a few hours ago after being close to death for two days, but really, Quint, you're going to have to name your son soon, or the poor child is likely to get stuck with Verra Hungry MacLeod for the rest of his life. Half the castle already calls the bairn by that horrid moniker."

Quint nodded. "Aye, my Beth. First thing on the morrow I'll give our son a right proper name, and it will nae be Verra Hungry, I promise. For now, go see our wee bairn fed, my love, and I'll be along shortly. At the moment, it does feel good ta be sitting upright once more. I'm afraid my poor arse is worse the wear for all the lying about it's done lately.

He watched her walk away, and a weight lifted from his soul.

At least his Beth wouldn't be in the great hall when Telford arrived. She'd already been witness this day ta more blood, gore, and death than any lassie ever should. And that more death was coming ta Brochel was simply a fact of life.

Though he was weak as a wee bairn himself because of the aftereffects of the poisoning, it would still fall upon his shoulders to face Telford. And God help any man who got in his way.

After all, he was laird. This was his castle and these were his people. If he had ta tie his sword ta his arm and use both hands in order ta lift it, he would. For only one man would be left standing and breathing when what was ta come was over and done with.

Chapter Twenty-Three

Quint had almost dozed off when the doors of the keep suddenly burst wide open and in marched Lord Fredrick, Viscount Telford, dressed in full regalia, with his nose stuck high in the air, and waving about a sheet of parchment.

He wasn't alone. He was followed closely by at least a dozen well-armed men and what looked to be both ship captains.

"As close confidant to King Charles," the viscount shouted. "And as the legally appointed guardian to the widow, Lady Elspeth Frasier MacLeod, and her poor fatherless child, I claim this castle and all surrounding lands for the crown. God save the king."

Quint cleared his throat as he slowly stood. "Ye might be a tad premature claiming what's nae yours ta claim, Telford. As ye can see, the lady is nae a widow, and neither is the bairn fatherless. But if ye think ye man enough ta take what's mine, then I welcome the challenge."

If the situation hadn't been so grave, he would've enjoyed the shocked look on not just Telford's face, but the man's entire entourage. But there'd been nothing remotely humorous about anything that'd transpired this day. The state of affairs concerning the viscount was tenuous at best, and anything could happen at any moment. Especially considering one life had already come to an end because of this bloody, stupid business.

And the day was young.

For a moment, fear clouded the viscount's eyes, and Quint was glad to see the man at least had the intelligence to be afraid. But then they cleared, and what was left in their wake was pure arrogance.

Quint sighed as he gripped the hilt of his sword. So much for common sense.

"I seem to have been misinformed, laird." Lord Fredrick chuckled. "I could've sworn I was told you had departed this life due to poisoning, I believe." He tsked. "A woman's choice of weapon. A man would've run you through."

The viscount made a production of stepping over Marta's dead body, as if she were no more than a pile of dung upon the floor, instead of the person he'd conspired with. "But it does seem I've made at least one error"—Lord Fredrick glanced back at the dead woman—"in judgment."

Quint had ordered Marta's body not be removed on purpose. He'd wanted the Englishman to see what became of traitors in Scotland.

Telford, however, didn't blink an eye. He simply kept talking, as if a body in the middle of the floor were an everyday occurrence. "I must admit I'm not quite as pleased to see you so lively as I probably should be. After all, we do both have our orders we take from someone above us, don't we? I mean, you do as the MacLeod demands of you, and I do as my king wishes of me. And right now, my king wishes Brochel, so it seems we have a quandary. But my father once told me, if you want something done right, do it yourself."

"Well then…" Quint sighed. "We do have a wee

problem. Brochel is mine, and I'm nae willing ta part with it, with me wife, nor me bairn."

Every Scot in the hall rose and unsheathed their swords, including John Iain and Alec.

The viscount merely raised a single eyebrow. "Do call off your guard dogs. That is unless you wish a slaughter right here in the middle of your hall. Though I have but a dozen men standing at my back this very moment. I have two ships at my beck and call, and both captains here to do the calling if need be. This is between you and I, MacLeod, and no one else dare get in the middle of *our* business."

Quint nodded, and his fingers itched with the want to get down to that business.

"And as far as taking your wife? Oh, I certainly am planning on doing just that, over and over and over after I'm through dispatching you. Perhaps this very day and perhaps even in your bed. She's to be my third countess, you see? The other two were barren useless bitches, but because of your efforts, I already know this one isn't. I suppose I should thank you for that before I kill you. Good breeding stock is ever so hard to find. Don't you agree?"

A hatred like nothing he'd ever felt before poured though Quint, and it was all he could do not to spring forward and cut the viscount down where he stood. But too many of his own men were standing between them, and he wouldn't chance someone other than Telford being wounded because of his lack of fortitude right now. He first needed to take a few deep breaths in order to garner the strength it would take to hop over the board and past his people. For then and only then, would he be face to face with the man he was about to kill.

So instead of leaping as he wished to do, he settled for taking those deep breaths while informing the viscount of his plan. "I'm going ta enjoy spilling ye blood this day, Telford."

The viscount laughed. "Right there is the true beauty of my plan. You won't be spilling anything, you see? Especially not my blood. For you wouldn't dare strike a peer of the realm and the king's closest advisor. It would be the same as declaring war upon England. A war that would ultimately turn your laird, John Iain, and many of your other countrymen against you."

Telford drew his sword. "Though I doubt a filthy Scot will be wise enough to heed my words, you, Quinton MacLeod, should be a good chap and simply stand still while I run this blade through your heart. Then we can both be done with this nasty business. For if you do not, I'll see to it every living soul on the dirty little isle will no longer be living at all."

He smiled once again as he sauntered toward the board and Quint. "And if you're real good, and you stand very, very still without flinching, perhaps Lady Elspeth and I will even name a child after you someday. Though not my heir of course. He'll be little Lord Fredrick, Viscount Telford the second. Sounds wonderful, doesn't it? Perhaps I'll even be so kind as to allow your son to serve mine, as it should be."

Quint leapt over the big table, his fury adding to his strength as his sword came down quick and hard against the viscount's. "War or nae, ye'll not live long enough ta see it. And ye be wrong. My wife will nae ever bear ye children, and my son nae ever serve ye or yours like a dog. For he will someday be laird of

Brochel in my stead. And the only serving of any kind he'll be doing is ta serve ye up your death if I fail ta do it myself this day."

The viscount didn't look near as arrogant now. As a matter of fact, his face turned ashen white, and he swallowed convulsively. "You hit me. You actually hit me. How dare you strike a peer of the realm." He turned toward his men. "Kill them all," he ordered. "Kill them now."

But his men simply stood watching the drama unfold.

"I said kill them," he shouted again. "And protect your better as you've been paid to do."

Every Scot sword in the room raised in ready for the onslaught, but none came as one of the viscount's men stepped forward. "You do not pay us enough to die for your sorry ass, Lord Fredrick. You were a big enough man to start a fight with a Highlander laird. You can finish it yourself."

To a man, the viscount's guards lowered their weapons to the floor in surrender.

****

Beth smiled as Duncan reached out a single finger and stroked the fuzzy head of his baby cousin who was feeding contently at her breast.

"He has the tiniest hands, I've ever seen, ye ken?" The child's eyes sparkled with awe. "And they be both so verra perfect. But then everything about Verra Hungry is perfect, because he is the son of ye and the laird. He has ten little fingers just as he should, and both his feet are without flaw. Nae like mine." Duncan sighed. "And though he be so much smaller than I, I ken he'll grow inta a greater man than I can ever hope ta be. Aunt Marta said it was his destiny while mine is ta always be a useless cripple."

If Beth could've brought Marta MacLeod back from the dead just for the pleasure of killing the woman herself, she would've done it. How could an adult, no matter their grief, be so unkind to a small child? Perhaps she couldn't bring the woman back and punisher her, but she could offer words of truth and comfort to Duncan.

"Nonsense," she said. "You are and will always be important to Brochel, to me, to Quint, and especially to Verra Hungry. Someday you will be steward of this castle, and it will be you the laird depends upon to see his business done. It is a great honor, Duncan, and one your laird has decided you and only you are worthy of."

She took a deep breath. "As far as your aunt, Marta will no longer be around to say unkind things to you. She's…"

The little boy nodded. "Aye, I ken she be dead. Bronwyn told me." He suddenly teared up. "Do ye really think she be telling my mither right now how it was me who killed her? For that's what she said she'd do first off after she died and was reunited with her sister. I do nae want my mither ta hate me. I did nae mean ta do it. I swear I did nae."

Beth gathered Duncan as close into her arms as her dozing infant would allow.

"You listen to me." She forced back the tears in her throat. "Because this is the very last time we are ever going to discuss this matter. Mothers do not hate their children, no matter what. And your mother certainly does not hold you to account for her death. She wanted you, she prayed for you, she loved you with all her heart, and she gladly gave her life to see you born. Sometimes women die in childbirth, but it isn't the child's fault, ever. So there will be no more guilt on your part concerning the matter, do you hear?"

He slowly nodded his head, and she squeezed him even closer. So close the babe began to squirm. But Beth ignored Verra Hungry for the moment. She could calm him once again with a tit if need be. But what troubled Duncan wouldn't be quite so easy to fix.

"You are a precious gift from God, and don't you ever forget that. I love you, and Quint loves you. You may not have been born of my body, but you are now my child just the same. We are your family, and you are ours and will always be. In our eyes, you are beyond perfect just as you are, and we are both so very proud to have you in our lives."

She took a deep breath and calmed the day's turmoil spinning through her mind. "If anything, your mother is smiling down from heaven this very moment and bragging to her sister about how very smart, loyal, kind, and perfect her son is. For that's what a mother sees, Duncan, because she looks first with her heart and then with her eyes."

A commotion in the hallway outside the nursery drew both their attentions, and Beth hurriedly opened the door. Bronwyn stood on the other side with her bright red hair hanging in her eyes, and visibly winded as if she'd run a race.

"My lady," she whispered while trying to catch her breath. "Ye best come quick. Ye husband just attacked the viscount, and I fear more blood is about ta be shed."

Beth handed over the sleeping infant into the arms of old nurse. "Keep Duncan here with you, too."

Duncan looked as if he would argue, but she stopped whatever he'd been about to say with a shake of her head and a handful of words. "I must hurry, but you will stay here with Bronwyn and Verra Hungry. You are their guardsman, remember? And I, and your laird trust none other with that task."

Beth could tell he still didn't want to do as she commanded, but in the end, Duncan MacLeod stayed behind with his little sword drawn and ready as she ran toward the stairs.

****

The sound of metal upon metal as the downward stroke of Quint's sword met the resistance of Telford's rang throughout the great hall.

Sweat beaded Quint's forehead, and his arms felt as heavy as if they'd been made of lead, but he continued his advance, parrying, and pushing the viscount closer and closer toward the door, in hopes of forcing the man completely out of his keep and far away from his wife and child.

It was no easy feat. Telford was much more skilled with a sword than Quint had first thought. Either that, or he himself was much weaker than he realized.

His thoughts were consumed with the fact he dare not lose, for though he'd gladly give his life for his people and for his wife and child, losing would mean a lifetime of horror for everyone he loved.

He slipped on a puddle of Marta's blood, his legs wobbly from the effects of the poison and the two days spent abed. And just like that, the viscount was upon him, slicing a deep line down his face from eyebrow to chin.

In the back of his mind, Quint registered Beth's

scream at the same time his warm, sticky blood began seeping down his neck and on to the collar of his tunic. He ignored both, though. Ta take his attention off his adversary would mean the sealing of his own fate.

"Yield, Scot," the viscount shouted. "Or I'll slice you up one piece at a time instead of being merciful and ending your useless life with a single stroke. For you can't win. What you don't know is, I've been the king's fencing champion three years running."

Quint glanced quickly toward Beth who stood at the top of the stairs. If this moment was truly going to be his last, then he wanted her face to be the final thing he saw of this world. He wished desperately that he could go to her right this moment and kiss away the worry line stretched across her brow.

But he couldn't. He wouldn't leave her here all alone in this world, in this time. And especially not at the mercy of a madman.

So he turned his attention back to the viscount while he dug deeper, pulling strength and determination from the very depths of his soul to keep on fighting for what was rightfully his. For what he refused to give up.

"'Tis a generous offer, Telford." Quint said. "But I'm afraid I must decline."

Their swords clashed again and again, until both men were beyond winded and the viscount's arm visibly shook. Still, neither man yielded. With a quick spin to his left, Quint caught Lord Fredrick off guard and was almost surprised to find his sword pressed firmly against the bounding pulse of his adversary's neck.

"Yield, and I'll let ye live ta return ta England and ye king." Quint panted for a good breath. "But do nae ever again step onta the shores of Raasay. For if ye do, I'll finish what ye started today and war be damned."

The viscount nodded and lowered his sword. Quint darted a glance once more toward Beth in order to assure his wife their problems with Telford were finally over and they could now get on with their lives.

But the look of horror on his Beth's face had him spinning back around, and just in time to see a dagger fall from the viscount's hand and clatter uselessly to the floor. Nae even a heartbeat later, the man slumped over dead with a long blade sticking straight out of his back.

One of the ship's captains shrugged. "He was going to stab you while your back was turned, and after he had yielded no less. I cannot abide the actions of a coward. Especially not one who'd once been related to me by marriage."

Quint shook his head. "The viscount is ye relation?"

The ship's captain nodded. "Yes, I'm the brother of one of those first two useless, barren wives of his. My baby sister was so full of hope and life before he got his hooks into her. But in less than the span of a full year of marriage to that monster, her battered and broken body was found one cold winter morning at the bottom of a very high tower." The captain took a deep breath and cleared his throat. "He said she jumped to her death because she was so ashamed she couldn't give him a child, but I've always suspected it was he who tossed her out that window."

Moisture clouded the captain's eyes. "My little sister was a good Catholic girl, you see. She would never have taken her own life." The man hung his head. "I should've helped her when she came to me begging.

Instead, I sent her back to her husband as the law demands, though I saw for myself the bruises and the depth of her despair." He took another deep breath, and his entire body shuddered. "Perhaps now, she can forgive me and rest in peace."

Every man in the hall, English and Scot alike, nodded and sheathed their swords as the other ship's captain spoke up. "Well, I think it's a damn shame poor Lord Fredrick, Viscount Telford, died of the bloody flux before ever reaching the shores of Raasay. But I'm glad the rest of us made the journey just to give you his congratulations on the birth of your fine son. As soon as we clean up this mess upon your fine floor, I for one am looking forward to trying a taste of what you chaps call *uisge beatha*. I've been told, Scot's whiskey is as smooth as liquid fire flowing down your throat and warming your innards as it goes."

Englishman after Englishman nodded.

"Aye," said one of them. "It's always a shame when a lord such as Telford comes to such a shitty end. And that's just what we'll all be telling the king if'n he asks. Though I doubt he will. He's a little preoccupied with trying to keep his throne at the moment. Now, what was all that talk about whiskey?"

****

March 1644

Beth stood upon the parapet with Quint's arms securely about her waist and breathed in the early spring air. Just a hint of the newly blooming heather was carried upon the wind along with wisps of peat smoke, but it was enough to make her heart soar. That, and the secret she held close to her heart. The long winter was all but behind them, and a bright new beginning with the man she loved stretched out before her.

She still missed Ben and Brian, of that there was no doubt. She'd always miss them, and someday she'd give them that apology they so deserved. But she couldn't bring herself to regret her decision to remain in the past with Quint. A love like this one was much too precious a gift to throw away, no matter when or where or whose body she had to possess to find it.

And Quint was right. Her sons would understand, and they'd want her to be happy. Out of respect for them and their memory, she had every intention of being happy, very happy, and for as long as possible.

"What ye be thinking so hard on, my Beth? When we snuck away up here, I thought it was ta make love, not simply enjoy the view. I have a powerful need ta be inside ye."

The rumble of his warm, familiar Scottish brogue sent shivers of her own need racing along her spine, and she leaned back into his embrace. "I was just thinking about how happy I am, husband."

He chuckled. "And which happy is it ye be this day? The happy that the sun is shining? The happy of what we are about ta do? Or the happy that our wee bairn is napping and we got ta steal away a few precious moments ta ourselves? Or is it ye are simply happy that ye husband desires ta show ye exactly how happy he is ta have ye as wife?"

He grasped a breast while nuzzling her neck, and Beth squeaked as the outline of his stiff cock came in contact with her backside. Heat spread through every fiber of her being. "I am happy that you are happy." She giggled. "Especially since you were all but growling at everyone last evening, even your poor little son."

"Poor little son," he sputtered. "I swear that wee devil knows when I'm within arm's reach of ye and yells the castle walls near ta toppling if I dare try and touch his sainted mither. And then the moment I give up, the bugger's sound asleep and as sweet looking as an angel straight from the bosom of God."

Beth smiled. She couldn't help herself. Quint was right, Verra Hungry— She shook her head, she had to stop thinking of their son as Verra Hungry even if the child's favorite pastime was eating. He had a name now, a real honest-to-goodness name, and had for some time.

Quint's complaint was a valid one, though. John Dougal MacLeod did seem to realize every time his father came near, that he'd be expected to share his mother's attention, and if there was one thing the young lord of the manor wasn't into, it was sharing.

She wiggled her hips against him. "Well, at the moment, our wee John is sleeping peacefully and has no idea we've slipped away. So what was that about showing me how happy you are to have me as your wife?"

He quickly bent her over the parapet, lifted her skirts, and plunged deep into her waiting warmth. Liquid fire flowed through her veins.

"My God, Beth, how I love ye," he whispered. "Ye are my heart, my soul, my everything."

She meant to answer him back. Really she did. But then he shifted slightly to the right, and his thick cock embedded itself even deeper. All Beth could manage to do was hold on and moan with the pleasure of it.

A sense of euphoria filled her as completely as he did. This was her time, this was her place, and here with this man was where she truly belonged. His strokes slowed and became more purposeful. Deep, long, hard thrusts that had the very roots of the hair on the top of her head tingling and her toes curling.

Her mouth went dry, and her limbs went weak.

"Thought I'd find the two of ye up here," Bronwyn yelled. "Verra Hungry seems ta be verra hungry again, and ye know as well as I, he won't take a tit that is nae his mither's. Howling his head off, he is. About ta make the whole castle deaf."

Quint stopped midstroke, groaned, and pulled out. "I'm nae gonna survive that bairn's childhood. Ye just wait and see."

Beth chuckled, turned in his arms, and whispered, "Oh, we'll both survive this one, but it's the one to come in the fall that concerns me. Two nursing weans at the same time will certainly cut deeper into our, umm, private time, Laird."

At first, her husband looked confused, and then understanding dawned. "The one ta come in the fall? As in another one? Already? God help us both if he's anything like his brother."

She scrunched up her nose. "Oh, I doubt we'll have to worry about that. I'm pretty sure she'll come with her own very unique set of demands. And I'll bet anything that, in no time at all, she'll be giving her big brother a run for his money."

Quint simpy shook his head. "Like I said, God help us both."

Epilogue

Isle of Raasay, Castle Brochel
Summer 1690

A gentle nudge drew Beth from her thoughts, and she glanced up at the solemn face of her oldest son, John Dougal MacLeod. A smile tugged at her lips. So like his father he was. The same dark brown wavy hair, the same stormy blue eyes, even the same gentle smile. And just like his father before him, now the laird of the MacLeods of Brochel.

God above, how she missed Quint.

"Mither, 'tis time ta go."

She shook her head. "I'm nae ready yet. I need a few more minutes alone with ye da." Beth motioned toward the crowd of people standing around the freshly turned grave. "Ye be a good lad and take ye brothers, ye sisters, the wives, the husbands, and all the grandbairns back ta the keep. I'll be along shortly."

John Dougal's shook his head. "I cannae be leaving ye out here all alone, Mither."

She tsked at him. "I know my way back. I've lived on this isle for close ta fifty years, ye ken? There is nae a pebble upon the ground I'm nae familiar with. Do nae be treating me like one of ye bairns, Verra Hungry."

John Dougal chuckled at the nickname his mother insisted upon using every time she felt the need to remind him who was really in charge. "Me bairns, as ye call them, Mither, are all full grown men themselves, and each and every one would have my hide, and rightly so, if I was ta leave their dear old granny sitting out in the cold. 'Tis still ta early in the year ta be at the mercy of the elements for verra long."

As a reminder, the chill wind off the sea whipped about the small family cemetery, and Beth wrapped her shawl tighter about her shoulders. "I'll have my own private time ta say goodbye to ye father, and that's all there is ta it. A woman does nae live with and love a man as long as I have Quinton MacLeod and not give him the words of a proper goodbye."

Duncan tapped John Dougal on the shoulder. "Ye ken there's nae use arguing with her, Cousin. It's a waste of good breath. I'll stay close by until she's ready ta go."

Though at first, he looked as if he'd disagree, finally, John Dougal nodded, bent to her level, and kissed Beth on the cheek. "I love ye, Mither."

She patted him on the cheek. "I know ye do, Son, and never forget I love ye, too. Every single one of my children is more precious than the world to me."

"Aye, we ken. Ye tell us every day without fail. Even when we give ye reason ta be vexed with us." He turned, gathered the crowd, and slowly, they made their way back down the path leading toward Brochel castle.

Duncan cleared his throat and pointed as he hobbled toward a small corpse of trees off to the right. "I'll give ye your privacy then, my lady. I'll be right over there when ye have need of me."

"Thank ye," she said.

What a fine man Duncan Macleod had become. Not only had the sad, little crippled boy kept his word and diligently guarded John Dougal's back, but he'd also become a most studious steward for Brochel and a patient teacher to the children who lived upon the isle. He'd married one of old Annie's many granddaughters, the little red-haired one, and together they'd raised a large boisterous family consisting of a lovely daughter of their own, and four braw sons. All perfectly healthy, all full grown now, and all with families of their own.

She glanced around the isle. "Oh Quint, look at how ye wee village has grown and prospered. I know you've only been gone from us for the span of two sunrises, but I swear those grandbabies and great grandbabies of ours have grown at least an inch. Time passes so quickly. Every day speeds by. I miss ye, my love, and God willing, I'll see ye again soon."

The last words he'd spoken to her fluttered through her mind like the costal breeze, only much warmer. "*I'll be waiting for ye on the other side, my Beth, but take ye time getting here, ye ken? And when ye do get ta where I'm going, we'll dance among the stars and take a stroll upon the moon just like those men ye once told me about. My Beth, my heart, thank ye for keeping ye promise and staying with me all these many years. I once told ye all life was a gift and nae ta be wasted, but in truth, ye were always a gift more precious than my life ever was ta me.*"

Weariness washed over her, and Beth laid her head upon the cold stone of the bench she'd been sitting upon. Though she hadn't thought about him in years, she called out to Fate. "Tobias, how I long for ye to come and take me to them now. I'm so ready."

The air around her began to shimmer. "Are you certain this time, madam?"

Beth sat straight up, and her mouth gaped open. Right before her eyes stood Fate, Tobias Moiré, third generation event manipulator, and he looked exactly the same as he had the last time she'd seen him.

She couldn't help herself. She smiled. "Tobias, how have ye been?"

Not much had changed since the last time she'd laid eyes on him. He still wore what appeared to be the same long white robe, and his brown hair was as disheveled as it ever was. Even his wire-rimmed glasses appeared to be the very same pair she'd last seen him wear.

The little man glared at her. "How have I been, you ask? How do you think I've been? I'm a Fate, and I've been busy, of course. While you've been happily lollygagging about in the past, I've had wars, disease, hatred, and all manner of human conditions to deal with." He pointed to the large-faced watch gracing his wrist. "But that's beside the point. Time isn't to be wasted. Did I hear you correctly, madam? You are ready to be reunited with your children as we agreed?"

"Oh yes," she said with a sigh. "And with Quint, too."

An understanding came over her, and Beth glanced back down at the bench she'd been relaxing upon only moments before. There lay what remained of Lady Elspeth Frasier MacLeod's lifeless body. She looked perfectly peaceful, serene.

"Umm, dead again, I take it?" Beth cringed.

Fate nodded, and his smile held a hint of sadness. "I'm afraid so, madam. Nothing fancy like a thousand-year-old rock toppling over, mind you. Your death this time was simply Lady Elspeth Frasier MacLeod's turn.

A turn, I might add, that had no need whatsoever for my particular talents. And at least in this instance, it won't take a full crew in hazmat suites to clean up the mess."

Beth shuddered.

From his pocket, Tobias Moiré pulled the same high-tech smart-phone-looking thingy he'd used on her the first time and began pushing buttons. "Our agreement was I'd reunite you with your children, and that is precisely what I intend to do. Quinton MacLeod, however, was never part of the equation."

Beth braced herself for the feeling of floating up and away in the ever-growing pool of nothingness she'd experienced last time. Right before it completely enveloped her, she managed to shout. "But they're all in Heaven waiting for me. Reuniting me with one will reunite me with all three. Won't it?"

His voice was no more than a whisper, but his response carried upon the wind. "We shall see."

****

"For the love of God, would ye please stop kicking the back of my seat? I already have a headache." Beth snapped her mouth shut and grasped the steering wheel with both hands. Large metal objects—cars—whizzed by her at amazing speeds.

"I'm hungry," Brian whined.

She took two deep breaths and glanced into the rearview mirror. Her heart almost stopped for the third time. There sat Ben and Brian, in the back seat, in their little baseball uniforms, very much alive.

Oh God, her boys. She bit her lower lip to keep it from trembling and forced herself to answer. "We're all hungry, honey."

Rain beat down faster, and Beth probed her memory for the instructions of how to turn up the wiper blades. She glanced at the passenger side of the front seat, and there sat Tobias Moiré big as life.

"What's going on?" she hissed.

Fate turned his face toward her and smiled. "You did as I asked you to do and gave Quinton MacLeod his heir, and now I've kept my word and returned you to your children. A deal is a deal, madam."

Beth glanced quickly into the back seat.

Fate chuckled. "Don't worry. They can neither see nor hear me. Only you can."

"Why? Why here? Why now? I can't do this," she whispered. "I can't watch my children die a second time. I can't. I won't."

Tears filled her eyes, and she swiped them away. The car swerved to the right, and she fought to control it. This driving stuff was a lot harder than she remembered.

Fate shrugged. "Then don't."

Beth took her foot off the gas, but the car didn't slow. She applied the brake all the way to the floor, but the vehicle didn't change speed. Frantically, she looked toward Fate. "Make it stop."

He shook his head. "I can't. The journey you've begun must be completed." He pointed upward. "Not my decision. His."

"Can we have mac and cheese when we get home?" Ben asked.

Beth gulped. "Sure, why not."

"Why do you do that?" Brian argued. "You know we can't have mac and cheese. What'd Dad say last time?"

Ben huffed from the back seat beside his brother. "I don't care what Daddy says. He doesn't have to eat it if he doesn't want to."

Brian kicked the back of Beth's seat, again. "Oh yeah? Well, I bet you'll care when he throws it on the floor or at Mom again. Won't ya?"

She could hear the fear in her young son's voice, and like the last time, it broke her heart all over again. "Don't worry about it, Brian. I'll make ye, I mean your father a nice big baked potato to go along with his steak. Just the way he likes it."

She glanced in the rearview mirror at her sons. God, how she'd missed them. Both blond and handsome with dark brown eyes and winning smiles. Ben, with a smattering of freckles across his nose and ridiculously oversized ears, and Brian, with his rosy cheeks smudged with dirt.

"Give it back," Ben suddenly yelled.

Beth jerked out of the contemplation of her near perfect children and back into reality of the moment mode. Her voice shook. "Brian, give your brother back what you took, please."

"I just wanted to look at his stupid catcher's mitt."

Her eight-year-old still sounded whiney, and what a wonderful sound it was.

Ben's piercing screech went right through Beth's heart. "How many times do I have to tell you, I don't want your greasy paws on my stuff? Give it back like Mom said."

Beth took a deep calming breath and slowly blew it out as she gripped the steering wheel harder. "Brian, give your brother back his mitt now, please."

Instead of doing as she'd asked and just as she

expected, Brian tossed the catcher's mitt into the front seat and out of his brother's reach. It landed on the passenger side floor board. Right at Tobias Moiré's feet.

"Mom!" Ben whaled.

Beth gulped, but this time she didn't overreact, and she didn't say the things she'd longed to beg her children's forgiveness for. Instead, she looked right at Fate and tightened her seatbelt. "Not this time. If I can't avoid what's coming, then I'll make sure I stay right here in this car with them."

The event manipulator chuckled. "Whatever you wish, madam. I'm simply a passenger, and I'm immortal."

She ignored the little man and turned her head slightly toward her children. "I'll get your mitt when it's safe to pull over, Ben."

Fear gripped Beth's heart as she once more faced the oncoming traffic and their oncoming fate.

But this time, the lane was clear.

There was no dark pickup truck with its headlights blinding her and its tires swerving dangerously forward. No need to slam on her brakes and veer. No need to throw her free arm over the backseat in hopes of somehow shielding her children from what was about to happen.

Nothing.

There was nothing at all in her line of vision except a long stretch of wet Miami highway.

Beth drove a couple of more miles for good measure, and when the turn off to the road where she'd shared a home with Burt came into sight, she took her foot off the gas pedal. This time, the car slowed. She gently applied the brakes, pulled completely onto the gravel shoulder, and allowed the car to come to a stop.

She turned off the engine.

Unbuckling her seatbelt, Beth leaned over, picked up the mitt, and tossed it back to Ben. He grinned, and her eyes filled with tears. How? How could now be so very different from before?

Tobias Moiré cleared his throat. "Because, as I've told you before, time really is a circle, madam."

She tore her gaze from her children and stared at Fate. "What?"

The event manipulator rolled his eyes. "You were wondering why, this time, there was no accident, weren't you?"

She nodded.

"Well," he continued. "It is because time truly is a circle. Changes made in the past are like tiny ripples upon a pond. They spread out and trickle down through time so to speak. When Lady Elspeth gave Quinton MacLeod his heir, a series of events was set into motion that directly affected Bethany Ann Anderson and her children."

Tears ran down her cheeks, and Beth worked to swallow the lump forming in her throat. "How?" she finally choked out.

"Mom, are you okay?" Brian sounded scared.

She glanced over the seat at her small son and smiled. "Yes, honey, Mommy's fine. I—I just need a minute." To Fate, she whispered, "Go on."

Tobias nodded. "One of Elspeth's and Quinton's great-great-great-whatever grandsons now sits upon the night court bench in Miami. It was his turn two days ago when a certain drunk driver appeared before him.

Instead of being released with a summons to appear at a later date, he was held over for trial. Something about a well-known family inclination to detest and punish those who imbibe to excess and cause harm to others. I do believe he once was quoted as to have said that particular inclination had been passed down through many generations of MacLeods.

"Therefore, madam, since the man who was responsible for the accident in your previous life now sits rotting in a jail cell where he belongs, he could not possibly be on this stretch of highway this evening, causing harm to anyone."

Beth took a deep breath and stared through the windshield. "I suppose I should start this car and go home. Shouldn't I?"

Fate nodded. "It is where you live."

"I can't go back to the way things were with Burt. Especially after the life I've had with Quint. I won't."

Fate nodded again. "No, I suppose you cannot."

She started the engine and eased onto the road. "When will I get to see Quint again?" Suddenly, she gasped. "Oh my god, my children, my grandchildren, Duncan, they're all dead now, too, aren't they?"

Fate sighed. "It has been almost four hundred years, madam. But as I've said, there is no passage of time in Heaven. When you get there, and it's not my place to tell you when that will be, they will all be waiting for you. And it'll be as if you were with them this very morning."

"I was," she sobbed.

"Mom," Ben whispered. "Who you talking to? You're starting to scare me."

Beth shook her head. "Sorry, honey. I was talking

to myself. You know how I get sometimes."

She laughed a little brokenly.

Fate patted her hand. "You'll be fine, madam. Just remember the MacLeod motto and hold fast. By the way, what do you plan to do about your present husband, Burt?"

The rain was no more than a mist as she pulled into the driveway and turned off the engine. The boys immediately jumped out of the car.

"Go change out of your uniforms," she shouted. "Give me a minute, and I'll be in to get supper started."

They headed for the front door and disappeared from sight.

What was she going to do about Burt? She couldn't live with him even another day, and in this century, it was illegal to simply kill his stupid ass. What then? What were her options?

She looked straight at Tobias Moiré and smiled. "I'm going to walk through that door and feed my children, and then, later tonight, after Burt's asleep, I'm going to pack up myself and my kids, put us all in this car, empty all the accounts, and find a new place to live until I'm free to take myself and my children to Alaska. I divorced the creep once. I can certainly do it again. It's just, this time, I'll be a whole lot smarter about it."

Fate chuckled. "So, he doesn't frighten you anymore?"

Beth shook her head. "If living with Quinton taught me anything in the almost fifty years we were married, it's that I have no reason to fear anything or anyone. He helped me understand I'm strong, smart, and capable. Burt Anderson is in for a very big surprise when he wakes in the morning."

"And after you rid yourself of your deadbeat husband? What then, madam?"

Beth thought for a moment and smiled. "First, I'm going to raise those two little boys to be fine, honorable men, the same way Quint and I raised our children. And then, I'm going to sit back and enjoy the show as they fall in love and marry. I'm going to bounce a brand new set of grandbabies on my knee. And when the good Lord does sees fit to call me home, I'm going to run straight into Quinton MacLeod's waiting arms when he meets me at Heaven's gates. After all, he did tell me not to hurry."

Tobias Moiré, third generation event manipulator, better known as Fate, began to shimmer. "That sounds like a splendid plan, madam, and I do wish you luck. But for both our sakes and just to play it safe, I implore you, please stay out of Scotland."

With a tinkling of laughter upon the wind, he was gone.

Beth opened her car door, breathed in a lungful of muggy Miami, Florida, air, looked toward the heavens, and blew a kiss. "We'll be back together before you know it. I love you Quinton MacLeod, and I love our family, our entire family with all my heart, and I always will."

She sighed. "But right now, there are two little guys inside this house who need their mommy more than you need me to take a stroll through Heaven or even upon the surface of the moon, and I know you understand that better than most."

Beth smiled. "I also know that, of all the people who've lived in any time period ever, you're the one who understands best when I say, I am a MacLeod and

I will hold fast."

She straightened her shoulders, stiffened her spine, put one foot in front of the other, and headed into the house. It was time to get the next chapter of her gifted, very unusual, completely blessed life started.

About the Author

Hi, my name is Maxine Mansfield and I write fantasy, erotic romances. I live in the far northern state of Alaska where the summer days are long and the winter nights even longer. I have one very special man, his three equally special children, and our six delightful grandchildren in my life. Not to mention a very bossy African Grey parrot named Gabriel. Oh, and gnomes! Many, many gnomes!

~*~

Visit Maxine at

www.maxinemansfield.com

~*~

To chat with Maxine Mansfield and other Wild Rose Press authors of erotic romance, join us at www.groups.yahoo.com/group/thewilderroses.

Also Available

Tamed by the Fire
The Academy Book Four
by Maxine Mansfield

http://amzn.com/B00G60TGS0

Kitrina Dragonheart is a hunted woman, but the last thing the savvy rogue wants is to partner in a quest with the arrogant but oh-so-sexy prince who deflowered her. But when the threat extends to her legacy and her loved ones, she has no choice but to accept his skills as an extraordinary warrior. Now if she can just get past the distraction of his touch.

Barbarian Zander Hammerstrike vowed to protect Kit with his life. But who's going to protect Zander from the sensually sassy human? She's playing havoc on his sanity—as well as his libido—and she's on the verge of stealing his heart...again. He can't let that happen. As future ruler of Alaria, Zander must take a barbarian wife to keep the bloodline pure, and Kit being human...

Destined from birth to follow different paths, their love seems impossible, but does the Dragon Heart Opal have other plans in store for the pair?

Also Read

Going Deep
Immortals Book Three
by LJ Vickery

http://amzn.com/B01AJ78F8W

Dagon is unredeemable in the eyes of the gods he betrayed centuries ago, but now, the Mesopotamian sea god is truly screwed. The answer to his redemption, his Chosen, is finally within reach, but the powers-that-be have stepped up their war against the Earth-bound gods, and he's literally ripped from her arms. Thrust into the Underworld, he is forced to battle demons, and his body is ravaged beyond endurance. Perhaps it's for the best. Intense physical pain might be the only thing that can make him forget her.

After a hellish youth, bartender, Holly Abelard is just trying to get through life. At least, that's what she thinks until the guy she's hot for announces he's a god, and she's his mate. She's barely coming to terms with that revelation when the sexy hunk is sucked into the Underworld, and she's left in the hands of a league of super gods. But Holly isn't giving up on getting Dagon back. That isn't to say she doesn't have her doubts. Had he really sported fangs and scales? What the hell? Or should she say what in Hell, because that's where she'll have go to find him.

Thank you for purchasing this
publication of The Wild Rose Press, Inc.
If you enjoyed the story, we would appreciate
your letting others know by leaving a review.
For other wonderful stories, please visit our
on-line bookstore at www.wilderroses.com.

For questions or more
information contact us at
info@thewildrosepress.com.

The Wild Rose Press, Inc.
www.thewilderroses.com

Stay current with The Wild Rose Press, Inc.
Like us on Facebook
https://www.facebook.com/TheWildRosePress
And Follow us on Twitter
https://twitter.com/WildRosePress

She didn't expect to die…she sure as hell didn't expect to wake up in another woman's body or in the bed of a seventeenth century Highlander…

Beth's eyes flew open as warm hands gently shook her awake. "Elspeth, are ye or are ye nae still a maiden?"

She stared up into the stormy blue eyes of Lard Quinton MacLeod and shook her head no, then nodded yes.

"Which is it?"

She cleared her throat. "I swear to you, m—my lord, Elspeth Frasier MacLeod's body is still untouched by any man."

Quint smiled as he slowly brought his lips to hers. He chuckled. "Nae for long it isna."

The heat of his kiss as his lips captured hers burned Beth with a passion that seared her to the depths of her being. She was helpless, defenseless against the onslaught. She opened in surrender as his tongue slipped between her lips. It was heaven.